MADDY GOES TO

HOLLYWOOD

Maureen Martella was born and brought up in Co. Dublin with five sisters and a brother. Having moved to England in the sixties, fallen in love with an Italian and returned home to Ireland five months' pregnant, she continued to travel after having her children, ending up in Bel-Air where she worked as assistant to a mortician. She now lives in rural Ireland.

MAUREEN MARTELLA

MADDY GOES TO HOLLYWOOD

Published in the United Kingdom in 1999 by
Arrow Books

1 3 5 7 9 10 8 6 4 2

First published in the United Kingdom in 1999 by William Heinemann

Arrow Books Limited
Random House UK Ltd
20 Vauxhall Bridge Road, London, SW1V 2SA

Random House Australia (Pty) Limited
20 Alfred Street, Milsons Point, Sydney,
New South Wales 2061, Australia

Random House New Zealand Limited
18 Poland Road, Glenfield
Auckland 10, New Zealand

Random House South Africa (Pty) Limited
Endulini, 5a Jubilee Road, Parktown, 2193, South Africa

Random House UK Limited Reg. No. 954009

A CIP catalogue record for this book is available
from the British Library

Papers used by Random House UK Limited are natural, recyclable products made from wood grown in sustainable forests. The manufacturing processes conform to the environmental regulations of the country of origin

Typeset by SX Composing DTP, Rayleigh, Essex
Printed and bound in Germany by
Elsnerdruck, Berlin

ISBN 0 09 928057 4

To Dominic

Prologue

It's eight fifteen a.m., Los Angeles time. The sun is already hot. I climb, naked, out of the pool, slip into a bathrobe and retreat to the dim coolness of the ground-floor study. Gloria's study. This was her favourite room in the big sprawling house. She's all around me here. In the neat, leather-bound scripts, in the awards that litter the big desk, in the gold-framed photos lining the walls. My sister Gloria, laughing fit to burst. Skiing fearlessly down a steep, snow-covered slope. Gesticulating widely, on a crowded film set.

I sit in her well-worn leather chair and start the tape. Before I go I want to get it all recorded. Let Carlos know exactly how I feel. How I felt when that first letter arrived from Hollywood. How it started the chain of events that changed all our lives. I want him to know that Gloria and I made our own choices here. Most of all, I want him to know that everything we did, Gloria and I, even the most shameful, was almost inevitable given where it all began.

Ballyshannon

Mother never liked Gloria. She liked me even less. She didn't actually neglect us, not where the basic necessities of life were concerned. We were probably as well fed and clothed as any other child in the rough, rural landscape where we grew up. And just as severely punished for any minor misdemeanour, real or imagined. I can clearly remember spending a whole night sobbing, because Gloria was huddled outside in the numbing winter cold, locked in the old cow byre, because she had dared to sneak out to a teenage dance against Mother's explicit orders. Gloria was coming up to her sixteenth birthday that week. I was eleven, and my eyes remained tomato-red and swollen for the best part of the following day. When questioned about this, I said I had sties coming on. Mother rubbed her thick wedding band so hard against my swollen lids that it was all I could do not to cry out in pain.

Father was convinced that Mother's quick action had saved me from the terrible embarrassment of spending the rest of the Christmas holidays with both eyes disfigured by ugly, pustulating sties.

Gloria laughed so hard at this she almost wet herself. That was the most endearing thing about Gloria, she could find humour in anything. Nothing was ever so serious that she couldn't wring a laugh out of it.

Mother never laughed. Never. And Father walked around the farm, winter and summer, muttering 'It never rains but it pours' at every minor, or threatened, set-back. He never once connected his farming failures with anything but cruel destiny.

But Gloria knew how to laugh.

She even laughed the day father got bacteraemia. Of course, we didn't know it was bacteraemia then, and neither did he. We didn't even know it was blood poisoning. After all, he had only gone down to the low pasture to measure what was left of it after the County Council had commandeered several prime acres to facilitate a new road to the West. Father didn't trust what he called 'slick County Council surveyors' when it came to measuring precious farmland. But then Father didn't trust anyone. He was using his favourite measuring tool, a long piece of bailing wire, when he cut his hand where he already had a bit of an abscess. Nobody knows for sure if he cut it on the bailing wire, or the vicious hawthorn that was in full spring bloom that day, but it turned into blood poisoning, and he died full of abscesses and wheezing from the lungs.

He mightn't have, if he'd called a doctor. But Father didn't trust doctors either. And the strangest thing of all was that his cross-border collie, Runt, who had never really liked Father all that much when he was alive, wouldn't let the undertakers into the house to remove his body when he finally died.

They had to shoot Runt to gain access. I was twelve then.

I was nearly thirteen when Gloria ran away. She was seventeen.

I hung around the post-box for weeks afterwards,

convinced that she'd contact me, somehow. She didn't.

And it was a long, long time before she contacted Mother. Twenty years, to be exact. I was a married woman by then – Mrs Turlough O'Toole, the unproud mother of identical twin sons. And our farm was viable for the first time in three generations. Turlough had made a better fist of Hawthorn Farm than my father or grandfather ever had. Mother adored him beyond measure. Or sanity. Turlough, not Father. He was the son she'd never had, the son she'd always dreamed of having. When I gave birth to twin boys, ecstatic doesn't even begin to describe how Mother felt. At the Christening, I actually caught her smiling. That could have traumatized me for life. That, and the terrible post-natal depression I was suffering from at the time.

Mother took charge of the babies. She revelled in it. She was a better mother to the twins than she'd ever been to me. Or Gloria. I tried not to be jealous.

The doctor said I should hold off on having any more children. That suited everyone including me, because times were hard and I clearly wasn't cut out to be a mother. Hadn't my own mother taken her time in discovering her maternal instincts? And when she did, it was a little late in the day for some. I suppose she could be best described as a born-again mother.

Turlough didn't mind who looked after the babies, once the burden didn't fall to him. He probably felt he had enough on his plate, what with the tillage and the sheep, and introducing the new Friesians and all that, twice a day, milking and sterilizing. Whatever his faults, he never neglected the farm. He was a doggedly hard worker. Amazingly self-disciplined.

And he didn't go around moaning all day, the way Father used to. Or drink like Grandfather.

Turlough only got drunk at Christmas and he only ever moaned about money. He was totally dedicated to making the farm pay. He seemed to find endless satisfaction in the strenuous physical work this entailed. And in the milking parlour, as I was to discover later.

One promising spring evening when the twins were coming up to seven months old and I was feeling somewhat recovered from my post-natal depression, I dressed the three of us in our Sunday best and pushed their heavy pram across the yard, and down into the milking parlour to surprise Turlough.

I surprised him all right. But not half as much as he surprised me.

There he was, hard at work in the darkest corner, his trousers around his ankles, his luminous white arse bouncing up and down, and up and down, above fat Marion McCauley, who only came in to give him a hand with the milking.

I had a bit of a relapse after that. I took to my bed for a fortnight and gave up walking the twins. And I never again set foot in that milking parlour.

If Mother know what Turlough was up to with fat Marion, she never let on. But then Turlough could do no wrong in her eyes. He was king of the cows, was Turlough.

I was still taking the anti-depressants when the letter came from Gloria.

The postman drove right up to the front door and knocked loud enough to waken the dead. He said later that this was because he half suspected the airmail letter might have been wrongly addressed.

It was postmarked Hollywood, USA. And clearly addressed to Ms M. Mullin, which Mother took to be her, because her proper name is Margaret even though everyone calls her Hanna because her mother's name was also Margaret and people used to get them mixed up.

Mother snatched the letter from the postman's hand and slammed the door in his face before he could ask any embarrassing questions. 'Nosy old bugger,' she said, scanning the page. Then she sat down and poured herself a large whiskey, even though she despises people who drink. 'Here.' She practically threw the letter at me.

It was brief and to the point. Gloria was sorry for not getting in touch sooner. She had been busy. She was now working in Hollywood. A script-writer. She hoped we were well and would dearly love to hear from us. At the top of the slim page was her Los Angeles address, printed out in solid black letters, beside her personal phone number. Below this there was a business address, complete with another, extended, phone number. A fax number followed. And below this again was yet another line of letters, a complex code for an e-mail address.

All in all, this took up more space than the actual letter did.

'I thought she was working as a barmaid in London?' Mother appeared dazed. 'Mary Kilmartin's brother saw her there. He said she served him two large Jamesons in a snug in Fulham.'

'That was nineteen years ago, Mother.'

Turlough came in from the yard. He scraped his

dung-splattered boots on the wire mat by the back door, before dropping a can of buttermilk on the scrubbed table.

'There's a letter from Gloria.' Mother's voice was doom-laden.

Turlough had never met Gloria. He had only come to work in our parish some years after she had run off. He spared a quick glance at the single page, but didn't appear to be at all impressed. 'What would your sister be doing in Hollywood?' He stared accusingly at me.

'She's a script-writer,' I said proudly. 'Didn't you read it?' I picked up the letter reverentially.

'A script-writer?' He swallowed a mouthful of buttermilk. 'Is that what they're calling it now, script-writing?' Little ribbons of creamy yellow buttermilk trailed down his unshaven chin. He made no attempt to wipe them away. I knew that when he came in for lunch, in three hours' time, they would still be there, hardened now into thick white blobs on the rough red stubble that was practically his trademark.

Despite Turlough's protests and Mother's unease, I wrote back to Gloria. I told her Mother was thrilled with her meteoric rise in the world. I lied about Turlough as well. But not about the twins. I told her how remarkably plain they were, ugly even, and how well the farm was doing. I gave Turlough full credit for everything. I signed the letter 'with fondest love, your dearest sister, Maddy'.

Romantic nonsense, Mother would have called it, had she known.

Within a fortnight a second letter had arrived, this one by express post, which didn't mean a lot in

Ballyshannon, as the express post travelled in the same little green van as the regular post. But this one was addressed to Ms Maddy O'Toole, Hawthorn Farm, Ballyshannon. I thought I'd burst with pride.

After that, hardly a week passed without a neat little blue and red edged envelope dropping into the post-box. And all for me – Ms Maddy O'Toole, Hawthorn Farm.

I wasn't sure if it was my undisguised glee in being the recipient of all this exciting American mail or simply the fact of its arrival, but Turlough became even more sullen and moody as the weeks passed. He finally exploded. 'Planning on coming back, is she? Back to claim her share, now that the farm is doing well?'

We were in our cramped bedroom under the sloping eaves, where every sound carried clearly into the rest of the house, especially into Mother's bedroom just below. But for once I didn't care. I sprang to Gloria's defence. 'You don't know my sister. She'd give you the coat off her back if you were in need of it.'

He didn't reply, just leaned across me to switch on the radio. Then he deliberately turned up the sound.

Nothing unusual in that: the late-night weather forecast and the weekly beef prices were the only things guaranteed to hold his attention in our bedroom these days.

I turned over and went to sleep.

When the bundle of glossy photographs arrived everyone was intrigued. Even the postman. 'Sign here please.' He looked at me as if he was hoping I'd open the big manila envelope then and there on the rain-drenched doorstep.

'Close that door,' Mother yelled from the kitchen.

The twins actually looked up from their plates when they saw me tearing open the envelope. Then the photographs tumbled out and their eyes immediately glazed over.

Turlough also pretended to be completely uninterested. But this didn't prevent him from closely scrutinizing every single photograph, before blithely dismissing them. 'What interest would I have in photographs of a fancy American house?' He went back to his breakfast.

He was still convinced that Gloria had some sly ulterior motive in suddenly contacting us. 'Why now, after all those years of silence?' he insisted.

The photos *were* mostly of Gloria's house, if you could call it that. It was more like a palatial mansion, in glamorous Beverley Hills. A turreted mansion tucked among acres of lush green gardens, with a while-balustraded terrace running the full length of its imposing front. At the back it had a whole linc of french doors, opening out on to a wide, pink-tiled patio, the steps of which curved grandly downwards until they came to a halt just feet away from a glittering swimming pool shaped like a large kidney.

All this could be seen clearly in the coloured aerial photos.

'Who in the name of Jaysus would send you an aerial picture of their house? I ask you!' Turlough sneered.

'She's obviously . . .' I began.

'Nuts!' he said. 'Anyway, how do you know that's her house? You only have her word for it. She could be the scullery maid there, for all you know.'

Mother sat tight-lipped, turning the heel of a Fair Isle sock.

'How do you even know that's your sister?' Encouraged by Mother's silence, Turlough got well into his argument, paying more attention to me than he had for the previous six months. 'How long is it since you've seen Gloria? That woman could be anyone. Anyone at all!'

And the thing was I knew he could be right. The woman in the photos didn't look at all like the Gloria who had run away into the night all those years ago. This one could be twenty-five, Gloria would now be thirty-seven now, going on thirty-eight.

In one eye-catching shot she was lying on a pink sun lounger, her blonde hair casually tied back, her long sun-tanned legs stretching out for ever, towards the camera. She was wearing a mocking smile and not much else.

Gloria had been going on for plump when she ran away. And getting plumper.

There wasn't an inch of spare flesh on this woman's trim body. Then again, we Mullins didn't run to fat with increasing age. Mother was still slim as a racing whippet. And there was something about the woman in the photo, something uncannily familiar that I couldn't quite put my finger on. I peered closer.

'She's the spitting image of you.' Mother sounded angry.

'Me?'

I don't know who was the most shocked by this daft notion, Turlough or me. We banged our heads together in our rush to re-examine the photo. It was the most intimate contact we'd had in a full year.

Mother turned out to be right. If you discounted the sleek blonde mane and the smoothly tanned skin, and the movie star figure, the woman in the photo did look a bit like me, or rather I looked a bit like her. Without the glamour, etc., etc.

'She looks like a tart,' Turlough growled.

I picked up the bundle of photographs and hared it up the stairs.

'Where are you running to now? Off to spend the rest of the day gawking at glamorous Gloria, are you?' he called after me.

Which just goes to show how little he knew me. I was far more interested in gawking at the man who was in one of the photos with her. He was leaning against a wrought-iron table by the sunlit swimming pool, wearing dazzling white swimming trunks and holding a tall iced glass in his bronzed hand. Gloria was leaning against him, clinging on to his tanned body like a blood-starved leech.

Even with the bright Californian sun forcing him to squint at the camera there was no mistaking the handsome face of Carlos Garcia. Or the rest of him. I should know. For the past three years I had probably spent more time looking at Carlos Garcia than I had at any other living creature. I had sat, wide-eyed, no more than four feet away from him every Friday night, as I watched him play the divine Rick Hein in *People in Jeopardy*, my favourite television drama.

Friday night was sacrosanct in our house. It was the one night of the week every member of the family got to do exactly what he or she pleased, without any interference from the others. Turlough attended the Ballyshannon IFA meeting, where he had gone from being an ordinary member to being its elected treasurer, a highly coveted post, I don't think. The twins went kick-boxing in the church hall – their one chance to do severe physical damage to other teenagers without fear of reprimand. Or any legal consequences. And Mother retired at nine thirty, with a steaming cup of Horlicks and the latest hot-off-the-presses edition of the *Sacred Heart Messenger*. And me? I spent my Friday nights watching Carlos Garcia take off his clothes.

That's what he mostly did in *People in Jeopardy*. Not in the actual court-room scenes where he played the charismatic, compassionate lawyer so superbly. He kept his clothes on in those scenes, usually dark-grey or sometimes elegantly tailored navy suits, with just the merest hint of a pin-stripe. In those scenes he moved like a sleek-muscled panther, having first stood stock still, in order to draw the court's full attention, before suddenly swivelling to turn his big brown eyes on the jury and plead for mercy for his always innocent clients.

Sometimes he made long impassioned speeches about inequality, and how the poor and the dispossessed found it wellnigh impossible to obtain true justice, due to the increasingly complex and ever spiralling costs of the cumbersome law machine that the American judicial system had become.

But like millions of women world-wide, who kept *People in Jeopardy* at the top of the television ratings, I sat waiting impatiently for him to take his clothes off.

I can't remember a single episode where I was disappointed. I had watched him remove his garments so often I was more familiar with every line of his beautifully proportioned body than I was with Turlough's. And I had been married to him for fifteen years.

Standing by Gloria's kidney-shaped swimming

pool, Carlos Garcia was, if anything, even more attractive than he appeared on television. He smiled up at me now, squinting into the sun, his nether regions encased in the tightest pair of swimming trunks this side of decency. I took a deep breath.

Mother's head appeared around the door. 'Are you sick?'

'I . . .'

'You look sick.' And she was gone.

Dream On

I scoured Gloria's letter for his name, without success. Not once in the long missive that accompanied the photos did she refer to him. Not once. It was hard to believe that any woman could get within touching distance of Carlos Garcia and forget to mention it. Especially when she took up half a page with boring trivia about her Porsche Carrera 911.

'Whatever that is,' I said aloud in frustration.

'A heap of junk,' Turlough said, over my shoulder. He drove a twelve-year-old diesel jeep.

For the following week I watched the post like a hawk. When the blue and red envelope finally arrived I slipped away from the house and down to the old cow byre, the scene of Gloria's terrible punishment all those years ago. She had certainly come a long way from a cow byre in Ballyshannon, my big sister. From being a ready target for Mother's quick temper, the constant butt of her cruel tongue, Gloria had managed to become a highly respected script-writer and the proud owner of a mansion in Beverly Hills. Not bad for a girl Mother used to call a witless cretin.

I was half-way along the second tightly written page before I found the name I was looking for. There it was, simply written, Carlos Garcia. I don't know what I had expected, capital letters maybe? A long line of exclamation marks? Neon lights? There wasn't anything to alert me to what was coming next. His name was written in the same bland ink as the rest.

Carlos and I met almost ten years ago. He was a bit player in the old Twentieth Century-Fox studio then, just starting out on his career. But there was something about him. I couldn't get him out of my mind. I knew he had something special. Star quality, I suppose. Whatever. But he was so naïve! I had to take him in hand. I introduced him around. Took him to places where he ought to be seen. Smartened him up a bit. He was so easygoing you wouldn't believe. But I have to give him credit for being a fast learner. His career took off at a phenomenal rate. He's almost overtaken me now. But not in the earning stakes, Maddy. Ha, ha. Not quite! We've been living together for nine years and it's been pretty good. Our dreams have become a little tarnished, I guess, but then whose dreams haven't? And I have to admit that Hollywood is not the best place to find personal fulfilment.

I almost fell off the wall with shock.

Carlos Garcia, the sexiest man on prime-time television, was living with my sister? My sister Gloria, who never even had a boy-friend in Ballyshannon. Who was always a bit of a joke among the boys with her thin hair, her too plump body and her permanently bruised fists, from fighting all comers. Gloria, who used to climb into my bed, after Mother had reduced her to tears with yet another hiding, and swear that she would one day live alone, in a mansion on a hill with nobody to answer to. Nobody to tell her what to do, ever again.

'I'll do it, Maddy. I swear I'll do it!'

And she had. She had got her mansion and I knew that nobody would dare order her around in it. But she wasn't living alone. Gloria had the gold ring. She was living with *Carlos Garcia*!

All those Friday nights, when I had gone to bed with my pulse racing, my head spinning with seductive images of him making love to yet another stunningly beautiful Hollywood actress, he had been going home to Gloria.

According to my TV guide our national electricity grid had once been in grave danger of failing, plunging the whole country into darkness, because of an unprecedented surge in demand by overheated women all rushing at the same time to make a calming cup of tea, after a particularly hot love scene between Carlos Garcia and a very famous actress.

And he was living with my sister?

It was the sheer injustice of it that got me. Not the fact that the national grid had almost failed us, but that I had stayed with Mother, after the bacteraemia killed Father. I had kept my promise to him. Listened to her cursing him for not trusting the Council surveyors. For using the rusty bailing wire to measure the low field. I could have run away – I was smart enough to earn a living even then. But I didn't.

I had stayed with the farm that had been in our family for five generations. Hurried home from school to assist old Miley with the milking. Helped to till fields and dip sheep. I had taken all the abuse Mother could give, all the vicious put-downs. I had never answered her back, or demanded my own way. Never once did anything to shame her in our little community. I had remained untouched and virginal, pure as the driven snow, until my wedding night, because Mother and Father Brennan, our parish priest, said it was the only thing to do.

Gloria had probably whored around Hollywood.

I had carried and given birth, in indescribable agony, to two of the ugliest children the nursing staff at St Columcilles Hospital had ever laid eyes on. I had received eight agonizing stitches in my senses, because their heads were so big. Not the nursing staff at St Columcilles, the twins.

Gloria had remained childless and unstitched.

And see how had things turned out for us. Where was my reward for being a good girl? For obeying all the rules? For staying to help out on a farm everyone said was doomed?

I got Turlough O'Toole, the late-night weather forecast and fat lamb prices every second night of the week.

What did Gloria get?

Runaway Gloria got to write scripts for *People in Jeopardy*. *She* got a mansion in Beverly Hills; a kidney-shaped swimming pool and Carlos Garcia in her bed every night.

Gloria had already mentioned a brief marriage and a swift divorce in one of her earlier letters. This had set Mother running for her purse. She handed Father Brennan a fiver to say mass for all sinners. But everyone knew who she meant.

To give him his due, Father Brennan did say that in his opinion divorcees didn't necessarily carry the mark of Satan any more. Then he winked at me.

But he took the fiver all the same.

*

Mother decided it was her belated maternal duty to watch *People in Jeopardy* at least once.

I did my best to dissuade her. But she has never been an easy woman to convince, as anyone who has tried to stop her using the AI man will testify.

'It's very . . . American,' I warned, as she settled herself in front of the television set, her knitting at the ready.

How else could I have put it? How could I tell a woman who boasted that in sixteen years of marriage her husband had never once caught her undressing, let alone naked, that in practically every episode the breath-takingly handsome Carlos did the horizontal jitterbug with some of the most alluring women in Hollywood?

'I hope he's a good actor, that's all,' she said.

I muttered a quick prayer to St Jude, the patron saint of lost causes.

The theme music for *People in Jeopardy* came on; a catchy little tune called 'Night Moves', which had been in the hit parade on both sides of the Atlantic for months on end.

'Is it a musical?' she asked hopefully, her needles beginning to click happily.

My heart sank.

The first ten minutes of the programme were taken up with a dramatic court-room scene where Carlos was battling away against mindless bureaucrats who were intent on forcing a group of elderly people out of their rent-controlled apartments. Carlos, or Rick Hein as he was called, had discovered that the real villain of the piece was in fact a powerful conglomerate, which stood to gain trillions when it knocked down the apartment building and replaced it with a glass-walled office block.

Mother nodded encouragingly to Carlos every time he spoke and her needles clicked in support whenever he won a salient point.

If I hadn't been a regular fan of *People in Jeopardy* I might have relaxed or even begun to thank St Jude for his saintly intervention, because we seemed now to be watching the only episode of the series where there wasn't a chance of Carlos getting his leg over.

Not one of his clients appeared to be under sixty. And Hollywood had a strict age code, I had noticed.

I was still apprehensive.

And then it happened, right after the second ad break, just as I had feared.

All through the earlier court-room scenes a feisty female lawyer had been eyeing Carlos up. And who could blame the woman? Although she *was* on the opposing legal team and supposedly Rick's mortal enemy. But it was a small court-room and she'd had to brush past him every time she wanted to interject, or cross-examine a hostile witness.

After the second ad break they walked together briskly towards an unused office. Carlos locked the door behind them. I knew what was coming. The feisty female lawyer started to unbutton his immaculate white shirt.

'Will I make us a cup of tea, Mother?' Too late. The female lawyer was already reaching for Carlos's well-tailored flies. And just in case the viewers misconstrued her intentions, or were completely brain-dead, the camera moved in to give us a lingering close-up.

'Jesus, Mary and Joseph, what's she doing?' Mother dropped a line of stitches.

'Maybe she's . . . dropped something?' I panicked.

'Don't you treat me like a fool!' Mother's face was turning puce with embarrassment.

Carlos and the woman lawyer were now thrashing around on a huge desk. He began tearing off her white shirt, sending little double-fronted pearl buttons flying in all directions.

'Oh my God.' Mother put a hand to her mouth as the female lawyer's huge breasts filled the small screen. 'Oh merciful hour! Oh sweet heart of Jesus! Don't let Gloria be watching this.'

'She writes the scripts, Mother,' I had to remind her.

'Gloria wrote . . .?' Her voice failed.

Carlos was now running his tongue along one huge, deeply bronzed breast. He didn't stop there, but continued on downwards towards the bottom of the screen.

Mother leaped to her feet. 'Sacred heart of Jesus. I've seen everything now.'

But she hadn't. She had barely left the room when the feisty blonde lawyer began trailing her tongue southwards on Carlos. The camera moved in for a close-up of his perspiring face, squashing between two dusty filing cabinets, then the scene faded.

We were in the middle of breakfast when the phone rang.

'Gloria? Oh Glo, is it really you?' Despite the American twang, I recognized her voice instantly. It was as if the past twenty years had never happened. We fell into the same old teasing pattern we had used, laughing and joking as if we had never been apart. 'Oh Gloria . . . it's as if you never went away. When are you coming over to see us?'

Turlough froze, mid-chew. The twins turned to listen, their ugly little faces, with their close-set eyes, mirroring their father's worried expression.

Mother put out her hand for the receiver. She had never been a woman to waste time on incidentals. 'Are you not ashamed to be mixed up in the kind of filth we had to watch last night?'

The twins stopped eating altogether, their loose mouths falling open, dropping half-chewed bits of toast on to the plastic table-cloth. When they realized she was only referring to a television show they lost interest. The twins never watched television. There wasn't enough violence on it for them.

Turlough and I sat motionless, like opposing statues, both of us straining to hear what Gloria was saying.

Mother had a habit of holding the receiver well away from her ear whenever she used the phone. She had a cousin who had died in the nineteen sixties from a stroke rumoured to be brought on by some kind of electrical charge running along a phone line. Turlough had often remarked that it was more likely to have been when he saw his phone bill, but none the less Mother had remained uneasy around telephones ever after. She certainly chose to hold them at what she considered to be a safe distance from her head.

This peculiar habit of hers made it a lot easier for the rest of us to overhear what her caller might be saying, when they spoke loudly enough.

Gloria's voice did carry. But it was completely calm and controlled. She might have been explaining her programme to a gathering of already interested businessmen. Her voice was completely neutral. Not a scintilla of emotion. Facts only.

People in Jeopardy was a realistic portrayal of modern American life, she said.

'Life in the sewer, you mean?' Mother's face was contorted with anger.

'Contemporary America . . . sixty million viewers . . . we've . . . prestigious awards . . .' The calm voice continued.

'Awards? For what? Spreading filth?' Mother was yelling now.

The call ended on that happy note. Twenty years on and Mother and Gloria were still mortal enemies.

I waited until I was alone to call her back. 'Glo? I'm so proud of you,' I whispered. Then I hung up, because Turlough always checked the phone bills.

It became a weekly routine. Gloria would phone, and she and Mother would cross swords viciously, the one cool and assured, the other practically foaming at the mouth because Gloria was beyond her reach. Then it would be my turn to talk, and Gloria and I would laugh and giggle until Mother's eyes narrowed into angry slits.

It was the same every Saturday morning. That's when she called. And always at the same time.

'Cheap rates,' Turlough remarked slyly.

I ignored him. Gloria and I began ending our conversations with, 'I love you, Sis.'

But I had to whisper, in case I was overheard.

When the two first-class tickets to Los Angeles arrived all hell broke loose.

'Who does she think she is?' Twelve hours later Mother was still going on about it. 'Does she think that because she has a swimming pool like a kidney

I'd want to visit her? In that den of iniquity? Contemporary American life is right. Contemporary filth is more like it.' She was practically spitting.

'She must be making some serious money all the same. I believe that programme is shown all over the world.' There was a definite note of respect beginning to creep into Turlough's voice whenever the subject of Gloria's career arose.

'What's that got to do with anything? Dirty money is dirty money. Would you put your hand to that sort of money?'

Turlough's face was a picture.

I took a deep breath. 'My sister has been nominated for an Emmy award in Hollywood. There are people would kill for that honour. We should be proud of Gloria. Proud to have a family member who can write award-winning scripts.'

'The day I'll be proud of what she does is the day I'll join your father in the grave.'

And all the way over in Ballycairn graveyard I swear I could hear Father trembling.

Turlough and I went to our room.

He turned on the weather forccast, although there was little need, as we could already hear the cold wind whistling around the eaves of the old house. It said there were gale force winds due in from the Faeroe Isles. I pulled on a warm jumper before getting into bed.

I detected a definite lightening in Turlough's step. This was either due to the fact that fat Marion was now coming in one extra day a week, or all the talk of the big money Gloria was supposedly earning in Hollywood. I knew how his mind worked. If she was earning millions she was hardly likely to want a share of a smallish farm in Ballyshannon, was she? None the less, he still slyly backed Mother whenever she denigrated Gloria. But then Turlough had always known which side his bread was buttered on.

The twins were forever on her side too, right or wrong. In so far as they were interested in anything outside of kick-boxing half the youth of the parish. Or punching each other around the yard.

'I want Gran,' one of them cried, when I tried to comfort him in the small hours, after he had woken from a bad dream. Probably one where he had failed to knock his brother unconscious.

'Coming, son.' I could hear her, flapping along the poorly lit landing, like a bat in flight, her old leather slippers slapping against the worn lino, the way they used to slap against Gloria's pale face whenever she dared ask permission to go out after tea.

She had never beaten me with quite the same enthusiasm. But then I had never gone against her. Even Turlough had been her choice. She had been the one to introduce the idea of marriage to him. We hadn't even gone out together at that stage.

Our cowman Miley had told Mother that Turlough O'Toole was said to be gifted with animals. 'He's a wonder with the beasts. A fair hard worker, too.' Miley was anxious to retire.

Mother pointed out the big redheaded man to me at Mass. She said I could do a lot worse. He wasn't bad looking. Some people might even consider him handsome, with his big wide shoulders and strong back. He started following me home at night, walking past our gate after evening devotions, even though the farm where he then worked was four miles in the other direction.

I began waving to him, I don't know why. He sent me a Christmas card. It had a silver manger on the front. And the oxen on it looked clean enough to be in the Spring Show in Dublin.

When he suggested a wedding in Rome, not because of any religious convictions but because it was cheap, Mother made up her mind. And Turlough and I were married. In Rome.

Almost a year later I had painfully delivered two babies at once, saving a considerable amount on expensive hospital bills. And as both were boys, Mother and Turlough were dumbfounded with delight. I had finally done something right. Something admirable for once.

That night I dreamed they had married each other.

'I can't go travelling to America at my age.'

'You're sixty-two, Hanna. The Pope was practically circumnavigating the globe in his mid-seventies.' Father Brennan winked at me.

'He's omnipotent,' Mother barked.

Turlough backed her up as usual: 'Who'd want to go to an award ceremony in a foreign flesh-pot anyway?'

'I would. Gloria is my sister. I'd like to see her getting an award.'

Turlough looked at Mother. 'We could always sell the other ticket.'

When Gloria rang, Mother was ready for her. 'So you think you're going to win an Oscar, do you?'

'An Emmy, Mother. Oscars are for movies.'

'An Emmy, an Oscar, what's the difference.' Mother hated to be wrong.

Gloria's hearty laugh rang out across the miles. 'About a million dollars.'

'What?'

Turlough sold the spare ticket. He bought me a new tweed suit and himself a new second-hand dairy sterilizer with the proceeds.

Fat Marion came up the yard to inspect it. 'Oh Mr O'Toole, it's massive. I can't wait to have a go at it.

I'll bet, fat Marion. I'll bet, I thought.

Mother stood over me, supervising my packing. When there was nothing left to do she still hung around, shifting from one foot to the other. She began to fiddle with the photo of Gloria that I had given pride of place on my dressing-table.

'She always shad poor skin. Not like a Mullin at all. And she certainly wasn't born with hair that colour.'

'Neither were you,' I muttered, glancing at her greying thatch.

'Don't you get cheeky with me!'

I was thirty-three years old and still forbidden to answer back.

'And would you look at the size of the chest on her. No one in this family ever had a chest that size . . . and as for that pool!' She held the plastic-framed photo up to her face for a closer look. 'I say she has to have that pumped every day.'

I'm almost sure she meant the pool.

'It's a selfish move, leaving Turlough to deal with the new calves.'

She definitely meant me. But since when had Turlough allowed me to handle a beast of his? Certainly not since fat Marion had been on the job.

'Don't you get into conversation with any strangers

over there. Americans aren't like us. They're all out for what they can get.'

Words of wisdom from a woman who had never travelled further than Ballycairn graveyard. And wasn't ever likely to.

My flight was at two-thirty. At twelve o'clock I took an extra Roche five, just in case. It was a mistake. By twelve-twenty the world was beginning to slide into slow motion and my mouth felt as if it was packed with cotton wool. Descending the crooked old stairway took me an age.

'Maaady?' Father Brennan was calling from the end of a long tunnel. 'Are you ready, deeeear?'

Turlough was too busy calving out of season to drive me to the airport. *And* he was having trouble with the jeep. The wire holding the exhaust pipe in place was threatening to give up the ghost next time it encountered a pot-hole of any reasonable depth.

I wasn't sure if I should kiss Mother goodbye or not. It wasn't something we made a habit of in our family. In fact, the only people you could legitimately kiss in public in Ballyshannon were the newly dead.

Mother saved me the worry by holding out a rigid dry-skinned hand. We shook goodbye, like two hill farmers after completing a sheep deal.

I looked around for the twins. Somebody said they were down in the church hall, training.

'For what?'

Nobody seemed to know.

'Say goodbye to them for me,' a hoarse voice said. It was probably mine.

And then things began to speed up again. Turlough coughed and aimed a half-hearted little peck at my left cheek, but I must have moved because it went way off target, landing somewhere between my new perm and my left ear-lobe.

I stared wide-eyed at him, wondering if he had ever kissed fat Marion on the perm. Not that I cared any more. The first time I saw them together I had been distraught, barely able to make it back to the house I was so upset. But over the following weeks I began to realize that I didn't even like Turlough. So why should I feel betrayed? And I would hardly miss his clumsy gropes under the sheets, what with knowing Mother was always lying awake directly below.

I resigned myself to a life of celibacy. Well semi-celibacy. With a couple of drinks inside him Turlough was inclined to remember his conjugal duties. But then he only drank at Christmas. And New Year.

'I've told Maddy to behave herself in America.' Father Brennan laughed.

Then we were in the car.

They were frowning in the window at me, Mother and Turlough. Then they straightened up, folding their arms in unison like those old married couples who mimic each other for want of something better to do. 'Don't forget your pills,' they chorused.

And I thought Mother looked bereft for a second. But that was probably a trick of the light.

I didn't imagine the fact that Turlough was clean-shaven. Fat Marion must have been coming in to do some extra work that day.

Father Brennan startled me by patting my knee, his big rough hand splaying out across the heavy tweed of my new skirt. 'Don't look so sad, Maddy. You'll have a great time altogether in America. Your sister will show you the time of your life!' He laughed as he swung the car out the gate, scattering hens in all directions. 'It'll probably be the ruination of you, going to America. You'll never be the same again once you get the taste of Hollywood.'

He didn't really mean it, of course, and neither of us realized it at the time, but he had never spoken a truer word.

Only it wasn't Hollywood I was to get the taste for.

At last LA

It wasn't as if I'd been expecting Los Angeles airport to be anything like as homely as Shannon had been, of course I wasn't. It was, after all, the gateway to Hollywood, as I had to keep reminding myself on the flight from New York whenever the two leather-clad men sitting opposite embraced each other. Or French kissed. And what they did over Albuquerque doesn't bear repeating.

Despite this, nothing could have prepared me for the scene I encountered after US customs.

Hordes of excited cameramen were milling around, jostling each other, vying for space in front of a line of burly policemen. And *behind* the blue-uniformed line was what appeared to be half the female population of America. All screaming at the tops of their voices.

Without warning the crowd suddenly surged forward, knocking the cops into the group of cameramen.

'Leonardo! Leonardo!' the sound was deafening.

I turned to find the cause of all this hysteria.

Hurrying along behind me, no more than a few yards away, was Leonardo DiCaprio being roughly escorted by an army of men in three-piece suits.

'Leonardo! Leonardo!' The screams became unbearable.

The police linked arms to form a human chain in front of me; their sweat-drenched backs threatening to burst through their short-sleeved shirts, as they attempted to hold back the hysterical crowd.

'Get back! Get back, for Chrissakes! Before someone gets hurt here,' one of them yelled.

I was doing my best to obey when I realized he hadn't meant me. Even if he had, I couldn't have obliged. I was now being pushed forward by Leonardo's minders. And he appeared even more frightened than I was. He also looked as if he shouldn't be out this late without a note from his mother.

He bestowed on his fans an obliging little wave and they went wild, screeching and clawing their way towards him. The police cordon almost gave way with the pressure. One more surge like that and we would all be in danger of being trampled underfoot.

A huge policeman, his mountainous stomach overhanging his tight bluc trousers, reached out and grabbed my arm, almost pulling it from its socket. 'This way, Ma'am, quickly. You shudda used the other door.'

Only his great bulk prevented me from being flattened when the crowd finally broke through.

He pushed me through a side door and locked it behind me, leaving Leonardo to the tender mercies of his adoring fans.

In the main arrivals hall I went searching for a ladies room. I couldn't let Gloria catch me looking like something the cat dragged in from the silage pit. Even before my encounter with Leonardo's frenzied fans I had been the only passenger in arrivals who looked worse than her passport photo. My tweed suit hadn't travelled at all well. And my new perm, which had looked so promising to begin with, had exploded in a disappointing frizz the second we got air clearance at Shannon.

Luckily my flight was early; I would have plenty of time to tidy up before Gloria caught sight of me.

'Maddy? Maddy?' an excited voice screamed and I was engulfed in a cloud of exotic perfume.

I turned. 'Gloria?'

She was a film star. From the top of her shining, beige-blonde hair, to her colour-co-ordinated five-inch stilettos, that had her towering above me in my flat brown brogues, she was dazzling. A Hollywood goddess in a pale-beige suit that looked as if it would require daily dry-cleaning.

She opened her arms wide.

I hesitated. 'It is you, Gloria?'

'Who do you think? You big eejit.' The exterior might be Hollywood, but the accent was pure Ballyshannon.

I burst into tears. In front of hundreds of strangers. Americans. I began to blubber like a baby. And I couldn't stop. And of course it might have been partly because my feet were swollen, and my ears hurt, and my perm was a disaster, and I was so desperately ashamed to be standing there looking gauche and ugly, compared with this beautiful golden-beige creature. But I think it was mostly because I was being hugged by the only person in the whole world who had ever truly loved me.

Then she was crying. This sophisticated woman whose lip gloss you could see your reflection in was crying, her face crinkling up, her dampening mascara threatening to destroy her beautifully made-up cheeks.

We stood in the middle of Los Angeles airport and howled.

And I have to confess that all the time she was crying and hugging me I kept thinking that she had Carlos Garcia. And I had Turlough. And now that I was far enough away from him I could finally admit the truth to myself – I hated Turlough O'Toole. 'Wear your new tweed suit,' he'd said.

'Let's get out of here, Maddy.' Gloria wiped her eyes. 'Let's go home.'

'To Ballyshannon?' I couldn't believe my ears.

'Not fucking likely.' She laughed.

I was determined not to giggle at the length of the stretch-limo that was waiting at the kerb. But I had to remark on it. 'How can it possibly stay up without support?' I gasped.

'That's the most frequently used defence in Hollywood, honey.'

It took me a second to read the wicked glint in her eye. 'She has a filthy tongue on her, that Gloria,' Mother used to say.

We clutched each other now, Gloria and I, and laughed so hard the uniformed driver began to look concerned.

'I thought he was Tom Cruise,' I whispered in her ear.

'I warned you!' She giggled with delight.

And she had. She had said Hollywood was so full of wannabes that you couldn't spit without gobbing on a Tom Cruise or a Robert De Niro look-alike.

Wannabe Tom was busy stacking my cases in the boot, so I picked up my little canvas holdall.

Then I almost fainted. 'Oh my God, Gloria, look,

there's Sylvester Stallone. Look! Over there carrying the black suitcases.'

'That'll be a porter.' She didn't even turn.

'No! It's definitely . . .'

'A porter. Nobody in LA carries their own baggage.'

I left the canvas holdall for Tom.

'You'll never believe who I saw in arrivals. Leonardo DiCaprio! The real one!' I boasted.

'Sure it was.' She stepped into the car. 'Did you have a rough flight?' She was staring at my hair.

We were purring along in the stretch-limo and I was trying not to ask too many dumb questions.

I had already checked out the fully stocked bar and the red push-button telephone, and the CD player fitted into the plush leather in front of me. Now I was looking at the fax machine. 'Is all this yours?' I asked.

'No.' She frowned. 'It belongs to Lilliput Productions.'

'Oh.' Lilliput was the company that produced *People in Jeopardy*. 'Do they own your house as well?'

'No, that's mine. All bought and paid for.'

She didn't say, *wrong again, Maddy*, but I knew she was thinking it. So when I spotted something that looked uncannily like the famous old Hollywood sign, way up on a shrub-covered hillside, I knew it couldn't possibly be the real thing. It looked far too realistic to be anything but a wannabe. So I didn't say a word.

I didn't want to appear like a complete ignoramus.

'Haven't you noticed the famous Hollywood sign, honey? We took this route specially, so you could have an unencumbered view of it. It's been there for over fifty years,' she chastised me.

Wannabe Tom glared at me in the driving mirror.

So LA wasn't all that different from Ballyshannon after all. Hard as I tried, I still ended up in the wrong. Every time. 'It just that it's so well preserved, it looks new,' I defended myself.

'Welcome to Hollywood, honey. The land of sweet illusion.'

The aerial photos hadn't done justice to Gloria's home. It was impossible to take it all in at once. The limo sped past a blur of towering palm trees, high electronic gates, and swept around the most magnificent turreted mansion, before coming to a halt in what might have been a national park.

This was Gloria's back garden.

'Big, isn't it?' She grinned, her eyes sparkling.

Big? The swimming pool alone could have facilitated the entire population of Ballyshannon – if they'd been able to swim. The garden was bigger than Country Carlow. If you got lost here they'd have to send in helicopters.

Gloria was delighted by my stunned reaction. Her cheeks became flushed with pleasure. And the more dumbstruck I became the happier she got.

She insisted on giving me a quick tour of the garden before we went indoors. 'Before the sun goes down,' she said.

I trailed along behind her as she tore around pointing out plants that might have been from Mars. She led me past masterfully designed flowerbeds the likes of which would only be seen at the Chelsea Flower Show. She dragged me along herb-edged pathways and over decorative little waterfalls, all the time talking ninety to the dozen.

'I know how you love the outdoors, Maddy. You could spend weeks exploring this garden.'

She was right. After a while I stopped to pull my shoes off my swollen feet.

The next thing I know Gloria is shoeless as well, her expensive high heels carelessly discarded in a giant clump of broccoli.

She ran barefoot through row after row of well-mulched vegetables, seeming not to care that her manicured feet were becoming covered in clinging damp loam.

When I tore off my sweaty tweed jacket, she threw back her head and cheered. 'Go for it, Maddy!'

We ended up chasing each other around floodlit statues of naked men; with large bunches of stone grapes. Giggling hysterically at the sight of vulgar little cherubs, peeing nonstop into the big swimming pool.

I can't speak for Gloria, but I hadn't enjoyed myself so much since we mitched from school, one golden September morning, and went blackberry picking in Ballycairn graveyard.

We were the Mullin girls again, united against the world. With nobody watching us, nobody telling us what to do.

I could have stayed in that garden for ever.

But Gloria had already run into the house, and what could I do but follow.

She had always been the leader. I was only the younger sister always trailing behind.

Wannabe Tom was standing just inside the big double doors, my cases in a heap by his feet. He scowled fiercely as I ran past him.

'Gloria? Where are you?' I called.

I was hurrying along a palatial, high-ceilinged hallway, not knowing which way to turn, when I suddenly collided with a tall, gaunt figure approaching from the other direction.

For one terrifying second I thought it was Mother and the laughter died on my lips. Then I recognized her. It was Mrs Danvers. There was no mistaking that tall sombre figure. Anyone who has even glanced at a single page of *Rebecca* couldn't but recognize the woman standing before me. She might as well have been wearing one of those little tin badges children flaunt on their birthdays and sometimes for days afterwards. The one that proudly proclaim to the world, – *I am five. Or Six.* Only hers would have said *I am Mrs Danvers.*

'Ah, Betty.' Gloria ran up, panting hard. 'I see you've met my sister Maddy.'

Mrs Danvers turned.

Gloria was a sight. Her neatly pinned hair had collapsed around her shoulders, like a carelessly made bird's nest. Long streamers of damp hair clung to her silk blouse, which was well on the way to becoming as grubby as mine. Her cheeks were cherry red and glistening with sweat. Her scarlet lipstick was smeared across her fine chin, where she had clumsily attempted to brush back a strand of falling hair.

Mrs Danvers stared at us without speaking. She allowed her gaze to trail slowly downwards, taking everything in, before coming to rest on our filthy, dirt-splattered feet.

I fully expected to be sent to bed without any tea.

But this was Gloria's housekeeper, not our mother. And she wasn't really Mrs Danvers, either. Yet I would challenge anyone who has ever read *Rebecca*, under the blankets with a torch, to come face to face with this woman and not feel a little shiver of apprehension run along their spine.

She was dressed in deep black, a little fringe of cream lace garlanding her skinny throat in a desperate attempt to take the harm out of her. It didn't work. Her ivory-skinned face, with its prominent cheekbones and deeply set eyes, might have been described as handsome. Not by me. The very look of her chilled me to the bone.

And yet I had no wish to be judgemental. Looks can be deceiving. Life has taught me that. I held out my hand and forced a smile. 'Pleased to meet you,' I said.

Her handclasp almost broke my index finger.

'Dinner is served, Madam.'

'Oh we'll need to shower first.' Gloria was all-American again, the wild girl from Ballyshannon no longer in evidence.

Mrs Danvers nodded, her eyes still riveted by our dirty feet.

'Don't worry about unpacking, Maddy. You'll find bathrobes and anything else you need in your room. Betty will show you the way.'

Was I to be left alone with her? I tried signalling my panic to Gloria with my eyes, but she had already turned away.

She led me upstairs, walking ramrod straight as if she owned the place. I had to keep reminding myself that this was my sister's housekeeper. She was a servant here. No more than that.

And I was far too old to be intimidated by a servant in my sister's house. I threw back my shoulders and adopted my most dignified walk, not easy given that I was still in my bare feet.

I wouldn't please her by gasping at the splendour of my room. Or even at my first sight of the king-sized bed, which was bigger than our kitchen scullery after we added the extension.

She didn't say a word, just laid out warm towels in the glittering bathroom, while I walked around, trying to give the impression that I was well familiar with exquisitely fitted bathrooms that had sunken marble baths, mirrored ceilings and goldfish-head fittings everywhere you looked.

I hardly glanced at the pink marble bidet.

I had been to Rome. I had seen a bidet before. The only difference with this one was that, in common with so much else here, it somehow managed to look sumptuous and sexy all at once. In fact, everything here looked sumptuous and sexy. Except for the endless reflections of my sweaty, fuzzy-headed self, staring back at me out of the wall-to-wall mirrors.

Mrs Danvers served dinner.

'Just a simple little meal, Maddy. I appreciate how exhausted you must be. Jet lag is a killer,' Gloria said, understanding seeping from every pore.

Our simple little meal began with cold lobster soup, with featherlight croutons floating on top. This was followed by thin slices of honey-glazed ham, with a selection of vegetables, most of which I'd be hard to put to name. And everything was so tastefully arranged on gold-rimmed plates that it seemed a shame to disturb it, just because you were hungry.

'Mmm . . . umm . . . ooh.' I couldn't help myself.

Mrs Danvers hovered at my elbow, filling and refilling my long-stemmed wineglass.

'Oh Gloria, this is . . . this is . . .' I was at a loss for words.

Gloria sat back to watch me eat. She looked like the cat that got the cream in the dairy.

Mrs Danvers didn't smile, but her icy façade did begin to look as if a mild thaw might be setting in.

I was still in raptures over my main course when I spotted the dessert. 'Oh my God!' It had to be the biggest chocolate cheesecake in the world.

Gloria giggled with delight at my reaction. 'You haven't changed one bit, Maddy. I told Dong you liked your food.'

'Dong?' I looked up, my mouth full of crispy vegetables.

'My cook. He's Vietnamese. Well his father was French.'

'Oh. These vegetables . . . umm!'

At Hawthorn Farm Mother was in sole charge of the cooking. I was a mere kitchen hand. She had always considered food to be nothing more than fuel to get a body through the day. Pandering to the senses was a mortal sin in her book. A good sharp boil was her remedy for what she considered to be the stubborn nature of most root vegetables in particular. If this tended to reduce them to a quivering, unrecognizable mass, then so be it. Food was to be eaten, not admired. Her most frequently used culinary aid was bread soda. She lashed a spoonful of this softening agent into practically everything she cooked. Especially the vegetables. She had discovered that the cooking time of any of them could be halved by the addition of a spoonful of bread soda. I must have been seventeen years old before I discovered that some people actually ate vegetables with their shape and taste still intact.

'Is she still using the bread soda?' Gloria cut into my thoughts.

I almost choked. We sat back and laughed until the tears ran down our faces.

'Has anything changed?'

'Well, she has Turlough to connive with now. They get along very well.'

'What about the twins?'

'They only talk to each other. Old Miley retired. We have a part-time milkmaid instead.'

'Is she any good?'

'She is at some things.' I thought about the scene I had witnessed in the milking parlour.

Mrs Danvers began to clear away the plates.

'That was delicious. Thank you Mrs Danvers,' I said.

There was a stony silence.

Gloria stared down at her dessert plate.

'I . . . I'm so sorry . . . I didn't mean . . .' I began.

An icy hand gripped my shoulder. I half expected to feel the cold metal of the dessert fork sinking into my back. Instead, she leaned across and placed a giant slice of cheesecake on the gold-rimmed plate in front of me. 'Cream, Madam?'

I shook my head, more in fear than anything else.

She glided out silently, moving as if she had well-oiled castors instead of feet beneath the long black skirt.

I threw down my napkin. 'I'm so sorry, Gloria. I don't know how I . . . I'm always doing it. The name just slipped out. I'm so sorry.'

'Don't be crazy. She loved it. Couldn't you tell? You've made her day.'

And it appeared that I had, because after that unintentional slip I became Mrs Danvers's favourite person in the whole world. After Gloria, of course.

Betty Buttoni was Mrs Danvers's real name. She was a failed actress from Buffalo – her description. Betty from Buffalo. Her one and only stage success had been playing Mrs Danvers in a Summer Stock production of *Rebecca*. She had, apparently, brought the house down. And never worked again. Not as an actress, anyway. But she had taken such a liking to the part of Mrs Danvers that she was loath to relinquish it. When finally forced to seek alternative employment, she took the part with her and became one of the most coveted housekeepers in Beverly Hills.

'Everybody wants Betty.' Gloria said. 'She's discreet, loyal and, best of all, unlikely to run off with anyone's husband. If you know what I mean.' She winked. 'And she never steps out of her role. The woman is a treasure. And you spotted it straight off. You've made a friend there, Maddy.'

I had also learned a never to be forgotten lesson about Hollywood. Anywhere else, Betty Buttoni might have been in grave danger of being certified. But here she could continue acting out her greatest success, day after day, night after night, even without the benefit of stage lighting or a paying audience. And for her trouble she gained endless admiration. *And* a hefty salary.

As far as Betty was concerned, acting was acting. If she couldn't tread the boards successfully she could play her beloved Mrs Danvers in a mansion that almost rivalled Manderley for imposing beauty. She relished her life here. And despite being regularly headhunted by half the avaricious matrons of Beverly Hills she remained loyal to Gloria.

To the bitter end.

Hollywood Heaven

'It's just the change of food. Or perhaps the heat,' Gloria said consolingly, when I complained of feeling queasy as we sat in the sun together. 'Move into the shade – you'll feel better.'

I hoped her diagnosis was right. The alternative was too horrible to contemplate. Queasiness in the morning? Nausea in the afternoon? What that might signal would be beyond endurance.

But I couldn't possibly be pregnant. You had to have sex to become pregnant. At least in Ballyshannon. And I hadn't had sex for well over a year. Closer to two if you didn't count the time Turlough got rat-arsed at the Irish Farming Association's Christmas dinner and tried to force me to lean over the dry-stone wall, by the old cow byre, on the way home. His version of urgent passion.

Fat Marion must have been incommunicado that week. Or away visiting her maternal cousin who had emigrated to the Ballymun flats complex in Dublin. That must have lowered the tone of the place considerably, having her cousin move in.

The last time I remembered Turlough being in such a state of sexual frustration had been on the long flight back from Rome after our wedding. Due to some oversight at the booking office, or more likely sly penny pinching on his part, we failed to get seats next to each other. He sulked for the first hundred or so air miles and then, although Christmas was months away, began breaking into our stock of duty free.

A large party of the Little Sisters of Perpetual Succour happened to be travelling on the same flight. They were returning from their annual pilgrimage to St Peter's in Rome and occupied all the seats around us.

If my memory serves, we were something like thirty-five thousand feet above Penzance when Turlough began reaching across, trying to touch my groin. The Little Sister beside me put up with his ham-fisted attempts for a full two minutes, before calling the steward.

He reported Turlough to the captain, who left the cockpit to have a word with him. A reporter from a tabloid paper also happened to be on the same flight and he got wind of the scandalous goings-on in tourist class. Except that in the time-honoured tradition of the tabloid press, he got it wrong.

Next day there was a blurry picture of Turlough on the front page of a scurrilous rag, with the caption: *Randy Farmer Tries to Assault Nun*.

Gloria and I were sipping iced tea on her glorious pink sun terrace when I told her this story. She almost choked on hers.

I rattled the ice-cubes in mine. It was not one of my better memories.

'What about Mother? What did she say when she read it?' Gloria finally stopped laughing.

'Don't be daft! Mother only admits to reading the *Sacred Heart Messenger*, you know that. Well, she does sometimes look at the *Irish Independent*. But only to check the death columns. She likes to be first with the *really* good news. *And* make her own corrections.'

Gloria raised her well-plucked brows.

'Well, they sometimes get the age *wrong*, don't they? Of the deceased. Or maybe they forget to add *and loving grandchildren*, or something of that magnitude. Mother makes corrections in the margins. She never goes any further than that, she's not one of those people who write letters to newspapers complaining about misprints or anything. She just likes to make her own corrections. Mark them out for her own satisfaction. You can always tell when she's discovered a mistake; she goes around nodding happily to herself. Gets a satisfied look about her. Her version of a smile, I suppose.'

'Jeeze, Maddy, you're making me homesick for the old place.'

I grinned. 'Oh it's a constant barrel of laughs all right. And, of course, Turlough wouldn't be without the *Irish Independent* every Tuesday. That's the day it comes with the free farming section. Beef prices, milk quotas and the coming week's weather forecast. Essential bedtime reading for all young marrieds.' I tried not to sound bitter.

'Why on earth did you marry him, Maddy? I was sure you'd have had a good career by now. Maybe something in the bank. Or even teaching.'

'Me?'

'Yes. You were always so clever. Always reading. My strongest memories are of you in the school library with your head stuck in a book. Always hungry for knowledge, you were, for information about exotic, far-away places. Places nobody else thought about, then. I never even considered the wider world until you began to tell me stories about it.'

'Are you sure you don't have me mixed up with someone else?'

'You used to tell me about the world, Maddy. I have the clearest recollection of that. I never bothered with books. That was you.' She seemed to be annoyed with me for not sharing *her* memories.

There was an uneasy silence between us for a few seconds.

Then she suddenly asked. 'Did you never even consider moving to Dublin?'

I played with the ice-cubes again. The sun was so hot it was melting them at an unbelievable rate.

'Maddy?'

'How could I have moved to Dublin? When you ran off it left us completely short-handed. I had to take over your chores as well as doing my own.'

'Jesus, do you blame me for . . .'

'I don't blame anyone. I'm just saying that I had to stay. Someone had to stay. She couldn't have managed the place on her own. Besides, Father would have haunted me if I'd deserted her.'

'Like I did, you mean?'

'No, I didn't mean that. You did what you needed to do at the time.'

'How do you know what I needed?' Her eyes were hard. 'Then or now.'

'All I'm saying, Gloria, is that I had to stay. Miley was getting older, the farm needed another pair of hands.'

She grinned slyly. 'So that's why you married Turlough.'

I wasn't going to be drawn. I hadn't come all this way to row with Gloria. I could get that at home any day of the week. I was hoping for better things in sunny California. I lay back on the sun bed and closed my eyes.

'So what do you do with your free time now that Superman is on the job?'

I had to laugh. 'Actually, he's not. At least not with me. He has a milkmaid.'

'What?' She sat up straight. 'In Catholic Ballyshannon? Is nothing sacred?'

'Oh you wouldn't believe the changes in Ballyshannon since you left.'

'What? Has someone invented the wheel?'

We laughed together. 'Not only that, we have a TV set.'

'Yeah! And mother watches *People in Jeopardy*.' She was serious again.

I nearly said, no she doesn't. I'm the one who spends all week waiting for Friday night when I get to watch your Carlos on the screen. But I didn't. I was afraid that I might give myself away if I said his name. By drooling at the mouth or something.

I rattled the ice-cubes instead and asked, 'When is this man of yours going to appear?'

'Carlos?' She smiled. 'You'll love him, Maddy, he's a babe. An absolute babe. But of course you've seen him on television.'

I felt myself blush.

If Gloria noticed she didn't comment. She probably attributed it to the heat. 'He'll be back in a few days. They shoot all the exteriors of *People in Jeopardy* in New York. That's where Rick Hein's office is set. This season we're going for more and more exteriors. It gives the show a more authentic feel. Keeps the viewers on their toes, I think.'

I thought it might have been seeing the divine

Carlos in close-up that kept most of the viewers on their toes. But I said nothing.

'Location work is notorious for running overtime. And the expense! You wouldn't believe the running costs of a location shoot, Maddy. Especially in New York. It's absolute hell, it can push you to the edge of bankruptcy.'

She began to explain the intricacies of costing a popular TV series on location. The trouble involved in bringing in crews, and equipment, and actors. 'And don't start me on wardrobe, Maddy. That can be the biggest headache of all.'

I thought about Carlos in the last scene I had watched him in. That hardly required much wardrobing, seeing that he had spent the whole time in bed with a semi-naked actress.

'If I'm there I make damn sure to keep the pressure on them.'

'Pardon?'

'When I go on location with him. I keep the pressure on the whole company. Time is money, I keep reminding them. On location, Maddy,' She frowned.

'Of course.' I had to force myself to concentrate on what she was saying. 'Would you have been with him in New York if I hadn't been coming over? Did I keep you here, Gloria?'

'It's my pleasure, honey.' She caught my hand and held it against her face, then began to move her soft cheek backwards and forwards against my palm, and for the second time in twenty years I felt so much love well up inside me I thought I might drown in it.

Mrs Danvers woke me next morning. 'Tea, Madam?'

I waited to see if my nausea would recur. It didn't.

And the dreaded jet lag seemed finally to have disappeared. Today I knew exactly where I was. I was in Hollywood, *home of the stars*. And of my sister Gloria.

I had a quick shower in the holy of holies, made a quicker dart down the already sun-scorched steps and dived feet first into the big kidney-shaped pool.

After a few ungainly dog paddles I turned on my back, luxuriating in the hot Californian sun. It beamed down on me from a blue, cloudless sky. Well almost cloudless. There was one tiny little gathering of white fluff trailing its way across the endless expanse of blue. I was trying to decide if it most resembled a sheep or a profile of Pope Pius the Twelfth, when a sudden little breeze rippled across the pool bringing the scent of summer roses in full bloom, *and* the appetizing smell of hot waffles.

If this wasn't heaven it would do for me.

Breakfast was laid out on the terrace. For one. On the pink steps, my wet footprints dried out almost before they could form.

Mrs Danvers draped a kitten-soft robe around my shoulders. Like everything else here, it reeked of unbridled luxury. 'Madam left the papers for you. She'll be back in time for lunch. Is there anything else you require?'

'No thank you, Mrs Danvers. This is perfect.'

'Thank you, Madam.' She preened, before gliding away in her peculiar silent fashion.

I gorged myself on the hot, honey-coated waffles, drank coffee to die for, then slipped off the robe and stretched out in the warm sun.

I don't know how long I slept, but I woke to find myself lying in the shade of a large white parasol, with

Mrs Danvers hovering nearby, fiddling with a jug of fresh orange juice. She filled a glass for me.

The slim glass was a replica of the one Carlos held in the photo that I kept under my pillow upstairs. It could even be the same glass.

I gave a long contented sigh and settled back into the soft pink cushions. 'Close the parasol please, Mrs Danvers, I want to get a tan.'

'Lunch will be ready in one hour, Madam.' She was now arranging a bowl of fresh fruit on the wrought-iron table.

'Oh God bless you.' I closed my eyes.

I was wondering how long it would take me to get a tan like Gloria's when I realized I was still in the shade. Mrs Danvers hadn't touched the parasol. I looked around, but she was gone. I suppose I could have got up and shut it myself, but that would have required far too much effort for a day like this. I closed my eyes and went back to my day-dream.

In it I was deeply tanned, confident, eloquent and two inches taller. And sharing a glass of champagne with Carlos. He was laughing at my jokes, as he stood in front of me in his white swimming trunks. I threw my head back provocatively, showing the long tanned line of my throat. He whipped the glass from my hand, then slowly and deliberately ran his tongue along the imprint left by my high-gloss lipstick, before placing it on the table. He moved closer, his eyes burning into mine.

Sister, Dear Sister

Gloria was doing her best, but it was clearly impossible for her to arrange a completely free day to spend with me. It wasn't her fault; she did everything she could. She rushed home between meetings, she postponed them, she hurried back at breakneck speed most evenings so we could have dinner together. Then she tore out again.

When she was home the phones didn't stop. She made it a firm rule never to use her mobile at home. Not that this shortened her list of callers. They simply transferred to her home numbers.

She apologized to me over and over for these frequent interruptions, constantly describing the callers as 'those persistent bastards'. Yet she still gave them her full attention. I suppose that's how she got to be the recipient of so many calls in the first place. She seemed to spend more time on the telephone and in negotiations than she did writing scripts.

I told her I understood, although I didn't. I said I didn't mind, even when I did.

But I couldn't expect her to put important business on hold just because I was visiting. It wasn't her fault that I had come alone. And yet, even if Turlough and Mother hadn't chosen the sterilizing machine over the trip of a lifetime I doubt it either of them would have been all that anxious to see Clint Eastwood's parking space.

Or even the Frederick's of Hollywood Museum, where Madonna's pointy-breasted corset was on central display.

It was Wannabe Tom who had recommended these treats to me and driven me to see them. He also took me to the apparently unmissable Petersen Automotive Museum that boasted a full four-storey extravaganza of two hundred cars and motor cycles. I got a migraine that day.

'I'm happy enough just being here,' I assured Gloria when she rang to check on how I was doing.

'Are you sure, honey? I feel guilty leaving you alone so much.'

'I'm not alone. I have Mrs Danvers.'

I wasn't lying. Standing not two feet away from me, Mrs Danvers all but levitated with pride.

Most of Gloria's important meetings centred around Lilliput Productions, the most famous of all being *People in Jeopardy*.

'You must be really proud of that show.' I encouraged her to talk about it.

'Well it may not be the best drama we produce, but it's sure as hell the most profitable.' She laughed.

'We?'

'Phillip and Nathan, my two business partners. And Robert Kennedy, of course.'

'Robert Kennedy?' My eyes popped.

She laughed again. 'Yeah, he's one of those Kennedys all right. But not the immediate family. He's some kinda second cousin to the real Kennedys. He's our junior partner. Between the four of us we own Lilliput.'

'I thought you just wrote the scripts?'

'I wish.'

We were sitting by the pool as usual. My choice. Despite her golden tan Gloria never appeared to be all that comfortable outdoors. I loved it. I couldn't bear to be indoors in such glorious weather, wasting all that hot sunshine. Even on those days when the peculiar LA smog threatened to invade the hills I still preferred being out in the garden.

'It relieves stress, everybody knows that,' she snapped, when I asked why she drove herself around like a lunatic, when Wannabe Tom was well paid to do it. She tipped a generous shot of vodka into her waiting orange juice.

Vodka was clearly another stress reliever.

It wasn't yet noon. I sipped my orange juice.

'Don't look at me like that, Maddy, you don't know the pressures I'm under.' She drained her glass.

'Why don't you have a swim, then. Everyone knows that relieves stress.'

She wasn't amused. 'I can't go swimming. I have a meeting. I can't walk into a boardroom full of pretentious pricks with my hair dripping. And what about my make-up? Have you any idea how much I paid to have this job done this morning?' She pointed to her expertly made-up face.

I didn't feel it was my place to mention the dozens of hair dryers that littered the mansion. I did attempt to say that her face, with its wonderful bone structure, would be beautiful even without make-up.

She dismissed this notion with a wave of her scarlet-tipped fingers. 'Jesus, Maddy, you have no idea.' She shook her head. 'Sometimes I think you imagine we're still in Ballyshannon.'

I glanced around at the spectacular house and garden. 'What?'

She had the grace to laugh. 'You know what I mean. Expectations here are pretty high. Mediocrity doesn't cut it in Hollywood.'

I sipped my juice.

'The pressure to be the best is relentless, the pace insane. Don't you believe all that shit about laid-back California. Laid back, my ass! Maybe for beach bums it is. But for anyone in the business the pace never eases. There's not even time to do what you gotta do. And I haven't broken into the movies yet. But I'm getting there, honey, I'm on the threshold.'

'Threshold? You're already at the top. I've seen all those awards on your desk.'

'Oh Maddy, you're so naïve.' She reached for the vodka. 'Sometimes I wonder what the fuck I'm doing in this place?'

'Well, that's understandable. Here you are, lying on a sun bed by your own swimming pool, while your personal chef prepares lunch and Mrs Danvers slavishly waits on you hand and foot. It's a tough life, Gloria.' I shook my head. 'I wouldn't want it.'

She frowned. 'Wouldn't you?'

I looked at her. 'Give me the chance. I'd never leave.'

'I might hold you to that, Maddy.' She grinned, tapped at her glass with her long scarlet nails. Then her expression changed and she had such a sad look on her face that it unnerved me.

'I thought you loved what you do? Don't you enjoy script-writing?'

'Writing is the easy part. It's going head to head with the pricks in this business that will land me in the funny farm. You have no idea, Mad, it's all pitching and bitching, and never knowing when you're gonna get shafted.' She sighed. 'My life would be so much simpler if I could spend all my time writing. Let the suits handle the rest.'

'Then why don't you?'

She narrowed her eyes. 'Let the suits handle my business? I can't trust those bastards with everything I've worked for.'

'What about your business partners? Surely you can trust them?'

'I guess. But it's not that simple, Maddy. The bigger the pot, the more watching it takes. Who said that? Some prick I suppose.' She poured another vodka. A double this time.

'But if it's all such a burden, why don't you just . . .?'

'Because it's *my* burden, Maddy,' she interrupted me, her face cross.

The big white telephone at her elbow had been flashing like a Christmas tree all the time we'd been speaking.

She picked it up. 'What?' she snapped, then listened for a second. 'No, I won't agree to those changes. I've already told you. That scene is pivotal to the whole . . . Well tough luck, Richie, it's my decision. Complain to whoever you like, it's my call.' She rang off.

Mrs Danvers stood waiting. 'Should I keep putting them through, Madam?'

'Fuck them, Betty. Put the machine on.'

They exchanged a look.

'Oh sod it! I'm going to take you out to lunch, Maddy. You came all this way and you haven't seen any real live movie stars yet.'

'I saw Leonardo DiCaprio,' I began.

But she was already half-way up the steps.

The restaurant was called the Ivy Room. I have no idea why. It looked more like a scented rose garden to me. Their cloying perfume hit us the moment we stepped from the limo. That and the icy disdain of the doorman when he saw my frightening frizz emerging from the gleaming car.

I had asked Gloria if it was all right for me to be seen in public with my hair like this.

'This is LA,' she snapped impatiently. 'They'll think you're making a statement.'

She swept past reception, ignoring the long queue, and marched on through the antique-filled restaurant with its cosy blend of chintz and cabbage roses, and straight out on to a red-bricked terrace clearly reserved for VIPs.

The *maître d'* practically asphyxiated at this unprecedented cheek. Until he saw who it was. Then he ran alongside her, his little legs working overtime to keep up with her long strides.

'Pleasure to see you. Pleasure to see you.' His accent was French. Or something.

Gloria ignored him.

She swept onwards, towards a prominent table in the middle of the terrace, then stood tapping her foot impatiently.

The *maître d'* and his sidekick raced to hold her chair.

I sat down without anyone's help. I was tugging nervously at my frizz when I spotted the famous face beyond Gloria's beige shoulder pad. 'Don't look now, but Arnold Schwarzenegger is sitting behind you.

And he's got two small children with him,' I whispered excitedly.

'Probably his dessert,' she drawled, intent on the menu.

It was like dining out with the Queen. Or the Pope, or somebody equally magnificent. The waiting staff collided with each other in their anxiety to facilitate us, until the *maître d'* herded most of them back into the no man's land that was the main restaurant.

There wasn't a table in the terraced area that couldn't boast a famous face. And those that weren't famous looked as if they should be.

Gloria glanced up from the leather-bound menu. 'Close your mouth, Maddy. And try not to stare.'

But how could I not when I had a clear view of Brad Pitt's peerless profile every time I turned my head. And further along the terrace I had spotted Sharon Stone, dazzling all comers, in a dress that looked as if it was melting in the heat.

Gloria showed no interest in the other diners. Although I saw quite a few of them glance her way. She was preoccupied with the menu, irritated by the constant fussing of the *maître d'*. 'He won't be joining me today, Kurt, so you can stop salivating.' She sounded uncannily like Mother. 'He's still in New York. This is my sister Maddy, I want you to look after her, as if . . .' she grinned slyly '. . . as if she were Carlos.'

Kurt blushed to the roots of his hairpiece.

'Carlos and his fans.' Gloria laughed. 'Never employ a man who is prettier than you are, Maddy. It's a killer.'

Two salads appeared in front of us. 'Your Caesar salads, ladies.'

'Carlos works for you?'

'Well, I am his employer. Go away.' She dismissed the hovering waiter.

'You're his boss?'

'You could put it like that. Eat your food, honey. This place makes the best Caesars on the West Coast. She stabbed her fork into something large and wobbly.

'Could . . . could I have a glass of wine, please?'

'Maddy, I told you, you can have anything you want.'

'Then I want a glass of wine. Is that all right?' I didn't fancy the look of the salads she had ordered. I thought we were going to eat some real food.

Gloria saw my expression. 'God, I'd forgotten how aggravating you can be. Why didn't you say you're not into salads? Why did you just sit there letting me order?' She was practically shouting.

'Is there a problem, ladies?' Kurt was back.

I thought Gloria would explode. 'Clear this away . . . yeah, the mineral water . . . everything . . . the salads . . . bring us a bottle of Pouilly Fumé Château Tracy.'

Within seconds we had three waiters scurrying around the table, clearing away plates, opening up Château Tracy and setting out fresh cutlery.

'Château Tracy?' I examined the label. 'Is this from Chigwell?'

She didn't even smile. 'Give over, Maddy. We're gonna start from fresh. This time you order exactly what *you* want, okay? And I'll join you. To hell with diets, and abstinence, and . . .'

'Who mentioned diets? I've never dieted in my life.'

'Jesus.' She covered her eyes. 'Bring me a bottle of brandy,' she said to one of the waiters.

I had a strong feeling this lunch was going to be a memorable one. And not just for the food.

I was right.

We ate spinach linguine with tomato and basil sauce, then prime rib, with Cajun spices and parsley-decked sweet potato. Now this was real food. This was worth crossing the Atlantic for.

Then, for some reason that escapes me now, Gloria ordered lobster. Lobster for two. As we had already got through the best part of two bottles of wine by then I was in no fit state to argue.

I began to nibble unenthusiastically at the lobster, then found that I couldn't stop.

The third bottle of wine complemented it perfectly.

We had almost finished the wine when she ordered the Sambucas.

'No way, Gloria. I couldn't swallow another drop.'

She drank both.

I prodded Kurt in the bum with my souvenir bread stick as we staggered out through reception. 'Was that Richard Gere I saw you talking to?'

'I hope so, darling,' he twittered. 'He paid his tab with Richard's gold card.'

'Give this man a tip,' I said to Gloria.

'Certainly.' She leaned over to whisper in his ear: 'Practise safe sex.'

The doorman leaped swiftly to one side, as if our condition were contagious.

'Our mother hates sex,' Gloria said to him in passing. 'And she hates us, because she had to have sex to have us.'

Give him his due, the man didn't bat an eyelid.

‘Yes, Ma’am.’ He held open the door for her.

‘I’m surprised she didn’t force us to have a clitrode . . . a clitero . . . what’s the word I’m searching for?’ she asked him.

‘Your car, Ma’am.’

She fell into the back seat. ‘Cliterodectomy!’ she shouted at the startled Wannabe Tom.

‘Sh, Gloria.’

‘It has to be said, Maddy. It has to be said!’ A big tear rolled down her beautifully made-up cheek.

And what could I do? This was my beloved sister, who had brought me all the way to Hollywood to dine with the stars.

We cried all the way back to the mansion.

Mrs Danvers was at the door, waiting. Wannabe Tom had obviously snitched on the car phone. Gloria ignored her proffered arm and staggered on through the hallway and out on to the pink patio, losing her bag and jacket, not to mention what remained of her dignity, *en route*.

‘Bring me a drink, Betty.’

‘Coffee, Madam?’

Gloria threw her a scathing look. ‘Bring me a drink!’ She plonked herself down at the small wrought-iron table by the poolside.

‘I have to go to the bathroom,’ I said. But nobody paid any attention.

When I got back Gloria was on the phone. ‘I don’t give a flying fuck about you or that stupid fucking farm.’

Oh my God, she was abusing Turlough. ‘Gloria please . . .’

‘Sit down,’ she hissed at me. ‘No not you, you self-serving turd. I have something to say to you. You have made shite of my sister for the very last time. *No*! You listen to me. Because she doesn't want to speak to you, that's why. I'm going to tell you now that if I have my way my sister will never ever set foot on that God-forsaken farm ever again. Do you hear me?'

I didn't doubt that even the partially deaf Tomasino, working in the distant herb garden, could hear her.

She struggled to her feet, as if this might lend more weight to her threats. 'I know who I am! Who the fuck do you think you are? What gives you the right to treat my sister like some kind of skivvy? Giving her no say in anything. Fucking Superman, I don't think! And I want to tell you that I never for one minute regretted leaving Hawthorn Farm. It was the best thing I ever did. What do you mean, hang up? Hang up? It's all the same to me, you miserable fucker.' She frowned at the receiver. 'They hung up.' She sounded surprised.

'Maybe you went too far, Gloria.'

'What?'

'With Turlough. He's not used to hearing women speak like that.'

'Turlough? I was speaking to Mother.' She stepped back, forgetting how close she was to the pool.

When she fell into it, still clutching the phone, I couldn't believe how little she actually disturbed its calm surface as she sank beneath the water.

It was several seconds before I realized she wasn't coming back up again.

Being from a family that mistrusted the medical profession as a whole and doctors in particular, I was amazed to see two doctors *and* a white-clad nurse rushing to attend to Gloria.

Dong and I hung around outside her door, waiting for their prognoses. Wannabe Tom paced the hallway. Only Tomasino was missing. He was probably still tracking his way out of the herb garden.

Apart from the medical contingent, Mrs Danvers was the only one allowed access to the sick-room. She had insisted that Carlos was not to be alerted.

I wondered why he would be; Gloria had only fallen into the pool. It wasn't as if she had contracted bacteraemia or anything.

There was a weak little cry from behind the closed door and I was instantly flooded with guilt. Was I being callous and unfeeling? Everybody else was in a tizzy. Practically hysterical with worry.

It seemed that in America falling into a pool was considered to be a very serious matter. Even if you were pulled out within seconds and you had enough French brandy inside you to protect you from an Arctic freeze-over.

Mullins had been falling into bog holes, and lakes and things, since time immemorial. Usually with a fair amount of drink inside them. And they had all lived to tell the tale. Mostly. Without recourse to any kind of medical assistance whatsoever.

'How is she?' I asked Mrs Danvers when she appeared, hollow-eyed, from the sick-room.

'She'll recover.' Her voice carried all the gravitas of someone who has peered into the void and beyond. But then that was her normal speaking voice.

'Thank God. Thank God!' Wannabe Tom closed his eyes and joined his hands in grateful thanksgiving.

Carlos, Close Up and Perfect

Falling into the swimming pool was probably the best thing that could have happened to Gloria. It forced her to take time off work. *And* switch off the phones. I was convinced that she needed a long rest and Mrs Danvers agreed with me.

So did Carlos. After some snitch called him in New York.

Two days after her unplanned dip in the pool I watched Gloria approaching it again. This time she was dressed for swimming. Or perhaps undressed is a better word. She had on the most minuscule bikini imaginable. She still moved in her usual hurried fashion, seemingly incapable of slowing down, even when she was supposed to be engaged in a leisure activity.

Seeing her up close, in the tiny blue bikini reminded me, if I needed reminding, just how thin she was. I had to keep telling myself that this was LA where you could never be too thin, or too rich. In Ballyshannon they preferred women with a little, or even a lot, of surplus flesh on them and if anyone became rich to any real degree they were viewed with intense suspicion, if not outright hostility.

Yet there was no doubt that despite being so startlingly thin, Gloria was strong as ever. Her gaunt arms sliced through the water as she outpaced me in the big pool. She was a powerful swimmer, much better than I could ever hope to be, even with all the practice I was getting.

'Come on, slowcoach, put some zip into it.' She was a full length ahead of me now.

'Where did you learn to swim like that?' I asked, when I finally caught up with her.

'Jamaica.'

'Where?' I swallowed a mouthful of water.

'Jamaica. A little place called Negril. There's an artists' colony there, in the north-west of the island. An old hippie hang-out. A true garden of Eden. For the privileged few. That's where Jean-Baptiste grew up, naked as a jay-bird.' She laughed.

'Jean-Baptiste?' This was a namc I hadn't heard before.

'My husband. He was Jamaican. Well, his father was North-African.' Her eyes were alive with devilment.

I climbed out of the pool, coughing.

'What's the matter, Maddy? The water too cold?' Shc was laughing outright now.

'Was he black?'

'Well he sho' wasn't white, honeychile.'

I started to laugh. Not at her funny accent, but at the thought of Mother's face if Gloria had arrived home in Ballyshannon with a Jamaican husband. Mother classed people from north Kerry as foreigners.

'Thinking about our dear and distant mother, are you?' She was beside me.

I nodded. 'What I'd give to see . . .'

'I know. I'm ashamed to say that might have been

part of the reason I married him. He deserved better; he was one of the coolest guys I've ever known. And talk about talented.'

'What happened? Why did you break up?'

'He couldn't take the whole Hollywood thing. And he wanted children. Couldn't wait to hear the patter of little feet. I told him to get a hamster.'

'Gloria.' I frowned.

'Maaady!' she drawled, laughing. 'He went back to London – that's where we first met. He's doing well I hear. I'm not surprised, he was always a better writer than I could ever hope to be.' She lay face down on the sun bed. With the water glistening on them, her shoulder-blades were like razors.

'You should have told him to pop over to Ballyshannon when he had a spare minute. Call in on Mother with the family album.' I was drying her back, before putting sun oil on it. 'Didn't you want to have children?'

'Can't have them,' she said lazily. 'God's punishment on me, for being a bad girl. All those wicked abortions, Mother would say.'

The bottle of sun oil slipped from my hand and slid along the tiles, staining their smooth pink surface. 'Sorry, Gloria.' In my confusion, I was all thumbs.

'No, I'm sorry, Maddy, that was nasty of me. I'm such a thoughtless bitch, just blurting it out like that.'

'You are not!'

'You don't know me, Maddy. You keep mistaking me for the little seventeen-year-old who left Ireland all those years ago.'

'How many?'

'Years ago?'

'Ab . . . abortions.' I had trouble with the word.

'Two.'

'You must have had good reasons.' I tried to keep my voice steady.

'Oh I did. Two perfectly good reasons. Greed and ambition.' She laughed bitterly. 'There's something wonderfully symmetrical about that, don't you think? Two perfectly good reasons. For two bad abortions.' She turned away.

'Were they . . . was it Carlos?'

'Christ no. He's far too much of a puritan. It was long before I met him.'

The knot in my stomach began to unravel slowly. 'You were only a child then.'

'Hardly.' She closed her eyes against the bright sun.

I watched her sleep, her narrow shoulders rising and falling rhythmically with her quiet, easy breathing. She was right, I did still think of her as the sixteen-year-old I used to hear crying in the night. Or maybe the seventeen-year-old who had hugged me fiercely the day before she ran away, although all Mullins were honour bound not to show emotion in public. She had waited for me outside the school and we had walked home in silence. At the farmyard gate she had suddenly grabbed me and held on, as if she would never let go.

I couldn't imagine that girl readily consenting to an abortion. Not the one who used to run frantically around our kitchen, glass in hand, intent on catching every wayward wasp and releasing it back into the yard before Mother got to squash it with a newspaper.

And she could never understand my fear of spiders.

'They're so defenceless.' She would try to entice me to hold one on my palm. 'They can't hurt you.'

That's the girl I saw, sleeping beside me.

Mrs Danvers brought coffee. She checked the big parasol to make sure Gloria wasn't getting too much sun. It was becoming hotter by the minute now.

I didn't really want coffee, but I didn't want to offend Mrs Danvers either, when she tried so hard to please us. I sipped at the brimming cup until she was out of sight.

It seemed that I had only closed my eyes when she was back again. This time with the big white telephone. 'It's Mr Garcia.' She shook Gloria's shoulder gently.

Gloria sat up, startled. 'Carlos?'

I don't know why it was such a shock, hearing her talking to him. He had been calling regularly since I arrived, but she usually took his calls in her study when she was at home. This was the first time I had actually heard her speaking to him. It embarrassed me beyond belief.

'I switched it off . . . with Maddy . . . we've been swimming . . . no she's crap.' She grinned at me. 'I'm kidding, she's great, I can't tell you how good it is to have her here . . . it's so good for me . . . I love her to death . . . so will you, baby . . . I can't wait for you two to meet . . . no, just tired . . . what? . . . And you believe him? . . . He gossips like an old woman.' She laughed, then she was serious again. 'How is the shoot going . . . no, don't tell me, Bobby has already been on . . . no, I told him to do his fuckin' job . . . I know, I know, but that's the business we're in.' She was becoming agitated. They were clearly in serious disagreement about something. Her voice rose angrily as she walked up the steps and into the house.

I stretched out in the sun. It was really hot now. But that's how I liked it.

Turlough was fond of saying 'Fools get what they deserve'. Especially when he heard of a prize milker getting a blocked udder or a supposedly healthy cow aborting mid-term, for no apparent reason. He didn't mean the animals were fools; Turlough had unfailing sympathy for animals. His problem was with people.

He never forgave carelessness. Especially when it caused a preventable illness. Luckily he wasn't around when I got sunstroke. I had no one to blame but myself, I knew that. Gloria had warned me often enough about the dangers of exposing my white skin to the hot Californian sun. She was boringly repetitive about it.

Mrs Danvers didn't actually voice her opinion, but she spent her time silently adjusting the big parasol, determined to keep me in the shade.

But how was I to know that a single afternoon in the sun could have such serious repercussions? And over such a long time.

It was the dizziness that first alerted me. Then the nausea and the terrible pain across the top of my head. Then my whole body felt as if it were on fire. I looked like the boiled lobster we had eaten in the Ivy Room, except for two narrow white strips where my borrowed bikini had covered me.

'Oh dear, we are in a state.' Mrs Danvers lost her customary cool.

'Holy shit,' Gloria said.

It was six a.m. One of Gloria's doctors arrived at twenty past. This was her favourite, Dr Wright.

He told me off in his wheezy English voice, warning

me about the dangers of skin cancer. Then he asked if my periods were regular.

While I was still trying to make the connection between sunstroke and regular periods, he prescribed rakes of pills, lots of fluid and recommended that I sleep in a cool, dark room. And presumably use tampons, as required.

He gave Mrs Danvers a jar of something that looked suspiciously like dog sick to plaster all over my body.

I tried to protest.

She ignored me, rolling up her sleeves and getting on with the job. She didn't stop until I looked like an Alien from the *X-Files*.

'Holy shit!' Gloria repeated when she saw me.

Mrs Danvers tut-tutted and washed her hands. Every time she looked at me she had 'just deserts' written all over her face. 'You have got to stay in a cool dark place for six to seven hours.' She made me sound like a failed home brew.

'Ow,' I protested.

'What about the basement?' Gloria quipped. 'We could grow mushrooms on her at the same time.'

'Ow,' I said.

'Don't cry, precious, you can stay in Gloria's room if you want.' She was laughing openly now. 'Put her in my bed, Betty. *Mine* is the coolest room in the whole house.' She grinned wickedly at me.

Her only legacy from our long afternoon in the sun was a slight deepening of her already glorious tan. 'I've got a script conference at seven,' she said. 'I'll be home for lunch.' And she was gone.

Mrs Danvers tucked me up in Gloria's bed, then gave me an unmarked pill.

I hoped it was cyanide.

It must have been close to lunch when I woke. I could hear someone moving about in the bathroom. They came out, leaving the adjoining door slightly ajar to allow a narrow shaft of light to fall into the darkened bedroom. I could just about see the outline of the tall straight figure approaching the bed.

Jesus, she was going to put more of that stuff on me.

I dived under the covers.

What happened next is not altogether clear in my mind. That may be because of the pill Mrs Danvers had given me, or perhaps the whole scene was simply too traumatic for my brain to record it properly. But I need to recall it as best I can, because what happened in the room that day was to impact on the rest of my life.

And on everyone else's in the big mansion.

This is how I recall it.

I'm hiding beneath the crisp sheets, my body still plastered with the smelly gunge that has been prescribed to cool my burning skin. My wild, unintentional Afro is standing on end thanks to the tossing and turning of the past miserable hours.

Suddenly, there is a hand tugging at the sheet, threatening to uncover me. I grip the sheet, holding on for dear life, thinking that if I made it difficult enough for her she might go away and forget all about rubbing in the vile embrocation.

There is another tug at the sheet. This time I lose my grip slightly and it's pulled back a little, enough for me to be able to peer over it.

That's when I realized that the person pulling at it was most definitely not Mrs Danvers. The tall figure in the semi-darkness was a man. There was no doubt about that, because he was stark naked. He was also a person of rare and indescribable beauty. Even in the dull half-light that much was obvious. And there was something even more obvious about him. It wouldn't have taken a degree in physiology to comprehend that sleep was the last thing on his mind. From where I was cowering behind the sheet his agenda was stunningly obvious.

His slender hands tugged harder at the sheet. And so began a spectacular little tug of war. First he gained ground, then I did, and finally he won.

I was uncovered.

But instead of slipping in beside me he paused and squinted at me in the dim light, then reached across to the bedside table.

For one insane second I thought he was reaching for a gun, because we were, after all, in California. But he wasn't. He was reaching for the light switch.

And when I found myself sitting in a pool of bright light I wished it had been a gun, because this beautiful man, this incomparable Adonis, took one look at me and began to scream at the top of his voice.

Then he's running like a startled hare, fear fuelling his long muscular legs as he tears across the big room and out into the hallway, yelling as he goes.

And that is how I first came face to face with Carlos Garcia. The man I had dreamed of and lusted after for three long, lonely years in rain-swept Bally-shannon.

I knew I couldn't go on avoiding Carlos for ever, although I did my best. I locked my door and refused to step outside my room for the rest of that humiliating day, and for most of the following morning.

And I wouldn't allow anyone in. Without identification.

Gloria lost patience with me. 'For God's sake, Maddy, you're acting like a stupid kid. So you saw each other naked? Big deal. You're a married woman, for Chrissakes. Don't tell me that seeing a horny man approach your bed was a total shock?'

I didn't reply.

'What about Carlos? How do you think he felt? He was intent on surprising me.'

'He surprised me.' I sulked.

'Aw come on, Maddy, I love Carlos, but when it comes down to it, honey, they all look pretty much the same in the buff, don't they?'

Gloria had clearly left Ballyshannon far too young.

'I'll give you twenty minutes. Dong has made a special lunch for Carlos. He's only got a couple of hours left before he has to head back to New York. He wants to meet you, honey.' She smirked. 'I know you've already met, but this time things will be different. You'll be dressed for a start.' She was trying not to laugh. 'Stop sulking, Maddy.'

'Is he . . . laughing at me?'

'Why would he laugh?' You could give him a bad time. Come on, honey, it's important to me having you two meet. I've left a dress out for you. Twenty minutes, okay?'

Mrs Danvers was my saviour. She worked miracles on my Brillo-pad hair. With a few flicks of some electric tongs and half a dozen giant hairpins, she forced it into a shining French pleat at the back of my head. The effect was extraordinary. It made me look almost glamorous.

The vile concoction had showered away completely, leaving my skin fresh and clear. In the pale-cream dress that Gloria had left out for me I appeared to be nicely tanned, a feat I had never before managed, not even in the hottest summer in Ballyshannon.

Mrs Danvers swept my lashes with black mascara, painted my lips bright pink and I was ready.

She put a hand on my shoulder as I stood admiring her handiwork in the full-length mirror. 'Very nice, Madam. Very nice indeed.'

Fulsome praise from a woman whose favourite lines were the scathingly uttered: 'Mrs de Winter would have ordered a wine sauce, Madam.'

He was standing with his back to me when I walked in.

'Carlos, this is Maddy, my baby sister.' Gloria's voice deepened with emotion, as if I were somebody to be proud of instead of some kind of genetic embarrassment.

He turned and looked straight at me. And my heart stopped. I know a lot of people say that and it's not really true, it's just an expression they use. But when I say my heart stopped I mean it. The sight of him, standing there in front of the big open fireplace, made my heart miss a beat. And if it had never started again I wouldn't have cared, because I had finally got to see him in the flesh. Perhaps not as much flesh as I'd seen yesterday, but today's circumstances were so much less embarrassing. And in the bright clear light of day he was as perfect as I had always dreamed he'd be.

He was breath-takingly handsome. Tall and gentle-eyed, and with the most beautiful smile this side of paradise. And, of course, fully dressed. In a dark-grey business suit that must have been fitted by experts. Lucky experts.

He held out his hand, and the first words he ever spoke to me put Byron and Shelley and even the great Yeats to shame. He caught my hand and said: 'Hi, Maddy. I've heard so much about you. Welcome to Hollywood.'

And I looked up into the smiling, chocolate-brown eyes and was lost to Ballyshannon for ever.

Although it hardly seemed possible, Dong had actually managed to outdo his previous best with this special lunch for Carlos. Sadly, I had to take everyone else's word for this as I might as well have been guzzling yesterday's dog sick for all the impact the feast had on me.

I sat at the table like a zombie. I put food in my mouth, chewed and swallowed it without having the faintest idea what I was eating. Or even if I was eating.

'Have you seen anybody eat like our Maddy, Carlos?' Gloria asked proudly.

'I like a woman with a hearty appetite.' He smiled across at me.

And my skin began to burn again, although I hadn't been in the sun for forty-eight hours.

'Here in LA, women live on salads,' he said.

'That's because we can't afford to put on an ounce of weight. Fat is the only true sin in California. In LA,' Gloria corrected herself.

'You two don't have to worry about that. It's not in your nature to gain weight,' he said.

Since we had sat down to eat I had managed to

avoid his eyes every time he spoke to me. I knew this probably made me appear sly and shifty-eyed to him. I had also managed, somehow, not to speak directly to him. To be honest, I was incapable of doing this. But that didn't prevent me from darting sneaky looks at his beautiful face when I thought he wasn't looking. But I was so terrified that he might be able to read my sinful thoughts that I had to keep my eyes averted whenever he turned towards me.

'What do *you* think, Maddy?' Gloria was beaming at me.

What did I think? About what? What? All I was capable of thinking, just then, was that he had the most perfect mouth I had ever seen. And that God must have sat up for years, planning those brown eyes.

But most of all I was thinking, and hoping, that Dong's chili sauce wasn't dribbling down my chin. If there was anything I despised it was a sloppy eater.

He didn't have the tiniest smudge of food on his perfectly chiselled mouth.

'Is mother as slim as ever?' Gloria was asking.

'Absolutely.' See, I could chat away to Gloria easily enough. It was just when I looked across at him that my brain seized up.

'More wine, Madam.' Mrs Danvers knew. I could tell by her eyes.

'Thank you.' My voice was a squeak.

'How does your husband feel about you coming here?' he asked.

'Who?' Another squeak.

'You husband, Maddy. Turlough.' Gloria laughed.

'Oh. Yes. He won't miss me.'

Carlos looked shocked. 'A whole month and he

won't miss you? I can't believe that.' The brown eyes were appraising me.

'He . . . he's ca . . . ca . . . calving,' I whispered.

'He's . . . ?' He leaned towards me, clearly perplexed by this new form of language.

'Calving, honey,' Gloria said in her best American accent. 'The cows are calving. On the farm.'

'Oh.' He sat back. He smiled and I noticed for the first time that one of his eye-teeth curved slightly inwards over its neighbour, and instead of this tiny flaw diminishing him in any way it made him even more attractive. And sexy. 'I see. I'd still miss you if you were my wife.'

Crash. My wineglass smashed against my plate, spewing gallon after gallon of bright-red wine across the delicate lace table-cloth. The vulgar red tide swept on like a river in flood, until it finally ran out of table and had to settle for dripping over the edge and on to Gloria's lap, where it happily soaked into the beige silk dress that she had paid a small fortune for only a few days ago.

Before I could stab myself and do us all a favour, everyone attempted to kill me with kindness. Gloria and Carlos both said it didn't matter one bit. Both of them insisted that it was always happening to them.

In a pig's eye, it was. I could just see either of these two perfect people clumsily smashing a fine wineglass against their dinner-plate because they were so overcome with lust for someone they knew they could never have.

I crept downstairs in the dark. I was in need of something to settle my grumbling stomach. Or maybe my dented pride. And food had always proved to be a great comfort in the past.

The big fridge was stocked like a Friday morning supermarket. Plastic containers of milk lined the wide doorshelves. There was full-fat, semi-skimmed, chocolate-flavoured, goat's milk. Goat's milk? My stomach grumbled again.

I paused with my hand on the door, before reaching past the goat's milk to the full-fat. There was a soft footfall behind me.

I swung round empty-handed.

She was standing in the dark, with only the thin light from the open fridge illuminating her bloodless face.

'Mrs Danvers, you scared the wits out of me.' Did the woman never sleep?

'Can I help you, Madam?'

'I . . . I need . . . milk?'

'Sit down. I'll get it for you.'

'Oh would you? I'd be so grateful.'

She poured semi-skimmed milk into a glass tumbler. It wasn't crystal, I noticed.

'Is Madam asleep?'

I grinned. 'Well, he's long gone.'

Our eyes met over the glass.

'I would do anything for her.' Her face was completely expressionless.

'So would I. She's my sister.'

'I mean anything.' Still no expression.

'So do I.' I frowned.

'I hope so, Madam. I hope so.' And she was gone.

La La Land

With Carlos filming in New York for three consecutive weeks without a single break and the date for the Emmy awards fast approaching, Gloria's life took on an even more frenetic pace. She was a human whirlwind. Unstoppable.

She dashed in and out of the mansion like a whirligig, hardly pausing to catch a breath. When I asked if I could do anything to help she looked at me as if I had completely lost my marbles, then rushed back into her study to make yet another important phone call. All Gloria's phone calls seemed to be important. Or at least from important people.

Her every waking hour was now dedicated to winning the precious Emmy. Nothing else seemed to matter.

'But surely it's out of your hands?' I asked. 'Won't some committee or other now be deciding who wins and who doesn't? Isn't that how these things usually work?'

She didn't even answer, just threw me one of her scathing looks.

I didn't understand. It wasn't as if it was the first time she had been nominated for an award. Her desk was littered with little statuettes and plaques of all sorts. There were two Golden Globes and various other prestigious awards, all commending her writing skills, all naming her as a writer of great merit. And substance. It didn't appear to me that she needed any further assurance of how talented she was. But what did I know? I was just a farmer's wife from Ballyshannon.

She did take time out from a busy day to introduce me to her hairdresser. He practically fainted at the sight of my frizzed-out perm, clutching his forehead dramatically as if the sight of it caused him physical pain. Then he gave his considered opinion. To the hushed salon. 'Disgusting!'

'We already know that José.' Gloria didn't embarrass easily. 'We're here to ask what we can do with it.'

'Nothing.' He clutched his forehead again.

'Ah, now come on, you can do something with it.'

'With this!' He flicked at it dismissively. 'No.'

I stood up. I'd had enough of being being humiliated by a man who wore a skirt over his trousers and blonde streaks in his hair.

'Sit down,' he commanded.

'Sit down, Maddy.' Gloria echoed. 'He's the best.'

'It all come off,' José said.

He was Cuban. He claimed to have left his five sisters and a broken-hearted girl-friend in downtown Havana when he shipped out to Miami. If he had a broken-hearted girl-friend I was Fidel Castro.

Before you could say Bay of Pigs, he was wielding a razor like a man possessed.

'Gloria? Help!' I cried.

But Gloria had her own problems. She was having her face peeled in the next cubicle.

'You are young Audrey Hepburn. Those big eyes . . . like frightened little fawn.' Gloria had already told me that José had watched too many old movies before he took the rowing boat out of Havana.

The slashing razor missed my perspiring scalp by a fraction of an inch.

Gloria loved my haircut.

I hated it.

She gave José the Cuban a great tip.

I hid behind her and directed a low blow at him. 'Long live the revolution,' I shouted and ran out of the salon.

Gloria thought it was a hoot. Her word.

My cropped haircut turned out to be a great success. To my total surprise everyone liked it. Even Dong. 'Liddle boy! Liddle boy!' He tittered uncontrollably.

I still hated it until Carlos touched it and said, 'Wow.'

I never let it grow again.

Looking at it in the main bathroom mirror during one of Gloria's parties I had to admit that it did make me look a bit like a 'liddle boy'. It also made my eyes look big and startled. But then again that could be the new added-fibre mascara Gloria's beautician had recommended.

The door flew open and three giggling women crowded in behind me.

'My Gawd, did you see her in that last movie? That shower scene? I thought I'd die.'

'Yeah, if that was her ass I'm Snow White.'

'Oh please, Lindy, not that old fantasy again.'

They cackled loudly and continued gossiping away as if I was invisible.

'She can forget that Emmy.' One of them squirted

half a gallon of hair spray on her already rock-solid fringe.

I caught my breath.

'Damn right. She can go to every god-damn party in town. Even throw a few herself, that still won't make her a decent . . .' the tallest woman stopped to outline her pouting lips in shiny red lipstick '. . . actress.'

I was already at the door when I heard one of them ask: 'What about Gloria? Do you think the other writers will vote . . .'

I rattled the doorknob as if I had difficulty opening it. I didn't want to hear gossip about Gloria. I had recognised one of the women, although she obviously didn't recall meeting me. Gloria had introduced us at a ridiculously formal charity function, where I had spent most of the afternoon ducking behind the curtains.

'Be nice to her, Maddy,' Gloria had whispered. 'Her husband is the head script-writer on *Carter's Celestial Voyages*. He has a vote for the Emmy and rumour has it that he's the most pussy-whipped man in town.'

I had forced myself to chat to the terrifyingly tall woman, using every ounce of charm I possessed, to oblige Gloria. I had smiled at her until my jaws cramped. She clearly didn't remember me at all. Still determined to help Gloria in every way possible, I smiled widely at the blonde amazon now, hoping this might trigger a memory of our long chat at the charity lunch. It didn't.

I slipped out.

The door was closing behind me when I heard her say: 'That girl with the silly smile, I know her from somewhere. Did she play the leader of the Morons in

Demons from Mars?'

I went back to the living-room.

'Stephen is seeing a shrink again,' a thin white-haired man was confiding to his burly baggy-eyed companion.

'Trouble with the movie, huh?'

'No. He says he's having marital problems.'

'Screwing around, huh?'

'I guess so.'

Baggy-eyes shook his head and sighed at the terrible inevitability of it all.

One of the hired waiters offered me a glass of champagne.

Gloria's partners were standing by the big fireplace, a little apart from the milling throng as usual. The youngest of them appeared to be completely out of sorts tonight. He looked bored and irritable, ready to run. This was Bobby Kennedy, the only person whose energy output even came close to matching Gloria's. No wonder they were friends.

I liked Bobby; he never seemed to mind that his famous name was always good for a laugh at the duller parties. It was certainly a conversation stopper among newcomers when he walked into a room, because he was the spitting image of his dead uncle once removed.

'A dead ringer for his dead uncle,' Gloria had informed me, before we met.

It was true. He always had that slightly edgy look that seemed to be the main component of any photo I had seen of his famous relative.

He had trapped me in a corner one night and told me all about the Bay of Pigs and how history had misjudged the Kennedys. 'It's those damn newspapers,' he drawled. 'They've always had it in for us, portraying us as power-mad lechers.' While he was speaking his hand slid downwards towards my behind, forcing me to rearrange my stance in order to keep it out of his range.

Our conversation had begun with me telling him about José the hairdresser and had somehow turned into a lecture on Cuban–American relations. Not to mention a groping session.

I wasn't sure what had turned him on, whether it was all the talk about war, or my new short haircut. But by the end of that particular evening I was an expert on Cuban–American relations. Or the lack of them. And also at removing his big knuckled hand from my person. Bobby was a true Kennedy and no mistake.

But I liked him. He was different from the other powerful men in Gloria's set. He could laugh at the strangeness of Hollywood. And he wasn't at all intimidating, once you managed to get his hands under control. He told bad jokes in his slow Boston drawl and kidded me about Ireland. But he was one of the few people I met who didn't think it was attached to England. Or Scotland. Or even Wales. Bobby had a degree from Harvard. He was a lawyer. Smart.

He was also Carlos's best friend.

Wannabe Tom told me that they had been buddies for years. They played tennis together in LA. And squash in New York. Neither of them was a true Californian, he added.

There was a slight edge to his voice when he said this. But then Wannabe Tom had a nasty jealous streak in him.

I crept up behind Bobby now.

'Just look at him, the stupid prick! I could kill him,' he was saying to the sombre bespectacled Philip, his senior partner in Lilliput Productions. 'As if he can't get it in New York whenever he wants it. If Gloria catches him at it he's a dead man.' He ran a finger across his tanned throat.

Philip nodded in silent agreement.

They were watching Carlos, who was standing directly across from them, practically surrounded by women. He was smiling down into the face of a famous actress whose pneumatic breasts were reputed to have cost three thousand dollars. Each.

I watched as she deliberately trailed a red-taloned finger across the front of his dress shirt, just above his belt buckle. He leaned towards her so she could whisper in his ear. Whatever she said, he certainly likcd it. His hcad was nodding, likc a puppct on a string.

'Stupid prick,' Bobby repeated, not knowing I was standing there listening.

I slipped away and went down to the kitchen.

Hours later I bumped into red talons, the great whisperer, in the upstairs corridor. She was coming out of one of the bedrooms, wiping white powder from the end of her perfect little Hollywood nose. She gave one last deep sniff as we approached each other, almost jolting her gigantic frontage from its precarious moorings.

'Howdy.' She grabbed my shoulder to steady herself. Then she flashed me a wide, dazzling smile and moved on.

Howdy? Had she been watching old cowboy movies?

Wannabe Tom had also told me that watching old cowboy movies was one of Carlos's favourite pastimes in New York.

I couldn't make up my mind whether to go back downstairs to the party or not. I knew Gloria would kill me if she heard I went to bed this early. When she held a party it was all hands on deck; you participated or else. I decided on a compromise. I selected a vantage point on the landing from where I could watch what was happening below. I could even wave to them if I had to.

There was a group of people gathering there now. Someone important was either coming or going. Suddenly the group parted like the Red Sea to allow Barbara Farrington to take her leave of Gloria and Carlos. Barbara was head of one of the biggest studios in Hollywood.

'She's kinda on the same level as God,' Wannabe Tom had confided in awed tones. Then he spoiled it by saying, 'But she always reminds me of one of those old queens down on the strip.'

The party practically stopped for Barbara's departure. It was a great coup to have her attend, as she was known to be highly selective in her choice of friends.

She kissed Gloria warmly on both cheeks. 'Thank you, darling. Much love.'

She kissed Carlos on the mouth. 'Umm . . . you delicious man.'

The hired butler, yet another wannabe, led her to her waiting limo, grovelling unashamedly every inch of the way. 'Watch your step, Madam. Careful there. That rail is . . .'

Bobby Kennedy pushed the door closed behind

him, trapping him outside. The crowd in the hallway broke up, considering this to be a great joke altogether.

Gloria and Bobby gave each other the hand slap known as a high five, then she disappeared back into the living-room. The ever gracious, ever smiling hostess. My sister Gloria.

Bobby looked up and saw me. 'Hey, Irish! Is that where you've been hiding all night? You get down here and join the party.'

I waited until I was close enough to him to be able to whisper. 'Fuck off!' I said under my breath. That would teach him to call Carlos filthy names in my hearing.

I can't remember when I have ever seen anyone look so shocked. It was as if Mother Theresa had lifted her shawl and given him the finger. 'Maddy?' He was incredulous.

I hurried down to the kitchen.

I was eating sugared melon balls when Carlos appeared.

'What did you say to Bobby?' He seemed amused.

'Nothing.' I continued eating.

'Are you angry with me, Maddy?'

'No.'

'Yes you are. What's the matter?' He was so close that I could see little flecks of amber in his brown eyes. 'What is it?'

'Mr Garcia, you are needed upstairs.'

He sighed. 'Okay. See you, Maddy.' He turned to leave.

Mrs Danvers watched me watching him.

'I'm off to bed,' I said, pushing the melon balls aside.

The live band had struck up again. It was playing 'Night Moves', the oh so familiar theme music from *People in Jeopardy*. I might have been back in Ballyshannon waiting for the programme to begin; checking to see that Mother was safely tucked away in her room.

The music followed me upstairs. I left my bedroom door open so I could listen.

Every now and again loud whoops of laughter broke out below. I knew what that meant. It meant Gloria was back in the hallway. You never had to look for her at a party; all you had to do was listen.

Wherever there was the loudest laughter, the most raucous bellows, the hisses of mock embarrassment, you could be sure Gloria was somewhere in the middle of it. It was as if someone flicked a switch at party time and turned her on. As if some disembodied voice called out, 'Audience, lights – cue Gloria.' And there she was, entertaining the world.

She had told me, several times, that actors are a breed apart, a different species from the rest of us. And yet when it came to entertaining she was the best actor of all.

My long-lost sister was a constant source of amazement to me. There seemed to be no end to her talents.

She was everything I would like to be: beautiful, self-confident, talented, sexy. And most of all, Carlos Garcia's lover.

I lay in bed thinking about this and the coming Emmy awards. I wasn't looking forward to them. Not because I thought Gloria might be pipped at the post or anything. She was going to win the Emmy, no question. She was the best script-writer in America, everyone said so. She was going to win and I already knew whose name she was going to mention in her acceptance speech.

At least I'd get to sit beside him and applaud her.

And still I wasn't looking forward to it. In fact, I was dreading its approach.

Because my return ticket was booked for the following day.

Emmy or Not Emmy

Carlos flew in from New York an hour before we were due to leave for the awards ceremony. He had had practically no sleep, on account of a late shoot the night before. But this didn't prevent him looking better than any human being has a right to.

Gloria and I had spent the best part of the day being tortured in a place called Transform U. They had waxed our legs rigorously and steamed our faces cruelly, or maybe vice versa, I can't remember. They certainly steamed our hair and then, most unbelievable of all, wrapped us up for forty minutes in hot bandages.

Two other women were in the throes of being wrapped when we walked in. One of them seemed close to fainting from her ordeal. I kept thinking of *The Curse of the Mummy's Tomb*, a film Turlough had taken me to when he was trying to convince me to marry him.

But Gloria refused to let me leave. 'Trust me, honey, the results will be worth it, you'll see.'

So we were wrapped and eventually unwrapped. Our faces were made up. Our nails painted. And our hair washed, set and 'teased' without mercy.

Gloria turned out to be right, as usual. The results were worth it. For her. She looked like Miss America by the time they were finished with her.

I could have sued for misleading advertising.

Gloria laughed when I said this. 'You look beautiful and you know it,' she insisted.

Loyalty had always been one of her best traits. That's why it had come as such a shock when she disappeared, all those years ago, without a word. It was something that was never far from my mind. Why had she never contacted me?

'Why did you never write to me?' We were in the back of the limo on our way home to get dressed for the awards when I asked her this.

'What?'

'When you ran away. Why did you never write to me?'

'God, you are a funny little creature, Maddy! What a time to choose to start asking about that.'

'I'm sorry. It just popped into my head,' I lied.

'I wrote you dozens of letters. Some I posted, some I didn't. I knew she wouldn't give them to you anyway. You must have hated me, Maddy.'

'I couldn't hate you. Nothing could ever make me hate you. I just missed you so much. I was so lonely.' My lip began to quiver.

'Don't you dare make me cry, Maddy O'Toole! Not after I've spent a bloody fortune on all this fuckin' make-up.'

We were still laughing when we reached the mansion. Wannabe Tom opened the door for us, his eyes not leaving Gloria's face. He never said, but I always suspected him of having the biggest crush on Gloria.

With sixty minutes to go I still hadn't settled on a suitable dress. I had already tried on and refused, almost every evening dress in Gloria's vast wardrobe.

'That's it. I can't possibly go!' I cried.

It wasn't vanity that had me behaving like this, it was nerves. I looked ridiculous in Gloria's clothes. They were all so dramatic, over the top. I couldn't carry them off, especially with my cropped hair.

'I look like a female impersonator,' I moaned when I tried on yet another extravagant number encrusted with mock diamonds.

Gloria tried not to laugh, but even she had to admit that on me the big halter-necked dress was a failure.

It was Mrs Danvers who finally came up with a demure little black number that even Mother couldn't have found fault with.

Until I put it on. What had looked simple and innocent on a hanger took on a whole new aspect with a woman's body inside it. It was blatantly sexy. It made me look as if I had a better figure than Gloria, which was saying something.

The cutaway back was as dangerously low as the wickedly draped front, exposing far too much tanned flesh for a God-fearing woman from Ballyshannon.

Gloria applauded when I walked into her room.

Mrs Danvers practically smiled.

I tugged at the black velvet bodice, trying to pull it up a little higher, because my chest kept trying to make a bid for freedom.

Gloria slapped my hand. 'Stop that, Maddy. It's too well designed to fall down.' I think she meant the dress.

And I have to be honest; I did like the look of it on me, even if it was inclined to be immodest. I never got a chance to show off my two best features in Ballyshannon. How could I? Washing down the yard or spreading silage hardly called for an eye-catching *décolletage*. And even indoors I settled for jumpers. My chest had to come to Hollywood to get an airing.

Mrs Danvers and Gloria disappeared into her dressing-room to sew Gloria into her new Christian Lacroix dress.

That's when Carlos arrived. I heard him first. Running up the stairs. I stayed where I was, transfixed in front of Gloria's full-length mirror, admiring myself in the low-cut dress.

He came into the room and paused for a second. Next thing I know he's pressing his lips against my bare shoulder. And it's not my imagination this time. This is really happening, it's not some wild fantasy, born out of need. He really is kissing me, moving his mouth slowly along my back, and I'm about to faint with pleasure.

'Oh baby. Come on, we've got plenty of time before the car gets here.' He was drawing me towards the bed.

He thought I was Gloria! Even with my cropped hair he mistook me for the most attractive woman who had ever come out of Ballyshannon. I was about to protest, I swear I was, when I felt him shaking with suppressed laughter.

'Sorry, Maddy, I couldn't resist, you looked like a startled colt when you saw me come in. As if you expected me to pounce on you.' He threw himself on to the bed, laughing like a drain.

'Carlos Garcia! Are you stoned?' Gloria stood over him, resplendent in her new dress, her scarlet-tipped hands on her hips.

'Just a little bit, baby. Come here.' He held out his arms.

'Jesus Christ, are you mad? You know how

important this evening is to me. Do you know who's going to be in our party?'

'Sure, the big man himself, Herbet Dwight Goldman. And do you know something else? He'll be stoned too. If he has any sense.' He fell back, laughing again.

'Jesus Christ, how did Bobby let you get into this state? What are we gonna do?' She turned to Mrs Danvers.

'Don't worry.' Carlos laughed. 'Nobody'll notice. Maddy couldn't tell I was stoned. Could you, Maddy?'

The chocolate-brown eyes were smiling into mine, sending me dangerous signals. Of course, he *was* out of his head.

'What the fuck would she know? She lives in the asshole of the world!' Gloria almost spat. Then she was slapping him around the head, calling him names, filthy, racist names that I couldn't believe my sister would use. 'You stupid spic! You fuckin' wetback . . . You . . .'

I put my hands over my ears.

Mrs Danvers stood there, keeping well out of it. So did I. But I did it out of sheer funk. She did it from superiority of character.

I had admired her before, but she rose hugely in my estimation that day.

My sister had a truly remarkable vocabulary. I suppose it was necessary in her line of work. Tools of the trade, so to speak. She certainly used it to good effect in her *People in Jeopardy* scripts. You could always tell when she had written the teleplay. The language could only be described as ripe. But to hear such words coming from her pretty mouth was hugely offensive.

It had no effect on Carlos. No matter how vile her language became, how vulgar her threats, he just laughed. And this made her worse.

'You can stay here. I'm not going to be seen with you. You think I'm going to walk up to that podium with the whole auditorium laughing at me? You stupid fucker! You know how hard I've worked for this night? All that damn party giving.'

'All those asses you had to kiss.' He giggled.

'You bastard!'

'Ass-kissing to win a stupid award.' He made kissing noises.

'Well you'll never have to do that, will you, pretty boy? Because pretty boy actors don't get nominated for awards. It takes real talent to be nominated, never mind win.'

Mrs Danvers flinched.

'Pretty boy,' Carlos echoed and laughed even harder.

I had spent three years watching Carlos act. I had studied his every movement on screen during that time and in my judgement not one of those performances even came close to matching the one he gave the night of the Emmy awards. He was superb. Beyond criticism.

From the moment we stepped out of the stretch-limo he was on stage, everything a Famous Star should be. He was courteous and charming, patient with the press. Obliging to the waiting photographers, turning this way and that without complaint. He waved to his fans and signed endless autographs. And all the time smiling. Not the silly grin that aggravated Gloria so much in the limo that she threatened him with her Gucci bag, but a smile that was fit for the front page of any magazine. Or newspaper.

He charmed everyone in sight.

Except Gloria. 'Oh, now he decides to act,' she muttered. 'Maybe next time he could try it in front of the fuckin' cameras.'

I thought this was uncalled for. She had told him to smile and behave himself. Ordered him to. Now that he had, she still wasn't satisfied. Maybe there was no satisfying Gloria. Or perhaps she was just plain jealous.

The press had ignored us as we walked ahead of him. Gloria was the nominee, the most important person in our party, but it was Carlos's picture they wanted. His smile on the front page. He was The Star.

'This way, Carlos. Look over here. Smile! Again!'

He had been right about nobody noticing the state he was in. When we were finally seated among the specially invited guests, no one seemed to realize how stoned he was, or if they did they didn't care. I caught Bobby darting a sideways glance at him once or twice, but that was all.

Carlos's behaviour was impeccable.

So was Gloria's, when they finally announced the winner of the award for best writer of a drama series. It made me proud to be her sister.

She sat, surrounded by her colleagues, looking almost regal in her cream silk dress, her hands clasped loosely in her lap, a genuinely interested look on her face as the nominees were listed, one by nerve-racking one. The names rang out and a short excerpt from each writer's work was shown on the big screens above us. Gloria was so relaxed it was hard to believe the scenes we'd endured in the mansion before we left. Or the difficulty she'd had memorizing her acceptance speech.

Then the announcement came. And everyone held their breath. I was so excited I almost leaped to my feet before her name rang out.

'And the winner is . . . Michael Halson . . . for *Goodbody Brown.*'

It was like the feeling you get just before your ears pop on an aeroplane, that strange sensation of being shut off from the rest of the world, even though you can still see it all going on around you. Those few numbing seconds when you are locked in your own little soundless bubble, before the world breaks through again and reclaims you.

The applause was deafening. I wondered if I had heard wrong, mistaken the name they'd called out.

I turned to verify this with Carlos and was almost shocked to see Gloria still sitting there, her chin held high as someone else strode past to the winner's podium.

She was applauding just as enthusiastically as everyone else. Smiling and nodding her head, as though she had been waiting all these weeks for this exact announcement. As if she had never expected any other name to be called out but Michael Halson's.

I held my breath, afraid to exhale in case I broke down in tears and disgraced her. Frightened that I might run up to the podium, grab the award from the hands of the smiling impostor and carry it back triumphantly to the rightful winner.

When the applause died down and the impostor began his modest and thoroughly boring speech, I saw Carlos slip his hand between the seats to squeeze Gloria's in silent comfort.

If I loved my sister with all my heart at that moment, I loved this man with my whole being.

The announcements went on. And on.

What appeared to be an endless parade of overdressed people strode up to the winners' podium to thank their colleagues, their families, their agents and, in one absent-minded case, I think a psychiatrist.

Or perhaps that one was meant as a joke. I was beyond caring. All I knew was that Gloria didn't get to hold one of the coveted little statuettes and Michael Halson had carried the one for best writer, head high, back to his cheering colleagues.

And still Gloria smiled. She applauded each and every winner enthusiastically. And graciously. In between cracking ribald jokes with the people sitting closest to her.

A bearded man came to speak to her, clutching the award for Best Director.

Gloria kissed him warmly, her eyes moist.

'Next year, Gloria,' I heard him say. 'If there's any justice.'

So at least she got to see an Emmy close up.

If only it had been hers.

There were so many parties that night that we were spoiled for choice. Instead of appearing despondent, Gloria shone with a wild manic energy, which put the rest of us in the shade. If Carlos seemed to be watching her apprehensively I tried not to notice. I was just glad to see her enjoying herself.

We skipped from gathering to gathering, Gloria receiving so many tributes you'd swear she had won.

Everywhere we went people approached her saying, 'Such a shame, Gloria, everyone knows you should have won.'

This happened so often that I began to wonder why she hadn't. If everyone thought she should have got it, how come she didn't?

'The luck of the draw,' Bobby muttered, looking as downcast as only a Kennedy can.

And of course the inevitable happened. We had only stepped in the door of one of the more raucous parties when we spotted the impostor. He was centre stage, dancing wildly, his brand-new Emmy in one hand, a blonde nymphet in the other.

He rushed over to Gloria, leaving his dancing partner stranded mid-boogie. He hugged her and repeated the mantra of the night. 'You should have won, darling, everyone knows that.'

I thought he was going to give her the Emmy. He didn't even give her a drink.

By one thirty most of our party was ready for bed. But not Gloria. She was wrapped around some man from Romania who hardly spoke a word of English, but who had won for best lighting technician, or putting a plug on a camera, or something.

'Is she all right?' I asked Carlos, who was chewing at his lip.

'I don't think so,' he said. 'Let's go get her, Bobby.'

Between them they practically manhandled her back to the table.

'Let go of me, you bastards.' She seemed to be annoyed.

'Gloria, I have to get some sleep,' I said. 'My flight is tomorrow.'

She was suddenly full of remorse and concern for

my well-being. 'Oh Maddy. And we haven't had a chance to speak all night.'

'I've got to be on the set in three hours.' Carlos said quietly.

'I have to talk to Maddy,' she snapped, reaching for my hand.

'We can talk in the car, Gloria.'

I sat in the limo watching her bid emotional goodbyes to several people whose names she couldn't even remember. But I felt sorry for her. She was being so brave. Drunk, but brave. She finally climbed into the car and across me, piercing my instep with one of her deadly stiletto heels.

I waited until the three of us were settled into the roomy interior before turning to her. 'What did you want to talk about, Gloria?'

She was fast asleep, her head on Carlos's shoulder, his jacket covering her like a blanket.

His eyes were closed too, but something told me he wasn't sleeping.

I looked out at the darkness.

Gloria Bares Her Soul

Gloria crept into my bed at six a.m. I wasn't asleep. I had been lying awake, staring at the ceiling for what seemed like hours. Day-dreaming. This was the last time I would wake up in this beautiful room, I was telling myself. The last time I would lie here knowing that Carlos was sleeping only a few yards away down the corridor. Life was so cruel. Why couldn't I, just once, have something I wanted? Why couldn't it be my turn this time?

Then Gloria was in my bed and I was ashamed of being so selfish. She had lost out on something she had worked hard for. And she had done so in public; my disappointments were private and only I knew about them.

She put her head on my shoulder and I curled my arms around her thin body. She began to weep silently, the way she used to all those years ago in Ballyshannon. And I was the bewildered little sister again, comforting her as best I could without quite knowing why she needed comforting. Right now I wasn't sure if she was crying because she hadn't won the Emmy, or because I was leaving in a few hours' time.

I turned out to be wrong on both counts.

'I hate her, Maddy,' she suddenly said.

'Mrs Danvers?' I whispered.

'No!' She rounded on me. 'Mother.'

She sat bolt upright, as if she had just this very minute made a momentous decision. 'There's something I haven't told you, Maddy.'

The familiar knot began to form in my stomach. I wanted to say, don't tell me please, leave things as they are, I'll be gone in a few hours. I don't have to know *everything*.

'Let the hare sit,' Father used to say when he sensed trouble brewing. I wanted to say this to Gloria now, but it was too late; she had begun her story.

'Remember the old tin-roofed cowshed? At the back of the yard?'

'That's long gone, Turlough had it knocked down years ago.' I tried distracting her.

She wasn't listening.

'Father and I were in there one night. It was freezing cold. One of our best heifers was about to calve. We were afraid to leave her alone because her first calf had been stillborn, yet there was nothing much happening with her, so all we could do was watch and wait. And it was so fuckin' cold. I can't remember ever being so cold, before or since. Whenever I think of that place my predominant memory is always of the bone-chilling cold.'

'You always felt the cold more than any of us. Mother used to remark on that.'

'Mother!' She spat the word. 'She'll say whatever suits her. She's hardly an oracle of wisdom, is she?'

'I . . .'

'Father and I were in the cowshed. He put his arm around me and I clung to his waist, and then, because I was so cold, I snuggled underneath his big grey coat to keep warm. Remember his big grey coat, Maddy? The one with the long ragged tear under the arm?'

She didn't wait for an answer. 'He wrapped it around me so tightly, squashing us together. And I liked it, even though I hated the smell of tobacco that always clung to him. My teeth finally stopped chattering and I looked up at him, and he patted my head, the way he used to pat Runt. You know that absent-minded way he had of doing things. I think half the time he didn't know if it was one of us or the dog he was patting. His mind was always elsewhere. Away in the distance. But for some reason I began to laugh. And, quite unbelievably, Father laughed back. Father? Laughing? And then she was there. She must have come up on us in that sneaky way she had, as if she was hoping to catch us doing something forbidden. When she suddenly appeared in front of us, Father and I both gave a start and leaped apart, as if we were guilty of some wrongdoing. And I'll never forget the look on her face. She hated me. She whacked me across the head with her big Aran cardigan and told me to get into the house. She made my life hell from that day out. Called me a no-good. A little tramp. I was thirteen years old, Maddy, I had spent my whole life on Hawthorn Farm. I didn't know a damn thing about men and women, and what went on between them, you know that.'

She looked down at me, lying there in the soft, warm bed.

'I know what you're thinking, Maddy. Do you imagine I haven't gone over that scene a million times in my own head? Asked myself the same question, over and over. Could there have been something? Something I missed? Was I so naïve . . .? I swear to you, Maddy, the man never behaved in any way towards me except as the absent-minded father he always was. It was her warped mind, which twisted everything. She made everything dirty. I'm surprised she allows you and Turlough to share a bed in her house.'

I thought about the little room under the eaves, the way Mother's room was positioned four-square beneath it. How every noise carried.

'She's a frigid woman, Maddy, in every sense of the word. Can you recollect the word love ever being used in that house? Ever?'

I didn't answer.

'I know she's from another generation and I know they married her off to Father when she was young enough to be his granddaughter. You remember those horrible stories about her having to wash his false teeth before they retired for the night? But that doesn't excuse the way she treated me. I'll never forgive her for the way she punished that little thirteen-year-old. And for what? For something that only existed in her own sick mind. I began to believe I was guilty of something. If my own mother hated me so much I must have done something terribly wrong. Or maybe there was just something dirty about me. Perhaps I deserved to be punished. When Father died I even wondered if I might have been, somehow, to blame. Crazy!'

'Is . . . is that why you ran away?'

She tossed back her hair. 'When I got to London I behaved the way I thought dirty people were supposed to behave. I slept with anything that moved. I didn't care who they were. What they were. Anybody would do. The nastier the better.'

'Gloria . . .'

'Do you want me to lie?'

I turned away.

'I wasn't a tart or anything. I didn't charge. At least, nothing more than a couple of vodkas. With Coke. And the more they hurt me the better I felt. I couldn't sink low enough, couldn't find the level I knew I deserved. When I had that first abortion I was hoping they'd leave me torn and bruised and bleeding and . . . They didn't. They couldn't have been gentler or more caring. They even arranged counselling for me.'

'Who . . . who was the father?'

'How should I know? It could have been any of a dozen men. Some filthy drunk, or wino, or horny cabby, anyone.'

'Gloria.' I tried not to cry.

She got up and crossed over to the big window. When she tugged at the heavy silken cord the drapes flew open, flooding the room with bright sunshine. She stood there in the sunlight in her little cream nightie, her long bleached hair tumbling past her thin shoulders.

She was smiling as she swung around. 'I met Jean-Baptiste through my counsellor.' She grinned wickedly. 'He was her boy-friend. Came to collect her one day and bingo! We connected. It happens, Maddy. There were fireworks between us that first time. So he dumped her. We dumped her. He already had a visa for the States. Been commissioned to write a screenplay. We were married in Las Vegas, in the most vulgar ceremony imaginable. Delicious!'

She laughed gleefully. 'The minister looked like Elvis. In the desperate years. He was squashed into a white boiler suit. What a sight! Try to imagine two pounds of sausage meat forced into a one-pound skin. And he had a lazy eye. Not a good omen, Maddy.

You couldn't be sure who he was looking at half the time. I left the place convinced that he'd married Jean-Baptiste to a witness we had dragged in off the street. I though I'd wet myself laughing.' She wiped her eyes.

'Shame the marriage wasn't as much fun. *It* was a disaster. Once we rolled off each other we had nothing left to say. And he hated Hollywood so much. He began to wake up every morning with the same cry, "What are we doin' here, man, are we craaaazy?"' She mimicked a lilting accent. 'I told him he'd have to compromise, for a while at least. Write the kind of scripts they wanted. He wouldn't. He wanted out. But I liked LA. There was a kind of freedom here that you couldn't get anywhere else, not even in London. I felt I could walk, naked, down Sunset Boulevard with a feather in my ass and no one would turn a hair. Don't worry, I didn't.' She grinned. 'But I did write a script. And the rest, as they say, Mad, is history.'

'What about your husband?'

'Oh he buggered off, back to London.'

She noticed my shocked reaction to her glib tone. 'I did try to make it work, Maddy. I even went to Jamaica with him for a romantic weekend. But you're missing the point. I had finally found something I was good at. I could write,' she said gleefully.

'When did you have the second abortion?'

'What is this? The fuckin' Inquisition?'

I lowered my head.

'He'd already left. I didn't wanna contact him.' Her voice rose. 'I was midway through a deal. I had written an excellent script and . . . oh you'd never understand.'

'I might.'

'I had a chance to prove myself. Be somebody. If a major Hollywood studio was willing to pay big bucks for something I'd written, even if it was for TV, that proved something, didn't it? Well I thought it did. I could produce an item that people were prepared to shell out a lot of dollars for. I couldn't let anything get in the way of that. I had to be out there fighting. Doing the deal. That's how it works here. Any sign of weakness, or hesitation and . . . I had no choice, Maddy. I was alone, no one to turn to. I couldn't afford to have a child. I had too many battles to fight.'

'Battles?'

'It's different for you. You bend with the wind. I can't, it's not my nature. People admire what they imagine is my strength. But it's not strength that keeps me going, Maddy. It's anger. Without that I'd be nothing. I have to hold on to my anger. You're different, Mad. You have an inner calm that keeps you on an even keel.'

'An even keel? Me?' I squeaked. 'I let everyone walk on me.'

'I don't think so, Maddy. Not when it comes to something you really want. Maybe you just haven't found that yet.'

I felt myself blush.

'Oh look at you blush. I love you, Mad. Don't go back to those selfish bastards. They don't deserve you. Stay here.'

'Here?' I echoed.

'Here with me. I need you, Maddy.'

I spluttered, 'Nobody needs me.'

'I do.'

There was a knock on the door. 'Madam?'

'I need you, Maddy, you can't even imagine how much.'

Mrs Danvers came in. She hesitated for a second, before approaching the bed.

'Think about it, Maddy.' Gloria turned and walked out.

'Did you wish me to start packing?' Mrs Danvers's eyes were alive with curiosity.

'What . . .?' My head was spinning.

'Should I start your packing?'

'I . . . I suppose.'

I was having a final walk around the garden, taking my leave of all my favourite plants, when Gloria came running towards me along the lavender-edged pathway. Gloria never walked when she could run. I held out a small sprig of lavender to her. I had cut it for remembrance.

She gave it a quick sniff, before discarding it to link her arm through mine. 'Lavender is an old woman's scent.' She grinned when she saw my expression.

'I like it.'

Normally she would have had a witty retort. Not today. Today we walked in silence. This was unusual for her. She liked to fill every second with words. We were almost back at the house before she spoke again. 'Maddy?'

'Don't tempt me, Gloria, you'll get me in terrible trouble.'

'Trouble? What can they do to you? Cut you off without a penny?'

We laughed together.

'I'll give you a weekly allowance.' She mentioned a sum that was far in excess of the monthly income of

Hawthorn Farm, then misread my shocked reaction. 'I could give you more?'

'It's not the money. It . . . it wouldn't be right.'

'For whom? You? You love it here, that's obvious. And we love having you, Carlos and I. *And* the rest of the household. Name one person who gives a damn about you at Hawthorn Farm.' She frowned. 'Do you think anyone there would miss you?'

I thought about the twins. Remembered how badly I felt when I learned that they had gone down to the church hall the morning of my flight, without even coming to say goodbye.

'Who'll miss you?'

'Nobody.' I couldn't lie.

'Then stay. It would mean so much to me.' She stood in front of me, blocking my path. 'Please. Give it a try. If, by the remotest chance, you became homesick you could always hop on a plane. I won't hold you prisoner. Shackle you in a dungeon, or anything.'

I grinned.

'Then you'll stay?'

'No, I . . .'

'Please stay with me, Mad.' She caught my arm so forcefully it made me wince. 'When I saw that bastard collect the Emmy I felt doom-laden. As if some kind of terrible curse was about to descend on me. As though it was some kind of omen, telling me my luck was running out. Can you understand that, Maddy? It's dumb and archaic, I know, but it's there in my head now and I can't shift it. That bastard took my luck when he collected that Emmy. It was mine, Maddy, it belonged to me. And he got it. It never rains but it pours. Remember? Stay with me, Mad.

Don't make me beg.'

'You don't have to beg me. I love you. You know that.' I tried to hug her.

She held me at arm's length, her grip surprisingly strong. 'Will you stay then?'

'I . . . but everything is arranged . . . how can I cancel my flight . . . and . . . ?'

She was a whirlwind. A mobile phone seemed to materialize out of nowhere. Her fingers dialled at record speed. 'Janet? Hi, it's me, I want you to get on to Pan Air. Yeah. My sister's ticket. Well whoever. You'll find all the details in my desk diary. Yeah. Cancel it.' She looked at me. 'That doesn't matter. Just cancel it.'

She rang off. 'Done.'

'Gloria Mullin, you're nuts.'

'It's in my genes, honey. In my genes.' She spun round and round, laughing wildly. She could have been twelve years old.

Carlos didn't seem too surprised to hear that I was staying on. Perhaps living all this time with Gloria had made him immune to such sudden turnabouts.

Mrs Danvers behaved as if it was the most natural thing in the world to be asked to unpack my suitcases not two hours after she had so expertly packed them.

Dong's reaction was the most heart-warming of all. He came into the dining-room carrying a painstakingly iced fruit-cake. The thick Royal icing above the deep layer of smooth almond was sculpted into a winter snow scene that drew gasps of admiration from everyone who saw it.

Somebody had told Dong of my lifelong passion.

'Kek for liddle boy.' He chuckled

He held his masterpiece aloft as Mrs Danvers switched off the lights. A single pink candle burned amid the pristine snow scene, dripping pink wax on to the gleaming white. If I'd had any doubts about my decision to stay on here, the sight of that lovingly iced cake put them all out of my mind.

I was eating my way blissfully through a wedge of my special treat when Gloria phoned Ballyshannon. She had volunteered to tell them that I had been unavoidably detained in LA. She had concocted a thrillingly dramatic story about an encounter with a diving board. I had broken my foot, so the story went, after insisting on diving from the highest board at the Beverly Hills Hilton.

It was a heart-rending tale. Full of drama and pathos. And blood. Not for nothing was my sister an award-winning script-writer.

She came back into the room with a satisfied smirk on her face.

'Did they ask to speak to me?'

'No. Turlough did wonder if you could sue the Hilton for compensation.' She scooped up a thick slice of cake and bit into it, still looking pleased as punch.

'Maybe they thought my broken foot would prevent me coming to the phone?'

'Ever the optimist, Maddy. Ever the optimist.' She rang for Mrs Danvers. 'Bring me a bottle of champagne, Betty.'

'Er which . . .?'

Gloria stretched like a cat. 'I don't mind. You choose.'

Gloria's Party

When Carlos arrived home from the studio the bottle was empty.

'Did I miss the celebration?' He turned it upside down, his beautiful eyebrows shooting skywards.

'Plenty more where that came from.' Gloria grinned, ringing for Mrs Danvers again. 'Betty, call a few people for me, will you? Bobby and Phil, and maybe Sara and . . . you know the drill.' She glanced at Carlos. 'What about Herman? Ah, call everybody. Tell them we're having a little party.'

It never failed to amaze me, the things Mrs Danvers was required to do for Gloria. And always without question or hesitation.

Carlos looked at me with an amused expression on his face. 'Did you know we were having a party?'

'Not until this minute.'

We commiserated with each other as Gloria ran upstairs to change. 'Won't be a sec, folks, don't start the fun without me.'

As if.

A full forty minutes later we were still sitting there waiting. The conversation wasn't exactly fizzing. Carlos took a couple of phone calls to relieve his boredom. Once or twice I thought of something to say, then reconsidered and stayed silent.

Carlos glanced towards the hallway and sighed in

exasperation. He picked up a bottle of champagne and began to shake it. Hard.

Mrs Danvers stood by, two fluted glasses at the ready.

'I guess you won't be running upstairs for some time to come, Maddy.' The bottle popped, sending a spray of champagne into the air.

Mrs Danvers repositioned the glasses.

'What do you mean?'

'Your poor broken foot, that will take some time to mend.' He finished pouring the bubbling drink.

We both drank up far too quickly.

Mrs Danvers busied herself lighting the tall candles on the mantelpiece. She dimmed the big central chandelier and walked around placing coasters on every possible inch of furniture.

Soft music filled the room.

Carlos poured me another drink.

And still Gloria hadn't come down.

The champagne was beginning to take effect on both of us. Carlos teased me about my make-believe accident with the diving board. And I watched his mouth as he spoke. To my absolute delight, he dropped to his knees in front of me and took my foot gently in his hand. Shoe and all. He bowed his head over it, as if he was about to kiss it.

It was a joke of course. To him. A joke to pass the time while we were waiting for Gloria to come down and liven things up.

He had no idea that I would have broken my foot with an axe to have him kneeling at my feet for real. I stared longingly at the top of his head. His hair was jet black and I knew it would be soft to the touch. My fingers started to move of their own accord.

The doorbell rang loudly and he was on his feet.

At the impromptu party I finally got to dance with him.

Despite the champagne I was determined not to show myself up. I tried to keep cool and not tremble too noticeably, or stare too blatantly. Or bite him on the neck just below his perfect chin.

He was wearing jeans and a casual T-shirt, but he smelled of expensive cologne. And sex. Well, that's not quite true, but he did smell of expensive cologne – a light, musky smell that made me think of sex. Of course, if he hadn't been wearing cologne I would have still thought of sex, because no female with living red corpuscles in her veins could dance this close to him and not think about it.

When he smiled lazily down at me, his brown eyes twinkling, I could have sworn he was thinking about it as well. But then wishful thinking can really power the imagination.

'Come and dance with me, Irish,' Bobby interrupted us.

It was that kind of party. Worse luck.

Everybody there was a close friend of either Carlos of Gloria. Mostly Gloria. The whole thing was totally informal. Their friends wandered around wherever they pleased. There were couples strewn all over the place. On the floor rugs, on the big squishy sofas, even out on the terrace, although it wasn't a warm night.

The rest of them danced and flirted to the low blues music that Gloria had quite a penchant for. The smell of marijuana was everywhere.

The atmosphere was completely relaxed. Laid-back, Gloria called it. There was none of the hawk-eyed networking I had seen on other occasions here. None of the continuous peering over shoulders to check out each newcomer as he or she arrived. This gathering wasn't remotely like the pre-Emmy parties Gloria had hosted. This was fun. And not just because I got to dance with Carlos.

'So you're not going back to the old country, then?'

'What?'

'You're staying in LA?' Bobby asked.

'Not for ever.' I laughed.

'That's not what I heard,' he said. But Bobby was a tease. He sometimes liked to pretend that he thought Ireland was overrun by leprechauns and that all Gaels danced around fairy forts, come the first stroke of midnight. I half believed him until I learned that he had a Masters in European History, as well as his law degree. He was also fond of playing the 'Irish boyo', even though it was well over a hundred years since his ancestors had swapped the soft green fields of Wexford for the lure of the New World.

'How are things back in the old country?' he asked.

'How are things in the cocaine trade?' I retorted.

'Ouch!' He pretended to be mortally wounded.

The cocaine jibe wasn't really on, but what the hell; he had interrupted my slow dance with Carlos. When I had overheard his remark, at an earlier party, about Carlos 'getting enough of it in New York' I had assumed he was talking about sex, probably because, when it came to Carlos, that was the one subject always uppermost in my mind. But Bobby had been referring to cocaine.

It was Wannabe Tom, as ever, who enlightened me.

'Bobby Kennedy supplies Carlos with whatever he wants. And he likes a toot now and again.'

'Is it true that you supply Carlos with . . .?' I began.

'Sh, if Gloria found out she'd kill us.'

'I should hope so.'

'Anything that might damage his looks is a no no. Lilliput Productions has far too much invested in him to allow . . .'

He went on and on, telling me how valuable Carlos was to them. I had heard Turlough describe a prime heifer in much the same terms, the little calculator in his brain quickly figuring how long she could viably produce a decent quota before he'd sell her off. To the abattoir.

'It's not as if he does it regularly, him being such a damn puritan,' Bobby was saying.

This was the second time I'd heard Carlos called a puritan. It hardly jelled with the image I had of him as a sultry-eyed sex god.

Bobby laughed at my puzzled expression. 'How are things in the cocaine trade?' He mimicked my accent. 'You're such a funny girl, Maddy.'

'Woman.'

'Okay, you're such a funny woman.' He pulled me closer, his hand sliding down towards my bottom. 'How about a kiss between friends?'

'I'm not that funny,' I said, and walked away and out of the room.

When I got back to the living-room everyone was in stitches.

Bobby had apparently made a very entertaining speech, insulting the Emmy awards and praising Gloria's long-running battle with a major Hollywood studio. I made it in time to hear the final line – 'So here's to my friend and hero, Gloria Mullin! The woman with the biggest balls in Hollywood.'

There were whistles and cheers.

Judging by her loud laughter, Gloria evidently appreciated Bobby's remark.

I didn't. I saw Carlos watching me and it crossed my mind that he would think me such a little prude for not appreciating the joke. But it wasn't the lame joke that concerned me. It was the way Gloria was behaving.

I didn't like Gloria much when she was drunk. I knew what would follow. She would become more and more foul-mouthed as the night wore on.

With a few drinks inside her my sister was so lovable. She was everyone's favourite, witty and smart, and always hilariously funny.

But too much drink and she became someone else entirely. She could turn bitter and nasty. And no one escaped her vicious tongue.

It was like heresy to admit it, even to myself, but she sometimes reminded me of Mother.

'I've known Gloria longer than any of you guys.' Bobby was back on his feet again after sitting on Gloria's lap to kiss her soundly. 'I know when the creative juices are beginning to flow. I recognize that Celtic glow that infuses her poetic soul.'

Everyone cheered.

'I can see it in action right now. You're already hatching your next little creation, aren't you, Glo? Go on, 'fess up.' He hiccuped loudly. 'You're among friends.'

All eyes turned to Gloria.

Drunk as she was, she gave nothing away. She just

smiled and sipped her drink. Gloria could be quite the Sphinx when she chose.

'Is it a movie?' Bobby was insistent.

'Is it a plane?' Carlos was beyond caring.

'Is it a book?' someone asked. 'A novel?'

'You'll all know soon enough.' Gloria looked smug. 'I can tell you that it will be my most surprising production to date.'

That got everyone excited. They were, after all, in the same business. Everybody wanted a guess. In on this new game. Ideas came thick and fast. People were shouting each other down, determined to have their opinions heard above the others.

Even the couples who were well stoned became interested. It turned into a noisy free-for-all.

Nobody noticed when I crept away. Not even Carlos, who was now stretched across one of the big sofas looking thoroughly bored.

I would have given ten years of my life for another dance with him. But nobody was dancing any more. It was all Hollywood games now. An insider euphemism for business.

I watched him for a second before leaving. He was so handsome. How could Gloria be in the same room as him and choose to spend her time talking business crap with Bobby Kennedy? Was the woman blind?

Gloria had too much, that was her problem. She was so spoiled that she couldn't see the wood for the trees.

Outside the door I practically fell over Mrs Danvers. 'What are you doing at this hour?'

She straightened up and began to rejig an already perfect flower arrangement.

At one o'clock in the morning?
'Why don't you go to bed?' I asked.
'Madam might need me,' she said haughtily.
Like I said, Gloria was thoroughly spoiled.

The Deal

One of the nicest things about Hollywood was being able to breakfast in the sun. I did this almost every day, filling up on the most appetising waffles in existence. I could eat my way through mounds of these feather-light delicacies at a sitting. Usually after I had smothered them in a rich honey sauce that clung to the palate, until it was washed down by the best coffee in the universe.

After a lifetime of Mother's salty grey porridge and pale milky tea, this American breakfast represented the height of decadence to me. I couldn't get enough of it.

The morning after Gloria's party I was midway through such a breakfast when Mrs Danvers interrupted me. 'Madam wishes to see you.' She made it sound like a Royal command. 'In her study, please,' she added mysteriously.

I was so intrigued that I pushed aside my plate.

I found it surprising that Gloria was working so early this morning. She couldn't have had much sleep, because the party had continued well into the small hours and beyond. And she surely had the mother of all hangovers.

I knocked on the big oak-panelled door.

'Come in.' It was a formal invitation.

I peeped around the door, deliberately pop-eyed to make her laugh. She didn't.

She was sitting behind her desk wearing a big fluffy dressing-gown. This was serious stuff. Gloria never ever wore a dressing-gown around the house; she was one of those women who seemed to wake up fully clothed and ready to go.

'Sit down, Maddy.' The desk light glanced off her gold ear-rings.

This, at least, was reassuring. If she was wearing ear-rings, she hadn't descended into complete sloth. But she was definitely nervous. And Gloria was never nervous; it wasn't in her nature. She could be sad, even melancholy at times, but never nervous. Gloria was the queen of self-assured sophistication. Even when she fell into the pool, fully clothed, she gave the impression that the pool was at fault, not she.

I was the one who became edgy at any excuse. It was happening now. Her nervousness made me nervous.

She leaned forward, her big eyes searching my face. 'Did you sleep well, Maddy?'

Did I sleep well? Had she called me away from my breakfast to ask me that?

'Yes thank you,' I replied, the benefits of a convent education showing.

'Just the . . . the noise, I hope it didn't disturb you.'

'No.' I was becoming really suspicious now. What had she called me here for? I racked my brains to think of something I might have done that annoyed her. Something that made her sorry she had asked me to stay on. Was it Carlos bending over my foot last night? But that was just a joke. It wasn't as if he would ever want to kiss my foot or any other part of me for real. I tried to remember if Mrs Danvers had been in or out of the room when it happened, but I couldn't recall. I had been too mesmerized by the sight of the top of his head, the feel of his warm thumb on my instep.

'I wanted to ask you something, Maddy.' She was looking really stern now.

I was definitely guilty of something.

'Did you ever have a dream, Maddy?'

'A dream?' Mrs Danvers couldn't have reported on my dreams. Even she wasn't that good an eaves-dropper.

'You know. Did you ever hope or dream about having something that might be way out of your reach?'

Oh my God, she had found the photo of Carlos under my pillow. I knew it was a mistake keeping it there. I knew.

'Maddy?' Her whole brow was furrowed as she waited for my answer.

'No!' I didn't mean for my denial to come out quite so loud.

'You have never dreamed of having something . . . beyond you. Wanted it desperately?'

I hunted around for a way out. 'Mary Kilmartin's mother kept a relic of Padre Pio under *her* pillow. That was hardly . . .'

She looked startled. 'What . . .?'

'Padre Pio the stigmatic. The one with great healing powers, and hands and feet that bled. From holes in the palms. And soles,' I added helpfully.

'What are you talking about?'

I looked down at my lap.

'Padre Pio?' She frowned. 'What has he got to do with anything?'

'You're right. She died anyway.'

'Who?'

'Mary Kilmartin's mother. You remember. You said that she looked terrible when she was laid out. And you were right, she did. Although she was never all that attractive when she was alive.' I was babbling on.

'Jesus!' She got up to pour herself a drink.

'You want me to go home, don't you?' I said to her back. 'You're sorry you asked me to stay on. I don't blame you. If I were you I'd tell me to go home.'

'I don't want you to go home. The exact opposite. I want you to stay here as long as you like. For ever, if you wish.'

I went light-headed with relief.

She sat at the desk again. 'But there *is* something I was to discuss with you, Mad.' She seemed to be having trouble finding a spot for her glass on the crowded desk. 'There is something very serious that I want us to talk about.'

'How serious?'

She smiled. 'Very. For some time now, I have been considering . . .' she broke off to clear her throat '. . . I have been thinking about having a baby.'

'A baby? Wow! That would be great.' Then I remembered. 'But you can't, you said, after the second abortion you . . .?'

'You're right.' She cut across me. 'I can't have one the usual way.'

'So you're thinking of . . .?'

'*In vitro* fertilization? No. That's not an option for me.' She shook her head. 'But there is a way I could have a child. It would take a lot of planning. A lot of organizing. Goodwill even.' She was fiddling with her glass again. 'And a lot of effort. But you know me,

Maddy, I never take things lightly. In fact, I have been accused of over-researching in the past. So you can imagine how much work I've already put into *this* idea. I think I must have read every word written on the subject. So much so that I've become quite an expert.' She laughed.

'Ha, ha,' I joined in. 'Are you talking about adoption?'

'No. Not adoption.' She was firm.

'Not adoption.'

'But what I am considering would entail a legal adoption. At a later stage.'

This appeared to be the big give-away. She looked at me as if she thought I would now know exactly what she meant.

I hadn't the faintest idea what she was talking about.

'I would also take care of all medical and financial aspects. See that they were scrupulously adhered to. I would handle all that myself. But not without an open discussion first. That goes without saying.'

'Oh, right.' I still hadn't a clue what she was going on about. I did notice that her hands were beginning to tremble. At the time I assumed that she was suffering from a hangover.

She wasn't. Her head was perfectly clear when she dropped the bombshell.

'I'm considering surrogacy, Maddy.'

'Surrogacy?' Jesus Christ, she must be desperate, I thought.

For the first time in years I appreciated how lucky I was to have the twins. Even if they didn't know I was alive half the time. At least I had experienced something Gloria never would. The wonder of childbirth.

Even if it was agonizing. And I had to have all those stitches. I had actually brought two new human beings into the world, two children who would carry my genes into the next generation. Poor Gloria would never get to do that.

In a sudden burst of compassion, tempered, it has to be said, with a tincture of pride, I reached out to her. 'You do whatever you have to do, Gloria. Pay no heed to the sceptics. Surrogacy is just as valid a way to bring a child into the world as any other.'

She clasped my hand so hard her nails bit into my flesh. 'I'm so glad you feel that way, Maddy, because I want you to have a baby for me.'

There was a big grandfather clock in the alcove by the window, a valuable antique I'd been told. It had come with the house. It stood there like a beacon from the past among all the modern high-tech equipment in the room, the state-of-the-art computers and telexes, the editing machine, the video recorders. *And* the battery of telephones that sat on the desk. All the essential components of Gloria's working life. The clock began to chime. Eight o'clock. Eight melodic chimes. I counted them.

Then I looked around for the camera. There was bound to be a camera somewhere. Pointing directly at us, I shouldn't be surprised. To catch my reaction. Because this was a joke; Gloria was having me on.

I gave a nervous little laugh. 'Ha, ha. Very funny, Gloria. Where's the camera?'

'I'm not joking, Maddy.'

I knew that. Even when I was saying 'where's the camera' I knew she was deadly serious. There are some things you don't joke about. Not if you grew up in Ballyshannon.

And it was the brazen cheek of it that got to me then. Her cool assumption that she could even ask me such a thing. *I want you to have a baby for me.* What was I supposed to reply to that? *Certainly, Gloria, will one be enough*?

What in God's name did she take me for? She ran off twenty years ago, leaving me to deal with Mother and an unworkable farm. She had condemned me to twenty years of drudgery. Now she was asking me to have a child for her?

What did she think I was? Some kind of brood mare? A farm animal whose body she could lease for breeding purposes? A lab rat forever at her disposal?

I was well aware that she saw me as awkward, pathetic Maddy. The nonentity from the *asshole of the world.* Gauche Maddy, who spilled wine all over her designer clothes and who, despite her sister's best efforts to civilize her, was struck dumb whenever Carlos walked into the room. I could accept all that, it wasn't too far from the truth. What I couldn't believe was that she considered me to be a feckless half-wit, who would lease her body out as a baby incubator.

'Carlos is as anxious as I am, even more so. He wants to have a child pretty badly.'

'Carlos?' My voice was a squeak.

'Yes, he so wants this.'

'He knows you're asking me to . . .?'

'Oh, yes.'

'He approves?'

'He thinks it's a wonderful idea.' She was all sisterly softness now, her body language mimicking mine as she leaned forward. 'He's thirty-six, Maddy. He's come to an age when you begin to think about such things. Reflect on them. You come to the realization that you're not immortal. That maybe you should be working on something you can leave behind.'

'Working?'

'You know what I mean.' She played her trump card. 'Oh Maddy, Carlos would be forever in your debt if you did this for him.'

My mouth went dry. 'But it's crazy.'

Gloria could sense weakness a mile off. Maybe that's what made her so successful in Hollywood, knowing when to push home an advantage.

She was around the desk in a flash, pulling up a chair to sit in front of me. 'But it's not, Maddy. I have investigated it thoroughly. You know me, a stickler for detail. When you've had time to think about it you'll see that it makes perfect sense. Do you know that siblings have more in common genetically speaking than even parents and their children? In that way you and I are probably closer than any two human beings could possibly be without being identical twins. Do you know that it's a proven fact that ninety-five per cent of women who act as surrogates say that it enriches their lives?'

If I'd been thinking straight and not just about Carlos I might have questioned the quality of their lives before the surrogacy. Although, given the quality of my life up to then, this might well have supported *her* argument.

'You'd make a perfect surrogate, Maddy. You have all the attributes. You've already given birth without complications. You're in your early thirties. You're healthy. You're calm – not at all neurotic. You're perfect!'

'I am?'

‘Yes. And this time you’d have every comfort. You’d be surrounded by love. By people whose every thought would be your well-being. We would be there to facilitate your every need. Your welfare would be paramount.’

‘But I . . .’

‘Don’t answer too quickly, Maddy. Think about it. Think. I want to give Carlos a baby. You have it in your power to help me do this. It’s my dream. My dearest wish. I’ve been thinking about it for such a long time. You have children, you can’t believe the pain of wanting to give someone a child and knowing you can’t.’

Gloria had spent years in Hollywood. She’d had a lot of practice at pitching her ideas to some of the toughest men in the business. I must have seemed like a pussycat compared with them. She played me like a violin. Of course, I didn’t know that then. She knew when to sit back. When to push. When to offer me refreshments. She knew when it was time to let a little tear escape from her eye. When to pull my heart-strings.

I still said no.

She ordered lunch. To be served in her study. Only in retrospect do I realize that she knew that if I left the room she would have lost me.

We were now sitting side by side on the leather couch by her bookshelves. She was drinking vodka. I stuck to straight fruit juice after the wine we’d had at lunch. I had a feeling I’d need to keep a clear head.

Despite her drinking, Gloria’s concentration never wavered. Not once. When it came to producing cold hard facts she could still annihilate me. ‘Let’s discuss this hypothetically, Maddy. That's all I want from you now. Just give me some hypothetical thoughts.'

Oh Gloria, was there ever such a shrewd negotiator?

She had spent the last hour wearing me down. Telling me all about surrogacy. Painting it in such glowing terms. Praising it from every angle, making it sound so exciting that you'd wonder why anyone would want to have a child any other way. She made it seem like the answer to every woman's needs.

My reply was hardly balanced. 'That's a load of crap,' I said.

'Maddy, I'm not trying to talk you into anything now. I'm just putting a hypothetical argument. Now you put your side.'

And what harm could it do, I asked myself. She *wasn't* pushing me any more, all she wanted now was to discuss it *hypothetically*.

'Okay. Supposing, just supposing, I agreed. We're talking hypothetically now. You know how I feel about all things medical. The sight of a needle makes me want to throw up. There appears to be an awful lot of medical intervention in surrogacy, from what you've told me.'

'Oh there doesn't have to be.' She grabbed my arm.

'Of course there does.' I was beginning to enjoy this. 'For a start, there's all that messing about with tubes to facilitate the insemination. Ugh!'

'It doesn't have to be like that.' Her eyes were shining. 'A friend of mine, who now has the most gorgeous little five-year-old, went the natural route.'

'The natural route?' I sipped my juice.

'Yes. Her husband and the girl . . . you know.' She was becoming nervous again.

'They actually . . . did it?'

'It took a couple of times, but it worked. And nobody was any the wiser outside their small circle of friends.'

'She actually let her husband . . .?'

'She wanted a baby pretty badly, Maddy. And they *were* all consenting adults. We're hardly living in Victorian times.'

I swallowed hard. 'Are you suggesting that Carlos and I would have to . . .' I waved my hand about.

'Don't be offended. Please. It's just a thought. I wouldn't dream of attempting to cajole you into doing something you might find morally repugnant. Or against your ethics. I fully appreciate how staunchly Catholic you are still. But I don't think the Church would disapprove of you having a baby for your sister. After all, they are pro-life, aren't they? Supposing you did decided, hypothetically speaking, to go with this idea, well all the better, surely, from the Church's point of view if you . . .'

I couldn't hear her any more. Her voice had faded. The whole room had disappeared.

All I could see were the clearest images of Carlos and me lying naked on a huge king-sized bed, Carlos leaning over me, his brown eyes with the little amber flecks burning with desire, his hands touching me, his mouth coming closer . . .

'. . . I'll give you my word he is the gentlest, most considerate man. He would in no way embarrass you. And I'd go away, Maddy, for days, weeks, whatever it took. I promise you, you would not be embarrassed. I fully appreciate the pitfalls and complexities of what we're discussing. I know it could be fraught with . . .'

'I'll do it.'

'What?' She seemed shocked.

'I said I'll do it.'

'Oh Maddy . . .' She leaped at me, hugging and kissing me, almost throttling me in wild delight. 'You won't regret it, I promise you. You won't regret it.'

Of course the whole idea was insane – my brain recognized that. But my body had its own agenda.

I left her study with my pulse racing. Then half-way along the hallway I almost turned back and yelled 'tricked ya', the way we used to when we were kids and wanted to welsh on a promise.

Then I remembered how Carlos had looked the day he had approached the big bed in the semi-darkness. I had to take several deep, cleansing breaths after this. If I didn't stop thinking about it, I knew I could end up with a paper bag over my head.

Mary Kilmartin said this had once happened to a girl she knew in school, after a Rolling Stones concert in Slane Castle. Mick Jagger had, apparently, touched her up and she began to hyperventilate. This girl, not Mary Kilmartin. They had to put a paper bag over her head to save her life, Mary said.

And Mick Jagger is one *ugly* man.

If ugly Mick Jagger could make you hyperventilate, imagine what the divine Carlos Garcia could do to you.

Disappointment had always been an integral part of my life. I had married Turlough, hadn't I? *And* given birth to twin boys. And fat Marion had taken over my job in the milking parlour. I was used to disappointments.

But the days following my pact with Gloria were some of the most disappointing of my life. I'm not sure what I had been expecting. I knew Gloria would have to fill Carlos in on the unusual variation we had settled on. And I fully realized that wheels would have to be set in motion, so to speak, before Carlos and I would actually *get together*. But I had expected that something would change.

There would, at least, be some recognition of the agreement between us. A sly handclasp as we passed on the stairs, perhaps. A meaningful look over the honey-smeared waffles. A quick wink over the flower arrangements.

There was nothing. He left for New York within hours of my talk with Gloria. I didn't even get to see him go.

I was walking around the garden in a trance, my head full of romantic images of him and me, and what we would say to each other when we came face to face, when I heard his car drive away. I continued my walk, my heart like lead. My arms full of the blood-red roses I had picked to decorate my room.

Gloria was also driven away soon afterwards, sitting in the back of the limo like a victorious queen. But at least she came to say goodbye. And thank me repeatedly. In fact, all she was short of was kissing me on the lips.

Despite the momentous decision I had made nothing changed for me in the big mansion. I passed my days much as I had until then. I spent time with Tomasino in the garden. And Dong in the kitchen. And Mrs Danvers still waited on me hand and foot by the swimming pool.

Sometimes when I allowed myself to think of what was to come I had to leap into the water to cool off.

Even if I had only just emerged from it seconds before.

There had been one minor change. I had removed Carlos's photo from beneath my pillow. You couldn't tell who might be on the snoop nowadays. I didn't want anything rocking the boat. I was now forced to dream about him, without recourse to his smiling image in those sinful white swimming trunks.

That's what I was doing by the pool, one sweltering afternoon, when Gloria suddenly appeared beside me. It was now two full days since our little talk in the study.

'I've made an appointment for you to see Dr Wright.' She smiled happily, as if she was imparting good news.

'You what? I don't need to see a doctor.'

'It's just a quick check. We want to be sure everything is in full working order.' She laughed. But it was an apprehensive little laugh, as if she wasn't altogether confident of my reaction.

'Is Carlos having a quick check to see that everything he has is in full working order?'

It was the first time I had seen Gloria blush. Even when we were kids she had never burned scarlet like me. 'I . . . I'm sorry, Maddy. I'll cancel the appointment if you wish.'

I did.

And she did.

For the first time in my life I had a sense of power. A couple of words from me and Gloria had backed down. Gloria Mullin never backed down from anything. Not even Mother. And here she was, afraid to offend me. I'm ashamed to say it made me feel good.

It appeared that there were to be all kinds of perks

going with this agreement. A whole lot of added bonuses that I hadn't even thought to consider. I lay back in the warm sun, under the cloudless sky, and mulled over my future prospects.

Conception can be a tricky business. Who is to say, with absolute assurance, when any particular woman is at her most fertile? I had broken all the rules last time by becoming pregnant on the final day of my period. The doctor had dismissed my claim. He said I must have got my dates mixed up.

I had assured him that anyone who had sex with Turlough O'Toole was not likely to get their dates mixed up.

Not that sex with Turlough was in any way memorable. It was just that it occurred so infrequently you'd be bound to recall the dates.

There were other aspects of conception to be considered.

'There's no guarantees that it will work the first time out of the trap,' old Miley used to say when we were trying to increase our herd by natural methods.

Sometimes we had to collect Mick Naughton's bull for weeks on end to get the job done on Hawthorn Farm. Then Mother discovered the AI man and she was made up. No more nasty, sweaty business between all those dirty, smelly animals.

Mother liked everything to be clean. Sterile.

I mulled over how long it might take me to conceive this time. Months perhaps? Years even, if I was lucky.

I had a sudden vision of Carlos approaching my bed, looking exactly as he had the day I'd had sunstroke.

I hit the pool again.

Closer and Closer

'I said her foot is not improving,' Gloria bellowed into the phone.

Part of our new arrangement was that Gloria would deal with all inquiries from Ballyshannon. In fact, she would make regular phone calls, in case they became too curious. Or troublesome.

'The Emmy? What's the Emmy got to do with Maddy's foot? Her foot! That's why I'm calling you. Who cares about the fuckin' Emmy?' She stamped her beige shoe in exasperation. 'I'm calling to tell you that your daughter's foot is worse. What's an Emmy to you anyway? Don't you care that your daughter is in unbearable agony?' Gloria was becoming more and more affronted because Mother wasn't showing the proper amount of sympathy for my non-existent injury.

'Why do you get so upset, Gloria? It's not as if I have a real injury.'

'She just makes me so fucking mad. Her and her precious fucking Turlough.'

Then she was hugging me, her temper forgotten.

'I'll never forget what you're doing for us, Maddy. You have no idea how much Carlos wants a child.'

I found an array of vitamins beside my breakfast waffles. Everything from folic acid to vitamin C, to a peculiar-looking mess that turned out to be dried seaweed. 'What's all this?'

'Gotta get you in fighting form.' She was almost trembling with excitement.

'But we already know I'm fertile,' I protested when she once again began to mention her favourite gynaecologist.

'Of course you are, honey. Just one teensy-weensy little blood test. Please?'

'Fit as a fiddle,' she announced gleefully when the results of the test came back.

'That's what Mother said about Father the day after he cut his hand on that vile hawthorn.' I rubbed my arm where the needle had punctured the skin.

'That was just a small cut.'

'He died of severe blood poisoning, have you forgotten?'

'Oh Maddy, you're not going to turn into a hypochondriac, are you? Your arm was punctured by a sterile needle, for God's sake.'

See, all her talk about keeping things natural and now she was into sterile needles. And the Lord only knows what else. What was natural about sterile needles? I asked myself.

I hoped I wasn't going to regret this deal.

Then Carlos came home. And I would have punctured my arm with a number nine knitting needle to get my hands on him. Especially after he said, 'How are you, Maddy? Are you okay, honey?'

He called me *honey*. The only thing Turlough ever called me was you.

I couldn't sleep that night for thinking about it. *Honey*!

Carlos was home to discuss who should, and shouldn't, be told about the plan.

I couldn't have cared less who was told. They could have put it out on CNN if they wanted.

We only got RTE One and Two in Ballyshannon. And sometimes when the wind was blowing in the right direction we got a blurry BBC One from Northern Ireland.

Carlos was all for discretion. He felt that 'the plan', as he called it, should be kept between the three of us and go no further. 'It's our private business, we should keep it to ourselves. Let's not give them something to talk about out there.' Carlos was a great fan of the old *Hill Street Blues*.

'Don't be so fuckin' paranoid.' Gloria dismissed him in her usual ladylike fashion. 'This is LA, for Chrissakes. Nobody is ever surprised at what anyone does here. No one in LA will bat an eyelid.'

Carlos's agent went ballistic. I wasn't party to his exact words, but I do know that he slammed out of the room after they told him what we were planning to do. When he came back they said he was reeking of whiskey, and talking about lawyers and writs, and God only knows what else. Then he slammed out again.

They came home. Faxes flew backwards and forwards like snow on the wind. And every phone in the mansion lit up.

In the end, Herman turned up at the door. 'Have you completely lost it, Garcia?'

I could hear him all the way down the hall.

'Why don't you just slit your throat and be done with it? Or we could announce that you're a Commie and have you burn Old Glory on prime-time TV? How does that grab you. Huh? Huh?'

Mrs Danvers and I hardly had to eavesdrop he was shouting so loudly.

The study door suddenly flew open and a scowling Herman appeared. 'God-damn stupid sonofabitch.' He aimed a kick at a nearby antique chair.

Mrs Danvers and I busied ourselves adjusting the cut flowers.

'All right, Herman, you win!' Gloria bellowed after him.

And so it was agreed. We would be discreet. Tell nobody. I would remain out of public view behind the big electronic gates that separated us from the rest of the free world. When the time came, Gloria and Carlos would announce that they had adopted a baby without giving any further information.

They would, however, give the impression that the baby came from northern Europe.

Neither of them seemed too thrilled with the idea of such subterfuge, but it was apparently the lesser of two evils. Going public would without a doubt, according to shrewd little Herman, scuttle Carlos's brilliant career for ever.

'Can't you see the headlines?' he had bellowed. 'Three in a bed in Hollywood mansion! Carlos Garcia screws sisters in Hollywood love pact! I know what you're gonna say. That's happenin' every friggin' night of the god-damn week here. But not with my clients, it don't. Those broads who watch Carlos Garcia on TV all wanna think they might one day have a chance of leaping into the sack with him. And trust me, the last thing they wanna imagine is that when that happens, they'll turn over in the friggin' bed and bump into another friggin' broad.' He had to pause to wipe the spittle from his mouth with a huge tartan hanky. 'You can have all the friggin' beaver you friggin' want, Garcia, but you'd sure as hell better screw them one at a time. *If* you want to stay top of the ratings.'

'You're making it sound as if we planned an orgy.' Gloria was appalled by Herman's crude language. 'This has absolutely nothing to do with *sex*! This is about a loving sister giving her sibling a chance to fulfil a long-held dream.'

I focused hard on a little whorl on the Persian rug beneath my feet. It's always advisable to concentrate on an inanimate object when you're desperate not to give yourself away I find.

'You know there's nothing between Maddy and Carlos.'

Eyes on the Persian rug again.

'It don't matter a damn what I friggin' know. What matters here is what the friggin' public *think* is going on. And if you want him to hold on to his career . . .' he stabbed Carlos in the chest with his stubby little finger '. . . you'd better keep this quiet.'

Gloria pursed her lips.

Carlos said nothing.

I riveted my attention on the rug.

It didn't worry me that I would have to stay hidden in the mansion when I began to show. I loved being here. If I had been given the choice I would never have gone beyond the garden. I had no interest in the fancy shops on Rodeo Drive. It was Gloria who enjoyed running amok there with her gold card.

I had even less interest in the expensive restaurants where she insisted it was imperative to be seen. The first couple of times I had enjoyed the experience, but it soon became tedious, watching all those perfect people pose and table hop, and try to catch sight of themselves in every reflective surface.

I preferred messing about in the garden with Tomasino. Or swimming. I was becoming a competent swimmer. It was something I had never dreamed of doing at home. People in Ballyshannon only used the sea to fish. Or emigrate.

Tomasino had warned me that the temperature in LA could actually drop below sixty in winter. I didn't tell him that was sometimes two whole degrees above what we considered a sultry summer's day in Ballyshannon.

Mrs Danvers was party to the baby plan from the very beginning. She was known for her discretion. Gloria said we could trust her with our lives.

Another statement that was to ring in my ears a long time later.

Gloria was a formidable organizer. She drew up a plan that a four-star general might envy. She pinned a huge wall calendar behind her desk, with little red flags to remind her when to phone Mother. To keep her from becoming suspicious.

The broken-foot scenario couldn't remain simple. It would have to be broadened out to give us the required nine months plus, she said. She planned to say that the foot had to be rebroken and reset several times. Knowing Mother's opinion of doctors, we knew how readily she would accept this explanation.

Gloria decided that Wannabe Tom couldn't be trusted with our secret. He had to go. He was given two months' wages, in lieu of notice, and three perfectly good suits that Carlos had no further use for.

I suspected that he was none too pleased with this

arrangement. Apart from the fact that Carlos was at least a foot taller than he was, all three suits were well out of fashion.

I don't know what peeved him the most, getting the sack or Carlos's cast-offs. I do know that he spat on every car in the drive before he left.

But life went on and Wannabe Tom was barely out the gate when Carlos was off to New York again.

Gloria may have wanted me to be in optimum health for the big moment, bursting with vitality and well-being. I, on the other hand, had my own agenda.

I began to use skin-softening creams all over. Morning *and* night.

I had my legs waxed. And my hair cropped short again. This time I allowed José to add the warm highlights he'd been recommending for weeks on end. I was now used to my new gamine look. Except that I thought of it more as brazen and began to act accordingly.

When I caught the cab driver watching me admiringly in the mirror I hardly even blushed. He insisted on helping me with my bags, although they were no weight. When my skirt slid way above my knees as I stepped out of the cab I didn't even attempt to pull it down.

I hurried up to my room to begin a series of bust-firming exercises. I had picked up the magazine containing them in the beauty salon. On my word of honour, this was the very first time I had taken something that didn't belong to me.

It would not be the last.

Mrs Danvers gave me a neck massage most evenings to calm me down.

I trimmed my pubic hair also for the first time in my life. Then I did something else for the very first time. I stood in front of a mirror, stark naked, and examined my body.

This I would never have dared do in Ballyshannon. Before I was married it would have been a sin against modesty. Afterwards, Turlough would have sent for a priest. Women had been burned at the stake for less not all that long ago. Ballyshannon farmers' wives do not stand naked in front of mirrors. Or their husbands.

I stared hard at my unclothed self. It wasn't a body to be ashamed of. The breasts were high and firm, even though I had only begun the exercises yesterday. My waist was slim enough, if not exactly the hourglass shape much favoured by the glossy magazine I had *borrowed*. My newly trimmed pubic hair formed a neat little golden triangle, modestly blurring the edges of the pale fat lips beneath it.

My legs were as long and slim as Gloria's. In fact, except for the gamine haircut, I now looked more like the woman in the photo Gloria had sent us than she did.

And Carlos was due back from New York at the weekend.

The arrangement was that Gloria would leave the mansion and stay in the Regal Biltmore for the weekend. She wouldn't be slumming or anything. The Biltmore had a twenty-four-hour room service, a state-of-the-art health club, a Jacuzzi, a sauna and a tile and brass inlaid swimming pool for those who had need of such things.

Dong was going to the YMCA, even though he was

a Buddhist. Tomasino was visiting his brother in Pasadena.

Gloria had arranged everything with the precision of a military take-over. It was all perfectly timed. Except for the main event, of course. Something had to be left in the lap of the gods. Gloria had taken everything else into consideration, leaving nothing out. Not forgetting a thing.

Except one. The weather.

After the event, when I had time to reflect on it, the irony of this wasn't lost on me. Here I was in LA, immersed in a plan to fulfil a dream, and it all nearly came apart because we forgot to check the one thing I had spent the past fifteen years listening to. The weather forecast.

I was watching the frightening downpour from the living-room window when Carlos came speeding up the drive in a cab. It was the last cab to venture up this high that night.

I had never witnessed such a storm. Nor, apparently, had LA. It was judged to be the worst in living memory.

The airports were shut down. A terrible accident had closed the San Diego freeway. The highway patrol advised people to get back indoors as soon as possible. Lightning had brought down trees and telegraph poles, and there were live electricity cables snaking across at least one rain-drenched highway.

On TV there were frightening pictures of cars, buses and trucks stuck in mudslides. Commentators stood knee deep in floodwater recommending that people remain indoors and not travel.

Carlos was truly fortunate to have made it home

before the roads became impassable.

'DO NOT TRAVEL, EXCEPT IN AN EXTREME EMERGENCY.' The TV commentator had to shout to be heard above the howling wind.

Gloria's cases were stacked in the hall, all ready to go. She didn't believe in travelling light. I had seen families of twelve emigrate with less baggage than she needed for a weekend in the Biltmore.

She was on the phone when it suddenly went dead.

There was still the possibility that she could make it to the hotel. It was no great distance.

'There are reports coming in of landslides in the Hollywood Hills,' a powdered anchorman announced happily from the safety of his air-conditioned studio.

And that was that. It would have been utter madness for her to set out after hearing that news flash. Whatever else she might be, my sister Gloria was certainly not mad. Although I was well on the way myself. My big night was going to be ruined, because she hadn't had the foresight to check the weather forecast.

Where was Turlough when you needed him?

I was sulking in my room when she appeared. 'This doesn't have to change anything, Maddy. Have you any idea how big this house is? The West Wing is practically in another time zone. You could fight a guerrilla war over here and nobody in the other wing would be any the wiser.'

I felt she might have chosen a more romantic simile.

Her next idea was more in line with my hopes. 'I'll sleep in the West Wing. You know me, two little pills and I'm lost to the world. I wouldn't awaken if there were fireworks going off over here.'

*

Timing was crucial according to Gloria. The 'big event' couldn't be postponed.

Her electrical calendar had noted that this was the most opportune time, hormonally speaking, for Carlos and me to do it.

Hormonally speaking? I was getting pretty tired of all this LA speak.

'It's your most fertile period, Maddy.'

Was that so? Then how come I had conceived twins on the final day of my erratic monthly period? A guaranteed safe time according to the rhythm method approved and sanctified by the Holy Roman Catholic Church? And how come my husband, half out of his head on Bushmills whiskey and not exactly a prime stud at the best of times, had managed to impregnate me when it was all over before I realized it had even started? And here was my childless sister trying to convince me that she was some kind of fertility expert. What did she know about fertility? The only thing she was an expert on was abortions.

I knew that any time would have been the right time for Carlos Garcia and me.

I had been avoiding him since he dashed in through the rain. I had actually hidden in the broom cupboard, when I heard him coming along the hallway as I was making a run for the stairs. So much for my new-found confidence. My new brazen image.

I didn't know how he felt, but coming face to face with my sister's lover, knowing what was ahead of us in a couple of hours, was something I couldn't cope with. Yet.

Relaxing in a softly lit bedroom after a few drinks was one thing. *Especially* with my newly trimmed pubic hair. But meeting him in the brightly lit hallway, with his calfskin valise and his expensively tailored *People in Jeopardy* suit, was another story altogether.

So I ran.

Mrs Danvers was in the big kitchen chopping something. She was very fond of chopping. She took one look at me and pulled out a chair.

A bowl of steaming soup appeared at my elbow.

I have absolutely no idea what kind, but there was certainly alcohol in it. A lot of alcohol. I didn't refuse it.

The kitchen was far too quiet without Dong's happy chatter. And with only the loud intermittent crashes of thunder to break the uneasy silence, the atmosphere in the big mansion was becoming one of brooding menace, I thought.

The Main Event

The plan had been to allow Carlos and me to pass some quiet time together before the actual event. First we would bask in the sultry flower-scented air in the garden. Perhaps even swim in the warm pool. Then a companionable little walk around the aromatic herb garden, uninterrupted even by kindly old Tomasino, until we were relaxed enough to head for bed.

The reality couldn't have been more different.

First, only a raving lunatic would have ventured outdoors on an evening like this. Second, the electricity went down. Third, the only person who could work the fickle generator was in Pasadena visiting his octogenarian brother.

But Gloria wouldn't be beaten. After the first wave of mild hysteria, when we all ran around trying to get the lights working, it was she who suggested lighting the big fire in the living-room. She lit the candles herself and the room began to take on a warm, romantic look in the soft, flickering glow.

We ended up sitting around a log fire, all three of us. Drinking champagne.

Never mind that the champagne was warm, on account of there being no electricity to work the fridges. And the big logs were drenched, at least on the outside, which meant that they began to give off choking clouds of thick grey smoke instead of much needed heat.

Nobody spoke.

Once or twice Gloria cleared her throat, creating the impression that she was about to say something deeply profound and memorable. But her cough always frittered away into a weak silence, leaving all three of us even more embarrassed than when she began. I think it might have been nerves that triggered her coughing. Or perhaps it was the wood smoke.

One of the logs suddenly burst into flames.

'There now, isn't that cosy.' Gloria beamed as if she was personally responsible for natural combustion.

Nobody answered.

I began to wish I were back in Ballyshannon. At least we checked the weather forecast there.

The big clock in Gloria's study started to chime, its melodic sound echoing along the silent hall. Ten chimes. Ten o'clock. Bedtime in Hollywood for working actors.

At ten thirty we were still sitting in the exact same positions.

Then Mrs Danvers brought some light relief. Tea. I had forgotten about the gas in the kitchen.

'I'd forgotten about the gas in the kitchen,' I said to Gloria.

'Yeah. Me too.' And she expounded on the benefits of having a gas hob. This appeared mostly to consist of being able to have tea when the electricity was down.

'We came close to having a big electrical failure in Ireland once,' I began.

Then I remembered why our electricity grid had threatened to shut down and it didn't seem the appropriate time to tell that particular story. They waited for the punch line, but I went silent.

The logs were now burning at a fierce rate. I moved back from the heat to sit in the shadows. Mostly because the flames were bright enough for Carlos to spot my reddening face.

He turned to see where I was going. I sat down quickly on the edge of a nearby coffee table, terrified that he might assume I was rushing up to bed.

But that one glance was enough for me to understand how nervous he was. He actually looked pale in the warm firelight; his face taut and strained.

Of course, given that he was sitting here with his lover on one side and her gauche sister on the other in the middle of a storm-wracked LA, and he was under orders to impregnate the sister, it's probably not surprising that he was feeling nervous. And everyone gets stage fright sometimes.

But he was the famous sex symbol. The great lover. Or was that just an act?

'I think we could all do with a brandy.' Gloria swept out, holding a candelabra shoulder high, like one of those spoiled Southern belles in a Civil War movie.

I was now sitting in complete darkness. Carlos turned to look at me, but he obviously thought I had run away as well, because he sighed loudly and ran both hands nervously through his beautiful black hair.

And it was the sight of those trembling hands that did it. Or maybe the warm darkness. Whatever, a huge wave of pity overwhelmed me, motivating me to do something that I wouldn't have believed myself capable of. I walked towards the fire and stood beside him. I put my hands on his shoulders and began to massage them the way Mrs Danvers had taught me, pushing my thumbs hard against his neck, making the same slow circular movements she used to relax me.

And his reaction was practically instantaneous. Practically. After a couple of seconds he caught my hands and kissed them, then pulled me forward until I was on the rug in front of him. He began kissing me gently, his lips feather light against mine.

I was the one who opened my mouth first, so that he would kiss me deeper and harder.

And then I was on fire. I wanted him so much I would have made love to him right there on the hearth rug, no matter who was likely to interrupt us, even the candelabra-holding Southern belle. He was the one who kept slowing things down, moving his hands gently across my breasts and opening my blouse so carefully, while I wanted to tear at it. Then he was kissing my throat and I could feel the tip of his tongue moving slowly down between the cleft of my breasts. And my nipples were so hard and erect they hurt.

I wanted to scream, 'Now, now, please,' but he was intent on arousing me even further. I put my hand impatiently down to touch him and it wasn't as if he needed further arousing. If Turlough had ever got an erection like that he'd have called the *Guinness Book of Records*.

I don't know if Gloria ever came back with the brandy, but we didn't need it now.

We stumbled up the stairs in the dark, stopping every couple of seconds to kiss in that wonderful way he had, of almost caressing my lips with his tongue. Each time he did this I wanted to eat him alive.

But he was the one in control, which was lucky,

because if it had been left to me I would have had him then and there on the open stairway.

He preferred to undress me slowly, by the light of a single flickering candle. And then have me undress him, although I was all thumbs because I was trembling so much with desire.

When he finally entered me we were both in such a state of arousal that I began to climax almost immediately, making him gasp with my strong movements, until we came together with such an explosive release that I honestly thought we were responsible for the deafening crack of thunder which crashed across the sky at that very moment.

And this beautiful man, who could have any woman he wanted, raised his head, stared at me in wonder and said, 'Jesus . . . Jesus!' And Gloria had told *me* he was an atheist.

I looked up at him, at his perfectly sculptured mouth, which was wide open because of his heavy breathing, showing his renegade little eye-tooth, and what was I to do? I had learned tonight never to waste a given opportunity. I ran my fingers through his thick hair, pulled his head back down to me and put my tongue in his mouth.

His response was immediate. Well almost.

If I could, I would have taken his whole body inside me that second time. But greed is one of the seven deadly sins and I had committed nearly half of them since coming here. Anyway, what he was already giving me was more than enough. I couldn't remember ever having experienced such sinful physical pleasure before. And I had once eaten a whole nine-inch meringue cake, sandwiched together with whipped cream and topped with chocolate and forced strawberries, in Beweleys of Grafton Street on Ash Wednesday.

I had to bite my tongue several times to prevent myself screaming out in ecstasy. Or perhaps it was his tongue I was biting. We were at that stage where it was difficult to tell what bit belonged to whom.

If it was his tongue, he didn't raise any objections and that was all part of his magic. Part of what made him such a sensational lover. Here was a man who didn't expect me to draw the line anywhere. Nor I him. Whatever gave us pleasure was not only permissble but positively encouraged. It was the most gloriously abandoned and sensual night of my whole life. So far.

I woke to find that the storm had passed and the sun was blazing into the big room.

Carlos was still beside me.

He was lying on his back, stretched out like a satisfied child, his arms thrown wide, his hands relaxed and open. His breathing was deep and even, his smooth olive-skinned chest rising gently with every quiet inhalation.

I traced the line of his perfect brow with my finger, touched the long black lashes that fanned out to his cheek-bones. How could any man be so handsome? It seemed almost unfair that one male should have so much, when there were so many ugly people in the world.

He stirred slightly when I touched his mouth, making a little grunting sound. I wanted to eat him. I wanted to lock the door, and not allow a single living soul to enter this room and interrupt us.

'Madam? Madam?' There was a knock on the door. 'It's twelve thirty, Madam. Will you be requiring lunch?'

Had she been standing there all night?

I kissed his open mouth again. He stirred and smiled slightly in his sleep.

God he was beautiful. He was . . . *Rick Hein.*

'Madam?'

The door handle rattled.

The front terrace was carpeted with fallen leaves and dying flower petals. And one of the big palms by the gate looked as if it might have suffered some terminal damage. Otherwise things were pretty much as they had been before the storm hit.

The electricity had come on at six, I was told. Gloria had left at seven and I was to avoid the pool until Tom Selleck had finished cleaning it. All right, it wasn't the real Tom Selleck, but I defy anyone to tell the difference.

Mr Selleck was done by the time I was ready for my swim. He flashed me a gleaming white smile from beneath his yard-brush moustache and climbed into an even whiter van. I waited until the gates closed behind it, before dropping my robe and diving naked into the cool water.

I had to do something to stop me exploding with delight. I couldn't let the sharp-eyed Mrs Danvers see how much last night had meant to me. My nocturnal fandangos with Carlos were supposed to be on par with a true Hollywood business deal, i.e., a lot of screwing, but no personal satisfaction. At the very least I had to give the impression that I had sacrificed myself for love of my sister.

*

I was in the dining-room when I heard his footsteps behind me.

'Hi, Maddy.'

I kept my eyes glued to my plate. 'Good-morning . . . afternoon,' I corrected myself quickly.

He put his hand on the back of my neck.

'Your lunch is ready, Sir!' The crisp voice made us both jump.

'Thank you.' He sat down next to me.

She stood opposite, her hands clasped in front of her long black skirt, her hollow eyes daring us to misbehave.

She needn't have worried. The atmosphere at the table was leaden. My fault.

I was immobilized with nerves. So aware of his body and its proximity to mine that I was even more gauche and witless than I'd been the first time we'd sat at this table together. I didn't glance once in his direction.

When he spoke to me I stuttered and stammered, or worse still, pretended to be so busy slurping my thick pea soup that it interfered with my hearing.

I could sense his growing puzzlement. Last night, in the dark, nothing was taboo between us. I had been a complete slut. A wanton degenerate. And now I was playing Sister Immaculata of the Holy Rosary, with my eyes modestly lowered and my knees tightly crossed, determined to allow only the purest of thoughts to enter my meekly bowed head.

If I dared glance at him, even once, I knew the pious mask would slip. I would be in severe danger of leaping on to his wonderful body causing a startled Mrs Danvers to send for a fire hose to separate us.

'Is everything all right, Maddy?' His voice was low, worried.

'Super! Super!' I have absolutely no idea why I used that awful word. It didn't even belong in my vocabulary. Maybe it was the pea soup that did it.

We got through the lunch somehow. In an agonizing silence, it has to be said.

Mrs Danvers finally cleared away our plates and began to pour strong black coffee into our waiting cups. When she filled Carlos's she did it so fast that much of the dark, rich coffee ended up in his saucer. She didn't offer to clean it. Or to replace the flooded saucer.

She moved away, to stand across from us again, hands clasped tightly, at waist level this time, knuckles gleaming whitely against the severe black of her outfit.

'I've got a meeting at two.' Carlos pushed his chair back. There was definite regret in his voice, no doubt about that. But I still guessed that he couldn't wait to get away.

He was probably already regretting the deal. Wondering how in the name of Jesus he had ever consented to such madness.

'I have a meeting,' he repeated, looking at me. 'It's . . . pretty important.'

What did he expect me to say? Maybe he did have a meeting. People in Hollywood were always having meetings. And they were always important. Perhaps he didn't have a meeting. It could be just an excuse, because he couldn't wait to escape to the Biltmore. To go running to Gloria. To ask her, 'What in the name of Christ are we going to do about your dimwit sister? Because I have to be frank, my dear, I wouldn't go to bed with her again if you gave me Paramount Pictures.'

Mrs Danvers caught me crying in my room. 'You need your hair washed,' she said.

I sat in the sunken marble bath while she knelt above me, shampooing and rinsing and massaging my scalp, better than any professional hairdresser.

'Out!' She held up a large soft towel.

I sat at the dressing-table while she brushed and blow-dried my hair, wielding the powerful drier like a machine-gun. And if she seemed to linger a little too long over the final brushing I didn't object. I found it soothing to be taken care of and fussed over, after that terrible fiasco of a lunch.

I was well relaxed by the time Carlos got back. Sitting in the living-room, all dickied up, watching TV. There was a talk show on, a popular one where the belligerent host sometimes confronted his guests very aggressively. They were big on TV confrontations in LA. Not at all ashamed that a famous TV host had once been shot. On camera.

I found this strange, coming from a country where people could talk congenially for hours on TV, then disappear off the screen to happily stab each other in the back in the nearest pub.

The subject of this talk show was women who dominate men. I had switched on expecting to see a group of high-achieving businesswomen, cellular phones at the ready. Or perhaps domineering mothers, acting like harridans. Displaying no shame in their relentless mastery over their grown sons.

I had forgotten that I was in Hollywood. On the

screen in front of me there were four heavily made-up peroxided women, all dressed in mind-blowing black leather. Thigh-high boots, steel-tipped bosoms and inch-long false eyelashes completed the picture. One of them was only a cut away from being a man.

The star guest, a balding professor of anthropology from a mid-Western University, had written a book on the subject. He stammered with suppressed excitement whenever he glanced in the direction of the leather-clad foursome.

Carlos came into the room just as the balding academic was denying that he had indulged in any type of sado-masochism while researching his book. The woman with the biggest steel-tipped breasts looked as if she didn't believe a word he said.

Neither did I. I flicked on the weather channel, looking for a thunderstorm.

Carlos didn't speak; he just came up behind me and began to massage my neck, in a perfect imitation of my approach to him the previous night. Granted, it wasn't a very original move but when you look like Carlos you don't have to be original to get results. I leaned back against him, my whole body ready to dissolve into his hands.

He guided *my* hand to his crotch. 'Okay, Maddy?'

It certainly was.

We went to bed without waiting for supper. If I hadn't known that Carlos was making love to me in order to have a child, I would have sworn that he was as hungry for me as I was for him.

This time we even got to laugh together afterwards, when he described coming home to find a strange grey-skinned creature hiding beneath his sheets. 'All

I could see were these huge frightened eyes and a Jackson Five hairdo. I thought the Martians had landed.'

I told him that he had looked pretty scary himself from my vantage point. 'I thought you were reaching for a gun.'

This cracked him up totally. 'You're so funny, Maddy!'

I hadn't meant to be. I *did* think he was reaching for a gun from the bedside table. But after this encouraging bout of laughter there was no stopping me. I told him stories about old Miley and fat Marion, and how things were run on the farm. He was the only person in all my time in LA who showed a genuine interest in how the farm worked.

Then he stunned me by confessing that he had always wanted to be a cowhand.

'Like old Miley?' I gagged in disbelief.

'Not exactly. My kind of cowhand rides horses and rounds up steers. I did some of that when I was a kid. But I guess it's not all that different from what old Miley does. Is it?'

I looked at him lying there, his beautifully styled hair ruffled against the whiter-than-white pillow, his smooth Californian skin gleaming like pale gold in the soft light. At his perfect features. The huge brown eyes rimmed with lashes that rivalled the dominating women's for length, and I laughed until my cheeks ached.

'What's so funny?' He sounded hurt.

'You a cowboy?' I said. 'You were born to wear Armani suits and Gucci shoes, and pirouette in front of a camera.'

He didn't even smile. 'I was born in southern

Texas, dirt poor. My dad was a wetback who spent his life hiding from the INS. He never learned to read or write. He couldn't apply for citizenship, even if the ranchers who used him as cheap labour would've allowed it.'

'What's the INS?'

'Immigration and naturalization service. If they'd caught him they'd have sent him back across the border pretty sharply.'

'What about your mother?'

'She died of pneumonia in a run-down trailer park. And she was American. Thirty years old. In the richest state of the richest country in the world, and she dies of something that a few dollars' worth of medication might have put right. They blamed my dad for that. He tried to get her a doctor. But the only one he could reach didn't make calls to trailer parks. He claimed later that he left a note for my dad. Telling how to get to a free clinic. My mom died that night. Drowned in her own body fluids. They blamed him. Chased him out of town. Poor bastard. Me too.'

'What do you mean?'

'They weren't married. You know what that makes me?'

Gloria hadn't told me any of this. She just said they met in a film studio. She hadn't told me that Carlos had been doing brief walk-ons because the woman he had hitched a ride with from El Paso worked in a casting office and promised to get him a job. Carlos had assumed she meant driving a truck for one of the big studios she seemed to know so much about. He had heard stories about the great money to be made trucking in California. Nobody was more surprised than he was when she contacted him and told him to get some photos together for a portfolio. He was about to become an actor. With her help.

He was being cast in more and more bit parts when he met Gloria. The day she spotted him he actually had three whole words in a scene in a horror movie. 'Oh my God!' was his world-shattering pronouncement when he saw the undead approaching him, lusting for his blood. This was the vampire, not Gloria.

Gloria took one look at him, and decided there and then that he was her Rick Hein. Rick was her creation, after all. She knew how he would react to an approaching vampire.

Gloria had gone on to put as much work into Carlos Garcia as she had into Rick Hein. It couldn't fail. With her writing talent and his looks and charm they were a winning team.

What Gloria hadn't foreseen or even intended was that Rick Hein/Carlos Garcia would become an international sex symbol, the fantasy lover of trillions of women world-wide.

'Maddy.' The big brown eyes looked straight into mine when he came.

I loved him so much I would have lain awake all night just watching him sleep. Afterwards. But my tired eyes wouldn't co-operate. Before I gave in I swore that I would give up my whole future, my whole life, if only I could have this one magical night with this one perfect man last for a little bit longer.

Of course, I didn't know then what the future had in store for me.

He Can Kiss in Any Language

When I woke I was alone. But the bed was still warm beside me and I got the faint, musky, male scent of him whichever way I turned. It was on my body. On my mouth. In my soul now, what was left of it.

I didn't have to look at the clock to know how late it was. I could guess that from the angle of the sunlight coming in the big windows. Country girls never lose the knack.

I showered and dressed quickly. By the time I was ready it was nine thirty a.m., which is practically midday in LA.

Gloria had been due back from the hotel at seven. I took a deep breath and tapped on her bedroom door. There was no reply.

Her study sounded like a war zone. The fax machine was humming busily. There was a loud male voice talking hard dollars on the speakerphone and a TV set was blasting out the latest casualty figures from somewhere in the Far East. And above all this there was the sound of Gloria's angry voice. She dismissed the man on the room phone with a sharp expletive and yelled at someone to turn down *that fucking TV*.

Only then did I hear Carlos's voice. He sounded almost as angry as she was. I had never heard him raise his voice before. To hear Gloria shouting everyone down was nothing unusual. Despite the modern technology she surrounded herself with, yelling still remained her favourite form of communication.

But it was quite a shock to hear Carlos yelling back.

'Everything isn't about you!' he was saying. 'I'm free to make decisions about my own lines.'

'Not while I'm writing them.' She sounded vicious.

It was the first time I had heard them row. Gloria would fight with her toenails, given the opportunity, but he was different. He never retaliated. I had watched him try to calm her down, many times, when her temper was on the rise. He seldom succeeded. She would continue throwing insults at everyone in sight. Including him.

She was really laying into him now.

No wonder he was so fond of location work. That had to be the secret of their long-lasting relationship. He worked, for the most part, on the East Coast. Gloria ran the world from LA. And they met up for romantic reunions every second or third weekend.

It was a life-style guaranteed to save wear and tear on any relationship. But Gloria seemed to need turbulence in her life; she thrived on it. Nothing she liked better than a good old screaming match. With whoever happened to be handy at the time.

I slipped out to the garden. Tomasino wasn't anywhere to be seen, but he had thoughtfully left the lightest garden spade where he knew I could find it. I began digging around the flowerbeds. I had always found digging to be therapeutic, loved the feel of the spade as it sliced through the compacted earth.

I worked on the flowerbeds for well over an hour, before hunger drove me back indoors.

*

When I passed her study they were still arguing. Over the same thing. His lines in *People in Jeopardy*.

I have to admit that I was completely on his side. And not just because I was having great sex with him. Well, there was that, of course. But the more I learned about Carlos the more I liked him. Liked him as opposed to just lusting after him whenever he came in sight.

Gloria had been right when she said he was gentle. And kind. He was also a considerate lover, never once putting his own needs before mine. But to be honest our needs did appear to coincide in that area. Nevertheless, he certainly made me feel like the most beautiful and desirable woman in California. Some job!

On our second night together, after we had completely and utterly exhausted each other, his eyes said he would have liked to carry on making love to me all night long.

Then he had fallen asleep.

'If you had taken the trouble to check my new contract you'd know that whoever writes the episode, I still retain full rights to veto the script. At least my own dialogue.'

'And who came up with that little gem, I wonder? Handsome Herman?'

'I don't see anyone else in my corner lately.'

'You've got to be kidding? It seems to me, Mr Garcia, that your corner is getting a little bit crowded lately. Of course, your ego does tend to take up a lot of the available space.'

'What the fuck are you talking about? What's gotten into you this morning?'

'Nothing's got into *me*!'

There was a long pause. 'Is that what this is about? Maddy and me? But that was your idea. Your little replacement for your lost Emmy.'

There was the sound of a loud slap.

'Don't you ever do that to me again.' Carlos's voice was a low growl. 'If you mark my face while I'm filming . . .'

Gloria laughed mirthlessly. 'Oh God forbid I'd damage the precious face. Hands off the face at all costs. Did you warn Maddy not to touch your face while you're doing it?'

'What the hell is going on here, Gloria? And don't give me that old PMT crap that you still feed Bobby. I know better, remember?'

'You bastard. Are you saying I'm less of a woman because they took out my womb? Is that what you're saying?'

'What? What the fuck are you on about? You'd better go back to that shrink of yours.'

'I've got a better idea. You get the fuck out of my house. I don't know how I've put up with you all these years. You pretty boy actor.'

'You're gonna say that once too often, Gloria.'

'Are you threatening me, pretty boy? Me? You wouldn't have a shirt on your back if it weren't for me. Try cutting it in front of a camera without my dialogue to bail out your wooden acting. You'd end up on a daytime soap with all the other pretty boys. Ten a penny pretty boys!'

'Jesus, you are a major bitch.' He didn't even sound angry, just weary.

Gloria was obviously contrite, but didn't want to give in too easily. 'Do you want to go over the lines or not?' She actually sounded unsure.

'Stuff your lines.'

'Don't be silly, Carlos, don't be . . . okay, I'm sorry, I apologize. Is that what you want to hear?' She sighed. 'I need a drink.'

'That's the last thing you need.'

I know it was despicable of me, eavesdropping on their private conversation. Well, row. But whom was I harming? And it's difficult to break the habits of a lifetime.

'You're right about that last line, Carlos. Rick should have it, after all it's practically his show. Perry has no need for another sharp line, it's not as if it's essential to his character or anything.'

'It's such a strong line. The wittiest put-down in the whole episode. Only Gloria Mullin can come up with a line as sharp as that.'

'Okay then. But you know it will mean rewriting that whole scene? I'll have to rewrite his lines as well.'

'Who's my baby?'

I turned away.

Mrs Danvers was standing at the end of the corridor watching me.

Tomasino and I were deadheading the climbing roses when Gloria came striding across the garden.

'Senora.' Tomasino bowed respectfully.

Gloria barely acknowledged him. 'God preserve me from actors.' She grabbed an exquisite pink rose, breaking it so roughly from the stem that some of its delicate petals fell away.

'Eh?' Tomasino frowned.

'Not you, Tomasino.' I smiled.

He turned back to his roses.

'They're like children, always demanding your full attention, always worried that somebody else might steal their thunder. Take the limelight from them. Crazy.' She shook her head. There was a small vein pulsating steadily in her neck. 'How are you, Maddy?'

'Me? I'm deadheading the roses.'

She smiled and held out the rose for me to sniff. And everything was all right between us.

We had lunch in the small dining-room. In here, where the french doors opened out on to the flower-filled patio, the air was always fresh. And there was so much lush greenery behind the little curved lawn that you might have been in Ireland, instead of sun-scorched LA. It was much less formal in here than in the large wood-panelled room where we usually had our meals. I guessed that Gloria had chosen to eat in here for a purpose.

Maybe she thought it would lend itself to a more intimate discussion.

But I had already decided that I wasn't going to be drawn on the subject of Carlos.

It would make things impossible between Gloria and me if she had any inkling of the way I felt about him. Better if she continued to think of me as demure little Maddy with no great physical needs. Someone Carlos would only have sex with as a favour to her. That way she wouldn't be hurt. And I could have all that pleasure without being racked with guilt. Not that I was, when I was with him. Then, nothing else intruded. He was the whole world. He was everything I needed. There was no past and no future. Just the present. For as long as it lasted.

He had left for the studio while I was clipping the

roses with Tomasino. I knew it was silly of me, but I was hurt because he hadn't searched me out to say goodbye. So much for no past, no future. But we had been so close the night before, and not just during sex. We had talked and talked, then lain awake for such a long time, looking into each other's eyes.

Before he fell asleep he had smoothed my hair back from my face so tenderly, with his beautiful hands. 'Sleep well, baby,' he had murmured and fallen asleep, holding me in his arms.

This morning he hadn't even bothered to say goodbye. And he wouldn't be back for five whole days, five *long* days. He was travelling to New York directly from the Hollywood studio, where they were working on some kind of 'voice-over'. Whatever that was and as if I cared . . .

I hoped it was the row with Gloria that made him forget to say goodbye.

She was pretending to be immersed in the trade papers while she ate, but I knew better. She was watching my every move from beneath her heavily mascaraed lashes, probably looking for clues as to how the previous night had gone.

I tried to keep my face as bland as possible.

Finally she broke the silence. 'I . . . I don't wanna be indelicate, honey, but . . .'

Even with the seriousness of the moment, the idea of Gloria claiming that she didn't wish to be indelicate was enough to make me smile. Gloria was a master of indelicate. Her raunchy tongue had people howling with laughter at parties, when they weren't running for cover. No subject was off limits where Gloria's acid wit was concerned. After all these weeks of observing her in action I was forced to agree with Mother for the first time in my life: Gloria did have a dirty tongue. And here she was, claiming that she had no wish to be indelicate. I tried not to laugh.

'How did it go? With . . . you and Carlos.' Her voice was a whisper, her expression that of your everyday furrowed-browed Jesuit.

I couldn't held it, I burst out laughing.

And after a moment's hesitation, so did she. 'That good?'

We were both convulsed.

I pulled myself together. 'I would say without a doubt that . . .' I paused '. . . I'm pregnant.'

And we giggled again, before beginning to eat.

That's how we got over what was probably the most embarrassing moment in our relationship. And I had given nothing away. To be fair, I don't think she really wanted any intimate information, not deep down.

And all this time later, I still remain convinced that although she maintained that everything to do with this conception business should be completely natural and open to discussion, what she really wanted was to pretend to herself that what happened between Carlos and me was as cold and clinical as if it had occurred in a petri dish in a science lab.

I didn't disillusion her.

The only other difficult moment arose when we had to decide if there should be a repeat performance the following weekend, instead of waiting a whole month, as Gloria's reading matter advised.

'It's up to you,' I said, focusing hard on my Boeuf Bourgignon. 'But given my history, I think I'm as likely to conceive at one time of the month as another. If we really want to increase the odds then I think . . .'

I didn't have to force the issue. Gloria was as anxious as I was, for different reasons, of course.

'You're right. I think we should avail of every opportunity,' she enthused.

'I couldn't agree more.'

We changed the subject then and ate a most satisfying lunch.

That week passed smoothly enough. Hardly a blip between Gloria and me. Things were looking good. I was becoming more excited by the day. Then nature played a cruel trick on me. I woke early on Friday morning to discover that my period had started.

For one insane moment I considered not telling her. Letting her disappear off to the Regal Biltmore again for the weekend, so that I would get to sleep with Carlos. It wasn't as if I'd be depriving her or anything. If there were something really hot between her and Carlos he would hardly have been as . . . as active as he was with me. And the Biltmore was an exquisitely beautiful hotel. More than comfortable, I had heard. It must have been if it met Gloria's exacting standards. So what harm would it do if she *were* to spend this weekend there?

Then my conscience began to prick me. Sleeping with Carlos in order to fulfil my sister's dream was one thing. Going to bed with him under totally false pretences was another story altogether. And besides, what could I say to him when the time came? 'Oh you're never going to believe this, but I just this minute got my period.'

I told her I was menstruating.

She looked at me so strangely it was hard to know if she was disappointed or relieved. I know which one I was.

She phoned Carlos to give him the news. And it was completely surreal. My glamorous sister in LA phoning her world-famous lover in New York to tell him that I was having my period. Expecting him to be devastated because of this lost opportunity.

At least I hoped he would see it as a lost opportunity. I certainly did.

Gloria and I wandered aimlessly around the big house for most of that weekend. When you have your heart set on something, when you have a special plan in mind and you are unexpectedly foiled, prevented from carrying it out, it becomes very difficult, wellnigh impossible, to turn your thoughts to other more mundane things.

Each of us was as jittery and irritable as the other, Gloria and I, ill at ease whenever our eyes met or his name came up.

She spent a lot of time in her study. The weather was too bad for me to work in the garden. There was a strong wind blowing across the dark blue hills, threatening to carry with it another full-blown storm. And despite the famous song I was now almost continuously singing to myself it was, once again, raining in southern California.

When I saw Mrs Danvers carrying a tray towards the study I waylaid her. 'Let me do that. I'll take her coffee in.'

Gloria was sitting at her desk, intent on her computer keyboard. She didn't even glance up when the door opened.

'Coffee, Madam?' I asked.

She looked up, startled.

'It's so difficult to get good help these days.' I put the tray on her desk.

She stopped working and stretched back in the big chair, her eyes worried as she watched me. 'Oh Maddy. What's happened to us? How do we get ourselves into these situations?'

I looked blank.

'Me, you and Carlos. Whose fuckin' stupid idea was that?'

'Yours?'

She grinned. 'Are you sorry?'

'Do you still want a baby?'

'More than anything.'

'Then I'm not sorry.'

I meant it. I wasn't sorry. Not just because the deal gave me a chance to sleep with Carlos, but because sometimes there was something strangely sad about Gloria. Despite her constant wisecracks, and her money, and her enviable life-style there was something melancholy about her. When you caught her unawares she had a forlorn, almost lost air. Even when she was exquisitely made-up and dressed to kill, and had people fawning all over her, I still felt it. But that could have been my Mullin upbringing. The old family motto rearing its ugly head. *There is no such thing as perfect happiness*.

'Well, if you're not sorry, hon, then neither am I.'

This was the feisty Gloria that I loved, the one who had taken on mighty Hollywood and won.

'Wanna be cheered up? Have a laugh?' She leaped up from the big leather chair and crossed the room to stand in front of a complicated-looking control panel.

Her thin fingers were sure and efficient as she rearranged a whole bank of different coloured switches, and mysterious knobs.

'Wait till you see this!'

A huge TV screen slid out of the wall. She flicked a switch and Carlos's image suddenly appeared, pacing backwards and forwards in the familiar court-room setting of *People in Jeopardy*.

Another flick of a switch and the film fast-forwarded to a softly lit bedroom scene.

Here Carlos was locked in a passionate embrace with a well-known actress whose full lips had always reminded me of the inner tubes of my old Raleigh bicycle.

Carlos looked deep into the actress's blue eyes. '*Ya lublu teba*,' he said.

I turned to Gloria, puzzled.

She raised a finger. 'Wait.' She hit another switch. There was a whizzing noise and several loud clicks, then Carlos was on screen again, in exactly the same scene. '*Ich liebe dich*,' he said passionately to the spreadeagled inner-tube woman.

This time Gloria didn't wait for my reaction. She hit her magic little panel again and once more we were looking at Carlos in full glorious colour, speaking passionately to the same blue-eyed actress. Only this time he was speaking in beautifully fluid Spanish: '*Te quiero . . .*'

Gloria zapped him in mid-speech. 'Pretty talented, our boy, don't you think?'

I didn't reply. I was remembering the first time I had ever viewed that scene. It had been a freezing cold night in Ballyshannon. Turlough had been giving a talk on mastitis at an Irish Farmers

Association meeting, the twins were kick-boxing each other in the church hall and Mother was tucked up in bed with her *Sacred Heart Messenger*.

That particular love scene had kept me going for a whole week that miserable, rain-drenched winter. I looked out at the warm Californian drizzle beating against the glass.

'He can do it in any language,' Gloria was saying. She gave her big, vulgar laugh. 'They can't get enough of him in Russia. Or Germany. Or Spain. And that's not even half the countries we sell to. The joke is the series was never intended to be a vehicle for Carlos. I had to fight like hell to get him a part in the first place. And we weren't discussing the leading role. Then we put him on the screen and powee! The letters began flooding in, all demanding to see more of him. The bloody series wasn't supposed to be erotic at all. It was never intended to have a sexy central character. That was the furthest thing from our minds at the outset.'

I found this hard to believe. 'Then how did it become . . .?'

'Market forces, honey. The more demand there was, the more lines I gave him. And Rick Hein began to take over the bloody show. The bigger he got, the bigger we made his part.' She sniggered. 'Not that he needs much help in that area, as you well know.' She twitched her eyebrows like Groucho Marx.

'Gloria!' I protested.

She poured coffee for both of us, handing me the china cup from the tray. She took the big mug that was almost smothered beneath a pile of papers on her desk. It had THE BOSS printed across it in big bold lettering.

'Nathan, Phil and I thought we had it all worked out. We were going to make a serious drama about inner city life. Cutting-edge stuff. We were going to write and produce something that would spotlight the underbelly of life in big decaying cities. Life among the poor and the voiceless. We were going to give them a voice. Dramatized, of course. But we were going to show the true urban struggle, the horrors they have to face, every single day of their lives.' She put on a deep, ponderous voice. 'We were going to highlight the perennial battles against bad housing, bad schools and corrupt politicians. And we were *not* gonna glamorize it in any way. It was gonna make for harrowing viewing.'

'*People in Jeopardy*?' I tried not to look shocked.

'Yes siree. Hard to believe, isn't it?' She grinned.

'But I thought *People in Jeopardy* was supposed to be . . .?'

'Junk? Can't blame you, honey, but that wasn't the plan.' She laughed. 'We knew we'd have to give it a hint of melodrama, couldn't sell it to the big networks otherwise, but we never saw it becoming what it is today. I knew we'd have to tread lightly at first, but the idea was to toughen it up as we went along. Then I put Carlos in it. That was my big mistake.'

'What do you mean mistake? He *is People in Jeopardy*!'

'Exactly.'

'He makes it!' I defended him.

'He sure does. It's top of the ratings now. I wish I could say it was the great scripts, or the avant-garde production that did it. It wasn't. We had forgotten that old showbiz maxim – sex sells. And do you know what sells more than sex, Maddy?'

I shook my head.

'More sex. I was pushed into writing more and more love scenes for Carlos. Or Rick Hein. The whole fuckin' world wants to see Rick Hein in the buff, or at least kissing the tits off some buxom starlet. But even that's changed. We now have long-established movie stars knocking on our door, begging for cameo roles. With Rick fucking Hein. And guess what? Carlos knows instinctively what the punters want. He doesn't analyse it; he doesn't want to know the psychology behind it. He just knows. How's that for smarts?'

'But he's not the one who owns the production company?'

'I didn't say he was an intellectual. I said he knows how to keep the punters happy.'

'That's mean, Gloria.'

'Mean? Do you know how much we pay him?'

I was shocked. Not by the huge money Carlos was earning, but by her attitude. She spoke about him as if he was no more than a paid employee, someone to whom she grudgingly handed over a monthly cheque.

It took me a second to recall where I had encountered this sort of thing before. Of course! Old Miley used sometimes to have to call at the farmhouse twice on Fridays before Mother would hand over his wages.

'He should be paying me,' she used to grumble, referring to the bottle of buttermilk and the small soda bread she gave him to take home with his wages.

He stood outside on the step in all weathers, while she counted out his money on the big wooden table in the warm kitchen. He never once set foot in our farmhouse. Not even when Father died, preferring, even then, to stand in the yard with the casual labourers from the surrounding farms.

Recalling this long-buried memory made me cringe.

'What is it?' Gloria asked.

'Do you know you sometimes treat Carlos the way Mother treated old Miley?'

'Whaaaat? Are you crazy? That dirty, filthy old man?'

'He wasn't always dirty and filthy. And he must have been young once. He couldn't have been born stooped and rheumy-eyed and . . . What would happen to Carlos if he lost his looks? If people no longer wanted to watch him on their screens every weekend?'

'Do you know something, Maddy, you're for the birds.' She laughed. 'Only you could think to compare Carlos to a rheumy-eyed old cowman.' She pressed a button and the big TV screen shot back into the wall. 'All I was trying to tell you was that I wanted to write important social commentaries, but the world prefers to see Rick Hein's buns. How's the coffee?'

'Cold,' I said.

'The story of my fuckin' life,' she said and rang for Mrs Danvers.

And that was the end of our conversation about the man I had assumed my sister was in love with. And I still couldn't figure her out.

Sweet Dreams Are Made of This

Life in the big mansion always had a slightly dream-like quality to it. For me, at least. Most days I'd walk around, fully convinced that I'd wake up any moment and find myself back in the chilly little room beneath the windswept eaves, with Mother earwigging below. And Turlough snoring like a chain-saw beside me.

After my two magical nights with Carlos this feeling began to intensify. Some mornings I was afraid to open my eyes for fear of what I might find lying next to me.

Then Gloria introduced me to her gym. She recommended it as the best place to work up a sweat and do a lot of heavy breathing. I waited for her to laugh. She didn't.

So I passed the second week of Carlos's absence in a flurry of sweat and heavy breathing. In the gym.

I doubled my efforts at the bust-firming exercises, only stopping when my whole torso threatened to go into spasm. I used electronic pads on my face, giving myself mild electric shocks that guaranteed to keep me wrinkle free until well into the menopause and beyond. I even tried rapid buttock clenching, to keep my newly discovered cellulite at bay, until Mrs Danvers caught me and asked sombrely if I was troubled by trapped wind.

I ran a gruelling five and a half miles, non-stop. Luckily this was on an indoor running machine or I'd never have found my way back.

After all this pulse-racing exertion I threw myself on to the exercise mat and ate a full layer of milk chocolates. Double centres.

This wasn't as contradictory as it sounds. The magazine that had so graphically described the bust-firming exercises also had a long article by an eminent Californian doctor. A noted guru to the stars. A reputed expert on the female libido, he claimed that widespread clinical tests had proven that large doses of chocolate, taken orally, can give a woman almost as much physical satisfaction as penetrative sex.

He lied.

Or his subjects did.

Then Carlos came home and the chocolate was redundant anyway.

Given the reputed unpredictability of my menstrual cycle, Gloria decided that we would have to trust my instincts regarding when it might be my most fertile period. This is how we fell into the happy routine of Gloria heading out to the Regal Biltmore every Friday, while I prepared to welcome Carlos home.

She waved goodbye quite happily, surrounded by a mountain of crocodile-skin luggage, her trusty laptop under her arm. But on her return she was frequently snappy and short-tempered. And as Carlos would have departed for New York by then, I got the brunt of this. I knew she didn't mean the nasty things she was saying, she was just becoming increasingly anxious. Impatient for results. Or perhaps the beds in the Biltmore weren't all they were cracked up to be.

Her temper tantrums didn't really trouble me. I was too taken up with Carlos.

I was consumed by thoughts of him, constantly day-dreaming about the time we spent together. It was all I could think of, day or night.

And instead of our growing familiarity causing our time together to become less exciting, as the weeks passed it somehow increased their intensity. Every minute was becoming more passionate and heated. It got to the stage where he was barely out of the car when he was rushing up the stairs, looking for me. And, to my everlasting shame, he frequently found me in bed. All ready and waiting.

He began catching an earlier flight whenever possible. On those nights he would arrive unwashed and unshaven, and hugely grateful for the hot, sudsy bath I'd have prepared for him. It was sheer good fortune that the sunken tub had more than enough room for two, I told myself. Because what could be more conducive to conception than two spankingly clean bodies?

I knew that watching out for his arrival from the top window had little to do with smoothing the rocky road to conception. But I did it anyway.

When he began ringing me on the car phone on his way from the airport, I understood that had even less to do with facilitating conception.

But hc did it anyway.

He taught me things about my own body, and its responses to his, that I had never before contemplated.

But despite all this frenzied activity, I remained remarkably unpregnant. Indeed, far from becoming rounded and motherly, and heavily expectant as per plan, I began to lose weight.

It was now more than two months into the deal and the only thing showing was my rib-cage. I was becoming a beanpole.

Not surprisingly, Carlos was the first to notice this.

He became quite concerned. Took to bringing me all kinds of sweet little titbits and feeding me encouragingly by hand, which naturally enough caused me to want him all the more, which in turn caused him to react in the way nature intended.

'My director is starting to complain.' He lay back in the tub, heavy-eyed, one Friday. 'He says I gotta get some sleep at weekends.'

'Can he cause trouble for you?'

'Like what? Have Bobby insert a special behavioural clause in my contract? No hot sex while filming.' He grinned.

'How did you manage before this?' I asked. 'You usen't to look so wrecked?'

He laughed until he almost choked on the soap bubbles. 'God, Maddy, sometimes I think you're the last of the innocents.'

And I blew on the bubbles and helped him to search for the soap. And laughed with him. Life was wonderful. And our bodies were extremely clean.

One thing I had to bear in mind. We would have to keep our mutual laughter a secret from Gloria. Frolicking in a sunken bubble bath is one thing. Shared laughter is another story altogether.

I had heard Gloria telling Philip from Lilliput Productions that it can be more bonding than sex. And just as titillating. Of course, they were discussing television ratings at the time, but just the same. And whatever Philip had replied must have been quite funny, because she had spilled vodka all over the phone, she was laughing so hard.

When I wasn't pregnant after ten weeks, Gloria consulted her calendar. And my home-made temperature charts. She had insisted that I keep them, taking my temperature at the same time every morning, marking it down in blood-red ink.

But I had never been inordinately methodical. It wasn't in my nature. Some days I just scribbled down the first figure that came into my head.

'I can't make sense of this chart.' She looked worried.

'I told you my cycle can be a bit wayward.'

'It certainly appears to be unusual, to say the least. According to this you've been ovulating three times a month.'

'See! And you didn't believe me when I said my cycle is peculiar.'

'Jeeze, Maddy, is it possible that you have been right all along?' She scratched her head with her long pencil. 'Could you have conceived the twins . . . separately . . . in the one month . . . is . . . is that possible?'

'What?' This was getting too complicated for me.

'Perhaps you should go to Carlos in New York?'

I had to sit down.

'I'm sorry, honey, but we've tried everything else. To be honest, some of the times when you said you should be fertile I did wonder. But looking at these charts, it's beginning to make sense. Perhaps you can conceive at any time of the month? I have heard stories from other women, women who swear they were caught when there shouldn't have been the remotest possibility that they would conceive.'

'Right.' I nodded.

Oh God, I'll go straight to hell. Then I thought about the way Carlos touched me, the way he held me afterwards.

'Christ, I'm beginning to think it's all a lottery. Maybe the New Agers are correct; they say you conceive when your body decides it's right. Maybe you should go to New York. For one night at least. To increase the odds.'

'I'll do my best. Try my hardest.'

'I know that.' She frowned. 'Are you sure these figures are right? They really look strange.'

'I'm positive.'

Oh my God, I am heartily sorry for having offended thee. And I detest my sins above every other evil. And if you'll just let me have this wonderful man for a little while longer I'll take a vow of celibacy for the rest of my life. And I'll never wish Turlough dead again.

'Okay then. Let's get this show on the road. Whenever your temperature begins to climb, regardless, we'll ship you out to Carlos. To hell with Dr Wright and all his talk of artificial insemination.'

New York was grey. And crowded.

I had arrived during rush hour. Everyone seemed to hate each other. It was as if they were all natural enemies. Especially the drivers. Except when they ganged up to block the way of vulgar-looking limos with tinted windows. I might have fared better in the depressing gridlock if Carlos had sent a less conspicuous car to collect me from the airport.

The Manhattan skyline was admittedly eye-catching. Even viewed through the tinted windows. It loomed out of the murky gloom in elegant New

World splendour. But I was still homesick. For LA.

When we reached the towering apartment block, the grim-faced driver swept the door open for me, after first looking up and down the busy street like a CIA agent on some kind of secret mission. He rushed me across the thickly carpeted foyer and into the waiting lift, without exchanging a word with me.

I felt like a tart being smuggled in to a wealthy oil sheik.

The lift whizzed upwards soundlessly, the doors shot open and I was deposited in a stuffy, airless corridor.

Take me back, I wanted to say to the granite-faced driver. But the lift doors had already closed behind me.

'Maddy!' Carlos was standing in an open doorway, wearing a white cut-off T-shirt and brief shorts.

And the whole place was suddenly drenched in sunlight.

He caught my hand and led me into the apartment. It wasn't anything like the Los Angeles mansion. It had one sparsely furnished bedroom and no sunken bath. It did have spectacular views over the brooding city. But the most compelling sight of all was still Carlos in his T-shirt and brief shorts.

'How was the flight?' He kissed me.

'Long.' I kissed him back.

'Tiring?' He kissed my neck.

'Not that tiring.' I helped him with my buttons.

He looked even better without the T-shirt and shorts.

We were lying in bed watching the news. There was

unrest in the Middle East. Two people had been killed in a terrorist attack. Saddam Hussein was sabre rattling again.

'Is this a repeat, by any chance?' I asked.

Without a word he flicked to another news channel. Local this time.

Somewhere in the Bronx, a child had been saved from a skyscraper ledge by the heroic New York fire department. When the firemen got back to their tender they found all their windows had been smashed.

I sighed.

'Wanna go out to dinner?'

'What do you have in?'

'Beer?' He laughed.

'Sounds nourishing.'

'This is the Big Apple, honey. They'll deliver whatever you desire.'

'Really?' I ran a finger along his stomach.

Next time we surfaced it was too late to go out. Not for New York, for us.

He ordered pizza. It was obscenely large. Weighed down with pepperoni and anchovies, and three kinds of Italian cheese. Real cheese.

'We'll never get through all that.'

We fought over the crumbs and washed it down with ice-cold beer.

'What are all those videos?'

'Cowboy movies. You wanna see some?'

'Will I have to get dressed?'

'Never.'

The movies turned out to be quite good. Although I kept missing out on big chunks of them, which made it hard to tell who was who as the cowboys tended to be interchangeable. Only the lawmen were easily distinguishable. By their big white hats.

'Hang on.' I pushed Carlos away. 'What's he doing there? I thought he was the baddie?' I pointed out a cowboy who was tethering his horse outside the marshal's house. And being greeted by the marshal's wife who wore a yellow bow in her hair and a big frilly apron around her fourteen-inch waist.

'No. He's the guy who lost his ranch earlier on, remember? The bad guys don't get to ride horses like that. You have to concentrate, Maddy. These movies are works of art. It takes a keen eye to appreciate such . . .'

I hit him with a pillow. 'You keep your keen eye on that side of the bed then. And stop distracting me.' I pulled the sheet up around me, covering up.

'Ah, you've had enough art for one night.' He tugged at the sheet and we began to wrestle for it, laughing hysterically as we tickled and pinched each other.

The phone suddenly rang. It was past midnight.

'Hello?' he snapped. 'Oh Bobby, what the hell are you . . .? Sorry, buddy, no can do. No, it's not possible. I can't. Don't be a wise ass. I'm in bed, it's gone midnight. Alone, what do you think? Yeah, well that's your overactive imagination. I gotta be up at five thirty. Well fuck you too, buddy!' He hung up.

'Let me guess, that was er . . . Bobby?'

'Clairvoyant as well? Is there no end to your hidden talents?' He pulled me under the covers.

'That's for me to know and you to find out.'

In the back of the limo next morning he took off his

long cashmere scarf and wrapped it carefully around my neck. 'You gotta keep warm, honey, this isn't LA.'

I watched him cross the sleet-drenched street, the collar of his long dark overcoat turned up against the abrasive New York wind. At the steps of the building used for the external court-house scenes for *People in Jeopardy* he turned to wave, even though he couldn't possibly have seen my face pressed against the tinted glass.

I kept my eyes firmly shut on the way to the airport, playing a silly game to prevent myself filling up. I pretended that it was his arm I could feel brushing against my neck, not just his warm, comforting scarf.

'Oh Rick . . . Carlos,' I tried not to cry. 'What are we going to do?'

'Are you all right, Ma'am?' It was a different driver this morning. This one was young. Friendly.

'Yes thank you.'

His eyes, in the mirror, were concerned. Round and almost childish with worry. He might have got the day off school to drive Daddy's big car.

'I'm fine,' I sniffed, clutching the scarf to my mouth.

'I could get you a coffee?'

'No thank you.' I closed my eyes again.

At the check-in desk at Kennedy airport I gave him forty dollars. It was all the cash I had.

'No Ma'am, there's no need . . .'

'Please take it.'

He put it in his pocket and dropped my small case on the weigh-in scales. 'You are checking this?'

'Yes.'

'Will you be okay?' He was still worried.

I gave him a little wave as I walked into the departure lounge.

He saluted me with a gloved hand. It looked as if he had stolen it from a grown-up. The twins would be his age in a few years.

The flight to LA was most uncomfortable. My own fault. I refused to unwrap Carlos's warm scarf from around my neck, even though the heat in the airline cabin was stifling.

A suave, middle-aged man sitting next to me stared at my breasts, every time I sighed. I covered them with the ends of the big scarf, but it didn't deter him. By the time we were approaching LA airport he was telling me his name, handing me his business card and insisting on my phone number.

I gave him my best chilling look.

He responded by moving his pin-striped knee suggestively against mine. I gave him Gloria's private number. That would teach him.

I was only in the door of the mansion when the phone rang. For a second I thought it might be pin-striped.

It wasn't. It was Carlos.

'He wants to speak to you.' Mrs Danvers's eyes were as inscrutable as ever.

'Hi.'

'Just checking to see you got back okay.'

'I did, thank you.' She was standing directly behind me.

'Are you all right?'

'I'm tired.'

He laughed. 'Join the club, the make-up department are threatening a walk-out. Someone put a sticker on my chair saying, *Give it up before it kills you*. I don't think they meant smoking.'

'Thank you for ringing,' I said, uncomfortably aware of Mrs Danvers at my elbow.

She held out her hand for the receiver.

'Maddy? Is that all you've got to say to me?'

'Mrs Danvers is waiting for the phone.'

'Christ!'

'Goodbye.' My lip began to quiver.

When I looked in the mirror I saw why pin-striped had been so intent on striking up an acquaintance with me. My hair was standing on end. My lips looked red and puffy, and there were huge black craters beneath my tired eyes. I looked like an overworked hooker.

'Get some sleep, Madam.' Mrs Danvers's face was a mask of disapproval as she watched me climb the stairs.

The day my period was due Gloria and I went shopping. I didn't really want to go, but had decided that it was marginally better than hanging around the mansion waiting to see if it was going to arrive. Or not.

Gloria felt pretty much the same, I think. 'I can't settle in to work,' she said. 'Can't concentrate.'

She dragged me through Polo/Ralph Laurens on Rodeo Drive.

'You won't believe the children's clothes they have in the Polo collection,' she said.

I didn't.

Then she had to visit a store called Fred Segal.

'Isn't he a film star?'

'That's George Segal.'

'Oh. His brother then?'

She didn't reply; she was too busy studying a pair of beige suede boots. 'They're Chanel. What do you think?'

'Do you get free perfume with them?'

'For Gawd's sake, Maddy, make an effort,' she snapped as we walked into a grotto full of glamorous baby wear on Wilshire Boulevard. There was everything for the well-dressed baby here. Especially if they had notions of becoming fashion icons before they were potty trained.

I spotted a little cowgirl outfit. For a newborn.

'What? No bras?' I asked, as Gloria pointed out bikinis, and sun-dresses, and skiing outfits, and baby jewellery, including silver ankle bracelets.

Then she spotted the lace-covered bassinet. 'Oh my Gawd! I gotta have it. I just gotta.'

The bassinet was so smothered in frilly white lace you'd be hard put to find room for the baby in it. This didn't put Gloria off; she was already flashing her gold card at the bemused assistant.

Watching her mountain of purchases grow made me uneasy. She was adding more and more baby items to the pile. Apart from the fact that we couldn't be sure if there was going to be a baby, I believed it was unlucky to shop for a child before it was born.

'That's a load of superstitious crap.' Gloria smiled at the assistant.

'I haven't even missed a period yet,' I muttered.

'You're pregnant, I can tell.' Gloria was running her hand lovingly over a pair of tiny lace tights. Edged with rhinestones.

'What do you mean, you can tell?'

'Something about the way you're walking, you have a pregnant walk.'

'What are you talking about? What pregnant walk?'

'Mother used to say that.' She picked up a rosy-cheeked doll and looked up its dress.

'Gloria?'

'She used to say that she could tell when girls were pregnant. Said they had a pregnant walk.'

'When they were six months gone, maybe.'

'No. Before they even knew they were up the pole.'

'She never said that!'

'You were too young. You don't remember.'

'Liar.'

'You have a pregnant walk, Maddy.'

I found myself checking my walk in the nearest full-length mirror. Walking smartly past it and then turning swiftly, as if I might be able to catch myself unawares.

There was nothing different about my walk. It was the same uncomplicated stride it had always been.

Gloria stood grinning at me. 'Tricked ya!'

'Gloria Mullin! And you accuse me of being childish?'

'I'm not the one walking up and down like a brain-dead mannequin in front of half of Wilshire Boulevard.' She grinned at an elderly couple who had stopped to gaze curiously at me, the man leaning on a gold-topped walking stick.

We were in the coffee shop when she asked, 'Do you think you might be?'

'I need the bathroom.'

She paled. 'Has it started?'

On the contrary, there was no sign of my period and although it was true that my cycle did sometimes behave a little erratically it usually favoured being early. I couldn't recall ever being late.

'Oh my God, Maddy, do you think it's possible?'

She was practically chewing her Gucci purse in the women's room.

'Anything is possible, but don't let's get ahead of ourselves, Gloria. All I know is that I should have started this morning.' I dried my hands on the perfumed towelette the attendant held out to me.

'Oh my Gawd! She's having a baby!' Gloria screeched into the face of a complete stranger, who had just come out of a nearby toilet stall. 'We're having a baby!' She put her arms around me and kissed me on the lips.

The woman gave Gloria a frightened stare, then looked from me to the huge pile of bags from the baby department. She rushed out with stopping to dry her hands.

'Nice one, Gloria, she thinks we're a couple of raving lesbians.'

'Cool.' Gloria laughed. 'We're having a baby, Maddy!'

'Hold on, I'm just a few hours late. That doesn't mean I'm pregnant.'

'But you are. I know you are.'

'From my walk?'

We both giggled.

Before we reached home she had almost convinced me.

'But what if I'm just late? I could be late.'

'I'm so glad I bought that bassinet. Wasn't it lucky we went shopping? Now we already have a start to our baby layette.'

'A start?' I looked at the mountain of purchases.

'All these pretty baby things. All ready and waiting.'

'I could be late!'

Not Only Late, but Cancelled

Two days passed and there still no sign of my elusive period. Going to the bathroom became an ordeal, with Gloria trailing behind me every time. 'Well? Is there anything? Let me see.'

I refused flat out. We had become close again over the past few days, but not so close that I was prepared to allow her to check my underwear for stains.

I went to bed and slept fitfully. Got up and fell asleep in front of the TV. Swam in the pool and became languid. Said good-night and was instantly full of energy again. And all the time Gloria was watching. Watching.

Days passed. I was stepping out of the shower, when I caught sight of the irrefutable evidence in the full-length mirror.

It had nothing to do with my walk, that had been a load of nonsense. But the signs were there all right, even at this early stage. A fine network of barely discernible blue veins traced their way across my breasts, culminating in a busy little intersection, around the already darkening nipples. Only once before had my breasts borne those unmistakable signs.

To quote Gloria, I was most definitely 'up the pole'.

She had already arranged for her doctor to do a pregnancy test.

'Not one of those vulgar home kits, Mad. Too unreliable. We don't wanna have our hopes raised, then dashed again because we used some cheap home kit. You're gonna have a proper clinical test.'

No need for that now. The startling blue veins were proof enough. For me at any rate.

But for some reason I was in no hurry to share my discovery with Gloria. I don't know why. Perhaps I wanted this baby to be mine alone, for a little while at least. The moment I told her it would become everyone's property. Like the twins. But I hadn't wanted a baby, so why was I becoming all maternal over a child that wasn't really mine anyway. I was only having it for Gloria. Not for me. All I had wanted was Carlos. I was prepared to carry a child for nine months and suffer all the indignities that pregnancy could bring, just to have Carlos. Well, to be honest I hadn't actually though of it in those terms in the beginning. All I could think of was having him. The chance of a relationship with Carlos Garcia blinded me to anything else. No matter how temporary that relationship was going to be, I wanted it. I wanted him.

I was pulling on my dressing-gown when the penny dropped. If I was pregnant, that was the end of my intimate relationship with Carlos. There would be no more reason for us to sleep together. This was the end. It was over.

I would never make love with him again. Never again open my eyes in the half-light of dawn and catch him sleeping. Never again get to watch as he stretched his beautiful body, in that dreamlike state between sleep and waking. Never again see that slow, warm smile light up his face as he reached for me, his eyes still heavy with sleep.

There would be no more listening for his footsteps on the stairs. No more wet little kisses at the nape of my neck. No more full tongue kisses the moment the light went out. No more passionate sex.

I dropped in a crumpled heap on the floor and howled like Runt the night that Father died.

'Maddy? Maddy?' Gloria came running. 'Oh my God, what is it, honey?' She bent over me, the colour draining from her face. 'It's started, hasn't it? You've got your period?'

Then Mrs Danvers was there, lifting me as if I weighed nothing at all. Putting me on the bed, making sure my dressing-gown was modestly closed.

She got a cold towel from the bathroom and draped it round my head, then wiped my eyes gently with a tissue. 'Do you feel ill? Do you need a doctor?'

I shook my head.

'It's all right, Maddy. Don't worry.' Gloria made a huge effort to hide her disappointment. It fooled nobody.

'It's not what you think.' I opened my dressing-gown. Wide.

The two women looked aghast, staring at me as if they feared I was becoming an uncontrollable exhibitionist.

'What . . .?' Gloria began.

'Look.' I pointed to my breasts. 'Can't you see?'

And they both knew. I didn't have to say another word. Not a single one.

I thought Gloria would have a heart attack with excitement. She gave a loud screech, and jigged up and down like a hyperactive two-year-old who had once split the twins' heads open with a John F. Kennedy coffee mug.

Mrs Danvers stood watching, two little spots of colour beginning to blaze in the centre of her bloodless cheeks. It was a frightening sight. Unnatural. For once she seemed unsure of herself, as if she didn't know which way to turn.

And I lay on the bed, my head wrapped like a devoted Hindu, my dressing-gown gaping open.

Gloria had completely lost control now. She was running about squealing, biting her nails, staring at me, then shaking me with unbridled joy.

In the end I was the one who said, 'Shouldn't we ring Carlos?'

'Of course. Of course. I was just about to suggest that.' She had stopped leaping about long enough to speak.

'Let's ring Carlos. Great idea. Oh my Gawd, I can't believe it!'

I fastened my dressing-gown and got to my feet.

Mrs Danvers handed Gloria the phone. 'Carlos? Oh my Gawd! I can't believe it. Oh my . . . oh Gawd! A real live baby! Can you believe it?' she was screaming down the phone. 'A real live baby Carlos. What do you mean calm down? It's so . . . I . . . believe it? I . . . I . . . can't . . . believe it! It's just too . . . it's . . .'

My sister, who had earned herself a small fortune with words, now seemed incapable of stringing two consecutive sentences together and making sense of them.

She frowned into the phone. 'Of course I am. She's okay. Healthy as a horse. Yeah . . . Looking good. Oh my Gawd, I can't believe we're finally going to have our very own little baby.'

I sat back on to the bed. I couldn't help thinking what's all this we stuff? I'm going to have the baby. I'm going to be the one suffering from day-long morning sickness. I'm going to be the one who grows fat as a pig, with ankles that swell up like helium balloons. I'll be the one getting heartburn. Maybe even piles. I'll be the one having to pee ten times an hour. The one whose breasts will become agonizingly sore when I try to breast-feed. And drip smelly milk when I don't.

'We're having a baby, honey. We're . . .'

Not going to have troublesome veins and vile stretch marks, I thought.

Mrs Danvers pulled the coverlet up around me. 'Is there anything you need, Madam? Would you care for some hot milk?' Her eyes were watchful.

No I would not care for some bloody hot milk, you bitch. And the only thing I need is not to be pregnant. I shook my head, keeping my mouth tightly closed and wishing I had the nerve to punch Gloria.

'I can't believe how lucky I am,' she was still screeching.

She was. If I'd had a knife I would have stabbed her.

With the phone still stuck to her ear, she tried to hug me. 'Aren't we lucky, Maddy?'

I could hear Carlos's voice on the other end of the line and my heart began to pound. But nobody thought to ask if I would like to speak to him.

He flew home on Friday night. By then, two doctors had confirmed my diagnosis. I was very definitely pregnant, they said. Both of them. Twice.

There was no turning back now.

Gloria was beside herself with joy. Although admittedly a little less hysterical than she'd been at the first sight of my blue-veined breasts.

She opened a magnum of champagne as we waited for Carlos to motor in from the airport.

When he walked into the room his eyes immediately sought me out. I tried to read his expression, but it was difficult, given that Gloria had spread herself all over him.

'Isn't it great, honey, can you believe it?' She tottered back unsteadily on her five-inch stilettos.

'Great.' He kissed her.

'Go and kiss Maddy. Go on,' she ordered magnanimously, pushing him towards me.

He kissed me full on the mouth.

But it was a strangely impersonal kiss. He might have been kissing a distant cousin at a family wedding he hadn't really wanted to attend, but couldn't get out of because his mother wouldn't let him.

'Okay, Maddy?' His eyes were concerned.

'Of course she's okay, she's only pregnant, you twat, the healthiest state for a woman her age to be in.' Gloria was now swaying openly, rocking backwards and forwards on her dizzyingly high heels. She was Lady Bountiful, lavishing her goodwill on the lower orders. She handed Carlos a brimming glass of champagne and offered one to me.

I was about to refuse, when Carlos beat me to it. 'Should Maddy be drinking?' he asked her.

The refusal died on my lips. This was the man who, a few nights ago, couldn't keep his hands off me. A man who had behaved as if I were the most important person in his life. Who couldn't wait to share his daily experiences with me and get my reaction to them. And here he was, speaking over my head? Directing his question to Gloria, as if I was some kind of short mental defective.

Should Maddy be drinking?

'She's pregnant, not joining a nunnery.' Gloria dismissed him.

I took the tall fluted glass and deliberately drained it in one go. 'More please,' I requested, trying not to cough.

But nobody heard me. They were too busy raising their glasses to each other to pay any heed to me.

I dropped the glass and ran from the room.

I told Gloria repeatedly that I didn't need a doctor. She wouldn't listen. Now *she* was treating me like a witless cretin, a mindless fool, exactly as he had. The mood was clearly contagious.

The perma-tanned obstetrician turned out to be even more patronizing than either Carlos or Gloria had been.

'Hormones kicking in already?' he asked cheerfully, slapping my exposed belly.

I was opening my mouth to reply, when he stuck a thermometer in it. He checked my blood pressure while I lay there, on view to the world.

I hoped it was sky high. Let them deal with that, the smug Californian bastards.

Should Maddy be drinking?

Carlos was outside the door, pacing nervously.

I couldn't wait to hear how dangerously high my blood pressure was. Wait until he got that bit of news. That would stop him in his tracks. He'd have to stand by helplessly, watching me die from some terrible pregnancy-related illness, knowing it was all his fault. When he saw me laid out, with the rosary beads entwined in my lifeless fingers, he would realize that without me life wasn't worth living. Being an actor, he'd probably throw himself on to my cold grave and wait for the photographers to arrive, before dying from exposure.

My blood pressure was normal.

So was my temperature. And my pulse rate. My own body was conspiring against me. I had no friends. Nobody loved me.

'We're bound to be a little over-emotional during the first trimester.' The white-suited doctor spoke as if this were a group pregnancy, which it probably was. He smiled at me, flashing his stunning Los Angeles teeth, and snapped his bag shut. It was real leather, I noticed, a smooth, well-cured mahogany, a perfect match for his evenly tanned skin, which still bore the tell-tale pocks marks of the teenage acne, which must have scourged him in this haven of beauty.

I preferred Gloria's other doctor. His skin always had a pasty look to it. Blotchy. Like a real doctor's.

The perma-tan one patted my flat stomach. 'Things will settle down soon enough. You'll be surprised at how good you begin to feel, once you get over this bad patch.' It sounded like the voice of experience.

'Have you any dietary tips for her? Should we be giving her any special type of food supplements?' Gloria sounded as if she was planning on entering me at Crufts. 'During the first trimester, I mean?'

I didn't hear his reply. It's difficult to catch what people are saying when you have the bedclothes pulled up over your head. I wiped away a tear with the back of my hand.

I did manage to make out their footsteps leaving the room. Their voices fading down the long antique-filled corridor.

'Maddy?' It was Carlos. He turned the sheet back gently. 'Don't cry, honey. Don't cry.' He put his arms around me and held me close.

I made the most of it, crying until his immaculate shirt-front was drenched with tears. And large blobs of fibre-thick mascara. Browny black.

He took my face in his hands. 'Do you want to have this baby, Maddy?' His voice was no more than a whisper, his brown eyes searching mine.

'Yes,' I gulped, drowning in his beauty.

'Positive?'

I nodded.

There were footsteps coming back along the corridor.

'Love you, Maddy,' he whispered, patting my cheek. And he was gone.

'Well, you've certainly made a quick recovery. There's a bright face. What's going on here?' Gloria was standing over me.

'Probably my hormones. You know how it is.'

But she didn't. How could she? How could she possibly understand the wild elation that was surging through every part of me after hearing those three magical words.

Love you, Maddy, he'd said. Without laughing.

I lay back in the soft, luxurious bed and trembled at the very idea of it.

Carlos Garcia had just said *Love you, Maddy. Love you, Maddy: Love you, Maddy.* Well okay, he only said it the once, but it kept echoing round my head like a starburst that went on and on into infinity.

What was a little discomfort, a little morning sickness, compared with the joy of hearing those three magical words from his lips. To hear him say them again, I would willingly suffer fire and brimstone, hell and eternal damnation.

I would happily endure body-wrenching contractions, humiliating hospital enemas, endless prodding and poking, even a bloody episiotomy, just to hear those three little words again.

Of course I was only five weeks pregnant then.

Baby Blues

I spent the following six weeks vomiting. Or so it seemed. There may have been brief moments of respite between the racking bouts of nausea, but I find it hard to recall any. Not even the sight of Carlos's handsome face peering around my door every Friday night could ease the terrible retching that racked my body from the top of my aching head to my pink nail-varnished toes.

'I thought morning-sickness only occurred in the morning,' he said naïvely, as he stood patiently by while I threw up in the pink marble bidet.

Gloria was at a script conference. Something really big, was all the information she would give me. But I had learned that in Hollywood something really big was always just around the corner. Her script conference had already run over by three full hours, so I had foolishly attempted to have dinner, *à deux*, with Carlos.

My bottom had barely touched the Louis Quinze chair when the smell of the French onion soup had me racing to the bathroom.

Carlos ran behind me, murmuring words of consolation. He thought.

'Why is it called morning sickness, then?' He was completely puzzled.

'How the hell should I know?' I groaned and threw up again.

When I finished, he was waiting with a cool towel to press to my forehead.

We sat on the floor together and he rocked me like a baby.

Even sitting on the bathroom floor, with deep frown lines desecrating his perfect forehead, he still managed to look divine.

I looked like the Wicked Witch of the West in every one of my endless reflections in the wall-to-wall mirrors.

He was full of gentle concern. 'Were you this ill when you were expecting the twins?'

I nodded, afraid to open my mouth, in case I threw up on his beautiful *People in Jeopardy* suit.

My first pregnancy had been a nightmare, but he wasn't to know that. For practically the full nine months before the twins were born I had spent half of every day with my head stuck down the toilet. It didn't do the twins any harm, the doctor said. They would have been indescribably ugly anyway, given their paternal genetics. Well, the doctor didn't say that, but I did.

They had weighed in at a healthy five pounds ten ounces and five pounds six ounces respectively, which gave cause for great celebrations in the delivery suite of St Columcilles Hospital, which was used to delivering much smaller babies on account of there being a lot of jockeys in the area.

During all those months of vomiting, nobody had once thought to ask me how I was feeling. Pregnant women were expected to get on with it, not indulge in self-pity, on Hawthorn Farm. I *was*, however, given a wide berth while I threw up.

And Turlough did once or twice give me an

inquiring look, when he saw me emerging, porridge-faced and trembling, from the draughty bathroom. But he had other things on his mind just then, what with the growing dairy herd and trying to get the dry fodder into the shed before the weather broke. And maybe even fat Marion.

Although I don't think their relationship had begun at that time, and she wasn't as fat, then, as she was to become later. Not that she could ever be considered sylphlike.

Except, perhaps, by a weather-crazed farmer.

So all in all, Turlough had his hands full that summer. And blocked udders couldn't be put on the long finger, the way a vomiting wife could. In his favour, he did take extreme care not to make any sexual demands on me during that traumatic time. But to be honest, I wouldn't have minded a little bit of attention in that particular area.

Carlos had a totally different attitude to pregnancy. He wanted to know everything I was experiencing. He wanted to be there with me. In the bathroom. And I was to find out later that his attitude to sex in pregnancy couldn't have been more different from Turlough's.

He brought all kinds of interesting little delicacies from New York every Friday. Their packaging was frequently as intriguing as the gifts themselves, with all sorts of absurd little ribbons and bows holding them together.

'He has them gift-wrapped,' Gloria snapped when I remarked on the care that he seemed to take over these thoughtful little presents. 'Any store will do that for a couple of bucks.'

This was after he had hidden a particular gift behind his back, when she insisted on being the one to open it.

'No, Maddy's got to open it,' he teased. 'She'll appreciate it so much more.'

'What are you talking about, Garcia? Every woman appreciates little gifts. And I wanna be the one to open this one.' She leaped on him, practically forcing him into a half-Nelson on the carpet, as she tried to prize the fancy box from his grasp.

But he held on bravely, until I put out my hand.

'I'll get you for this, Garcia.' Gloria giggled, as they lay panting on the floor. 'Maddy will appreciate it so much more,' she mimicked. 'What has Maddy got that I haven't?'

The present made that pretty obvious. It was a little basket of herbal tea, a special mixture of peppermint and camomile guaranteed to ease nausea in pregnancy.

I thought Gloria would choke, she laughed so much.

Afterwards we sat on the floor sharing a box of rich Belgian chocolates that had also come from a fancy New York store. These had arrived in a wildly ostentatious gold and silver box.

'Jeeze, we should have done this years ago, Mad,' Gloria said, licking melted chocolate from her bony fingers.

She was a complete puzzle to me. I could never quite figure her out. She was like quicksilver, as soon as you thought you knew which direction she was heading, she surprised you by taking an alternative route.

'He can't wait to get home these nights.' She had

munched her way through half a layer of the calorie-rich chocolates, after spending a whole week dining on salads.

I don't think she was ever jealous of Carlos buying all these little gifts for me. She was too caught up with the exciting prospect of having a baby in the house.

I might have been too, if I hadn't been so busy throwing up.

When the vomiting continued beyond the first few weeks, Gloria began to distance herself from me. This wasn't meant as a slight, I knew that. She just bored easily.

She was a woman who needed constant variety in her life. It was essential to her well-being. A vomiting sister might be a novelty, even fun, for a while, but long-term throwing up was decidedly unappealing. Enough to test anyone's patience. It certainly wasn't to be encouraged.

Carlos, on the other hand, was always there for me. When he was home.

'He's just naturally tactile,' was how Gloria dismissed this heart-warming trait of his.

'And so gentle,' I said.

She frowned, her big eyes narrowing suspiciously. 'He's an actor, Maddy, don't ever forget that.'

'Acting is his profession. I'm talking about the man.'

'Yeah sure,' she said impatiently. 'Be warned, honey, in his business those lines of demarcation can run pretty thin.'

'What do you mean?'

'Hi, folks.' Carlos was home, his well-developed arms laden with gift-wrapped boxes. He had something for everyone this week. Including the baby. 'Look what I found in F. A. O. Schwarz,' he announced, tearing open a huge red box.

He had bought a train set. For a nine-week-old foetus.

As the baby wasn't quite up to it yet, he had to be the one to painstakingly arrange the model railway line across the Persian carpet. He frowned in concentration as he fitted each intricate little piece into the next.

'For Chrissake, Garcia, why don't you give in and wear the bloody glasses.' Gloria was *not* a patient woman.

The big brown eyes flashed her a look.

The train set was a perfect scale model. It had everything a railway line could possibly require. Little waiting-rooms full of people, a neat station master's cottage, colourful flowerbeds, even a little black-and-white terrier, its plastic leg permanently raised against a free-standing lamp-post.

The train itself had a miniature steam engine, with a funnel that gave out little bursts of grey steam whenever you pressed a remote control button.

'Man, it's so cool. I always wanted one of these. Wow! Imagine the fun a kid could have with this?'

'Yeah, right!' Gloria said waspishly. 'She's gonna love this.'

His face fell. 'She?' He looked from Gloria to me. 'Is it a girl?'

We burst out laughing.

'Who the hell knows,' Gloria said.

'So it might be a boy?' he asked hopefully.

'Or both,' I said.

This time it was Gloria who gaped. 'Twins?'

'Twins?' Carlos repeated.

I raced to the nearest bathroom to vomit.

I didn't sleep well that night. I was unhappy with Gloria's reaction to the idea of having twins. Next morning, I waited until Carlos was in the shower to have a quiet word with her. I thought we should discuss the possibility of a double birth. 'What if I have two babies? What then, Glo?'

'Oh for Chrissake, Maddy, give us a break.' She sniffed and continued typing at an unbelievable rate.

'It could be twins. It's not unheard of for multiple births to repeat in families.'

'Multiple? Jesus, you're really scaring me now.'

'I want to know what you think.'

She swung the big chair round to face me. 'Well, I know one thing, I sure as hell don't want triplets, or quads or any of that multiple shit.' She ran worried fingers through her well-groomed hair, making it stand on end.

'Shit? We're talking about babies here.'

'You know what I mean, Maddy. I want a baby, not a fucking nursery class.'

'So what if I'm carrying twins?'

'I . . . let's wait until you have the scan.'

'What scan?'

'Everyone has a scan, Maddy.'

'Not in Ballyshannon, they don't.'

'We're not in fuckin' Ballyshannon. How many times do I have to remind you?'

'There's no need to be rude.' I moved towards the door.

'We'll talk after you have the scan, Maddy.' She was busy at the computer keyboard again, chewing savagely on a piece of gum. I had never known her to chew gum before.

There was a polite knock on the door. Carlos came in, drying his hair with a towel. He was wearing white tennis shorts. That's all. And they weren't fastened all the way to the top. He had obviously pulled them on too hurriedly to bother. There were little droplets of water glistening on the fine line of black hair that traced its way downwards from his belly button and disappeared into the white shorts. The sight of it almost unhinged me. It certainly took my mind off whatever Gloria and I had been discussing.

'What's happening?' He rubbed briskly with the towel.

'Ask Maddy, it appears she's having a multiple birth.'

His face lit up. 'Maddy?'

'I didn't say that. All I said was how would you feel if I had two babies?' I tried not to stare at the line of glistening black hair.

'Cool!' He was beaming all over his face.

'Relax, Garcia. Before you get the cameras out, it was just a hypothetical discussion.'

'Shame.' He grinned. 'I like the idea of twins. Two little cowboys. I'll let you get back to work.' He walked out, whistling happily to himself.

I sighed.

'You really like him, don't you, Maddy?'

'Well I'd hardly have . . . you know, if I disliked him.'

'How fond of him are you?' She was tapping at the keyboard as if she wasn't really interested in my answer.

'I . . . I like him as much as anyone can like an

actor.' I shrugged, lying and telling the truth at the same time.

She seemed satisfied with this. 'Don't you go falling in love with him, Maddy. Don't you go doing anything as silly as that, or I'll have to send you back to Ballyshannon.' She was smiling, but there was a look in her eye. And she had stopped typing.

'What? Me *and* the twins?' I teased.

'Lunch is served, Madam.' Mrs Danvers stood in the doorway.

Gloria saved her work, then came around the big desk, carrying her shoes. She had a habit of kicking them off while she worked, said it helped her concentration. She sat on the edge of a leather recliner, pulling them on, fastening the narrow suede straps around her slim ankles. The shoes were high-heeled, as always, and the palest, softest looking suede imaginable.

I stared longingly at them. We wore the same shoe size, Gloria and I, but I had never had the opportunity, or the nerve, to wear such blatantly sexy footwear. The ankle straps made her long slim legs look even longer.

I glanced down at my still flat stomach. I could forget about ankle-strap shoes. In a couple of months' time I'd be lucky to be able to see my ankles.

'What?' Gloria caught me watching her. 'What is it?'

'Nothing.'

We went in to lunch, Gloria towering over me in her six-inch heels.

This time it was the scent of Beef Wellington that triggered my nausea. Carlos followed me into the bathroom to hold my forehead.

'Are you okay, Mad?' Gloria had called after me as I ran. Then presumably continued eating the tender Beef Wellington that was her favourite weekend dish.

Mine too. After Carlos.

One morning, the nausea woke me extra early. Then it was over and done with surprisingly quickly. As in all things, practice makes perfect, I suppose. I actually felt as if I could stomach a real breakfast afterwards.

I was humming my way past Gloria's room when I heard the sound of dry retching. It was one my ears were well used to.

I knew she'd be alone. It was midweek, Carlos was in New York. I walked in without bothering to knock, or call out to her.

Her bed was empty. But there was a box of expensive chocolates on the bedside table. It was open, the top layer missing.

She was in the bathroom, a pale-grey ghost leaning against the unfortunately coloured primrose-yellow wall.

Mrs Danvers was mopping her brow. 'There, there, soon be better.' When she caught sight of me in the doorway, the hollow eyes blazed with anger. 'Get out of here! Get out!'

It was as if I had intruded on some kind of private ritual. Something I wasn't supposed to see.

I ran, without a word.

It was a full hour before Gloria came downstairs. She didn't look at all sick, but she wasn't dressed for work. She was all tarted up, wearing her most expensive Armani suit, her hair immaculately coiled away from her well-made-up face. I recognized that look. She was dressed for shopping. She had once told me that whenever you go shopping, you should always look as if you already possess everything you could possibly need. Or want. 'And never, ever, approach a restaurant looking hungry,' she advised me.

'Morning, Maddy.' She strode to the window to stare out at a bank of approaching clouds. 'Looks like rain.' The prospect seemed to please her. She was almost jubilant.

'Were you sick this morning?'

She grinned. 'Please. You're becoming obsessed with sickness.'

'No, I heard you . . .' Something in her eyes stopped me. I tried to backtrack. 'I was sick earlier on, I thought it would last and last, but then it was suddenly over.'

I blathered on, unable to stop myself sounding as if she and I were involved in some kind of vomiting marathon and I was admitting defeat.

She scowled at me.

'But I feel better now,' I finished lamely.

'Good. Then you can come shopping with me.'

Gloria knew how to punish.

'Ah, not again. You know how much I hate shopping.'

'What do you mean, not again? It's gotta be at least a month since I bought anything for this baby of ours.'

Irritation gave me the courage to speak out for once. 'Gloria, this baby is no more than two inches long. And it has feet like a tadpole. And arms like jelly. I shouldn't think it has much use for Gucci loafers or Cartier watches.'

'Everyone needs a Cartier watch.'

'Please, Gloria, anything this baby needs I'm already giving it. Trust me, I can feel the calcium draining from my bones as we speak.'

'Really?' She paled.

'Don't be daft!'

'Tsk. I just want to be able to give it something too.' She turned away, her lips quivering dramatically.

'Okay, okay. Whatever you want, Gloria. But no gold watches or diamond pinky rings until its bones are properly formed.'

'Diamond pinky rings.' She made a miraculous recovery, giggling happily as she checked *her* Gucci bag to make sure it contained her collection of gold cards.

She drove like a madwoman, as usual. 'I am being careful, Maddy. If we go any slower we'll be busted for kerb-crawling. And I've never crashed. Well, hardly ever.' She laughed. 'Does once count?'

The last time she had driven me we'd had to pull over to the side of the road because I was so nauseous. We just missed getting a ticket for illegal parking.

'She's having a multiple birth,' Gloria had pleaded with the gum-chewing cop.

'Not here, she isn't.' He waved us on.

This time we reached Rodeo Drive without incident.

'Is there anything you need, Maddy?' she asked, as she swept ahead of me into the world-famous Gucci store.

'An anaesthetic?'

She laughed so hard she almost missed the eye-catching display of handmade crocodile purses to the right of a tiny sale sign.

Me too, except that I missed them because my eyes were still riveted by the figure on the sale sign. It said seven thousand dollars.

'Would that be for the whole building?' I asked.

Gloria went into a paroxysm of giggles again.

But I had been quite serious.

He Loves Me, He Loves Me Not?

I was three and a half months pregnant when the morning sickness began to taper off. Within a week it had disappeared altogether. This was the best part of the whole pregnancy. I hadn't yet gained weight. To look at me nobody would guess that I was expecting. There was hardly a curve to my stomach, thanks to all that vomiting.

When I realized that the sickness was finally at an end I couldn't believe my luck. Not four months gone and I had already finished throwing up. It was a miracle. And I couldn't remember when my hair and skin had last been in such amiable condition.

Gloria and Carlos began to insist on taking me to all sorts of fancy clubs and restaurants. Presumably to celebrate the fact that I could now sit down to a meal without throwing up on the waiters.

There may have been another reason. Gloria hated staying home at night, especially on weekends. And Carlos had complained that she was leaving me alone too much. Taking me out with her was probably the lesser of two evils.

It was becoming pretty obvious that my pregnancy was beginning to seriously pall on her. Just as I was starting to enjoy it, she'd had enough.

Gloria had wanted a baby, not a pregnant sister.

I have to admit that I was revelling in all the extra attention I was getting from Carlos.

He hardly took his eyes off me when we were out, watching over me all the time with a concerned, almost paternal look. He worried about my comfort, no matter where we were. No matter how exclusive the club or restaurant might be or how solicitous the waiting staff.

He was continually anxious, fretting about my welfare.

Was I too hot? Too cold? Was the place too packed? Too humid?

Was my chair comfortable?

'Will you stop fussing, for Gawd's sake,' Gloria finally snapped. 'You're beginning to sound like a neurotic old biddy. She's not sick. Are you, Maddy?'

'No.'

'Thank Gawd for that. If I had to listen to you retching one more time, or get a whiff of that god-damn awful stink whenever I passed a bathroom, I'd have to shoot you.' She ran her eye along the extensive menu in the members-only club, then looked up to find Carlos glaring at her. 'Oh for Gawd's sake, look at the pair of you. Bambi and his mother, waiting for the bullet in the head. I was just kidding. They shoot horses, don't they? It was just a joke.'

Carlos didn't smile. Neither did I.

'Oh lighten up, Maddy, for Chrissakes. You're a bad influence on him. He's been moping around like a neutered spaniel since your test came back positive.'

Carlos was blessed with that wonderful olive-tinted skin, that dark colouring that doesn't flush easily, but when he caught my eye his colour heightened considerably.

I almost burst into song.

Carlos wanted a child – Gloria had told me that – so there was only one possible reason why he would be moping around since my test came back positive.

I watched him as he perused the fancy menu.

He became more and more uncomfortable under my gaze. He shifted uneasily in his chair, glancing every now and again towards the well-lit dance floor.

'Let's dance, honey.' Gloria threw aside her menu, almost decapitating the big yellow roses in the table centrepiece.

I watched them walk hand in hand across the crowded club. They made such an attractive couple. He was so handsome it was sinful. He overshadowed every other man in the vicinity. It was all I could do not to run after him and throw myself at him. Beg him to take me to bed again.

Instead, I sat there, prim as a nun, in my second-hand dress that Mrs Danvers had let out at the bust.

They were so elegant-looking, Gloria and Carlos, especially on the dance floor. Both of them tall and graceful, and so refined. Once Gloria kept her mouth shut. And somebody rationed her alcohol.

They were dancing, now, like well-trained professionals.

Carlos had told me that she paid for him to attend some kind of jazz and free-movement class, after seeing his original audition tape. He said he hated every second of it, that he was the class dud, always tripping over his feet. The teacher, who was thirty-eight to his, then, twenty-five, ended up giving him extra lessons every night. He didn't say in what.

Even in this exclusive Hollywood club, where there

was no shortage of beautiful people, heads swivelled when he passed.

I wondered what his admiring onlookers would say if they knew that the quiet, plain person in the sensible boring shoes, with the dress that had to be let out at the bust, was expecting his child.

'Maddy? Hey! What are you doing here all alone?' It was Bobby Kennedy.

'Bobby!' I was genuinely happy to see him. Bobby was always good fun.

The girl clinging to his arm clearly thought so too. She also looked like sixteen going on fifty, but turned out to be twenty-three. Bobby was almost forty.

I recognized her. She'd had a bit part in *People in Jeopardy* once. She had played an old girl-friend of Rick Hein's who had come to him looking for help for her wrongly accused brother, went to bed with him and then fell under a train. Or maybe she was pushed. That was the big conundrum that week. It stood out in my mind, because it was Holy Week in Ireland and there had been a huge public debate on the suitability of such a programme being broadcast so close to Good Friday. There was no great concern about the girl being mangled by a speeding train during Holy Week; it was the fact that she had exposed her breasts, while making love to the divine Rick Hein, that raised the ire of so many good people.

'Mind if we join you, Maddy?' Bobby was already holding out a chair for the girl who had fallen under a train. Or been pushed. She didn't look any the worse for her ordeal.

She was wearing one of those Wonderbras that forced her breasts up on to a viewing platform. Not that they needed much encouragement, especially given the dress she was almost wearing. The neckline barely skimmed her acorn nipples.

'This is Lou Anne. Have you two met?'

'No.'

'This is Maddy. She's Gloria's sister, visiting from Ireland.'

Lou Anne gave me the warmest smile. 'We have met. The night of the Emmy awards, don't you remember?'

I didn't. 'Of course. You were er . . .'

'Stoned. I know.' She tossed back her long mane of natural blonde hair and smiled her warm, friendly smile. Capped. She was extremely pleasant and totally unaffected. And . . . staring at Carlos as he danced past.

Bobby called the waiter. 'Bring us a bottle of champagne, Bollinger. Is that okay with you, Mad?'

I nodded.

Gloria and Carlos arrived back at the table in time to greet several other friends of theirs. And Herman. He was the only person there, apart from me, who wasn't stunningly attractive. He made up for this by escorting a girl with purple hair and a gold nose ring. By my reckoning she had to be at least twelve.

'Isn't she something? She's my wild child.' He smirked proudly.

'Your daughter,' I said, relieved.

This raised a huge laugh, which I hadn't intended.

Herman looked as if he'd like to stab me. He stuck his tongue out and waggled it at me in what he clearly considered to be a provocative gesture.

It made me want to throw up.

But the girl bent towards his tongue, intent on clasping it between what looked like her early milk teeth. I felt that Herman could at least have waited until she grew her permanent set.

Bobby saw my concern. 'She's twenty-one, Maddy,' he whispered. 'Her father is Kurt Stinger.'

'That obnoxious rock star? The one who bites the heads off live rats?'

'That's the one.'

'Poor girl. She won't start biting the heads off live mice or anything, will she?'

'I hope not.' He nodded to where Herman was filling her mouth with his fat little tongue.

The staff extended our table in a jiffy, magically transforming it so that it could accommodate at least some of the gregarious crowd who wanted to gather around Gloria and Carlos. The unfortunate rejects had to be satisfied with places at an adjacent table. Those lucky enough to be invited to join the inner circle were all involved, one way or another, in 'the business'.

Thirteen in all. An ominous number, I felt. So who said showbiz people were superstitious?

Gloria had shouted greetings and thrown wild 'Mwaa' air kisses at everyone as they arrived.

Carlos was more restrained. He shook hands all round. But he was clearly pleased to have the company, unexpected as it was. They were, after all, mostly his colleagues and co-workers too. He could relax with these people.

Lou Anne couldn't. She sat on the edge of her seat devouring Carlos with her eyes.

Gloria ordered more champagne. Then she and Bobby got stuck into a heated argument with Carlos's director about the merits of imported wines versus the Californian vintages that the director insisted were vastly underrated.

'I have no time for wine snobbery!' he boomed.

'Ah, you Americans are all the same. So bloody chauvinistic. And you have such uneducated palates,' Gloria said. This was the girl who was twelve before she tasted anything but buttermilk.

Lou Anne, who had managed to get a seat directly across from Carlos, didn't have much to say but she leaned forward a lot. Every time she did this her breasts threatened to annex the whole table.

Herman and his tiny 'wild child' were lost behind the central flower display. This was a cause for celebration in itself, because tongues appeared to play a large part in their relationship.

'What's the latest on the divorce, Herman?' somebody asked.

'Don't mention money.' Herman peered soulfully from behind the flowers. Then his 'wild child' enticed him back again.

'Poor Herman.' Carlos's balding director laughed. 'His wife understands him.'

Herman was on his third divorce, I learned. His wife was demanding a settlement of four million.

'Dollars?' I gasped.

'Well, it ain't rupees, honey! Herman never gets it right,' Gloria said. 'He lays the dumb ones and marries the brains, instead of the other way round.'

As the champagne flowed the conversation got louder. Gloria and Bobby reminded me of the twins. Competing at everything. Trying to top each other at telling the most outrageous stories. I wouldn't have been at all surprised to see them break into kick-boxing.

But the conversational topic never strayed far from 'the business'. I didn't mind, once I wasn't expected to join in.

The food was superb, so I just sat there eating. After all, I had nearly four months' vomiting to make up for. I practically ate the pattern off my plate.

Carlos picked at his food.

Lou Anne continued to lean forward.

After my first glass of champagne, Carlos had asked the waiter to bring a mineral water for me.

'What's this?' Bobby frowned. 'Are you not drinking, Maddy? What's going on here?'

'I . . .'

'She's not drinking,' Gloria cut across me.

'Okay.' Bobby shrugged and got back to the main topic. 'Are you going to write the sequel? Or tell them to shove it?'

'I can hardly tell them to shove it when I haven't been officially asked yet.'

'They're gonna ask you. Everyone knows that. It's the worst kept secret in Hollywood.'

'Yeah, like the Emmy award.'

'Emmy? What's an Emmy? You're going to be picking up an Oscar for *The Moonwalkers*.'

'Says who?' she said, but she looked pleased.

'Everybody,' Carlos and Bobby chanted together.

The Moonwalkers was a big feature movie Gloria had scripted. A buzz of excitement arose whenever it was mentioned. Even Herman, who had no connection with it as far as I knew, got the dollar gleam in his eye when the subject came up and the most blasé of Gloria's guests attempted to pump her for information about its release date. I was really looking forward to seeing it. But it was now in what they called post-production, so it could be ages before it was ready to be shown and Gloria never discussed her work with me. At least, not after that one time she showed me Carlos in action in all those different languages.

But I couldn't help noticing that she was already working hard on another *hot project*! *The Moonwalkers* might be finished, but she was becoming immersed in something that appeared to be connected with it. Was this the sequel that Bobby was so curious about?

'I'll need to fine-tune that contract before you sign it. Bartlem is known to be a high-octane shit when it comes to dividing the spoils.' Bobby was suddenly serious.

Gloria got that closed look she often adopted when her work was mentioned in public.

'When are you back in New York?' Lou Anne was leaning across the table as far as she could without her feet actually leaving the floor.

The young waiter's hands shook as he removed her plate from the shadow of her stupendous bosom.

'What?' Carlos's mind was elsewhere.

'Bobby said you're about to begin shooting the next series of *People in Jeopardy*? I was wondering when you go back to New York?' Lou Anne flashed him a dazzling smile.

'You wanna check that with Gloria. She's the boss.' He raised an inquiring eyebrow at Gloria.

Lou Anne took one look at Gloria's expression and drew back in fear.

Gloria leaned towards her. 'What is it you want from me, honey? Do you want me to give him permission to fuc . . .'

'*Gloria!*' Bobby and Carlos yelled like a double act.

Gloria laughed wickedly.

Bobby darted a nervous look at me. He never seemed altogether sure how to behave around me. One minute he was flirting outrageously, trying to look down the front of my dress, the next he was pulling himself together and telling me about his dear old mother as if she and I were twin souls or something. She had reared him on stories of Holy Catholic Ireland, the land of Saints and Scholars.

She attended Mass and Communion every single morning, determined to outdo old Rose Kennedy in the devotion stakes. She said the rosary twice a day. And she harangued her only son constantly, by phone, for his failure to adhere to the strict precepts of the Holy Catholic Church, or wear the specially blessed scapulars she sent him.

From all the stories I had heard I had formed the opinion that Bobby's mother was, most likely, out of her tree. A religious nut-case, in fact.

But who was I to talk? My mother went to bed with the *Sacret Heart Messenger*.

The lively blues music, which had been playing in the background since we arrived, suddenly changed without warning. We were now being treated to a loud rendition of 'Gangsta Rap'.

The young group, which had taken over the bandstand, was intent on bringing the house down. Or maybe just the roof.

'Oh wow! This is my absolute favourite!' Lou Anne began to jump up and down, and beat out a rhythm on the table with her smooth, twenty-three-year-old hands, her eyes still devouring Carlos.

'Good.' He smiled absently. 'Are you okay, Maddy?'

'Never better,' I said, tucking my rough work-hardened hands under the table.

The musicians were now happily singing about some 'Ho' or other. They were called 'The Dirty ol Mothers', Bobby told me. As if I needed to know that.

'Would you dance with me, Carlos? Please?' Lou Anne had to shout to be heard above the 'Dirty ol Mothers'.

Carlos looked startled, as well he might, because her magnificent chest was now jigging up and down only inches from his face.

'Go on, Carlos,' Bobby urged. 'She'll give me hell later if you don't.'

'Go on,' Gloria echoed, her voice already beginning to slur.

We all watched as they crossed to the dance floor, Lou Anne clinging to Carlos's side like an undulating sea barnacle.

'He's looking good. For a while there I was beginning to worry about him.' Bobby frowned.

'Me too,' Gloria said glumly. Then she brightened up. 'But everything is fine now, isn't it, Maddy?' She winked at me. 'We're all blooming.'

'Maddy doesn't look too happy to me. You wanna dance, honey? Let me show you how to dance to 'Gangsta Rap'.' Bobby got to his feet, swaying slightly.

We couldn't have been on the floor more than twenty seconds when his hands began to wander. He was like an octopus, every time you got one tentacle under control another began to slide southwards. I pushed him away and shuffled my feet to the 'Dirty ol Mothers'.

He suddenly bent towards me. 'Wouyoolaktegoot-wimme,' he said.

I smiled, thinking he was attempting a witty take off of the 'Gangsta Rap' lyrics.

He wasn't.

He stopped dancing. 'Would you like to go out with me?' he was bellowing as the music came to a sudden stop.

Several people around us began to titter.

And I started to giggle. I couldn't help it. Besides, while I was laughing he wouldn't expect an answer.

'I'm not kidding, Maddy. I'd like to take you out.'

I was still laughing. 'Isn't this out?'

The music started up again, a little slower this time and not quite so ear-shattering. Bobby held me close and far too tightly.

'I'm very fond of you, Maddy. I've told my mother all about you. She'd love to meet you.'

'I don't think so, Bobby.'

'She would. She said so.'

'I didn't mean that.'

He wasn't listening. 'I've told her you're a devoted Catholic. She's always wanted me to meet someone like you, someone from the old country who respects traditions. She has very strong views on women, Maddy. So have I.'

'Did you tell her about my husband?'

He ignored this, letting his hand slide down towards my bum.

'I don't want to dance any more, Bobby.' I caught his hand just in time.

He must have mistaken my sweaty grasp for a sign of encouragement, because suddenly he was leaning towards me, trying to kiss me, his tongue at the ready.

'Let me go!' I was pushing him away with both hands now, but he was too strong for me. His open mouth was almost on mine, his rigid tongue about to spear me, when someone pulled him away.

'Leave her alone, Bobby.' It was Carlos.

Bobby swung around, his face thunderous. 'Fuck off, Garcia. Get your own *chickie*!'

And the next minute Bobby was falling backwards and I hadn't even seen the blow. Somebody caught him and held him upright, and a flash went off, and then another. Then Carlos and a big fat man were holding each other by the lapels and snarling into each other's faces. And a camera went crashing to the floor.

I'm not exactly sure what happened next, but in the following few minutes somebody groped Lou Anne, who kneed him in the groin. After which several large men dressed in evening suits surrounded us.

I thought we were in trouble, but it appeared that the evening-suited men were there to protect us. Save us from any further harassment, which was a little strange, given the circumstances, I thought. We were led back to the table, with offers of free drinks all round.

The fat man and his camera, *and* the wounded groper, had all been thrown out. People were fussing around us, brushing Bobby down. Someone was putting ice on his mouth and he appeared to be completely dazed.

'What the fuck happened?' he kept repeating. 'What the fuck?'

Lou Anne draped her arm around Carlos's shoulders, leaning across him in such a way that her chest was practically blocking his airways. 'Are you okay, Carlos?'

Except for being in imminent danger of being smothered by a giant pair of mammeries he was perfectly all right. It was poor Bobby who was dripping blood on to the table.

Carlos shrugged Lou Anne off.

The next minute Gloria, who had been smiling drunkenly throughout all the excitement, was on her feet, screaming, 'You cheap little tart, what were you up to, out there on that dance floor?'

I paled.

'Nothing. I didn't do anything. Did I, Carlos?' Lou Anne pleaded.

Gloria ran around the table and gave her a resounding slap on her shocked face.

The poor girl hurried away in tears, a brace of wine waiters in hot pursuit.

'What did you do that for?' a shocked Carlos asked Gloria.

'For every woman over thirty.' Gloria grinned and held out her glass for a refill.

When Bobby took a blind swing at the hovering *maître d'*, Carlos decided we should leave.

The 'wild child' took her ear out of Herman's mouth.

'Wassa matter?' he asked.

I suppose somebody told him.

Next morning we were having coffee on the pink terrace when Bobby drove up. He was shamefaced. Saying sorry all round, while at the same time claiming to have no memory of what had occurred the night before. But he couldn't deny his burst lip.

It was repellent. With a huge purple bruise surrounding it, it looked like an overripe fig stuck on his face.

Carlos apologized for disfiguring him. 'I'm sorry, buddy.'

Bobby shrugged. 'I can't remember a thing.'

'Selective amnesia,' Gloria muttered loftily from behind the protection of her inky black glasses.

Carlos claimed not to know why he had suddenly struck out at Bobby. Not that it mattered, really. Carlos was a star. In Hollywood, stars don't have to have a reason for doing things. They are exempt from the petty restrictions and moral codes that bind the rest of us mortals. We have to live by the law of the land. They live by their own code.

So do gossip columnists. Every one of them ran the story. And they all got it wrong. Five different versions. I counted. And all wrong. They did agree on one thing. The cause of the fight had been some kind of male rivalry, over a rising young actress called Lou Anne Bechal.

Lou Anne didn't deny it. She was no fool. To be accused of starting a fist fight between Carlos Garcia and Robert Kennedy of Lilliput Productions was no burden to carry.

Her picture was in the *Globe* two days running, her name on everyone's lips. If she could make it into the *LA Times* she'd be laughing.

She might even get another part in *People in Jeopardy* on the strength of it.

And this time the train might miss her.

Bobby nursed his swollen mouth and looked puzzled. 'I still don't understand, Carlos, what the fuck happened? Why were we fighting over Lou

Anne? We can both have her any time we want. What was the problem?'

I threw a shocked look at Gloria, but she appeared to be asleep. Although it was hard to tell, given that half her face was hidden behind the big dark glasses.

Shattered Dreams

Gloria was locked away in her study. Entry barred to all. It was one of her 'do not disturb' days. You entered her domain at your peril at times like this. There had been so many of them in the past weeks I had lost count.

The coming baby was no longer the number one topic of discussion in the mansion. You were hardly allowed to mention it, in fact. If I hadn't known better I would have sworn that Gloria was sorry she had started the whole thing. Babies were the furthermost things from her mind right now. She had more important business on hand. She had finally been contracted to write the sequel to *The Moonwalkers*. Its working title was *Moonwalkers Two*.

When Carlos joked that she could have just as easily have called it 'The Moonies' she had almost snapped his head off. She was back in serious work mode, now, and nothing was allowed to distract her, especially not bad jokes. Or baby talk.

I pointed out a tastefully decorated nursery in a glossy magazine and said perhaps we could copy the clever design and she looked at me as if I had suggested we forge the US dollar.

When Carlos came home it was all she could do to sit at the dinner-table with us for an hour, before rushing back to her word processor again. I gingerly brought up the subject of my expanding waistline and mentioned the fact that I would shortly be in need of some loose clothing, and she looked me up and down and said, 'Are you crazy? You're thin as a whippet. I can't see any extra weight on you.'

She didn't actually say, 'Don't bore me with all this baby crap.'

But you'd have to be deaf not to hear it.

It was Sunday morning. I had just come back from my walk around the garden to find Carlos stretched full length along one of the big sofas in the living-room. I was feeling good. Blooming might be the word. Being outdoors always had a good effect on me. But there was something more today. Something was happening to me that had little to do with my surroundings. Or even the other people in the mansion. I was beginning to bond with this pregnancy. There was a kind of growing contentment about it all that I'd be hard put to explain. But it was definitely there. *And* something else I had never before experienced.

I was beginning to like myself.

Carlos was flicking through a film script. He sat up when I walked in. 'Close the door, Maddy.'

I pulled it shut behind me, cutting off the sounds of the household.

He threw down the script. A couple of loose-leafed pages scattered across the pale carpet.

I hurried to pick them up.

'Leave the fu . . . script, Maddy.' He caught my hand. 'What are we gonna do here?'

'About what?' I still remembered Bobby's remark about Lou Anne.

'Don't play games, Maddy, it doesn't suit you.' He kissed my hand.

And that's all it took. I wanted him so much it hurt and he knew it.

He pulled me towards him between his knees. 'Come here, baby.'

I knelt down. His mouth was warm and it tasted of sweet coffee. And his hands knew exactly how to arouse me. I didn't dare touch him, because if I did I knew there would be no turning back. He had no difficulty unbuttoning my blouse; it opened all too easily now.

I heard footsteps approaching the door. The handle being turned. I pulled away from him quickly, buttoning my blouse as fast as I could.

'What are we gonna do, Maddy?' He watched me.

'You can always go see Lou Anne,' I said.

'Wha . . .?' He appeared genuinely puzzled. 'What are you talking about?'

Mrs Danvers came in to collect the coffee tray. She piled his cup and saucer expertly on top of the little plates.

I turned to go.

'Don't go, Maddy, I wanna talk to you.' His jaw clenched angrily.

I held the door open for Mrs Danvers.

'Maddy?'

I walked her to the kitchen. Or rather, she walked me. She didn't even have to glance at my unevenly buttoned blouse to know what was going on. She knew everything. She knew that Carlos had been using his own room for months now when he was home. She was in charge of the house linen, she knew which beds were slept in. I had learned, ages ago, that Gloria and Carlos kept separate bedrooms in the big mansion. This was no reflection on their sex life,

Gloria had taken the trouble to assure me. They simply used their own spacious bedrooms for convenience, what with both of them having such demanding careers, and frequently keeping such diverse hours, that they would be constantly disturbing each other if they didn't.

It had been on the tip of my tongue to ask what kind of madwoman would object to being disturbed by Carlos Garcia.

'I've always been such a poor sleeper, Maddy.' She smiled. 'Easily woken. Carlos sleeps like the dead.'

That hadn't been my experience. The lightest touch on his skin and he was awake and ready for action.

But it was true that Gloria used a stunning medley of pills to help her sleep. *And* a black velvet eye mask. The first time I saw her in this I thought she was playing at being the Lone Ranger. Which would have made Carlos Tonto, I suppose.

Kemo Sabe!

She finally emerged from her study to join us for dinner that Sunday night. But it was obvious that her mind was still on her work. Or something. Whatever she was thinking about it wasn't pleasant. Not that she shared it with us. But Gloria's silence could speak volumes.

It didn't help that she walked into the dining-room to find Carlos and me circling each other like two dogs before a fight.

She froze us with a look. We sat down at the table in silence, all three of us.

We had almost finished the first course before anyone spoke.

'We're gonna have to tell Bobby about the baby,' Carlos said.

'Why?' Gloria's head snapped up.

'Because he's been hitting on Maddy, that's why.' He glared defiantly at me.

'Is that what happened in the club that night?' Gloria slammed down her spoon.

Carlos and I looked guiltily at each other.

'Is that what happened?' Gloria was the Grand Inquisitor demanding an answer.

'I . . . I guess.'

'Are you telling me that you and Bobby had a fist fight over *Maddy*?' I thought she was going to explode or at least throw her soup over him.

'I'd hardly call it a fist fight.' Carlos laughed.

'What would you call it, then?' I don't know when I had seen her this angry.

'For Chrissakes, Gloria, take it easy! When you thought it was over Lou Anne it was a great big joke.'

Her eyes were blazing. 'Yeah, well, I've been thinking about this whole baby business.' She took a deep breath. 'I've had to think long and hard about it. And I've come to the conclusion that it was not a good idea.'

'What?' Carlos asked.

'The timing is insane. It's all wrong . . . it's . . . not working. And now you tell me it's causing you and Bobby to fight? What will it be next? Pistols at dawn?'

'Gloria!' Carlos frowned.

'What do you mean, the timing is wrong?' My stomach was beginning to hurt.

'I mean the timing is wrong!' she barked. 'What do you think I mean?'

'The timing?'

'Is there something wrong with your hearing, Maddy?'

'You're the one who was in charge of the timing, Gloria.' Carlos was almost as livid as she was. But then he had been in a foul mood all day. 'We danced to your tune, remember?'

'Oh really? And was is it such a terrible ordeal for you? Was it?' Her face was like stone.

'What do you want me to say? What do you want me to fuckin' say, Gloria?'

I might as well have not been there. This was obviously a private argument. 'Maybe I should leave,' I said.

'You stay right where you are, Maddy,' she snapped.

'What's going on here, Gloria?' The nervous little tic was jumping in the side of his jaw.

'What's going on is I have no time for babies.'

'What?'

'Don't act so surprised. You know I have to get this new movie script out. *And* finish the *People in Jeopardy* scripts. Now they want me to become involved in the production of *Moonwalkers Two*. I'd be crazy to refuse. They're already talking about number three. I'm not going to have a free second for two years. At least.' She was trying not to sound excited.

'But you knew you were going to do *Moonwalkers Two*.'

'Yeah, the script. But who thought I was gonna become involved in the production? And now, as it turns out, I'm gonna be doing a back to back. No spare time in between at all. Who'd have thought the money would be coming in before the first one was even in the can? So we go straight into production and then on to number three.'

'What are you telling us, Gloria?'

'That I'm gonna be busy. Okay? I'm not gonna have any time for *babies*.' Her voice rose. 'That's out of the question now. I won't have time to pee for the next two years. I'll have to do that on the run.'

'So what are we gonna do here? About the baby?'

'We're going to have to come up with something, aren't we?'

'Like?'

'Well, if Maddy wants she could take care of the kid. She'd probably do a better job than I ever could.' She gave a nervous little laugh. 'She's had enough practice, for Gawd's sake. Twins? Jeeze! Can you imagine? It must have been a fuckin' nightmare.'

'So are you . . . ?' I attempted.

'Not gonna have a single free second? That's right, Maddy. And there is nothing I can do about it. I probably won't even be in the country in five months' time.'

'That's when I'm due,' I said stupidly.

'I know that,' she snapped, as if it was all my fault. 'We're gonna have to see what we can come up with. Course, nobody would force you to continue with the pregnancy, if . . . if you didn't want to, Maddy. You're in America now. Women have terminations every day of the week here.'

'Jesus, Gloria, what are you saying to her?'

She looked at him without flinching.

'I can't believe you said that.'

Again that unblinking stare, directly at him. It was the equivalent of a shrug. As if she was saying what can I do? I'm certainly not going to louse up my future for a baby. One that's not even born.

'You don't seriously expect Maddy to . . .' He stopped. 'Gloria?'

'I didn't plan it this way. It's just the way things turned out. Shit happens. What do you want me to do? Walk away from the biggest opportunity of my life? Would you?'

Her eyes were on Carlos again, challenging him, as if her business with me was already settled. Done. I didn't matter. My feelings were irrelevant here. I might have been at the table in Ballyshannon, sitting between Mother and Turlough as they bickered over some decision about livestock.

I began to shake. And it wasn't with fear. It was suppressed fury erupting from somewhere deep inside me.

I got to my feet, my hands holding my stomach. 'If you think I'd let anyone harm a hair on this baby's head you're insane. I'd kill you before I'll let you touch it now.'

There was a stunned silence. Carlos's jaw almost hit the floor. Gloria stared at me in disbelief.

'I mean it. You try doing anything to this baby and I won't be responsible for what I'll do to you, Gloria Mullin.' My voice was a growl. I was Linda Blair in *The Exorcist*.

'Maddy, take it easy.' She was completely shocked.

'Why? Because you're telling me to? Is that what I'm here for? To do your bidding? Come to Hollywood, Maddy. See my big house, Maddy. See who I live with, Maddy. Are you green with envy? Good. Now do me a little favour, Maddy. You can oblige me with a child seeing that I was such a generous sister, bringing you all the way to Hollywood. Showing you all these wonderful sights.'

'That's not the way it was.'

'Liar!' I almost felt my head swivel. 'You knew you

could talk me into anything. Little sister Maddy lives such a shit life she'll do anything to escape. And you were right. And I'm just as bad as you, because I went along with your plan for my own reasons. And now you don't want a child? It's inconvenient. What did you think it was? A sale-or-return deal? Do you think you can just give babies back, like a plastic doll in a box?'

'It was only a suggestion, Maddy.'

'A suggestion? Are you totally insane?' I was practically screaming with frustration now. 'What goes on inside that head of yours? Is there no room for anything that doesn't move your career forward? Was it seeing all that morning sickness that unnerved you? Too close to the bone for you, was it? Reminded you too strongly of shoving your fingers down your own throat when you want to bring your food back up?'

Carlos looked startled. This was obviously news to him. Had he lived with her all this time without knowing what she did? Not on a regular basis but often enough for me to cop on.

I almost felt sorry for her, but she didn't look as if she needed my pity. So I saved it for myself. I had escaped from one domineering harridan only to fall into the hands of another.

I was doubly convinced of this when she answered me, her voice chillingly calm: 'Spare me the hysterics, Maddy. I have never been a fan of melodrama. The bottom line is I'm not ready to be a mother. It's that simple. And uncomplicated. I'm not ready.'

'Well, fortunately for this baby somebody is.' I was practically spitting.

'If you'd calm down we might be able to discuss this rationally and come to some arrangement.'

'No we couldn't, you domineering, self-serving bitch!'

She almost fell off the chair as I strode to the door.

And Carlos? What about Carlos?

He was slumped at the table as if somebody had let all the air out of him. Like Mother had once done to a cheap blow-up Santa Father had brought home one stormy Christmas. With his airtight plug removed, Santa had spluttered around the kitchen for ages, before Mother caught him by the bobble and threw him into the stove. It was Christmas Eve. The stink of burning plastic had hung around the house for days afterwards.

Carlos was lucky I didn't do the same to him.

A Date with Destiny

With Carlos gone to ground in his New York apartment, Gloria and I maintained a surprisingly civilized truce. Given what had passed between us, we were amazingly polite to each other.

No doubt it helped that she was up to her eyes trying to get the new script finished and I was still suffering from the aftershock of actually confronting someone for the first time in my life. Up to then, I had been a master of cowardice, a black belt at avoidance. I was my father's daughter, no mistake. It was this baby who had forced me to stand up for myself. I had no choice in the matter. Thc thing was, I quite enjoyed it. I realized that I could get a taste for fighting for my rights. It was a good feeling. Pity my outburst hadn't resolved anything. I could tell that Gloria was still hoping I'd come round to her way of thinking.

Like hell I would. I was already planning my next move.

I needed to get Carlos on my side. Given his feeble protests the other night, this might not be easy.

I had expected him to erupt with righteous indignation. Leap to his Gucci-clad feet, dark eyes flashing fire, as I had seen him do so many times on TV.

It hadn't happened.

'What are you saying, Gloria?' he'd asked.

What kind of wimpy defence was that from the articulate lawyer of *People in Jeopardy*? The great crusader for peace and justice.

'What are you saying, Gloria?' That was the extent of his cross-examination. His questioning of the woman who wanted to destroy his unborn child.

I realized that no matter how repugnant he found her pronouncement at dinner, no matter how repulsed he was by it, in the end Gloria could probably talk him into anything. They had been together a long time, their careers were inextricably linked. She was his boss, for God's sake!

Who was I? Someone he'd slept with a few times.

Okay, someone he'd had great sex with a lot of times. But that was hardly a rarity for a man who could snap his fingers and have a trillion women leap into his bed, legs akimbo. Including, no doubt, the beauteous Lou Anne, who probably knew more positions than a Chinese acrobat.

I would have to find a way to get Carlos on my side if this baby was to get its rightful due.

Carlos's birthday was approaching. Gloria had already made it quite clear that she wasn't in the market for parties. '*Or any of that crap*. No time for frivolities until I finish this final draft,' she bellowed.

'Just a quiet dinner, Gloria? You have to eat,' I pleaded through the locked door of her study.

'All right, then. But just the three of us, mind. And only a quiet dinner. And straight home afterwards.'

'Perfect.' Was it my imagination or was her attitude beginning to soften?

'That's okay, then. I couldn't handle a party right now. All those coked-up assholes driving me crazy, drinking and smoking and wrecking my head. I need to remain *focused.*' She paused. 'Have you given any more thought to our little talk, Maddy?'

Our little talk! The woman was impossible.

'Maddy?' She opened the study door.

But I was already at the top of the stairs.

It wasn't until the day before his birthday that I finally came across the perfect gift for Carlos. I had gone, with Tomasino, to look at some new plants his supplier had brought in over the border. I suspected it was an illegal run, but that was none of my business.

I left them haggling over prices and wandered off to look at a nearby bric-à-brac stall.

And there it was, right in front of me, the perfect gift, exactly what I needed. From the minute I first laid eyes on it, squashed between the second-hand Barbie doll and the statue of Our Lady of Guadeloupe, I knew I had found what I was looking for. It didn't matter that it was second-hand and more than a bit grimy. I could polish it. The important thing was that it said exactly what I wanted it to.

I gave the seller the asking price of five dollars without quibbling.

'Tourist?' he asked in heavily accented English.

'Irish.' I smiled.

'Ah.' He nodded his head, as if this explained a lot.

I hurried back to Tomasino, clutching my unexpected find.

It was a little nickel cup. Not unlike the winning cups the twins used to bring home from their kick-boxing competitions. But this one had a different purpose. And I wouldn't even have to have it inscribed. The message was already there, on the base, small and not highly visible, but just as meaningful for all that.

I would give it to Carlos in front of Gloria. Leave neither of them in doubt as to how I felt. It would be my statement of intent. They could read the inscription together. But I wanted it to be in a public place because to tell the truth I was still a little in awe of Gloria. There was no knowing how she might react.

But with *The Moonwalkers* coming out shortly she would at least be forced to behave herself in public. Wouldn't she?

I felt really fortunate to have come across such an appropriate gift for Carlos. I mean, what do you give a man who has everything?

Gloria knew. She bought him an obscenely expensive Cartier watch. I knew what it cost because I had listened outside the door while she ordered it by telephone from Van Cleef and Arpels on Rodeo Drive. It was a known fact that Van Cleef and Arpels didn't handle any item below five figures.

It sort of put my five-dollar cup in the shade. But then I wasn't competing on that level. I knew Carlos now. Understood him a little better than I had at the beginning. I knew the way to his heart. Well, one of the ways.

I sat in my room admiring his present, giving it another quick polish. The little nickel cup might have no obvious value, but the inscription on its base was priceless.

In the tiniest little letters possible it said: *The World's Best Short-Sighted Father*.

*

The restaurant was called the Blue Pacific, a name that was to be indelibly engraved on my brain for the rest of my days. It was perched on a high cliff top overlooking the wind-swept Pacific Ocean. The blinding array of arc lights and floodlit palm trees that graced the stone-walled front entrance gave no hint of the cosy, almost intimate atmosphere that prevailed inside.

The dining-room was candle-lit and four musicians played so softly that I kept thinking someone had turned the volume down too far by mistake.

The *maître d'* led us past a row of little tables for two, each one tucked into its own discreetly lit alcove. Being three, we were shown to a slightly larger table, which was directly in front of an enormous picture window. At first I thought we'd be eating in full view of the outside world, then I realized that the window overlooked the darkening Pacific, which was crashing against rocks more than three hundred feet below. Only Spiderman could rubberneck here.

The velvet-clad menus were oyster-shaped. The wine list was champagne-coloured, which was pretty appropriate, given that this was what mostly featured on it.

I was admiring the etchings on the walls when I realized they were not intended for the prudish. If it weren't for some of the larger parties around us I would have thought this place was strictly for lovers.

'Christ, you'd think they'd turn on a few lights around here,' Gloria snapped. 'I can hardly read the fuckin' menu.'

Carlos started to say something.

'Yeah, yeah. I've heard it all before,' she anticipated him. '*It's one of the few places where I can eat in public, without being plagued by autograph hunters.*' She mimicked his deep tones, then pretended to yawn. 'Ho hum! The penalties of fame.'

I ducked behind the menu.

'Are you all right, Maddy?' Carlos asked.

'Jeeze! You're not gonna start that crap all over again, are you?'

The young couple at the next table were staring over. They were obviously honeymooners. If their chairs had been any closer together they would have been stacked on top of each other. Their clothes had that starchy post-wedding look that nobody in Hollywood would be caught dead in, except if they were starring in a Doris Day remake. And despite appearing to be desperately in love, they weren't groping each other with the careless ease of Los Angeles lovers. They were holding hands, as if nobody had told them the fifties were over.

'Tourists,' Gloria hissed, loud enough to be heard in the San Fernando Valley. 'How did they get in here? This place is going to the dogs.'

The couple had recognized Carlos the moment we walked in. Craned their necks to get a better look at him as we were led past their table.

He pretended to be oblivious to all this interest. But I could tell he was uncomfortable.

For a man who spent most of his life in front of a camera he had an almost pathological dread of being in the public eye. He had to steel himself to meet even the smallest group of fans face to face. After seeing at first hand the excitement sex symbols generated in public, I could well understand this fear. The craziness that a single dedicated autograph hunter could trigger in a crowded place was enough to put the fear of God into anyone.

Gloria seemed intent on making things worse for him tonight. Turning the screw by keeping her voice even louder than usual. She'd been building up to a row all afternoon, waiting for a phone call, which hadn't come. Gloria didn't take kindly to being kept waiting.

She snapped her fingers at a waiter to demand a double vodka before we ordered our food. She had already downed a couple of lethal-looking cocktails in the bar outside and God only knows how many snifters in her study before that.

Carlos made the mistake of giving her a disapproving look as she threw back the double.

'So?' she challenged him. 'What's the problem?'

He ducked behind the menu.

The three of us were picking unenthusiastically at our food when her mobile suddenly rang, shattering the quiet air of the restaurant.

She dropped her fork and barked impatiently into the receiver. 'Yes?'

Carlos and I pretended to eat, our eyes intent on our plates.

He actually swallowed some food, I noticed. I didn't.

Gloria was silent for a couple of seconds, as her caller spoke. When she replied her voice was icy: 'I told you if you changed that ending I'd slap a lawsuit on you.'

This was the long-awaited phone call. It concerned an ongoing row about *The Moonwalkers*. The film was already in the can, but somebody on high wanted the ending changed.

'Why?' I had asked naïvely.

'Because they're tight-assed bastards. That's why,' she'd said.

This was always possible, of course, but Gloria was never above telling a little fib or two when it suited her. She even admitted to it. 'Show me a person who says they never lie and I'll show you a liar,' she liked to say.

If the studio did want to change the ending of *The Moonwalkers* for no good reason she was perfectly entitled to feel hard done by, what with her having already worked so hard on the exciting sequel.

But as always with Gloria, there was more to it than meets the eye.

Bobby Kennedy had told me, in confidence, that the preview audience had given the film glowing reports. They were wild for it, bursting into spontaneous applause several times during the screening.

'So what's the problem?'

'The ending. They hate it,' he had whispered nervously, looking over his shoulder. 'But then, so do I. It spoils the whole movie. Everyone connected with it has agreed.'

'Except Gloria?'

'You got it.'

'Poor Gloria,' I'd said.

'Oh don't get me wrong,' Bobby had continued. 'It's a superb movie. The script is magnificent; it's the best thing she has ever written. We're talking sure-fire Oscar material here. *If* she can be persuaded to change the last two minutes.'

The Moonwalkers was an adventure story. Set in the distant future, on some fictitious hell-hole of a planet, a hostile world, with a savage, untamed landscape every inch of which proved to be a deadly threat for a group of scientists who had been marooned there. The two main characters begin the movie as sworn enemies. Mainly because they had once been married to each other. But also because, as scientists, they held rival theories as to the feasibility of finding viable life forms in such an inhospitable world. They are forced to put their personal feelings aside in order to survive. The last reel sees them staggering out into weak sunlight and stepping into separate rescue ships, as they respectfully salute each other.

A happy ending, I would have thought. But not happy enough for Hollywood. Or the preview audience.

Gloria wouldn't back down.

'The ending stays!' she yelled now into her mobile. 'They go their separate ways!'

Her caller presumably put his side of the argument.

Gloria flew into a rage, losing her head altogether this time. 'They can be as fucking happy as you want. Fucking ecstatic, for all I care! As long as they're fucking ecstatic separately.'

I think her caller disagreed.

'What the fuck would you know about it, you little pen pusher? These people are scientists, *they* have brains! They'd be rushing back to write papers on their findings, share their discoveries with the world. Not slipping each other the tongue like a couple of horny adolescents.' She took a deep breath. 'They go their separate ways. That's *my* final word. If he has a problem with that, tell him I'll see him in court.'

*

She ordered another drink. Carlos and I picked at our desserts.

She began loudly to belittle the movie business and everyone in it. Naming names. *And* body parts.

'Gloria, people are staring. Could you tone it down?' Carlos muttered under his breath.

'You shut the fuck up! It's not your script they want to mangle. Renew their vows, my ass! What kind of twats would renew their vows after the discoveries they've just made? They've come across something that will astound the world and what does Hollywood want them to do? Renew their fuckin' vows!' She was practically screaming.

The honeymoon couple was now staring open-mouthed at us.

'I think we should leave.' Carlos got to his feet.

'You sit down! We came here to celebrate your birthday and we're going to fuckin' celebrate it if it kills me. Waiter?' She clicked her fingers. 'Bring me two bottles of Krug.'

'Would this be a bad time to give Carlos his presents?' I asked.

Carlos feigned enormous surprise at the sight of the Cartier watch. He acted as if he was shocked to be the recipient of such an extravagant gift. 'You . . . shouldn't have,' he said to Gloria. Which went a long way to explaining why she was the script-writer and he wasn't.

She grabbed his wrist and began to remove his expensive Rolex. I had to turn away and look out at the ocean. I couldn't bear to witness even such a small act of intimacy between them.

'Maddy!' Gloria slapped my arm with the Rolex. 'Where's your present?'

Something about her expression made me freeze. I lost my nerve completely. What if she turned on me when she read the inscription? Told me to get the hell out of their lives? Threw me into the street with only my Gianni Versace on my back? What would become of me then? Would I end up a whore? Prostituting myself to visiting sailors? Living under a bridge in a cardboard box?

'Come on, Maddy.'

'I . . . I can't.' I had a sudden brainwave. 'It's still in my room.'

'Liar! I saw you put it in your purse.' She grabbed my bag from under the table.

'No! Please don't, Gloria.'

We fought over the raffia bag, while Carlos looked on in disbelief.

'Here it is. I knew you had it.' Gloria's eyes were mean. She handed the small box to Carlos.

The moment I saw the little cup in his beautifully manicured hands I knew I had made the worst mistake of my life. And it had nothing to do with my fear of ending up in a cardboard box under a rain-swept bridge.

It was the flashing Cartier watch on his elegant wrist that forced me back to reality. That and the cream Armani suit that fitted him like a glove. Not to mention the Ralph Lauren shirt, and the gold cuff-links that glinted in the candle-light with his every well co-ordinated gesture.

What had possessed me to think that this man would appreciate the worth of a little nickel cup?

Gloria had just handed him a watch that cost upwards of twenty thousand dollars. I had given him five dollars' worth of scratched nickel. He had tipped the doorman four times that on our way in. For saluting him. Where had I got the stupid idea that this money-drenched star would see the value of such a valueless gift?

I stared out at the sheer drop below. The blue Pacific looked most enticing.

'What is it?' Carlos was scrutinizing the little cup, holding it up to the light. He appeared to be completely baffled by it. As well he might.

'It's some kind of gag.' Gloria gave one of her nasty laughs. 'Stop teasing, Maddy, and give the man his present.'

My stomach began to hurt.

Carlos continued to press and prod every part of the little cup, turning it every way possible in his immaculate hands. He tapped it hopefully with his long, slim fingers, clearly expecting to come across some secret little compartment, cunningly concealing a priceless piece of jewellery from Van Cleef and Arpels.

'What the hell is it?' Gloria was losing patience. She made a sudden grab for it.

He held it beyond her reach, still tapping away, his brown eyes full of hope.

I wanted to shout *stop*, because the more he turned it, the cheaper and tackier it was looking. The Cartier watch didn't help. It continued to flash like fire against his bronzed wrist.

'It's . . . I know . . . there's a mechanism somewhere, isn't there?' He was completely intrigued now.

Gloria had lost interest. She was dialling again, ignoring the request from the *maître d'* to 'Please desist from using your mobile in the dining-room, Madam'.

So much for my big moment. My earth-shattering announcement. Neither of them had even noticed the inscription. Just as well, I suppose, because I didn't think I would be up for any more humiliating scenes tonight.

At least I had learned the truth about Gloria. And Carlos.

They were both looking for the *real* present behind the cute little cup, not knowing that it was there all the time in front of their noses. Each of them was as bad as the other. He'd seen the value of the Cartier watch all right. Hadn't missed that, had he? With his manicured hands and his Armani suit, and his haircut that probably cost more than a hay bailer.

What had possessed me to imagine that he and I could ever have a proper relationship? A few words spoken in the heated afterglow of sex had set me thinking that underneath all the glamour and glitz there was a simple cowboy from Texas. A cowboy who might have a special place in his heart for me.

In a pig's eye, he had.

He and Gloria probably laughed about my embarrassing naïveté when they were alone together.

He was likely bored out of his mind with me. Even Turlough found me boring. He'd rather have fat Marion in the draughty milking parlour than me in his warm bed.

'Excuse me . . . I . . . need . . . the bathroom.' I ran before Gloria could offer to accompany me.

Behind me there was a sudden hoot of laughter.

I sat on the toilet and wept. Big tears of self-pity running down my face. I stayed there for so long that somebody tapped on the door and a voice asked, 'Is everything all right in there?'

'Yes thank you. Just period pains,' I lied.

The owner of the voice offered me a packet of analgesics. And a tampon.

'No honestly, I'm fine now.' I blew my nose hard, sending shock waves thundering through my already aching sinuses.

I checked the watch that Turlough had got me from the Argus catalogue. It was still only nine forty. I would have to go back out there and sit through another humiliating hour with these two.

But that would be the end of it. Tomorrow I would leave the mansion. Go somewhere else. I had no idea where, but I wasn't staying in a place where I wasn't wanted. Where I was the butt of everyone's jokes.

It had been sheer wishful thinking on my part, imaging that Carlos felt something special for me. All he had ever wanted was to please Gloria. Whatever she wanted she had to get. Even another woman's child. And if the child got in the way of her career and she wanted to get rid of it he would support her, no matter what his own views were. Gloria was top dog around here. She had to be kept happy, whatever the price.

But he was stupid if he thought anyone could make Gloria happy. She was one of those people who carry their unhappiness around, like a badge of honour – *Look at me, I'm suffering*! You could give them the whole world and they still wouldn't be happy. It wasn't in their make-up.

And he was nearly as bad. 'I'd like to be a cowboy.'

Some cowboy! Riding the range in his Armani suit and Gucci loafers. Not many cowboys wear Cartier watches, I'll bet. Or have their nails manicured three times a week. Or their eyebrows plucked. Ha! He probably thought I didn't notice that.

My eyes were open now, even if they were all red and swollen. I was free from his spell. I would never again get all hot and bothered at the sight of him. I blew my nose one more time, then pushed open the heavy door.

He was standing outside, his face wreathed in smiles. 'Maddy? Why didn't you tell me about the inscription? I can't read anything so small without glasses. You know that!' He laughed, his beautiful face radiating happiness.

And I stood there, staring at him, my knees turning to jelly, my loins on fire.

He picked me up and swung me round with unashamed delight. 'What an epigraph!'

'You don't think it's . . . cheap and tacky?'

'As an epigraph?'

'The cup. Wasn't it . . . tacky?'

'Oh baby. It's so . . . real. It's the realest present anyone has ever given me.'

'Oh.'

God he was so beautiful! And sexy! I wanted to rip his clothes off.

'Maddy? Haven't you anything to say to me?'

I licked my dry lips. 'Er . . . Happy Birthday?'

He burst into laughter.

People were beginning to stare at us, but then Carlos was always worth staring at, never more so than when his head was thrown back and he was laughing. He somehow sent out signals that were picked up by every female within a hundred-yard radius.

They were gathering now, like the undead at the

smell of live flesh. Whispering and pointing. Giggling like schoolgirls. Moving in. If we didn't get out of here soon we'd be trampled to death in the rush from the powder room.

'Is it really you?' the woman nearest to him touched his sleeve reverentially.

Carlos gave her his most charming smile.

She rocked back on her heels, her eyes rolling in her head as if she was about to have a fit. 'It *is* you! It's Rick Hein!'

I had once seen Josie Murphy from the sub post office behave exactly like this when she claimed to have seen a vision of Our Lady on the gable end of Ballyshannon parish church. Father Brennan had told her to go home and get sense. And a good night's sleep.

'Let's go!' Carlos grabbed my hand and pulled me back into the candle-lit restaurant. He could have been leading me anywhere. I'd have followed him to the ends of the earth.

But he was only heading back to the table.

He had loved my present. Called it the realest gift he had ever been given. The man was a god, even if he did have trouble with his grammar. All TV stars probably had their eyebrows plucked. It was probably in their contract.

Gloria was still yelling into her mobile.

'We're gonna dance, Gloria,' Carlos said, drawing me along behind him.

She dismissed us with an impatient wave. 'Go! Go! No, not you . . .' she bellowed into the receiver.

The small nickel cup was standing by the discarded Rolex. They formed an odd little pair in the flickering candle-light. But for some reason the cup didn't look all that tacky any more.

Much.

It was sheer luck that the dance floor was so crowded. It meant that Carlos had to hold me dangerously close. You couldn't have passed a thread between our bodies as we moved together to the soft music.

It was absolute bliss to he held against him again without having to worry about throwing up on him. Or having Mrs Danvers interrupt us for no good reason.

And the lights were so low that when he began to caress my bare back I knew that nobody would complain, or become offended. Certainly not me. Then we were kissing, as if it were the most natural thing in the world for us to be doing in public.

We hadn't intended staying on the floor for more than one dance. Honestly. But when we headed for the table we saw that Gloria was still intent on her phone call, so what was the point in going back? Gloria hated people listening in to her business calls. What was there to do except have another dance? And then another . . .

We were both truly shocked when we discovered that we were practically the last couple on the floor.

She wasn't at the table when we got back. And everything had been cleared away: glasses, wine, the lot. The little nickel cup stood forlornly in the centre of the table. Even the fancy Rolex was gone.

We sat down without speaking, both of us acutely aware of our still curious audience at the next table.

They were gawking openly now, the young bridegroom attempting to catch my eye as I glanced around, trying to spot Gloria. She could be anywhere, haranguing any of the staff.

'I'll check the women's room,' I whispered to Carlos.

The bridegroom suddenly rushed over to us.

He was perspiring heavily, tiny beads of sweat standing out on his sunburned forehead. He rubbed his hands together nervously and I saw Carlos's jaw begin to tighten. But there wasn't an autograph book in sight, or a pen, and the boy was turning to me. 'Excuse me.' He bent towards me, practically dripping sweat. 'I . . . your mother left a message for you.'

'What?' Carlos sat upright.

The boy – he was no more than that – swallowed nervously, his brand-new wedding ring catching the light as he fingered his yellow tie. 'She . . . she said to tell you to . . .' his voice dropped until it was practically inaudible '. . . go fuck yourselves.' His red face flushed even redder behind his neat rimless glasses.

'Thank you very much.' I nodded.

'You're welcome.' He darted a quick look at Carlos, before rushing back to join his bride and hurry her away into the warm night.

Paradise Regained and Lost

We sat stiffly in the back of the cab taking great care not to brush against each other. I stared out of the window on my side. Every car we passed seemed to have two people in it, their heads close together.

We made a sudden stop at a red light. I was thrown forward and then fell back against Carlos.

'Okay, Maddy?' His mouth was close to my ear.

'Given the circumstances.' I nodded.

'Don't worry, Gloria's bark is worse than her bite.'

I turned to look at him in disbelief. And he began to laugh. Just a nervous little chuckle at first, then a proper laugh, but still tinged with fear. And then he was laughing uproariously, as if he was never going to stop.

And I couldn't help it, I joined in until we were both almost hysterical. I don't doubt that this was partly triggered by nerves, apprehension at what might happen when we got home.

It certainly relieved the tension.

'That poor bastard. Can you picture it?' Carlos wiped his eyes. 'Gloria in full flow? The woman who can reduce the toughest TV executive to a pool of quivering jelly in twenty seconds flat? Think of her hollering at that poor kid – in front of his blushing bride. Did you see his face? He looked as if he had never heard the word fuck before, let alone have to say it.'

I was still laughing. 'Wasn't he polite, though?'

'What about you? "*Thank you very much.*" Who else would say thank you for such a message?'

'What else could I have said? He was terrified.'

'He wasn't the only one.' He caught my hand.

'I can't believe he sat there waiting all that time. To deliver a message to a total stranger?'

'And what a message! But I can believe it. Gloria Mullin commands total obedience.' He was suddenly serious.

'Who's going to tell her he thought she was my mother?'

'Not me. She'd garrotte me. Then she'd track down that poor little bastard and disembowel him on Main Street Hicksville, or wherever he's from. Even if he did carry her message, word perfect.'

We got the giggles again. And then we were kissing. This time it was tongues and all, not restrained and polite like the kiss we'd exchanged on the darkened dance floor.

After a while, Carlos ordered the driver to pull over. 'We're in big trouble, Maddy. You know that?'

I nodded.

We sat there, like two teenagers who have broken curfew and are now too frightened to go home and face the music.

Carlos looked at me, his brown eyes dark pools of temptation. 'Wanna be in a little more trouble, Maddy?' He ran his index finger slowly along my lower lip.

'Might as well be hung for a sheep as a lamb,' I whispered, touching his beautifully tailored thigh.

'We're dead anyway.'

He gave the bored driver an address I had never heard of. Then we got back to the business in hand.

The cab pulled up outside a squat bougainvillaea-covered bungalow. 'One o one, Los Verdes. This is it, folks,' the cabby shouted. He hadn't recognized Carlos. Or perhaps working the night shift in Los Angeles made him too blasé to care who was misbehaving in the back of his cab.

All the same, Carlos waited until we saw its tail lights disappear around the corner before leading me a little further along the tree-lined road. 'Can't be too careful.'

We walked up a short pathway to a similar little bungalow, this one minus the flamboyant orange bougainvillaea. Carlos began searching through his wallet.

'Oh man, it's not here. I . . . yep.' He produced a door key.

'Who lives here?'

'One of our cameramen, but he's in New York. He is a buddy.'

The small garden was overgrown with weeds, the varnish peeling off the front door. And we almost fell over a pile of post in the dark hallway. But the place was cosy and warm, if a little dusty and unaired.

Not that any of that mattered. We weren't the dust inspectors. We went straight to bed.

Our love-making that night was even more intense that it had been before. I'm not altogether sure why. Perhaps it was after the enforced celibacy of the previous months. For me, at least. Or maybe it was the element of wickedness, forbidden fruit and all that. That had been missing from all our other assignations, seeing as they were all arranged and practically presided over by Gloria. This was our first genuinely clandestine tryst.

Whatever the reason, the lightest touch of his fingers was enough to have me gasping with desire. And his slow, teasing smile triggered impatient groans, which only stopped short of becoming encouraging cheers. His warm breath on the back of my neck was more arousing than a deeply passionate kiss might be from another man. And every cell in my body caught fire when he was finally inside me.

'You know what's happening here, Maddy?' His brown eyes searched mine.

'Great sex?' I smiled.

'Don't.' He frowned. 'You know what's happening.'

I turned away.

'I think I'm falling in love with you.'

'Don't make promises you can't keep.'

So he didn't. And I suppose I've only myself to blame. Me and my big mouth.

We didn't get any sleep that night, but then we hadn't gone to the little bungalow to sleep. I sometimes wonder now, though, how things might have turned out, if we hadn't been quite so greedy. Quite so hungry for each other. If we had got up and gone home immediately afterwards, instead of closing our eyes to catch our breath and then starting all over again. But we'll never know the answer to that.

All I know is that when Carlos pulled me towards his warm body again, happiness doesn't even begin to describe the way I felt.

We got the cabby to drop us a couple of hundred yards short of the mansion. It was almost dawn, pale light beginning to spread across the eastern sky. We crept soundlessly up the long driveway and around the back, like two cat burglars intent on dirty business.

When we reached the comparative shelter of the pink terrace we started a little dirty business of our own.

I was the first to come to my senses. 'Not here. This is crazy.'

Carlos leaned back and sighed. 'You're right. But we're gonna have to decide what we wanna do, you and me.'

'I know what I want to do, we just can't do it here.'

And he was laughing again and I wanted to eat him.

Looking back, I can only describe what I was feeling as akin to madness. Like a fever in the blood, it flared up at the least provocation. Or none. All it took was a glance or a smile to make me want him.

Watching him laugh, I thought for the hundredth time that night how impossibly handsome he was. Just looking at him was enough to make your teeth water. No man had a right to be *that* perfect. As well as being nice. And kind. And thoughtful. And Gloria's. That was the one thought I refused to indulge.

I looked up at the sky. It was turning the most magical shade of pinky red. 'See the colour of that sky? My father would have quoted, "Red sky in the morning shepherds warning!".'

'Did your old man not have *one* happy quote?' he asked.

'Think they're bad? You should have heard my mother's.'

We giggled together. Again, like two carefree teenagers.

Then suddenly he wasn't laughing any more. He made a dull, gasping sound, as if something had knocked the breath out of him. And he was staring past me, his face frozen in horror.

I don't know how long it took me to turn. It couldn't have been more than a second, but time had somehow slowed down so that it might have been a lifetime before I saw what he was staring at, down in the pool below us. And even then I refused to believe what I was seeing.

The beige shape on the water, the blonde hair trailing like grotesque seaweed behind it. The head bobbing gently as if it was nodding in the breaking light.

'Gloria!' I heard myself screaming.

Carlos was already half-way down the shallow steps.

He dived into the water fully clothed and I stood there, unable to move. Telling myself that this wasn't happening. This was some kind of fictional Hollywood drama being played out in front of me. It might even be an episode of *People in Jeopardy. Rick rides to the rescue . . .*

Then he was lifting her from the water, kneeling beside her, trying to resuscitate her, forcing air into her lungs. Struggling frantically to punch her heart back into life.

And I still managed to convince myself that it wasn't happening.

It wasn't my sister lying there on the pink tiles, her beige suit sodden with water, her face like the wax doll she had once carried everywhere with her around cold, wind-swept Ballyshannon. Gloria hated the cold, she wouldn't be lying here in the chilly dawn, her lips all blue, while Carlos yelled at me to ring 911.

When I finally managed to get to the phone my fingers repeatedly kept dialling 999. When nobody answered, I told myself once again that this was because it was all some silly dream. A nightmare. I would wake at any second now, to find Turlough yelling at the twins to get out of bed and bring the cows in for milking. Hear Mother clattering the wooden spoon against the big metal porridge pot as she dished out the breakfast.

Strong fingers prized the phone from my hand.

Mrs Danvers took over.

I looked up to see Carlos standing in the doorway, water dripping from his clothes. He was crying, tears running down his face as the water dripped on to the floor. I remember thinking that he would catch his death, standing there in the open doorway, drenched as he was, this early in the morning.

Then there was another sensation. A strange fluttering inside me, like butterfly wings beating against silk. The baby moved for the first time. And then I felt the warm trickle run down the inside of my thigh.

I was bleeding.

The Nightmare

'Gloria?' I could smell her perfume.

'It's all right, Maddy.' Mrs Danvers was standing by my bed, a black-clad cadaver, with her huge hollow eyes and fleshless cheeks.

'Gloria?'

She looked at me for a moment, without speaking. Then she said quietly, 'Gloria is gone, Maddy, you know that.'

It took me a second to recall what had happened. 'It's my fault. It's all my fault. I killed her.'

'Don't talk nonsense. Gloria had an accident. You weren't even there.'

'That's what I'm telling you. I let her die.'

She held a glass to my lips, preventing me from saying any more. Her hands were gentle enough, but her eyes said she hated me. Not as much as I hated myself, though. Nobody could possibly do that. I wanted to tell her that, so she would know. But I couldn't speak, because she was forcing pills down my throat. I have absolutely no idea what they were, but I swallowed them anyway, that's how bad I was feeling. I was convinced that she was poisoning me and I took them without complaint.

Next time I woke I could hear Carlos's voice on the landing outside. 'Don't let *him* in here. I don't want to see him.'

I needn't have worried. Carlos had no intention of

coming near me. He continued along the landing to Gloria's room.

'Does he know about the baby?' I caught Mrs Danvers's hand.

'The baby?' She frowned.

'That it's dead.'

'The baby isn't dead. The baby is fine. It's Gloria who . . .' Her voice broke and she turned away, her black-clad body suddenly racked by long, shuddering sobs.

I didn't know how to react to this. How could I comfort her? She was the one who did the comforting here. What could *I* say that would make *her* feel better?

And that's when I felt it again, the tiniest little fluttering, somewhere deep inside me. The baby was moving.

I reached out to her. 'Don't cry, Betty, we'll get through this, you'll see.' And the thing is, I really believed it.

Her eyes said she didn't.

Twenty-four hours later I was sitting alone in the small dining-room. I hadn't seen Carlos since the accident, only heard his voice that one time. There was a single place setting at the big table. All properly laid out with silverware and a napkin and everything. As if nothing had happened. As if I was dining alone because Gloria was out.

'You've got to eat,' Mrs Danvers insisted.

And strangely enough I did. I ate everything she put in front of me. I couldn't believe how hungry I was. I finished every course, clearing my plate each time. Then I was swamped with guilt for enjoying my food when my sister was dead. I decided to fast for the next twenty-four hours, as a penance for such unbridled gluttony.

Mrs Danvers brought in a big cream-covered flan and I burst into tears. 'Take it away, Mrs Danvers. I can't bear to look at it.'

'Yes, Madam.'

Pear flan was Gloria's favourite dessert. She would dig into one of these cream-covered flans after days of stringent dieting. I wandered into the living-room and turned on the TV, picking a station at random. There was a blues band guesting on a daytime chat show. They struck up one of Gloria's favourite tunes, 'Basin Street Blues'.

I couldn't go into the garden because she was everywhere I turned there. I especially couldn't walk past the swimming pool.

Maybe to punish myself I pushed the button on her CD player. The strains of a Beethoven piano concerto filled the big room.

My sister Gloria. A bundle of contradictions. Beethoven and Blues. Starvation diets and pigging out on cream-covered flans.

I cried until I had no tears left.

Mrs Danvers produced some more of her mystery pills.

'Are they safe? For the baby, I mean?' I asked.

'They're safe. But don't get too fond of them,' she warned me.

This was *after* she had watched me swallow them.

She had gone to the kitchen when the police cars arrived. She hurried back to the living-room, her face its usual mask of cool superiority.

'Detective Shawnessey would like a word with you, Madam. You don't have to speak to him if you don't feel up to it.'

A heavy-set man pushed past her. He flashed a badge of some sort. 'Detective Shawnessey . . .'

I didn't listen. I was too busy watching what was happening outside. A group of men had gathered by the pool. They were joined by a uniformed police officer. One of the plain-clothes men knelt down and began measuring from the water line to the curved top edge of the pool. Then two of them held either end of a taut metal tape, letting it span from the exit steps in the pool, to mid-way along its widest curve, where a white chalk mark ran across the tiles. The other man took a small black notebook from his pocket and began to write in it. He was black. Handsome. I suddenly thought of Jean-Baptiste. How would he feel when he heard about Gloria's death? Would he care? And who would tell him? Mrs. Danvers?

She had taken charge, after all.

She had already been in touch with Ballyshannon. While I was indisposed, she said. Indisposed? It was the perfect word for how I felt. They would have liked that in Ballyshannon. Maddy is indisposed. Gloria is dead and Maddy is indisposed. That's that, then. They'll blame me anyway. And they'd be perfectly right.

'Did they blame me?' I had asked her.

'Of course not,' she lied, like the well-rehearsed housekeeper she was.

'Miz . . .' Detective Shawnessey had been standing there all the time. But I had paid no attention to him. I hadn't heard a word he'd said.

He seemed to fill the room with his great bulk. Not that he was all that tall, he wasn't. Carlos would have dwarfed him had he stood beside him. But with his big square head and double chin threatening to overflow into a treble, he was a man who gave the impression of being a lot taller than he actually was.

His balding head glistened under the light. With sweat, I realized. He was sweating. Funny, that. I was freezing.

Shawnessey didn't look like a man to whom cleanliness was all that important. His clothes were shabby, untended, but his little blackcurrant eyes looked as if they could see straight into your mind and read your every thought.

'I'm sorry about your sister.' He made a humble gesture. It didn't suit him. Despite his shabby clothes, Detective Shawnessey was not a humble man. That was a façade, a trick to worm his way into your confidence. I met another man like that once. I had ended up marrying him.

I turned back to the window.

He coughed politely. 'I'm sorry, Ma'am, but I have to ask you a few questions.'

He didn't look sorry. He looked as if he enjoyed his work. Enjoyed prying into people's lives when they were at their most vulnerable, when they were seeing the world through clouds of pain.

'What time did you get home on Sunday morning?'

'Didn't Carlos tell you?' I was surprised.

'I'm asking you, Miz O'Toole.'

'I don't know the exact time. What has that got to do with anything?'

'It's my job to investigate your sister's death.'

So she really *was* dead then. I wasn't going to wake

up from this nightmare and hear her laughing at me. Or cursing a blue streak. Oh God, I wish she were here to curse me. She could yell at me all day if she wanted.

For the first time I noticed the other man, standing by the door. For some reason I turned to him. 'Would it have made any difference if we had come back earlier?'

He shook his head silently.

I rang for Mrs Danvers.

She came running. 'Have they upset you, Madam?'

I sniffed. 'I'm okay.'

'What have you said to her?' she asked Shawnessey.

Out by the pool the men were still measuring. Walking backwards and forwards across the seating area. One of them was so intent on what he was doing that he stumbled into one of the heavy wrought-iron chairs, hurting his knee. He kicked out at the chair, before going back to his measuring.

'What are they doing out there?'

Mrs Danvers held a brandy glass to my lips. 'Take a sip.' She glowered at the bulky detective. 'She's ill. Can't you see that?'

'I have a job to do. We have already been delayed here.' His little blackcurrant eyes said this was all my fault. 'Just a few more questions.'

'It's all right. I'm fine.' I indicated for Mrs Danvers to leave us.

She did. With great reluctance.

Detective Shawnessey sat down, without asking permission. His face looked tired, but his eyes remained sharp and watchful.

He looked like the O'Shaughnessys from the West

of Ireland, with his heavy black brows, that promised to meet in the middle but didn't quite make it. And his habit of staring at the ground whenever you tried to read his expression.

'I'm sorry you don't feel well, Miz O'Toole, but it's my job to ask these questions, you understand that?'

I nodded. I must have looked pretty awful because his voice softened a little. 'Did your sister come back to the house alone?'

'Yes.'

'You sound pretty sure?'

'She came back alone.' That was the one thing I was sure of.

'How can you be so positive? You weren't home, you were in the . . .' he glanced down at his notebook '. . . the Blue Pacific restaurant, with Mr Garcia.'

'I was in the Blue Pacific with Mr Garcia *and* my sister.' I swallowed. 'Until . . . .'

'What did you row about?' He sounded bored.

'Row?'

'In the restaurant. We have witnesses.'

'Witnesses? What is this?'

'Just doing my job.' He might have been speaking to a child. 'You can help me by answering the questions.'

'We didn't have a row. Gloria was arguing with someone on the phone. She can be . . . loud.'

He checked his notebook again. 'She said you and Mr Garcia should . . .' he coughed, '. . . go fuck yourselves. That doesn't sound as if the row was with her caller.'

'You didn't know Gloria.' For the first time I spoke of her in the past tense.

'Was she a good swimmer?'

'Yes. Excellent. But not when she was drunk.'
He wrote in his book.
'Was she drunk that night?'
'I don't know. Gloria could hold her liquor. But Mrs Danvers said . . .'
'Mrs Danvers? Nobody mentioned a Mrs Danvers?' He looked at the other man, who shook his head. 'How many people were here on Saturday night?' He checked his notebook again.
'Dong was away. So there was just Mrs Danvers. And Gloria, until . . .' I began to cry.
'Let me get this straight. You saw this Mrs Danvers?'
'Yes.' I sniffed.
'Ms Buttoni never mentioned a Mrs Danvers.'
'She's Mrs Danvers. Betty is Mrs Danvers!'
He exchanged glances with the man at the door.
'Betty Buttoni is Mrs Danvers?' He spoke slowly and clearly.
'Yes.'
'So there *was* only one person here when you and Mr Garcia arrived home? Is that right? Betty Butt . . .' he glanced at the other cop again '. . . Mrs Danvers? Have I got that right?'
I stared back at him. 'How many times do I have to tell you?' My head was beginning to pound with all these stupid questions.

I learned later that compared with the grilling he gave Carlos, Detective Shawnessey had let me off lightly.
Apparently he didn't like actors. Especially those who played clever lawyers on prime-time TV. He thought the cops had a difficult enough job without actors making fools out of them in TV dramas.

Smartass actors appearing on TV in three thousand dollar suits, trouncing the image of hard-working cops, was not something he cared for. Even if it was all make believe. *People in Jeopardy* was not top of his ratings.

So the man wouldn't be human if he didn't nurture a small hope of finding Carlos in some way responsible for Gloria's accident.

And he was, of course. But then, so was I, if we're talking about moral responsibility. But our morals didn't seem to feature in Detective Shawnessey's investigation. He was only concerned with proving that someone had deliberately caused her death, which was nonsense.

Saturday night wasn't the first time she had fallen into the pool when she had too much drink taken. I could attest to that. So could half of Hollywood. Stories abounded about Gloria ending up in the pool after late-night parties. Mrs Danvers and Bobby were apparently experts at fishing her out. But she had never learned to avoid the pool area when she had overindulged.

On every other occasion she had been lucky. There was always someone on hand to pull her out.

This time she had been alone.

And that *was* our fault. Carlos's and mine. If the three of us had left the Blue Pacific together, Gloria would still be alive.

Instead, Carlos and I had sneaked away to that grubby little bungalow.

If only he had mislaid the key. If only we hadn't started that second bout. If only we hadn't . . . All the ifs.

Including the biggest one of all.

Gloria would still be alive if I hadn't accepted her invitation to Hollywood.

She wouldn't have drowned in that cold water while Carlos and I were thrashing around on a grubby bed in Oakland, like two animals in heat.

Hollywood Mourns

The media had a field day with Gloria's death. Especially the press. It didn't start out like that. The first mention was quite dignified, given the circumstances.

AWARD-WINNING WRITER FOUND DEAD IN POOL was the news headline in the *Los Angeles Times*. Underneath there were a few brief paragraphs outlining her writing career. Nothing remotely salacious, just the bare facts. Most of the piece was devoted to her achievements in Hollywood. The awards she had won, the respect she was held in by her peers. They even mentioned her integrity. Twice.

LAPD INQUIRING INTO WRITER'S DEATH. The *Globe* was next, trying to make it sound a little more mysterious. But again there was nothing offensive, just the sort of information that could be found in Gloria's CV, if anyone cared to peruse it on the internet. This article did, however, mention that she and Carlos were 'long-time' lovers. This was inevitable, of course. In Hollywood, any relationship that lasted beyond a couple of years was considered worthy of comment.

After that, things began to heat up. Carlos's picture started to appear more and more with the story, especially in the tabloids. And in each consecutive shot he seemed to be wearing fewer and fewer clothes. And the headlines changed.

TV'S SEXIEST MAN MOURNS DEAD LOVER was one notable one.

MYSTERY DROWNING IN BEVERLY HILLS LOVE NEST was another.

Then the circus hit town. The mansion was besieged. TV crews and press journalists camped outside the big electronic gates, day and night.

After a couple of minor scuffles had occurred between reporters and people entering and leaving, Lilliput Productions arranged for a twenty-four-hour guard to be placed on the gates.

This made things a *lot* worse. A simple run to the market now meant that Dong had to fight his way through two sets of aggressors – the dreaded paparazzi *and* the armed security guards, who earned their fifty dollars an hour by manhandling everyone, friend or foe.

Dong resorted to smoking two medicinal joints to relieve his nerves after each stress-filled journey. That was his story, anyway.

Mrs Danvers resorted to a much less contentious way of dealing with the press siege. She took to ordering everything by phone.

Tomasino, who was three times Dong's age and twice Mrs Danvers's, proved to be the most resilient of them all. He drove through the gang at the gate in his old pick-up, without letting the speedometer drop below fifty, as he cursed them out of it in colloquial Spanish. He only slowed down once, and that was to spit on a particularly notorious paparazzo. Then he accelerated noisily along the tree-lined boulevard with two press cars in full pursuit, cameras clicking away as if he was some kind of borderline celebrity.

Our one true celebrity took to wearing dark glasses

everywhere he went. And a permanent scowl. His refusal to give interviews, or even acknowledge the clamouring press hordes, may have been the reason some of them turned against him and became so vindictive.

They hounded him day and night, without let-up. They even laid siege to his agent's office. When Carlos refused to give them a single quote, they fabricated their own.

DID I DRIVE MY LOVER TO TAKE HER OWN LIFE? was the caption beneath a photo of him with his head in his hands, as he was driven out through the gates on his way to the studio.

I was completely unaware of all these goings-on at first, too wrapped up in my own pain to pay heed to anything else. Even Carlos couldn't breach the protective wall I had erected around myself. Or perhaps he didn't want to. All I knew was that the sight of him was enough to increase my guilt a hundredfold.

We passed each other in the hallway some evenings, like two wounded animals. Heads lowered, eyes carefully averted.

We hadn't spoken to each other properly since he had lifted Gloria's body from the pool. And I had stood there frozen with disbelief, feeling the warm semen trickling down my thigh and assuming it was blood.

It was days before I even looked at a newspaper. When I did, I was horrified.

WAS CARLOS GARCIA IMPLICATED IN LOVER'S DEATH? This was the headline in a paper read by gossip-hungry millions across America. There followed a supposedly full investigation into Gloria's death, including interviews with her closest friends.

I didn't recognize a single name on the short list, until I opened the second page. And there he was, the snitch himself, giving his best Tom Cruise imitation. His little boy lost smile took up a whole quarter page. The heavily jelled quiff, which fell artfully over one blue eye, was almost two print columns wide.

But the most galling thing of all was that he was wearing one of Carlos's cast-off suits.

Wannabe Tom or, as he titled himself, a close personal friend of Carlos Garcia was spilling his guts to America. Or his fantasies. He was only short of claiming that he had witnessed wild orgies in the luxurious mansion.

Carlos told me that Gloria was an addict.

The lying little turd. I read the first two melodramatic paragraphs, citing drunken parties and drug taking, before tearing the paper to shreds.

Wannabe Tom would get his come-uppance for sure. I doubted that he would be giving many more interviews *after* he was sued for defamation of character.

Next morning Detective Shawnessey paid me a visit. He wanted to be the first to inform me that Gloria was a regular cocaine user.

'It's not true, I would have known. Are you telling me my sister was some kind of junkie?'

He gave a mirthless little bark. 'I didn't say she was a junkie. I said she was known to snort cocaine. Hardly a news flash in LA.' He rubbed his eyes wearily. 'I thought I should tell you before the wolves in the press pack got to you.'

'Why? Did you want to see my pain first-hand?'

He was actually insulted. 'I thought I made it clear to you that it's my job to investigate your sister's death, Miz O'Toole. That's what I do. I investigate.' His little blackcurrant eyes were hurt. 'I need to know everything that happened the night your sister died so I can decide if anybody should be held responsible.'

There was that word again. Responsible. 'Is somebody always responsible, Detective?'

His eyes held mine. 'Not always. Sometimes it's just circumstances. Nobody's fault. Just circumstances.'

I had been ringing Ballyshannon for two days without getting an answer. I finally got fat Marion. She was only too happy to tell me that Turlough was in Dublin for a full week, organizing a protest march against EC farming policies that were crippling small farmers. Or even big muscular ones like him.

According to her he had taken his favourite cow with him.

I held my tongue.

Mother was in Termonfeckin with the Irish Countrywoman's Association. Learning conversational French.

'Don't tell me. The twins are up in Belfast doing a peace course.'

'No! They are kick-boxing in the church hall.'

'Oh. So Hawthorn Farm hasn't completely fallen to pieces without me, then?'

'Oh no, Mrs O'Toole, we haven't even missed you. Everything is going like clockwork. I've never seen things go so smoothly. And the stock are all . . .'

'Yes. Yes. Thank you, Marion. Tell them I called.'

'Mrs O'Toole?'

'What is it, f . . . Marion?'

'I'm sorry for your trouble.'

Me too, fat Marion. Me too.

It was hard to believe that, of all people, it was Bobby Kennedy who was the greatest support to me after Gloria's death. I'd go so far as to call him irreplaceable, which was more than could be said for me, apparently. He spent hours in Gloria's study, fielding media inquiries and sorting through all outstanding business. He even dealt with the peculiar, not to mention truly bizarre, callers without a word of complaint. If it had been me, I might have strangled the man who wormed his way through the press cordon *and* the security men to arrive at the door insisting that he had a right to see Gloria's body, as they had been lovers in a previous life.

Caesar and Cleopatra, apparently.

Mrs Danvers was kept occupied finding places to put the hundreds of floral wreaths that were arriving daily. She filled the living-room to capacity, before resorting to lining the marble-floored hallway with the overflow. It got so every time you walked along it you had the eerie sensation of passing through an overcrowded funeral home.

'So many tributes. So beautiful.' Her voice was close to breaking.

I hated the wreaths. I hadn't known you could get funeral wreaths in the shape of a Packard Bell computer. Or a fountain pen. And certainly not of a packed court room.

I began to live in dread of one arriving in the shape of Rick Hein. In the buff.

'Perhaps we should have specified no flowers,' I ventured gently.

'No flowers?' Mrs Danvers was horrified.

She practically threw my dinner at me that night.

Cards of sympathy arrived by the vanload. And telegrams. Gloria seemed to have had friends all over the world.

'She was universally loved,' Mrs Danvers said, which wasn't quite true, but it was a comfort to see the esteem she had been held in by so many people in the film and TV industry. Even if some of them were sending wreaths that best belonged on a bonfire.

I pointed out a particularly vulgar-looking one to Bobby. It resembled a woman in some stage of undress. 'What is that one supposed to be, do you think?' I asked him.

'It's an Emmy,' he said, his face expressionless.

LA Blues

'Get on a plane and come straight back home after the funeral.' Mother was back from Termonfeckin with her French diploma. 'You don't belong in that place. Get back here where you belong.'

'Mother, I . . .'

Turlough came on the line. 'You stay there until the will is read,' he said. 'She's bound to have left you a few bob. Maybe she's left the twins something. She has no family of her own, has she? No husband to speak of.' He made it sound like an indictment.

I didn't reply.

'It won't kill you to hang around for another few weeks or so. Do you hear me?'

When I didn't answer he became worried. 'Don't you do anything stupid, now, like rushing home or anything like that. Think of the twins.'

I had been thinking of the twins quite a bit lately. Trying to work out where their future might lie. And mine. I wasn't sure if it was in Ballyshannon. But where, then? Ballyshannon was all the twins knew. It was their home. I wondered if they had been told about Gloria's tragic death.

Neither Mother nor Turlough appeared to be at all grieved by it. Turlough had never met her, of course, and she and Mother had never got on. Just the same, I would have expected her to be a little saddened by the tragedy. Show some sign of remorse or regret for the way she had treated Gloria.

She didn't.

Two sombre Mass cards did eventually arrive in the post. The one from Mother read: *May the Sacred Heart of Jesus grant you eternal peace.*

This from the woman who had ensured that Gloria would know no peace while she lived with her. And precious little afterwards.

Turlough's card said: *The Holy Sacrifice of the Mass will be offered for the repose of the soul of . . . Gloria Mullin.* Her name filled in, in leaky green biro. In the same leaky green biro he had signed his full name, Turlough O'Toole, as if there was some danger of him being mistaken for one of the Hollywood Turloughs.

Mother refused, flat out, to come to the funeral. 'I've seen enough of that place on television.'

I tried to assure her that Gloria's Beverly Hills home was a warm haven of good taste, a harbour of tranquillity, filled with French (I emphasized) period furniture and other spectacular antiques.

She wasn't interested. 'What about that dark chap? The one we saw on television? Is he still around?'

Yes, Mother, he's still around. He's very much around.

'Mother . . .?'

'Has the will been read yet?' Turlough was on the line.

Carlos wanted to send Mother a first-class airline ticket. He assumed that a lack of funds was the reason for her reluctance to attend the funeral of her first-born. It took me ages to convince him that what seemed like a complete lack of interest on her part was precisely that.

'But it's her daughter? Doesn't she care? Doesn't she feel anything?'

Carlos behaved as if Mother was rejecting him, not Gloria. He seemed to be doubly humiliated because Bobby was staying with us, which meant that he was privy to all our conversations. Bobby's good opinion carried great weight with Carlos. And here we were, in a mansion packed with tributes from all over the world, yet Gloria's mother was still holding out against coming to the funeral. Carlos's distress was painful to see.

'She's probably too depressed to travel,' Bobby said, when Carlos went on and on about Mother's reluctance to attend.

I was seeing a whole new side of Bobby lately; he had become a true friend indeed. He was always there to assist. And now he was saying exactly the right thing to help Carlos. If he kept this up I would be forced to forgive him all those embarrassing gropes, all those quick feels when he thought nobody was looking.

'That's it,' I said gratefully. 'She's probably depressed. And another thing you have to remember is she's not a young woman.'

'I guess.' Carlos sounded far from convinced.

'This broccoli is something else, Maddy. Fresh from the garden, is it? Vegetables are only worth eating when they are this fresh. Far too many chefs spoil them by overcooking. You know that guy in the Hilton?' He turned to Carlos. 'He reckons that if more people took the trouble to grow their own vegetables we would all live to be a hundred.'

Apart from the horrendous scenario he was evoking, Bobby was scoring new points with me by the minute for doing his best to distract Carlos.

But Carlos was like a dog with a bone. He refused to let go of the subject. 'We've got to get her here for the funeral. It's important.'

It took me ages to realize that this was his way of assuaging *his* guilt. If he could have Gloria's estranged mother weeping over her coffin he would have done something truly remarkable for Gloria. It would be his posthumous gift to her.

'Are you deaf? I said I'm not going,' Mother insisted.

And I knew she meant it. She might be broadening her horizons by travelling to Termonfeckin to learn conversational French, but she'd be damned if she'd fly to LA for Gloria's funeral.

That evening I tried consoling Carlos by regaling him with little tales of our childhood on Hawthorn Farm, leaving out the ones that might well have been penned by Edgar Allan Poe. But it was difficult to explain growing up there to someone who hadn't actually experienced it. I did my best to keep things light. Even amusing. That had always been my way, my mode of survival.

But it's quite difficult to describe someone dying from blood poisoning in a jocular fashion without sounding completely heartless.

Bobby stopped eating. 'The poor guy! But why didn't he call a doctor? Nobody should die from blood poisoning now.'

'That was twenty years ago and he couldn't stand doctors. He wouldn't have one near him. Brought us up the same way.'

'According to Gloria a whole team of doctors fought for his life,' Carlos said.

'Gloria!' I shook my head.

'That wasn't true?' Bobby asked. 'I think she told me that story as well. How they fought through the night. And he finally breathed his last as dawn was breaking.'

'He died at midnight.'

'That was Gloria,' Carlos said. 'She didn't believe in letting the truth get in the way of a good story.'

'Not even one doctor?' Bobby asked.

'After he was dead, maybe. Gloria was always a fantasizer. A born story-teller.'

Carlos nodded. 'Tell me about it.'

'Well, how long have you got?'

He gave me a little half-smile, his head tilted to one side. And my heart did a quick somersault. 'I didn't mean it that way,' he said.

'I know what you meant.' I looked down at the table. At his beautiful hands resting on the white cloth. At the way his long, slim fingers curved around the gold-rimmed plate the way they used to curve around my face when we made love.

He was suddenly aware of my eyes on him and the atmosphere between us became so charged that I knew Bobby had to notice it.

He didn't. 'Did you see that neat wreath from Stephen? And his card? I thought it was just about the coolest, most attractive one of all,' he was saying.

'Excuse me,' I said and hurried from the room.

'Oh I'm sorry, Maddy. I didn't mean to upset you,' he called after me.

He hadn't upset me. I had upset myself. I was covered in shame. My sister was barely cold and here I was, lusting after her man all over again. If Bobby hadn't been there God only knows what might have happened when Carlos passed me the salt. I knew I'd have to get away from the mansion or I'd condemn myself to burn in hell for all eternity.

I rang Ballyshannon. Nobody answered, although I let it ring for ages and willed someone to pick it up. Mother must have been out. Where could she be this time? Out line-dancing? The woman was turning into a social animal since I had left. And where the hell was Turlough at this hour? Seeing to his favourite cow, no doubt. It was all go in Ballyshannon these days.

The long delay in the funeral arrangements was making everyone jittery, especially me. I began dreaming about Gloria. Every night the same dream.

I knew she was in the pool, but hard as I tried I couldn't find her. I swam and swam, underwater, until my lungs began to protest. I rose to the surface, long enough to catch my breath, before diving again. This time I kept going, ignoring the burning pain in my chest, until I spotted her. But when I reached out to her the water clouded over with blood.

I burst to the surface screaming her name and suddenly she was there, right in front of me, laughing. Holding up a dead baby. 'Tricked ya, Maddy!'

I woke up wailing like a banshee.

Apart from my nightmares I also had the worry of my growing bump. I seemed to have become noticeably pregnant overnight. If things were delayed much longer my condition would be obvious to everyone who came to the funeral. And it wouldn't take a mathematical genius to work out that it couldn't possibly be my husband's child I was carrying. I might be of no interest to Hollywood, but there were some reporters here who would kill to get some dirt on Carlos Garcia.

It was Mrs Danvers who saved the day yet again. She produced a long black skirt, and finely pleated blouse, which more than disguised my bump. The only drawback was that dressed like this I looked like a mirror image of her. A little smaller and quite a bit younger, of course, but a chilling copy just the same.

'Are you uncomfortable with so much black?' she asked, seeing my expression.

Before I could reply she reached into her drawer and came up with a cream lace cravat, which she pinned at my throat.

The look was complete. I was now Mrs Danvers mark two.

'You look wonderful.' Her eyes were glowing with admiration.

When I walked into the kitchen Carlos did a double-take. 'Maddy? What the hell are you playing at?'

Dong almost dropped his wok. Then he began to giggle uncontrollably.

Mrs Danvers silenced both of them with a look.

When Barbara Farrington arrived to offer her condolences she took one look at me and burst into tears. 'Oh my dear.' She dabbed at her eyes with a mauve tissue. 'You don't have to wear deep mourning here. This is America! You're in the land of the free now. Get rid of those nasty old black things and get yourself into some pretty clothes. Have you seen Ralph Lauren's Polo collection yet? Made for you, my dear.'

'I can't,' I said sadly, thinking of my growing bump.

'Oh my dear, I understand. In Ireland it's *de rigueur* to wear deepest mourning for a full year, isn't it?'

I didn't tell her that in Ireland nowadays you'd be blinded by the array of colours at a funeral. Even the widows wore scarlet.

'I do admire you for respecting your long-held traditions. I couldn't do it.' She shuddered. 'Unrelieved black is a tad creepy for daywear, I find.' She darted a quick look at Mrs Danvers, who was standing directly behind me in an outfit that mirrored mine down to the last black pleat.

She held open the door for Barbara to leave, her eyes cold as flint.

But Barbara wouldn't be hurried. She turned to kiss me warmly on both cheeks. I had once watched her bid goodbye to Gloria like this. In this very hallway. My eyes began to fill up.

She caught my hand. 'Stiff upper lip, dear. Make Gloria proud of you. You keep your dignity. Show this town how a *true* lady behaves. It's been a long time since we had real class here.' She turned to go. 'If there's anything I can do, anything at all, you call me. I mean it, Madeline.'

I believed her. It was just hard to think this was the same woman who was rumoured to have shrunken heads nailed to her office wall, as a warning to junior executives who might be considering slacking off.

Barbara's silver limo was just pulling away when Detective Shawnessey arrived to tell us that Gloria's body was finally being released for burial.

Even he paled when he saw Mrs Danvers and me, standing side by side in the wreath-filled hallway.

Carlos came down the stairs at a run. 'Any further

developments in your inquiries, Detective?' He sounded sarcastic.

'You'll be the first to know,' Shawnessey said, his eyes still fixed on what must have appeared to him to be twin Mrs Danverses, standing amid a mountain of funeral wreaths.

Bobby was acting as family attorney. When Turlough heard this his first thought was that Bobby would be handing over whatever money Gloria might have left us.

What it actually meant was that he was empowered to ask for whatever information the investigators had gathered regarding Gloria's death. And, more important, the full details of the post-mortem examination.

He sat, grim-faced, in the flower-laden living-room, imparting as much information as he thought we could stomach right then.

It wasn't a lot.

There was apparently some unexplained bruising on Gloria's body. It was this that had caused Shawnessey to become suspicious. Bobby had an old school friend who was now a pathologist at a big teaching hospital back in Boston. He had sent him the relevant post-mortem slides and asked for his professional opinion.

His friend assured him that such *contusions* were not all that unusual in certain drowning victims. Especially those who had died in swimming pool accidents. It appeared that private swimming pools were not the safe playgrounds people assumed them to be.

'Certainly not when they're unlit after dark.'

Bobby's friend was scathing. 'Add to that the abuse of alcohol and other social drugs, and you have a potential death trap. An accident waiting to happen.'

He had collated data from hundreds of similar autopsies and a surprising number of victims had bruises that matched Gloria's.

'They are acquired when the victim panics and attempts to pull him- or herself from the water by grasping at the hard surround. Their inebriated state affects their judgement. Instead of swimming towards the safety of the steps, they reach out time and again for the water-drenched lip of the pool. Safety studies have shown that the people in the pool would attempt over and over again to pull themselves out of the water at impossible angles, regardless of how close they were to the steps.'

I tried not to cry.

Gloria's blood alcohol level was .19 per cent, which meant nothing to me.

Bobby saw my puzzled expression. 'That's almost double the .10 per cent that is the legal definition of driving under the influence of alcohol by the California Vehicular Code. It's a credit to her resilience that she battled so hard with so much alcohol in her bloodstream. But she couldn't have been thinking straight. She must have struggled for a long time, pulling herself up, then falling back into the water again. That's what caused the bruising on her arms and chest. It's likely that she continued doing this, until she was overcome by exhaustion.' He sighed.

He thought he was doing us a favour telling us this. Setting our minds at rest. Proving that it *was* just a careless accident. Nobody was to blame. He was absolving us from all guilt, Carlos and me.

What he didn't know was that he was sounding the death knell of whatever relationship there was between us. How could we ever touch each other again, knowing that the last time we were together Gloria had been fighting for her life in that cold water.

We couldn't keep enough distance between us as we sat listening to Bobby.

If Carlos had moved any further away from me he would have been sitting on the terrace.

I had only just closed my eyes that night when the nightmare came back. This time I could see big purple bruises standing out on Gloria's arms and chest.

'Help me, Maddy,' she was calling.

Funeral Surprises

The funeral passed in a blur, thanks to Mrs Danvers and her magic pills. I can clearly remember Bobby's hand gripping my arm, and Carlos on my other side clinging to my hand as if his sanity depended on it.

I recollect an array of black-suited men, hired to keep photographers at bay, walking in front of us like soldiers on parade.

But nothing else.

Oh there was one other thing, or rather two. I can remember Lou Anne Bechal's breasts, mostly because every time a photographer appeared Lou Anne blocked him with her chest. Some day I may even get to thank her for that.

Back at the house there were two lines of highly polished limos, parked bumper to bumper on either side of the driveway. People whose names I recognized from the flower wreaths and beautifully printed cards of sympathy now offered their hands in condolence.

I was the one who had insisted on a wake. Even if it was to be held the wrong way round. After the burial, instead of before. My sister deserved a wake. I wanted her life recorded, celebrated, by a gathering of her friends. Even her enemies, if it came to that.

To my surprise it was Carlos who did all the arranging. Not Bobby or Herman, or even her other two partners: Philip and the mysterious Nathan, who

I was fully convinced didn't exist at all, because nobody ever saw him in the flesh. He did everything by phone or fax. He and Gloria used to communicate daily by e-mail. When I told her my theory that he himself was a computer and not flesh and blood at all, she broke into gales of laughter.

'You may have something there, Maddy,' she said and e-mailed him again.

He sent an e-mail on the day of the funeral to say that he was unavoidably detained. And four magnums of vintage champagne, accompanied by four perfect tiger lilies. I don't know what this said, except perhaps that if he was a machine he was one with great style.

Everywhere you looked that day there were beautiful people. Famous faces. Actors and actresses, each one more attractive and gorgeous than the next. There were writers and movie moguls, and producers and directors, all dressed to kill, or perhaps bury is a more fitting word.

And, of course, there was Herman, who always looked as if he bought his suits ready crumpled in the Oxfam shop. Today's off-white mess being no exception.

Everybody raised a glass to Gloria. Most people had a story about her. Usually funny. And extremely well told. Sometimes acted out as well. She would have liked that.

As the afternoon wore on, some of the guests began to bitch and gossip, quite viciously, about those who hadn't made it to the funeral. Or the wake. Gloria would have enjoyed that even more.

When a bearded, teary-eyed man, whose name I can't recall, whipped out a flute and began playing a traditional Irish tune that was presently in vogue in Hollywood, as well as everywhere else on the planet, there wasn't a dry eye in the house. Except mine.

Gloria had hated this particular tune. 'Turn off that fuckin' crap,' she had screeched only a day or so before her death, when she heard it being played, on MTV.

When the bearded man finished his virtuoso performance I thanked him. 'Gloria would have loved that rendition,' I lied.

My jaws were beginning to ache from smiling at people I didn't know. And I was finding it unbelievably tiring, being stared at all the time.

I was in my room looking down at the uniformed drivers polishing the already spotless limos, when there was a soft tap on the door behind me. 'Yes?'

Carlos came in looking tired and heavy-eyed. He had finally discarded the dark glasses. 'How are you doing, Maddy?'

'To tell you the truth, I'm exhausted.'

We were both still guarded with each other. Carefully avoiding any real eye contact that might lead to anything more intimate. Cursory glances were acceptable. Quick shuftis from the corner of the eye, but nothing more. Certainly nothing that might incriminate us. Expose us as the lustful adulterers we knew ourselves to be.

'What about that Shawnessey going around asking people questions?' He stared down at the hard-working limo drivers.

'I didn't notice.'

'Oh. That's okay then.'

Some of the drivers had given up. It was far too hot to be polishing cars.

'Things will work out, Maddy,' Carlos said.
'You think so?'
'Bound to.'
We might have been discussing the weather, for all the emotion either of us showed. I had heard Turlough inject more passion into a talk on bovine TB.
'Carlos, I think I should tell you that I'm considering . . .'
The big brown eyes looked directly into mine for the first time and I was done for. My mind went completely blank.
He waited.
'. . . I . . . I've forgotten what I was going to say.'
'Maddy.' His hand reached out.
Bobby burst in without knocking. 'Did you see that bastard Shawnessey? The nerve of that guy! Walking in, just like that, to a private funeral?'
'Maddy didn't notice him.'
'Didn't you, honey? Oh poor Maddy. Poor little Maddy.' He put his arms around me, then grinned boyishly. 'Or not so little. You're putting on weight.' His hand slid downwards to check.
'Jaysus, Bobby, what is it with you? Even at a funeral?' I pushed him away.
'Sorry, Maddy.' He was genuinely contrite. 'I don't even know I'm doing it. Most of the time.'
'It's a disgusting habit.' He had gone way down in my estimation again.
Carlos got the wrong end of the stick. 'Bobby, everyone knows better than to tell a woman she's putting on weight.'
'Maddy doesn't care about stuff like that. She's not vain. Why else would she be dressed like this?' He

lifted the sleeve of my borrowed blouse. When he saw my expression he immediately tried to backtrack. 'I didn't mean that the way it sounds. I meant that you wouldn't waste your time trying to look better.'

'I'd drop it, Bobby, if I were you.' Carlos laughed for the first time since Gloria's accident.

Bobby wasn't stupid. 'What about Detective Shawnessey, what's he playing at?' he asked quickly.

Carlos was serious again. 'The guy's nuts. Off his trolley, if you ask me.'

'He's determined to make something more out of Gloria's accident,' I said. 'He must have little to do with his time.'

'He's just being a cop. They're creatures of habit. Give them an unexplained death and they automatically take a long hard look at the next of kin. It's what they do. It's nothing personal. It doesn't mean anything, it's just procedure. Besides, you two have nothing to worry about. You have an airtight alibi. Sorry to be so pedantic, but that's pretty important where cops are concerned. All Shawnessey has to do is ask anyone at the club. Isn't that where you two went after the restaurant?'

Neither of us answered. Carlos stared fixedly at something outside the window.

'Well? Won't the people in the club remember seeing you?'

'Maybe not.' Carlos cleared his throat.

'What do you mean, maybe not? People do tend to remember seeing you, Carlos.'

'Tell him.' I was tired of this cat-and-mouse nonsense.

'We weren't in the club, we were in Nicky Styles's house.'

'Nicky Styles? But he's in New York.'

Carlos didn't reply.

Bobby's expression was like one of those cartoon characters when they finally tumble to what's been happening around them. He froze, his high-roofed Kennedy mouth hanging open like a simpleton's.

Finally he found his voice. 'You two? In Nicky Styles's bungalow?' For a supposedly smart lawyer Bobby could be pretty slow on the uptake sometimes. And just as well he hadn't gone in for acting. Because, hard as he tried, he couldn't hide the look of disgust that was spreading across his face. 'I don't believe it.'

And whom did he vent his anger on? Whom did he look to blame?

'Maddy? What the hell has been going on here?'

'Would you excuse me, Bobby? Nature calls.' It hadn't, of course, but I scuttled into the bathroom anyway and locked the door behind me.

It was a spineless act without a doubt. But I was tired of feeling guilty. Of being responsible. Carlos had experienced as much pleasure as I had that night in the grubby little bungalow. Let him shoulder the guilt for a change. I was weary. Fed up. And pregnant. Where was his share of the burden? And anyway, who did Bobby think he was, with his look of moral superiority on his haughty Kennedy face? What was it to him what Carlos and I got up to in Nicky Styles's or whoever's bungalow it was. Hadn't he tried to grope me practically every time we met? Not Nicky Styles, Bobby. If it weren't for all those years of playing school hockey against the amazons of the Holy Faith, my right arm wouldn't be half as strong as it was and Bobby's sly gropes might have turned into occasions of sin. For him.

And yet, despite his roving hands and his sometimes lecherous eye, he did tend to have the aura of a defrocked priest about him. Probably something to do with his long-tailed Kennedy ancestry. Somewhere in his background there was bound to be a bishop or two. Whatever, I couldn't bear to see his face when he found out that I was having Carlos's baby.

'When were you planning on telling me? When the kid was in Junior High?'

'Take it easy, Bobby,' Carlos drawled.

'And Maddy? I can't believe it of her. Anyone but Maddy.'

I flushed the toilet again so I wouldn't hear the next bit. Then I was sorry, because they sounded as if they were about to fight.

I pressed my ear against the door jamb.

'. . . what *about* the other chicks?'

The cistern began to fill noisily. Damn and blast. I had to open the door a crack to hear what was happening.

'How many times have I saved your ass, Carlos? Did I ever flinch? Ever let you down? Point the finger? But you didn't think you could tell me? *You and Maddy*? I can't believe it. It's . . . it's . . . practically incest!'

'Thanks, buddy, And you wonder why I didn't tell you?'

The cistern began to rumble again. I punched it and kicked it into silence.

'What's gonna happen now? What the hell are you gonna do? Gloria's *sister*?'

The cistern hissed accusingly.

I could hear Carlos's voice pleading with Bobby, but I couldn't make out the actual words. I finally swallowed my pride and swept back into the room – just in time to see the door closing behind Bobby.

What *are* you gonna do, Carlos? I asked. But not out loud.

Instead, I said, 'I suppose you're sorry I ever came here?'

'No, of course not.'

But he could have said it with a little more conviction, I thought. And what else could he have said, anyway? He could hardly say, 'Eff off back to Ireland and take your bump with you, my life has fallen apart since you came here.' He might be thinking it, he probably *was* thinking it, but he would never put it into words. That wasn't his style.

Then I realized that he hadn't finished speaking.

'The baby is the one bright, shining light in all this darkness,' he was saying.

It was such a beautiful thing to say. It meant a lot to me. It would have meant a lot more if I hadn't heard him say it in the very first episode of *People in Jeopardy* to his then fiancée who was about to be killed with her unborn child by the wicked men who would turn Rick Hein into the brave crusading lawyer he was to become. And a man who was, for ever after, terrified to commit long-term to one woman.

'. . . a beautiful new life, Maddy.'

'What if it's ugly?'

He thought I was joking. He caught me to him and for the second time that afternoon he laughed out loud.

I stood there and forced a smile, thinking about the twins.

That's the picture Mrs Danvers must have seen when she pushed open the door.

If looks could kill, Carlos and I would have both been corpses. Lifeless cadavers stretched on the hundred per cent wool carpet.

'You have a visitor downstairs, Madam.' She finally spoke. 'From Ireland. Ballyshannon, I believe.'

I froze.

'A woman?' I gasped.

'A man. He's in the living-room.' She slammed the door viciously.

Welcome to Hollywood...

That walk down the stairs, the day of Gloria's funeral, was without a doubt the longest and loneliest walk of my whole life. Carlos had offered to accompany me, but I said no. I had to face Turlough alone. He had to be told the truth. I had never loved him. I had wasted fifteen years of my life because I hadn't been brave enough to admit this. Too intimidated by him. And Mother. He had never loved me; I had been nothing more than an accessory to Hawthorn Farm. The farm was his one true love. Even fat Marion was only a diversion. The farm was his life. Well, he could have it. Gloria's invitation had opened a door for me, I had stepped through it and I wasn't going back.

I couldn't tell what would happen with Carlos and me. I knew it was unlikely that we would spend the rest of our days together. He was a big Hollywood star; he belonged with the glitterati, among the glitz and glamour of show business. I belonged . . . I wasn't sure where. But I knew it wasn't back in my old life, being treated like a skivvy. I had changed too much for that. I was a different woman now. No longer the little mouse who had left Ballyshannon in the itchy tweed suit that her husband had chosen for her, with the fuzzy perm that she hadn't wanted in the first place.

I would be honest with Turlough for the very first time. Let him see my growing bump. I wasn't ashamed of it. This baby had been conceived in freedom. Not to mention the hottest, most orgasmic sex imaginable. How could I forget that?

I took a deep breath, threw my shoulders back, and walked into the crowded living-room.

'Maddy!' Father Brennan held out his arms.

I sucked in my stomach so hard it practically hit my spine.

'Well, let me get a look at you!' Father Brennan held me at arm's length.

I held my breath.

'Have you put on a bit of weight?'

He caught the look of terror on my face.

'Ah, you're all the same, you young ones, terrified of a bit of flesh.'

'Ha, ha.' I laughed mirthlessly.

'Well do you know what, Maddy? I don't know when I saw you looking so well. Hollywood agrees with you. You're looking robust. And the foot is obviously better.'

The foot? What was he on about?

'But who on earth persuaded you to have that little altar boy haircut? Ah, sure it'll grow out in time, please God. And what are you doing dressed all in black like an old biddy? There's no call to wear black nowadays. Your sister wouldn't want that, Lord have mercy on her. She's up there with Our Lady now – writing hymns for the angels, I don't doubt. Glorifying God's great heaven.'

He made it sound as if Gloria had made a positive career choice.

'Just look at all these lovely girls in their lovely clothes.' His eyes lit up as a bevy of miniskirted beauties passed by, their hemlines barely skimming their tanned thighs.

The girls were all smiling provocatively. At someone behind us. One of them throwing coy glances from beneath her spider-like lashes.

I didn't even have to turn. 'This is Carlos Garcia, Father. A friend . . . of Gloria's.'

He swung around. 'Rick Hein, is it? I don't believe it. Shure don't I watch you every week in *People in Jeopardy*! Wouldn't miss it for an audience with His Holiness!' He chortled. 'You're a fine-looking man off screen.' He pumped Carlos's hand. 'Tell me something, Rick . . . er . . . Carlos, you know that young girl who plays your secretary, the one with the red hair, is she as nice in real life as she is on television?'

'She's over there, by the bar. Would you like to meet her?'

Father Brennan actually blushed. 'Would it be possible?'

Carlos widened his eyes at me and led him away.

I let my stomach out.

After the first shock of seeing Father Brennan standing among the rich and famous I was glad to have him here, despite having to hold my stomach in every time he turned in my direction. His unquestioning belief that Gloria was now in a far better place was a great comfort, even if I didn't altogether share it. His simple words were a pleasure to my ears, after all the fancy logic I'd had to listen to about the frailties of human existence. Or the over-the-top quotes about karma and dharma and Buddha that had been repeated over and over again all day long by people who probably only cared about how much cocaine they could shove up their noses.

Father Brennan's face got redder and redder, as he chatted to the glamorous young men and women who filled the room.

Without exception, they all adored him.

'He's sooo cute,' one young starlet squealed. 'Don't you just love Russian priests!'

Gloria would have enjoyed this. Old Father Brennan becoming the star attraction at her wake. The man everyone wanted to meet. Press the flesh with.

'Could I see your rosaries, Father? My grandmother used to say her rosaries every day. But I think she called it the Angelus. Sooo cute!'

Another nubile young thing pouted in frustration as she was dislodged from Father Brennan's side by one of the girls who had been ogling Carlos earlier on.

'Upstaged by a priest.' Carlos grinned at Bobby.

'Yeah. And a Russian one at that.' Bobby was still feeling edgy.

But even he fell under Father Brennan's spell. They were discussing Rose Kennedy's unshakeable faith in the Almighty when Carlos interrupted them to ask Father Brennan to stay to dinner.

Mrs Danvers bared her teeth like a rabid bull terrier. 'I won't serve him. I refuse.' She also refused to say why. Two of the waitresses who were catering the wake agreed to stay on. At double their usual rate.

Blissfully unaware of the ruckus he was causing behind the scenes, Father Brennan continued to introduce himself to all and sundry, asking them questions even the *National Inquirer* might hesitate to put to them.

'You look familiar now. Are you on television?' he

asked a world-famous movie director, who liked nothing better than to appear in *Hello!* magazine amid the exotic splendour of his Moroccan palace. 'Oh I see. A director? Well, I suppose everyone can't be a star. Tell me now, what exactly does directing entail?' He linked arms with the notoriously egocentric man, leading him away from his little brigade of sycophants.

I thought the famous director would rebuff him in seconds, but when I next saw them they were laughing and chatting together like old school chums who had so much to catch up on that they had no time for anyone else in the room. Even the great man's fourth wife was dismissed when she attempted to interrupt them.

'He's been offered a walk-on in two separate movies.' Bobby was thawing out.

'He got a better offer from Kate Lubitch,' Herman announced. 'I think I'm gonna sign the bastard.'

'You leave that priest alone,' I warned them. 'Who's Kate Lubitch?' I asked Carlos.

'You don't wanna know.'

He was still fascinated by Father Brennan, but then everybody was. He was the star turn, entertaining each person he met. He worked the room like a professional, pocketing phone numbers by the dozen.

'Shame he missed Detective Shawnessey,' Bobby said drily. 'He would have gotten his number all right.'

'I got it.' Herman took out a huge filofax. 'It's 911.'

Even Bobby laughed.

Everyone Father Brennan spoke to ended up smiling. He addressed them all in exactly the same manner, from the twittering micro-clad starlets to the dourest cigar-chomping moguls who could destroy careers with a flick of a gold-bedecked wrist. They were all the same to him. He interrupted private conversations to introduce himself, his big countryman's hand offered high and low in warm friendship.

Before they left, people searched him out to say goodbye, shaking his hand as if they had known him all their lives.

He stood on the wide front steps, like Moses on the mountain, waving farewell to each departing car.

'Come in, Father, there are photographers all over the place,' I called from the shelter of the doorway.

'Ah shure they're only doing their job.' He dismissed my concerns and continued waving to an elegant redheaded woman, whose name kept escaping me. Although she seemed to be everywhere I turned.

'God bless you, Kate. Keep in touch.' He gave her a Pontiff-like wave, both arms bent at the elbows, two hands spread wide, as if he was imparting a blessing.

'Who *is* she?' I asked Bobby as the limo crept away, ferrying the ubiquitous Kate. 'Was she a good friend of Gloria's?'

'Not really.'

'Carlos, who is she?'

He grinned mischievously. 'She's a well-known Madam. Gloria used her once as a consultant on a series she was writing about hookers.'

'She's a hooker and you invited her to my sister's wake?'

He frowned. 'Gloria liked her. They liked each other. Didn't you see how upset she was at the funeral? I though she was gonna topple over into the grave.'

'Yeah, she was pretty tanked up all right,' Bobby said.

'Shut up, Bobby. And she's not a hooker, she runs an escort agency down in Malibu.'

'Well, thank God for that. She's not a hooker, then? She only prostitutes other women.' I couldn't keep the disgust out of my voice.

'You should have told me you wanted the mourners vetted for moral turpitude. If you had specified non-sinners only, you'd have had a pretty thin guest list, Maddy. You might even have had to stay away yourself.' He turned on his heel.

'You bastard! You come back here and say that to my face.'

Mrs Danvers came running along the hallway, her face even paler than usual. She looked as if she had seen a ghost.

'I could have sworn I heard her voice, coming from this direction.' She clutched her chest. 'It's all this reminiscing, it's too much for me. Excuse me, Madam.' She hurried away.

Too much for her? How did she think *I* was feeling? I thought I had discovered paradise. Now my sister was dead, Carlos had turned against me, Bobby thought I was a slut and the baby was doing bouncies against my bladder. And if I wasn't mistaken, Father Brennan had consumed far more alcohol than was good for him. If not something worse. He was acting in a very strange manner, for a priest. Talking about camera angles to a posturing director and befriending a hooker? A madam from Malibu? Asking her to keep in touch?

All I needed to crown my day was for Detective Shawnessey to come back and cuff me.

I had just stepped outside to draw some fresh air into my lungs when there was a sudden clattering noise above my head. I shielded my eyes from the sun to look up.

A huge silver helicopter was hovering over the mansion, the evening sun glancing off its whirling blades as it manoeuvred itself into position. I was wondering what for, when I saw the telephoto lens jutting out of the open doorway.

Then Father Brennan was standing directly in front of me. He raised his arms high in the air and I thought he was shooing the photographers away. Protecting me from them. He wasn't.

He was waving at them. 'Ahoy, the ship!' he called out in delight.

I ran into the house and up the stairs to seek the quiet sanctity of my bedroom.

The Camera Never Lies

'Where on earth did you disappear to last evening?' Father Brennan was sitting at the head of the long table in the big dining-room, eating his way through a mountain of scrambled eggs.

'I . . . I fell asleep.' What the hell was he doing here? He was supposed to leave last night. He had told all and sundry that it was crucial that he get back to his visiting parish by ten p.m. at the very latest. Of course, he hadn't specified which night.

He answered my questioning look. 'I gave Father Gonzales a ring. He said I should stay on here with you, it being so late and all. I don't drive too well in the dark, as you well know, Maddy.'

He didn't drive too well in daylight either, but that had never stopped him before.

'The morning traffic will have thinned out by now, Father,' I hinted broadly.

'No rush. When God made time he made plenty of it.' He shovelled another mound of scrambled eggs into his mouth. 'Sit down, Maddy. Have some breakfast.' He spoke as if he were the genial host and I the guest. 'You look drained. It's probably that awful black yoke you are wearing.'

I wasn't rude enough to remark on the long black cassock, which he still favoured after many another priest had discarded *it* as essential day wear.

He finished his eggs and began to help himself to

my favourite hot waffles, piling them one on top of another on his plate, until only two remained on the heated serving dish. 'Have some breakfast Maddy.' He gestured towards them.

'I'm not hungry, Father,' I lied.

Mrs Danvers was nowhere to be seen. I hoped she hadn't quit. She had been on the verge at least twice yesterday that I knew of. But then yesterday had been a bad day all round for everyone who loved Gloria. Today was bound to be an improvement. The law of averages would demand that.

I poured myself some strong black coffee.

'She's a funny woman, that housekeeper. She practically bared her teeth at me when I came down for breakfast.'

Father Brennan was used to warmer receptions from middle-aged housekeepers; he was quite a pin-up among that particular confraternity in Ireland.

'All I did was ask her why someone didn't talk you out of wearing those ugly black clothes. Her reaction was a little excessive, I thought.'

He might be friendly and warm to a fault, but sensitivity had never burdened Father Brennan.

'She believes strongly in wearing black for mourning.' I piled lie upon lie. 'After all, we only buried Gloria yesterday.'

'Of course. Of course. I'll remember her in my prayers.' He was eating again. Speaking with his mouth full, his jaws bulging with sweet waffles.

Maybe that's why I couldn't tell if he was promising to remember Gloria or Mrs Danvers in his prayers.

'Was that Carlos I heard leaving at the crack of

dawn?' He poured another layer of syrup over his remaining waffles.

'Probably. He works very hard.'

'A fine-looking man.' He glanced at me.

I blew on my coffee. He had unnerved me so much, I had forgotten to leave room for the milk.

'Is that all you're having for breakfast, Maddy? Black coffee?'

I didn't answer.

'Father Gonzales is coming back to Ballyshannon with me. For the rosary crusade.'

'That's good.'

'It is. I'll be here for the full month first. So we'll be able to see a lot of each other, Maddy. Please God.'

I kept hoping I had misheard him. What with his mouth full of waffles, and his tendency to mumble, I probably had.

'I said, I'll be able to see a lot of you during the next month, Maddy.'

The baby gave me a sudden kick, making me gasp.

'What's that, Maddy?'

'Nothing, Father.'

'Who knows, I might even persuade yourself and Carlos to come over to San Cristos for a crusade meeting one of these days.'

Only if you put an Uzi to my head, I thought.

'It's a sorry place, San Cristos. Crime is rampant. The young men there are in desperate need of strong role models. Would you believe half of them carry knives? And guns! These drive-by shootings are happening every day of the week. It's a sad place altogether. Moral fibre is a dirty word there.'

'Two words,' I muttered under my breath.

'You'd be shocked to the core at the goings-on there, Maddy.'

'Would I really, Father?'

'Oh you couldn't even imagine it, a good woman like you. The girls there have relations outside of marriage without giving it a second thought. They have babies without a husband in sight. What's the matter, Maddy?'

'I need some air.' I got to my feet.

'Wait up, Maddy, I'll come with you.'

We walked in a small secluded area to the rear of the herb garden. Tall eucalyptus hedges on both sides made this the one spot on the whole property that the prying lenses of the paparazzi couldn't reach. If they didn't resort to using helicopters, that is. I shot a quick nervous glance at the sky.

Father Brennan smiled. 'I find myself doing that as well. Keep expecting it to rain. Can't get used to this constant sunshine. It's a bit unnatural to the likes of us, isn't it?'

I didn't reply.

'It's hard to believe there's snow on the ground at home,' he continued happily. 'We'll never be fit for our changeable climate when we get back.'

The baby gave me another swift reminder of its presence. 'Aah.'

'Oh I agree, Maddy. There's a lot to be said for the changing seasons and every season does bring its own beauty, but it's nice to be greeted by the sun every morning, to feel it warming your weary bones. I'm thinking to extend my stay here, until the weather improves at home. Father Gonzales says there's always a bed for me in San Cristos. The man is a saint.'

'Oh no, he can't . . . ?'

'Believe me, Maddy, he is. You're looking pale. You need to get out more. You used to be a devil for the outdoors. Your mother would say if you want to find Maddy, don't waste your time looking in the house. You'll never find *her* there, she's off over the fields somewhere.' He frowned. 'There isn't anything troubling you, is there?'

'No, Father, I haven't a care in the world.'

It seemed as if I had only just got rid of Father Brennan when Herman arrived, in the worst temper ever. 'Where's Carlos?' he snarled, without even a greeting for me.

'In the living-room.' I hurried after him. Something dreadful must have happened.

He threw a paper on to the low coffee table in front of Carlos. 'Get a look at that and tell me it's not gonna hit the fan!'

Carlos picked up the paper and studied the front page. 'So Father Brennan has made the papers? Big deal. He'll love it. He missed his vocation, for sure. He's a born actor. A natural.'

'Look closer,' Herman hissed.

Carlos held the page wide, so we could examine it together. Underneath the heading – HOLLYWOOD MOURNS GIFTED SCREEN-WRITER – there were three pictures.

Two of them taken at the funeral. These were group shots of famous faces, every one of them wearing trendy black shades and sombre expressions, while still managing to remain eminently photogenic.

The third picture was something completely

different. And it wasn't taken at the funeral as I had first thought.

This picture had an almost cinematic quality to it, its scope was so wide. In it Father Brennan was standing on the steep top step of the balustraded mansion, both arms raised high in the air, his black cassock billowing dramatically in the whirling wind generated by the out-of-shot helicopter.

It was a striking photograph, its composition worthy of a true artist. It made the old priest look as if he was pleading with the heavens for an explanation of human suffering.

Carlos shrugged. 'So what? It's pretty dramatic all right, but whom can it hurt?'

'Look closer,' Herman snorted.

I spotted it first and my breath caught in my throat.

To the left and slightly behind the dramatically posed Father Brennan there was another, smaller figure, this one much less conspicuous. It was a woman in black, the wind also blowing hard against her clothes, forcing the thin cotton to curve around her obviously pregnant stomach.

'Oh my God!' was my first reaction.

Then I read the caption. *Gloria's devoted priest berates the heavens*!

There was no mention of me. Not a word. Herman was being paranoid. Most people wouldn't even notice the figure in the background. And even if they did they would hardly be interested in a nonentity like me. They certainly wouldn't be likely to check out my pregnancy. The only people likely to be interested in that were in Ballyshannon. And they didn't subscribe to the *Hollywood Reporter*.

'What's the problem?' I asked.

'The problem?' Herman practically spat. 'The problem is all it takes is for one cur of a journo to get curious and start sniffing around. Then he'll know what a real problem is.' He pointed to Carlos.

I expected him to dismiss Herman's ravings. He didn't. He sat there looking terrified, his face paling. 'What are we gonna do, Herman?'

Herman snatched the paper from his hand. 'Start praying, that's what you'll do.'

I reached out to catch Carlos's hand. I wanted to reassure him. Tell him that nobody in Hollywood would be interested in the woman in the photo. Why would they be, when the papers were full of beautiful people, looking glamorous *and* sad all at once?

So I reached out. And he recoiled from my touch.

Now I know people say that pregnancy brings out super-sensitivity in women. And there is some truth in that. So maybe when I say he recoiled, that's a bit too strong a word. But he certainly moved away. And he looked very uncomfortable. I'd go so far as to say that he looked as if he wished I'd never been born.

Or failing that, that he had never met me. Certainly that he had never made love to me and impregnated me so that I was now in a position to destroy his public image as the mourning lover. The devastated partner of the tragic Gloria Mullin.

Even Herman's expression was less hurtful. And he was sick as a parrot.

But the man who had made passionate love to me over all those weeks and months, the man who had caused me to have many a sleepless night with his soaring libido, the man who had been the cause of my third orgasm while my sister was drowning was now, whether consciously or not, moving slowly along the big sofa and as far away from me as he could possibly get without actually leaving the room.

'This is trouble,' Herman said.

You're telling me.

'Carlos?' I said.

Well, I think you should always give a truly stunning man a second chance, especially one who can give you three orgasms in a row. Fair is fair, after all. Tit for tat and all that.

But Carlos was either stricken by sudden deafness or he chose not to hear me. The give-away nervous tic was pulsating away in his exquisitely formed jaw. I almost reached out to soothe it.

The baby gave me a warning kick. *Back off*, it said.

'Will you excuse me?' I said. 'I need the bathroom.'

Silence.

I went upstairs and lay down on the big soft bed.

I woke to find my shoes being undone, gentle hands easing them off my feet. I didn't have to open my eyes; his touch was his signature. He was the only living being who could turn the simple act of removing a woman's shoe into an erotic experience. It took every ounce of self-restraint I possessed to remain passive while he undressed me and tucked me under the sheets.

I held out until I felt his warm lips on my forehead. It was a chaste kiss.

To hell with this, I thought, life is too short.

He lost two buttons from his Gianni Versace shirt-front that night. And they never did turn up again. He said I must have swallowed them. Nonsense.

But to this day it remains one of the great unsolved mysteries of my time in the big mansion.

What happened to Carlos's Gianni Versace buttons the night before Father Brennan came to the mansion and threatened to expose my adulterous behaviour to everyone in Ballyshannon.

Confession Is Good for the Soul

'And suppose you tell me where you *got* this information from, Father?' I was playing for time, doing my best to sound indignant. Innocent people always sounded indignant. At least on *People in Jeopardy*.

'From an American newspaper, Maddy. A dependable broadsheet. Not from a misleading gossip rag, as you keep insisting. Although where I got the information from is hardly relevant.' Father Brennan's cheeks were scarlet with repressed fury. Well, even more scarlet than usual.

'Of course it's relevant! Most of the papers here are no more than gossip rags. I'm surprised you'd even read them.'

'The picture was in the *Los Angeles Times*.'

That damn photographer! Why couldn't he have taken a lousy photograph, like any normal paparazzo? But no, he had to take a photo that was so well composed that every broadsheet in the country picked it up.

'Well, there you are, Father, anything with LA on it has to be suspect.' I tried brazening it out. But it was no use. I was doomed. I knew it and he knew it. I was now trying to defend the indefensible.

'Stop this silly game right now, Maddy. If you must

know, Father Gonzales gave me the paper. He thought I might like to see my photograph on the front page of the *Los Angeles Times*. He thought it quite a coup for an Irish priest. *He* thought it might give me *pleasure*.'

'And did it?' I asked cheekily.

'Is that the way you're going to speak to me?' He looked sad.

'What about the way you're speaking to me?'

'What did you expect? Congratulations?'

'You're the one always preaching that every life is precious. A gift from God.'

'Well now, Maddy, I think there might have been a little more than God involved in the conception of this particular life.'

'What's it to you anyway?' I hated being backed into a corner.

'I'm your priest, Maddy. Your eternal soul is . . .'

'None of your business. Anyway . . . I'm an atheist.'

'Is that so? And when did this great change come about?'

'When Gloria died.'

That stopped him in his tracks. I was quite pleased with myself for coming up with that one on the spur of the moment. 'Yes, Father, I'm an atheist thank God.'

'Don't be facetious, Maddy. It doesn't become you.'

I smiled. 'Doesn't it? And what does *become* me, Father? Being the ever obedient little wife and daughter? Never questioning my elders and betters?'

'I was hoping to see a little remorse.'

'What for? For bringing a new life into the world?'

'Have you lost all shame, then? Is that what coming here has done to you?'

I stared at the floor.

'Who is the father, Maddy?'

I glanced up. 'Would you believe my husband?'

'Maddy! Don't insult my intelligence. Please.'

'Since when are you an expert on pregnancy?'

'Is it that Kennedy chap?'

I couldn't help it, I burst out laughing.

'I knew it. He has the face of a lecher. Did Gloria know about this?'

'Know about it? I'll let you in on a secret. She set it up.' I smiled. 'Cross my heart and hope to die.'

'Oh Maddy, what's to become of you?'

I cupped my bump with both hands. 'I should think that's fairly obvious.'

'How you've changed. I never thought I'd hear you speak like this.'

'Like what, Father? Telling the truth for once? Don't pretend you didn't know how unhappy I was. What life did I have? You know how they treated me.'

'Who?' He seemed genuinely shocked.

'Who? Mother and Turlough, of course! You know how I worked! From dawn to dusk.'

'No more than Turlough. Or your mother. And she's twice your age. And Turlough works harder than any three men. He set Hawthorn Farm back on its feet when everyone in the parish said it was on the road to bankruptcy.'

'Turlough! He can't even throw me a civil word. And everyone thinks he's so great.'

'Isn't he, Maddy?'

'You know nothing about him.'

'You tell me, then. What is it that I don't know about him?'

I laughed. 'Do you know about him and fat Marion McCauley?'

He sighed.

'You knew. You knew! And you did nothing about it?'

'You were sick, Maddy.'

'So would you be if your man was riding fat Marion McCauley in the milking parlour.'

'There's no call for that kind of vulgarity.' His face flamed scarlet again.

'Damn right, there isn't!'

'What about your responsibilities? Your children?'

'When were they ever my children? They're more Mother's than mine. Always were. She made every decision that was to be made in that house. I was treated like a hired hand. Worse. Hired hands get paid at the end of the day. What did I ever get? Even the twins learned to ignore me. Copied what they saw around them. I didn't even get to mother my own children.'

'Is that why you . . . ?' He gestured at my stomach.

'Slept with a man who showed me more love and tenderness than I've ever known? Yes, Father, that could be the reason.'

I could hardly tell an anointed priest that love and tenderness aside, sometimes Carlos and I were so hot for each other we could barely make it to a place of privacy. No need to upset the man any more than he already was.

'I fully understand the human need for tenderness, Maddy, but what about duty?'

'I did my duty for thirty-three years, father. Where did that get me?'

'I'll pray that you come to your senses.' He sighed.

I stuck out my chin. 'Come to my senses? What does that mean, Father? That I'll disown my baby and go back to being an unwaged slave? What about love? Where will I find that?'

'God will provide. He always does.' He nodded sagely.

'Not for me, He didn't.'

'Don't blaspheme, Maddy. Don't add that to your other sins,' he said. But his face had lost the deep angry scarlet that had so unnerved me when he arrived.

He didn't offer to stay to lunch and I didn't invite him.

'Did he upset you, Madam?' Mrs Danvers appeared out of nowhere, a black wraith, at my elbow.

'I'm okay.' I tried to sound it.

'Madam wouldn't allow a priest into the house. Under no conditions.' It was a reprimand. 'She said a priest once refused to hear her confession. She never forgave him. Or went to church again.'

Her confession? My heart did a back flip. 'Oh thank you, Mrs Danvers. What would I do without you?'

She frowned and drew back, as if she was afraid I might embrace her.

I wouldn't have dared. Although she certainly deserved a big kiss. Not that she would ever guess why. She was a Methodist. She hadn't had the benefit of a grand Catholic education. She knew nothing of the Sacrament of Penance. That great Sacrament that enables the worst sinner to confess all his or her sins and be instantly forgiven, their sins stricken from the heavenly score-board. Once they vowed never to commit them again.

And make reparation, of course, which usually meant three Hail Marys and a firm act of contrition.

'*Mea culpa*!' I struck my breast dramatically with a closed fist.

She stared blankly at me.

'Don't worry about it.' I smiled. 'It's a Catholic thing.'

She was still throwing puzzled glances over her shoulder as she went back to the more familiar ground of Dong's kitchen.

I waved happily to her.

Carlos and Bobby were in the study, still wrestling with the maze that Gloria used to call a filing system.

'Did you know that Gloria hated priests?' I asked Carlos.

He peered out from behind a mountain of paper. He looked tired, despite having his beautiful eyes accentuated by the little round glasses he only ever used as a last resort.

He pulled them off before answering, 'Gloria hated *anyone* who wasn't in the business.' He sighed.

'That's true,' Bobby agreed, a little too quickly for my liking.

'But then she hated a lot of people *in* the business as well.' Carlos smiled, leaning back in the big leather chair as if glad of any excuse to get away from sorting out Gloria's papers. 'In fact, it would be a lot easier to count the people she didn't hate, rather than those she did.'

'Remember when she first met Herman?' Bobby grinned.

They both laughed.

'You've got to understand the way Gloria was,

Maddy. She only ever liked good-looking people. Young people. It was a thing she had. Old and ugly didn't do it for Gloria.'

'Don't be so horrible.'

'I'm just being truthful. Right, Carlos?'

'Damn tootin.' Carlos still fancied himself as a bit of a cowboy. Gloria mustn't have bothered to explain to him what that meant in Ireland.

'We were in the production office when she first met Herman,' Bobby said. 'You should have seen her reaction. She nods at him and walks out. Philip runs after her. "What are you doing, Gloria? That's Carlos's agent?" '

' "Is that who he is?" She pretends to be shocked. "I thought you were holding auditions for Snow White!" ' Bobby practically fell off his chair laughing.

I stood there waiting for the punch line.

'You had to be there, Maddy,' Carlos said.

'Poor Herman. Gloria never forgave him for being so badly put together. Or maybe it was for being so much older than the rest of us. And you've got to admit he does take ugliness to a whole new dimension.'

'What a cruel thing to say. You'll burn in hell for your wicked tongue, Bobby Kennedy.'

'I'm going to hell anyway.' He shrugged, stacking a pile of papers. 'According to your friend Father Brennan.'

'What do you mean?'

'He's been on to me, telling me that if I want to atone for my sinful ways it's my solemn Catholic duty to encourage you to go back to Ballyshannon. He said I'm a disgrace to the Kennedy name for doing whatever I'm supposed to have done. I wish I knew what the hell it was. I'd like to know if I enjoyed it.'

'Who does he think he is?' Carlos was annoyed. 'What did you say to him?'

'Told him it's nothing to do with me, where Maddy chooses to live. She's a grown woman. She makes her own decisions.' He laughed. 'He practically leaped down the phone at me, so I couldn't resist. I said, "I've sold my soul to the devil anyway, earning my daily bread in Hollywood, and Maddy has a right to do the same if she wants." I thought he was going to have a fit, he got so angry.'

Carlos's eyes widened with concern. 'Can he cause trouble for you, Maddy?'

'I'm not sure,' I lied. 'He is my parish priest. In Ballyshannon that means a lot.'

'Ha. Popish thuggery! I know all about that. They're worse than the Mafia, those guys.' This was the scion of one of the most prominent Catholic families in America speaking.

But I think he was joking.

It was Bobby who phoned with the first good news we'd had in ages. He rang to say that the Medical Examiner's office was going to hold a press conference. This was as a result of the unprecedented interest in Gloria's fatal accident. There had been so much ongoing press rumour and unsubstantiated gossip that the Chief Medical Examiner had taken it upon himself to announce his findings publicly and put an end to all the speculation.

Carlos was anxious to attend the conference. The Chief Medical Examiner had shown him extraordinary courtesy by inviting him.

Bobby advised him against going. He said his

presence would only provide renewed fodder for the scandal-hungry media. 'There's not a lot happening right now, Carlos, those guys will be on the look-out for anything that might give them a hot headline.'

'But I'd like to go, I feel it would be some kind of . . . closure.'

'I'm warning you, buddy, you can't trust those bastards. They've only just moved away from your gates. They'll be watching out for some angle. Someone to point the finger at. Not because they care, but to boost their circulation figures. You'd be smart to give it a miss.'

'I could go; I'll be your stand-in,' Herman growled. He was beginning to look more and more like Grumpy now that I had heard Gloria's opinion of him.

'Now there's an idea.' Bobby winked at me.

In the end, Bobby *and* Herman attended the packed conference. Standing in for Carlos like two proxy godparents at a christening that has grown too big for its boots.

Their appearance, by all accounts, proved a fierce disappointment to the waiting press. But then Herman had never claimed to be the most photogenic person on the planet, let alone in beauty-loving Hollywood. Whatever about Bobby with his strong Kennedy profile and proud upright figure, the sight of the vertically challenged Herman shuffling along beside him, in his shiny elevator shoes, his rotund little body puffing its way to the top of the room, must have been a right slap in the face for any photographer hell-bent on capturing the image of a sad-faced but devastatingly handsome Carlos.

Before the Chief Medical Examiner appeared, Herman took the opportunity for a little PR on Carlos's behalf. He told the waiting reporters that he was needed in New York all that week.

Lilliput Productions were in the middle of shooting some highly dramatic outdoor scenes for *People in Jeopardy*. This series would be even more exciting than the last, he promised. It would be compulsive viewing and Carlos was in every scene. If he went missing from the set, even for a day, dozens of other actors, not to mention technicians and ancillary workers, would be left twiddling their thumbs. The whole shooting schedule could be set back weeks. Months, even.

Carlos's presence on the set was essential, Herman said.

The Chief Medical Examiner turned out to be a fair-minded man. He showed an immense understanding of the trials and tribulations involved in the motion picture and TV industry, despite being from New Hampshire. He understood Carlos's dilemma perfectly. In fact, he sent his condolences to all the bereaved, said we could finally get on with our lives and put this terrible tragedy behind us.

'*No* foul play,' he emphasized to the waiting press.

Bobby was on the phone to me in no time, carefully recounting every syllable.

'But what about the actual cause of death?' I asked.

'You don't want to hear the medical evidence. What it comes down to is death by misadventure. Okay, honey?'

'Thank you, Bobby.'

Death by misadventure?

It struck me as a rather old-fashioned phrase. Like

something from one of the musty Agatha Christie novels Mother used to hide between the covers of the *Sacred Heart Messenger*, in case tales of mysterious goings-on in wealthy Protestant families might cause widespread corruption on Hawthorn Farm.

Death by misadventure. It was a fitting epitaph for a talented writer who had lived life to the full. It was satisfying, somehow, as Carlos had predicted, having an official closure, a legal stamp put on such a traumatic and guilt-ridden chapter of my life.

The press ruined it, of course. Accidental death, they called it. Which didn't have the same poetic ring to it at all. I decided to ignore them, and take the Medical Examiner's advice and get on with my life.

Mrs Danvers clearly felt the same. She did what she always did when she was feeling optimistic. She called in her army of contract cleaners and began a blitzkrieg against invisible dirt. There wasn't a corner of the huge mansion that she didn't order to be vacuumed, scrubbed or polished to within an inch of its life.

You couldn't cross the hall without bumping into some white-overalled man or woman doing something intriguing in rubber gloves. The cut-glass chandeliers were taken apart and put back together again, after being introduced to the modern miracle of soapless soapsuds.

I had to leave my bedroom when the furniture was removed, and the carpet shampooed and blow-dried even as I walked across it.

The terrace wasn't much safer. Out there, a couple of perspiring men were using power hoses to scour the tiles.

Carlos was in New York while all this was going on,

so I decided that this was the perfect time for a little cleansing of my own.

I went to confession.

I had already asked Bobby if he would drive me to San Cristos to see Father Brennan.

'What do you want to see him for?' He wasn't pleased.

'I want him to hear my confession.'

I swear I heard his lip quiver. 'Oh Maddy. You're such a good Catholic. You want to go all that way to confess to your own priest. Do you know how many churches there are between here and San Cristos?'

'Don't tell me, Bobby. Let me count them *en route*.'

'Oh Maddy, you're such a special person.'

'Aren't I, though? Can you pick me up around ten?' I had to hang up then, because the power hoses were inching ever closer.

Father Brennan greeted me with open arms. 'Good girl, Maddy. I knew you'd come to your senses.'

'Will you hear my confession, Father?' I kept my head bowed.

He slipped into the box.

'Bless me, Father, for I have sinned.' My voice seemed to echo around the empty church. 'I had an adulterous relationship and conceived a baby.'

'Go on, my child,' he whispered, his voice encouraging.

'This relationship was with . . . *my sister's lover*.' I cleared my throat. 'For this and all my sins, I am truly sorry.'

I began to recite the act of contrition I had learned in childhood.

And what could Father Brennan do? He was bound by his Holy Orders to forgive me in the name of Our Lord, because I was a repentant sinner. I was promising not to offend again, wasn't I? Even more important, he was bound by his Holy Orders never to reveal a single word I had said to him in the confessional.

'For your penance say the five sorrowful mysteries. Twice! Go, in Christ's name, and sin no more,' he hissed.

'Thank you, Father.' I ran like the wind out of the church, and down the steps and back to the car where Bobby sat waiting.

'Put the boot down,' I panted.

'Who's chasing you?' he asked.

'Never mind, just drive.'

Bobby insisted on treating me to lunch. I didn't want to go to one of the glitzy hotels or restaurants that Gloria and Carlos had always frequented, so we drove to a little bar near the beach. To my delight they served grilled seafood. And six kinds of beer, two of them non-alcoholic and three low calorie.

I drank bottled water. Bobby had beer. The real stuff with alcohol, and million of calories and everything.

I thought that I might feel strange among the scantily clad fit and beautiful who strolled up from the beach to sit under the cool awning. My dowdy black outfit was hardly suitable attire for such a place. But there were worse sights there than me. The most revolting being the muscle-bound men who looked as if someone had tied their bodies into knots for spite, and then cruelly refused to untie them.

I wolfed down the char-grilled fish.

'Nothing like confessing your sins to give you a hearty appetite, eh, Maddy?' Bobby laughed.

He could talk; he ate like a horse.

We had a lot in common, Bobby and I, apart from our huge appetites.

Our mothers, for instance. When we began to compare notes the similarities were amazing. Although they lived on different continents and their social standing was worlds apart, our mothers were practically interchangeable.

Both of them were ultra-conservative Roman Catholics with wills of iron. Both had married much older, weaker men. And buried them. Both believed that the most important attribute of a good mother was having the power to dominate your children completely. And never praise them, in case they lost the run of themselves.

'Did she ever compliment you? Ever say, well done?' he asked.

'Are you joking? What would she compliment me for?'

He shook his head. 'I won a Rhodes scholarship. It was a pretty big deal, then, even among the high achievers in my Ivy League school. She never once said, well done. That's all it would have taken. Two little words.'

'What about your father?'

'What about him? She was the spokesperson.'

'Mine too.'

We sat back and raised our glasses. 'Well done!' we said to each other.

'Well done!' a group of oiled body-builders behind us called out, obviously thinking we were celebrating some kind of victory.

Maybe we were.

Bobby had escaped from his stifling family circumstances by fleeing to the West Coast. I had escaped by breaking all the rules.

We spent the rest of that long lunch telling each other tales of our childhood.

I couldn't help wishing that I felt for Bobby the way I did for Carlos. It would have made everything so much simpler. Bobby could take time out from his busy schedule to accompany me to San Cristos. He could sit here having lunch, as if he had all the time in the world to talk to me. To make me laugh. To compare notes. And his blue eyes said he would like us to do more than that. I wasn't interested.

If it had been Carlos sitting opposite me I would have been watching every movement of his mouth as he ate the char-grilled squid. I would have been longing for him to touch my leg under the table.

I felt a hand on my knee. It was moving slowly upwards.

'Bobby Kennedy, if you don't remove your hand this instant I'll stab you with this fork.'

Both his hands were suddenly on the table. 'Let's order dessert.' He laughed.

Dealing with Bobby was so simple. With Carlos, desire always got in the way.

Bobby entertained me for a full hour with gossip about backstage Hollywood. He was so much fun. No wonder Gloria loved his company.

He wasn't at all like Carlos. He was like the brother I never had. Even his gropes were never quite serious. They were always tentative, as if he expected a rebuff. And I never disappointed him.

He seemed to have forgiven me for my deal with Gloria and Carlos. At least, for making it behind his back. In fact, I was convinced by his conduct today that he had completely forgotten I was pregnant.

Wrong.

'Gotta hand it to you, Maddy.' He leaned across the table, knocking his bottle of beer dangerously close to the edge.

'Watch out for your beer,' I warned.

'Never mind the beer. I really admire you, Maddy.'

'Oh no, you're not going to start that again.' I grabbed my fish fork.

'No, let me speak. When I think about what you did for Gloria. It was . . .' He looked as if he was about to cry. 'Not many women would do that for a sister. Especially one they haven't seen for . . . how long was it? Twenty years? You really are pretty special. It was such an unselfish thing to do, Maddy. And now Gloria is gone and if things work out for Carlos he'll be away for a whole year. You're going to have to take full responsibility for a baby you didn't even want. It's pretty unfair, Maddy. Carlos is my friend, but it seems to me he should be taking some responsibility, not hoping to disappear for a full year. Where will that leave you? Will you go home? Back to your mother? Carlos is not going to help you make any decision. All he can see is his career. Even if he weren't going on location I don't think he'd want to take any responsibility for a baby.'

He saw my shocked expression.

'Oh he'll support you financially, Maddy. But I wouldn't depend on him for anything more than that. He's not gonna be here, if he can help it. We both know he'd cut off his right hand to get that part in

Moonwalkers Two.'

No, I didn't know Carlos would cut off his hand for a part in *Moonwalkers Two*.

I knew nothing about that.

But then Bobby didn't know that Carlos and I were still having red-hot sex whenever he was home.

We drove back to the mansion in silence.

Bobby did ask 'Are you okay, Maddy?' a couple of times. But I didn't answer.

What Maddy Did Next

'The baby is doing extremely well, Maddy. Couldn't be better. But . . . let's talk about you for a change.'

Dr Wright sat opposite me in his swivel chair. He was whey-faced, a million worry lines fighting for space on his unnaturally high forehead. But that was his everyday expression. It was why I preferred him to the local breed of doctors. He always struck me as being a lot more trustworthy than the tribe of perma-tanned Supermen who masqueraded as learned physicians in LA.

Dr Wright was different. He was English. He behaved like a proper doctor, wheezing and sighing his way through every examination. And he looked like you expected a real doctor to look. As if he were about to collapse at your feet from overwork at any second. As if he carried the weight of the whole medical confraternity on his stooped shoulders.

He even smoked. In public! There are places in California where you could be jailed for that.

He was a genuine doctor.

'Maddy,' he wheezed. 'I knew Gloria for quite a long time. I was very fond of her. And I think she . . . trusted me.' Another worry line forced its way on to his already crowded forehead. 'But she never listened to advice. You're not like that, are you?'

'I might be.' I was wary.

'Well . . . I think what we need to do here is take stock.'

I knew I was in trouble. Whenever anyone in the medical world starts referring to *we*, when they really mean you, it's time to get the beads out.

'Am I going to die?'

'Of course you're not going to die, Maddy! What *we* need to talk about is . . .'

There it was again, the dreaded – *we*. Except that this time I think he did really mean we, as in he and I.

'So I'm *not* going to die?' I wanted to be absolutely sure; it's not as if death is a journey you can get a return ticket for.

'Now that's exactly the kind of thing I want to talk to you about.' He pointed a reproving finger at me.

I was completely lost.

'That air of nervous agitation that you have about you now. That's not at all reminiscent of the girl I first encountered in Gloria's house. The life you're leading these days doesn't at all suit you, Maddy.'

'Doesn't it?'

I thought about my leisurely days in the sun-drenched garden, the glorious food served to me by the ever solicitous Mrs Danvers. Every second or third weekend when Carlos got home and we invariably ended up in bed together. The beautician who came to the mansion to pet and pamper me beyond belief. My weekly manicures and pedicures.

There were women all over the world who would kill to be in my place.

'Why are you still wearing those silly black clothes, Maddy? You must be baked in them in this heat.'

'I'm not!' I lied. 'Anyway . . . I like wearing them.' What else could I say?

'You *like* having to disguise the fact that you're pregnant?' He held my gaze. 'Like some Victorian housemaid who has been seduced by the master of the household and has to hide her shame from the world?' He was really annoyed now.

'I . . .'

'You're being very foolish, Maddy.'

I stared at him.

'I feel I have a right to speak about this because . . . I allowed myself to be drawn into this silly idea of Gloria's. But I can't in all conscience turn my back on what I'm seeing. You can't continue to live like this, Maddy. It's an unhealthy situation you find yourself in. Not good for you or the baby.'

'What do you mean, unhealthy situation? I'm happier than I've ever been!'

'Are you really, Maddy? Are you happy to find yourself living so far from home? Living a lie? Having to hide your pregnancy from all but a tiny handful of people? Aren't you finding it a strain?'

'No.'

'So you're perfectly satisfied with the way your life is?'

'Are you perfectly satisfied with your life?' I snapped.

'I chose my situation, Maddy. Who chose yours?'

Who did he think he was? What business was it of his whether I was satisfied or not? And what did he know about satisfaction anyway? With his wrinkly face and his wheezy voice. I had Carlos. Sometimes. Of course I was bloody satisfied.

'Do you miss the farm, Maddy?'

'Are you joking? All that work?'

'Do you miss it?'

'Some days.' I brushed a stubborn piece of fluff off my long black skirt.

'And your sons? Are you in touch with them?'

'I sent them a couple of cards. I can never get them on the phone – they're always out.'

'What about your husband?'

That was the end of this conversation. Who did he think he was, giving me the third degree? He was as bad as Shawnessey. Give a man a little authority and he thinks it gives him domination over the whole world. And to think I used to like him.

Because of his morose exterior, people tended to get the impression that Dr Wright had no sense of humour whatsoever. They were right. But that was one of the things I had liked about him.

'Never trust a doctor with a sense of humour,' Father used to say. 'If you want a laugh you can always go to a music-hall.'

But Dr Wright's morose expression was getting on my nerves today. Even in a medical practitioner, extreme seriousness can become too much of a good thing.

If he didn't hurry up and write my prescription for mild anti-depressants, I would just have to leave without it. How would he feel then? Would *he* be satisfied *then*?

'I'd like you to think of me as a friend as well as your doctor, Maddy. To be honest, I feel somewhat responsible for the situation you find yourself in.'

There he was again with his *situation*. What was he talking about? And what was this friend business? I had enough friends, thank you. Just give me the bloody prescription and I'll go, I said. But not out loud.

Instead: 'I came here for a medical check-up. If I'd wanted a sermon I could have called my mother.' I opened the door. 'There are other doctors in West Hollywood you know.'

For the first time since Gloria's accident I went swimming in the big kidney-shaped pool. I had Dr Wright to thank for this. If I hadn't been feeling so vexed with him, I might never have ventured into it again.

I had often stood, looking down at it, during the past months. But always from a safe distance, usually from behind a window. Even then, it had caused cold shivers to run down my spine.

But once I was actually in the water, I found myself enjoying it. The weather was far too hot for me lately. And the water was so pleasant. So cool.

There was very little wind blowing in from the ocean today. LA needed its cooling ocean winds to make it bearable. I swam until all my anger drained away.

Mrs Danvers stood watching, like a big black mother hen. 'Your time is up, Madam.' She pointed to her watch. 'Can't have you catching cold now.'

In this heat? Where did she think we were? Ballyshannon?

She all but removed the top layer of my skin with her brisk rubdown. Then came the pills. Vitamins and iron and God only knows what else. She watched closely as I swallowed them, a peculiar look on her face.

I stared down at the last pill where it nestled in the palm of my hand. It looked exactly like the rabbit droppings that littered our orchard after Runt, the bunny's arch enemy, had gone to the big kennel in the sky.

'Did you ever see *Rosemary's Baby*?' I asked her.

'Very droll, Madam. Very droll.'

There, the strange expression had flitted across her face again. I knew what it was. It was a flicker of amusement. A tiny smile had almost broken out on her thin, bloodless lips. Not a proper smile, by any standards, but a close enough facsimile. Was it possible that she was happy?

'Betty?'

'Madam?'

It was gone.

'I thought I saw you smile, for a second.'

The hollow eyes met mine. 'You're a wicked girl.' And there it was again. A little glint of humour, in her eyes this time. She gathered up my wet things and strode back to the house. At the door she gave one quick glance over her shoulder to catch me grinning broadly at her.

The phone purred like a cat. 'How did the examination go? Did Dr Frankenstein give you a pass?' Carlos asked.

'An A plus. Top of the class.' I laughed.

'The baby?' This was the first time he had acknowledged its existence since the day of Gloria's funeral.

'Well, he did a couple of somersaults during the scan. But apart from that . . .'

'He?' There was a definite note of interest creeping into his voice.

'I said that without thinking. It's . . . it's what people say.'

'I guess.' It was as if I had confiscated his train set.
'It could be a boy.'
'Do you think so?'
'Well, long research has come to the conclusion that the chances are fifty-fifty.'
'You're in top form today.'
'Well, why not? I've just had a swim. The sun is shining. God is in his heaven and Mrs Danvers smiled at me. Nearly.'
'You make me wish I were there.'
'So hop on a plane. You can afford it.'
'Have you ever heard of a little thing called a career, Maddy?'
'Ye what?'
'Very funny. My contract says I'm in New York for the next month at least.'
'A whole month?'
'I'm not enjoying it, Maddy. I've had a lousy day. Everything went wrong on the set. Even the weather is against us. I've been hanging around in my trailer all day, waiting for the rain to stop. Damn rain has messed up the continuity again. Not one straight take in four hellish hours. I hate this business.'
'Liar. You love it.'
'Not on days like this, I don't.' He sounded completely fed up.
'Aw poor baby. Shame Mommy can't make it all better.'
'You could if you were here.'
I went all hot.
'Maddy? Are you still there?'
'Yes.'
'Come to New York and make me all better. I'm horny as hell.'

*

Of course I didn't go to New York. Imagine the trouble I'd have had disguising the bump on a five-hour flight to New York! And what would Carlos have done with me once I got there? Smuggled me into his trailer for a quickie, then chucked me out when the rain stopped and filming began again?

Still, the thought of being in a steamy small trailer with Carlos was tempting, certainly enough to give me a little warm glow.

I dived into the pool again, much to Mrs Danvers's disgust.

When he came home that weekend we had a huge row. It was probably my fault. Or maybe it was just too hot – the weather did seem to be getting increasingly warmer. I can't really remember how it started, or why. It might have had something to do with me trying to tell him about some of the things Dr Wright had said, and him trying to French kiss me at the same time. Carlos, not Dr Wright. And again, it's not as if I didn't want him to French kiss me, it was just that I didn't want him doing it at that particular time.

'What's wrong, Maddy?' He looked offended when I pushed him away.

'I'm trying to tell you something,' I said.

'Tell me tomorrow.' He bit my neck.

It wasn't a real bite, but it was enough to make me lose my rag. It was far too hot for neck biting. My hand just suddenly rose, of its own accord, and slapped him on the face.

It wasn't a hard slap or anything. Just a little mild, stop-biting-my-neck-please kind of slap.

He couldn't have been more shocked if I had kneed him in the groin. Full on. And I swear that idea had never even entered my head. Much.

He leaped to his feet. 'What the hell is the matter with you?' He was in front of the mirror checking his face.

'I was trying to get you to listen to me,' I said.

'You think the way to do that is to assault me?'

'You think that was an assault?' I had to laugh. 'You just *bit* me.'

'That wasn't a bite!'

'It wasn't a suck!'

And so it became a full-blown row over who had assaulted whom and whether a mild box on the ear – because that's what it actually was – constituted an assault. And whether *it* cancelled out the disputed nip on the neck, which may or may not have been a bite.

The last thing I heard him say as he slammed out through the door was 'something something bloody Gloria'. And I don't think he was complimenting me. Or Gloria. But I wasn't at all sorry. Not for such a little slap.

'Don't let people use you, Maddy,' Dr Wright had said. 'Hollywood has a way of chewing people up and spitting out the empty husk when it's finished with them. It's a way of life here, so much so that nobody even notices it happening any more. Except for those of us who remain steadfastly on the outside.'

'Could I have my prescription please?' I had snapped at the time, but all the way home his words had rattled round in my head. It irritated me beyond belief. *And* probably led to that very first row between Carlos and me.

*

The knock on my door woke me from the most wonderful dream. I was running barefoot through the long meadow on Hawthorn Farm. The sun was shining. It wasn't the relentless Californian sun that could curdle milk in two seconds flat, but the much gentler sun of Ballyshannon, which took a whole summer long, and a big chunk of autumn to ripen wheat or barley heads and make them ready for harvesting. I could smell the new-mown hay in the next field and when I climbed the high mossy bank that divided the two, the damp grass was like cool velvet beneath my feet.

Someone was calling my name.

'Maddy?'

I woke with a start. It was long past midnight.

'Maddy?' There was a knock on the door.

'Go away, I'm leaving in the morning.'

'Where are you going?'

'Ballyshannon.'

'Let me in, Maddy.'

'If I let you in, we'll only start to fight again.'

'We weren't fighting, you just hit me out of the blue.'

'See!'

'Okay, okay. We won't fight, I promise you.'

'What do you want to do then?'

'Talk?'

'Talking is acceptable. But only talking, mind you. You have to swear that you won't touch me. You have to keep your distance.'

'Promise.'

I unlocked the door.

We were in each other's arms before he kicked it closed behind him.

Pregnancy is no impediment to passionate and prolonged love-making. All it takes is a little more imagination, a little creativity. Or even a lot.

It so happened these were the two most frequently repeated words on my school report cards when I was growing up. Creative and imaginative.

Well, if I am to be completely honest, what they usually said was – *Madeline is highly creative, but she has far too much imagination for her own good.*

Just shows how little the nuns knew.

A Man's Career Is a Many-Splendoured Thing

Despite Dr Wright and his trouble-making innuendoes, everything was going pretty smoothly between Carlos and me, when Bobby arrived and dropped the bombshell.

It was mid-week; Carlos was in New York.

'Can you keep a secret, Maddy?' Bobby could hardly contain his excitement.

I looked straight at him, refusing even to dignify this with an answer.

'Sorry, Maddy, I wasn't thinking straight. I'm just so wired. Nobody knows yet, not even Carlos, but . . . he's got the part. He's got the lead in *Moonwalkers Two*.'

'Oh my God. How do you know?'

'Herman. He swore me to secrecy. He's on his way to New York to tell Carlos face to face.'

Lucky Herman, I thought. Out loud I said, 'Carlos will go out of his mind with delight.' This was true. All Carlos wanted to talk about lately, all he had been hoping for, was a chance to play this great movie role. The heroic Dr Mezzin in *Moonwalkers Two*.

The role of the century, he called it. But then I couldn't help noticing that the role of the century seemed to come around with great regularity in Hollywood. Every three months or so, by my reckoning.

We were in bed when I first asked him about the Dr Mezzin role. He was more than happy to talk about it. He told me how he had studied the character. What the character's motivation was, how he would speak, comb his hair, what he would drink, what he would think, in any given situation. He told me what his background might be. He forgot to tell me how often he had a bowel movement.

When I asked him what he would do if he didn't get the role his reply was pretty straightforward.

'I'll kill myself.'

Anywhere else you might laugh, but this was Hollywood.

He wouldn't actually have killed himself, of course, but the statement gave some indication of how passionately he wanted this much coveted part. Watching him reading the script for the umpteenth time, when he could have been having sex, made me realize that while he might draw the line at killing himself, it was not necessarily beyond the realms of possibility for him to kill somebody else to get it. Like one of the other actors who were up for it, for instance. Especially one whose name was being touted all over town as being born to play Dr Mezzin.

'He's a dork,' Herman said when Carlos voiced his fears about this.

'He's an Oscar winner,' Carlos countered.

'He got the sympathy vote that year. His wife had run off with the pool boy.'

'What about the Golden Globe?'

'He got that because she came back.' Herman was Carlos's number one fan.

I was always a little jealous of him. Sometimes I felt he had more opportunities to be intimate with Carlos than I had. Not intimate in the same way, of course, but it's an irrefutable fact that sharing the same dreams and ambitions can draw people even closer than sex. And now Herman would get to see Carlos's face when he imparted the great news.

I had to sit home and imagine Carlos's expression changing. Picture his handsome face lighting up with delight, his big brown eyes widening with shock and excitement, a bit like his reaction to some of the manoeuvres I got up to in bed. At least I had that over Herman, he would never get to see the way Carlos responded to some of those little tricks.

He phoned me at nine p.m. Los Angeles time. That meant it was the witching hour in New York. He was in a night-club celebrating with the cast and crew of *People in Jeopardy*.

He sounded drunk. 'Guess who's gonna be playing Dr Mezzin in *Moonwalkers Two*?'

'Al Pacino?' I feigned innocence.

'You're talking to him, Maddy!'

'Al Pacino? My God, you sound just like Carlos.' I squealed.

'Maddy!' He wasn't amused.

'Congratulations,' I said quickly. 'Well done. Well done. You deserve it.' I don't know why I said that, I suppose it's just something you say when a person gets something they want very badly. The truth was that any of the five actors who were up for it would have deserved it just as much. Maybe even more, I thought disloyally.

'*What did you say*?' He was yelling to be heard

above the loud music and the glee-club gaiety in the background.

'*I said you deserve it*!' I bellowed, practically bursting my own eardrums.

'No need to shout, Maddy, I can hear you perfectly.'

'Good,' I said.

'*What*?'

'*Well done*! It's quite a feather in your cap getting that part.'

'*A feather in my what*?' He was completely serious.

Before I could reply there was a sudden loud explosion of vulgar bump-and-grind music, in my ear. '*I hope that's the radio you have on*,' I shouted.

This time he did laugh. '*It's just a little celebration. The crew insisted.*' His voice was almost drowned out by loud cheering. Then came Herman's unmistakable nasal whine. 'Carlos, get back here, you won't believe these figures.'

'*I hope he's talking about the ratings.*'

'*What*?'

I gave up. 'Good-night, Carlos. Ring me tomorrow. Oh wait, who's got the female lead?'

He was gone.

It was all over the papers next day. Not just who was going to play Dr Mezzin, the lead role in the biggest man-against-the-elements survival blockbuster since *Indiana Jones*, but who had been chosen to play his sparring partner, or love interest as they called it in the business. And for love interest read *sex*.

I wasn't altogether naïve about the behind-the-scenes goings-on in Hollywood. I read the *Hollywood Reporter* regularly. And I had been to enough parties with Gloria to be able to work out what was what. And who was doing what to whom.

It was Herman who told me what co-stars expected of each other.

It wasn't always great acting, according to him. 'There is more rumpty tumpty goin' on between co-stars in Hollywood than there is between the average married couple in Pennsylvania,' he said.

That was the very day Carlos's future co-star was pictured in every single paper I looked at. And in every pose imaginable. Including some where she was in varying stages of undress. And there was *so* much of her to undress – the beauteous and truly voluptuous Lou Anne Bechal.

Bobby's secretary took her time putting me through.

'Maddy? What is it, honey? Where's the fire?'

I didn't waste time. 'Did you know *she* was getting the female lead?'

He didn't beat around the bush either. 'She's a good actress, Maddy.'

'Is that all she's good at? Come on, Bobby, we're friends, aren't we? You can tell me.'

'Well I hear she makes a killer martini.' He waited for me to laugh.

Maybe when hell froze over. 'That should come in handy in the jungle. Where is it they're planning on filming? The Congo, isn't it?'

'Er . . . no. It's a little too hot there at the moment.'

'It's a jungle. What did they expect?'

'I mean politically. The area they were considering has been overrun by Tutsis.'

'Oh well, Lou Anne should feel right at home there, then.'

'Tutsis are dangerous African rebels, Maddy!'

'I see. So they'll be filming somewhere safer then, somewhere closer to home?' This was good news. It would enable Carlos to get back on a regular basis, which meant that our relationship *could* be ongoing. I knew there would be no long-term promises, but I lived in hope. Who knew where it might end, if I was around for long enough, I told myself. If I had learned anything since coming here it was that Carlos always took the line of least resistance. In his private life, anyway.

Divinely handsome he might be *and* a sensational lover, but there was no doubt that he wasn't the most imaginative of souls when he didn't have a Rick Hein script in his hand.

Bobby was mumbling something now. 'Er em . . . I eh.'

'What?'

'They won't actually be filming closer to home. Well, only if . . .' he gave a forced little laugh '. . . well, only if you happen to live in northern Australia.'

'Tell me you're kidding, Bobby.'

'You'll laugh when you hear. They're gonna be filming in Papua New Guinea.'

I didn't laugh.

'Some of the crew are already over there. It's a perfect location.'

'For what? Parakeets?' I screeched.

'For *Moonwalkers Two*. Something to do with the light. Dieter says it has some kind of unique quality to it. Possibly to do with the lack of air pollution, or gas emissions, or something along those lines. Don't ask me, Maddy. I'm not a cinematographer or a lighting cameraman. But Dieter *is* the best in the business, and he's a stickler for accuracy and realism.'

'Accuracy and realism? It's set on a fictitious planet, for Christ's sake. How can he claim the light has to be accurate? Who the hell knows what kind of light there is on some bloody fictitious planet? The place doesn't exist, for God's sake. Gloria made it up. They could film the damn thing on the back lot of the studio and nobody would be any the wiser.'

'That's not true, Maddy, and you know it. Dieter is a craftsman. An artist!' He couldn't seem to make up his mind.

'You knew, didn't you? You knew she was going to get the second lead and that they were going to film in bloody *New Guinea*!'

'I thought *you* knew, Maddy. It wasn't exactly a secret. The kids on the strip are talking about it, for God's sake.'

'I see.'

It seemed that everyone in Hollywood, except me, was aware that *Moonwalkers Two* was expected to take a whole year to shoot. Anyone hoping to get a part knew they would have to clear their diaries for twelve months at least. Those in starring roles maybe even longer, what with pre-publicity and costume fittings and the like. Carlos would be in New Guinea for twelve months with *Lou Anne Bechal*!

'I can't believe you didn't tell me, Bobby.'

'I thought you knew. That's what I meant when I praised you for being so cool. I couldn't believe the way you were dealing with the *baby business* all on your own, without once complaining that you had gotten a raw deal. Not a word of self-pity that Gloria's death had left you in such a horrendous situation. I was amazed how you were managing. Any other woman might have been suing the estate for compensation.'

'Don't put ideas in my head, Bobby.'

'You wouldn't! Oh Christ, say you wouldn't, Maddy.'

I said nothing.

'*Maddy*?'

Just to frighten him I hung up.

The phone rang almost immediately. 'Don't scare me like that, Maddy, this is the state of California.'

'You don't know what scared is. I thought Carlos would at least be there until I had the baby. I didn't expect anything more than that.'

Liar liar pants on fire Maddy.

'Just to have someone there who would have an interest in the baby until it was born and I could decide what I'm going to do.'

'He's an actor, Maddy, he has to go where the roles take him.'

'So I'm to have the baby alone.'

'I'll be there for you, Maddy.'

I don't bloody want you, I want Carlos, I said. But not out loud.

'Maddy, just a word. I'm sure Carlos will take care of you financially, but don't expect anything more from him.'

'What do you mean?'

'Well, he's a nice guy. I like him a lot.' He paused. 'I just wouldn't want him marrying my sister, if you know what I mean.'

'No, I don't,' I lied.

'Gloria was okay with it, but she was a one-off. She gave him a lot of rope. Once he kept his little dalliances away from LA, and the newspapers, she could handle it. Not every woman could.'

'Are you telling me not to get any romantic ideas about Carlos?'

'Well, I don't have to tell you that, Maddy, do I? You're too smart for that.'

Was he being sarcastic?

I went walking in the garden to clear my head. Help myself think. It began to rain. It rains something like two days a year in LA. And both of those times had to be days when I needed the weather to be kind. Maybe even LA was trying to tell me something.

I ignored the rain, walking the narrow pathways trying to get things in perspective. I could hang on here, see how things turned out. But I would be completely dependent on Carlos's goodwill. I could go back to Ballyshannon and – surprise, surprise – be dependent on Mother's goodwill. Who had coined the phrase 'between a rock and a hard place'? What about my baby? Where would my baby be best off? Living in a squat in LA?

I was now drenched to the skin, my clothes a dead weight dragging against me like leaden rags.

Mrs Danvers came running to lead me back into the house. 'You'll catch your death out here.'

'I wouldn't be that lucky,' I said.

I phoned Ballyshannon, taking care to ring at a time Mother couldn't possibly find fault with. They would be getting up from the supper table just about now, the day's work finally over.

The phone rang for ages before it was picked up.

'Mother? It's Maddy.'

'God Almighty, do you deliberately choose the

worst time to phone? It's like a madhouse here. One of the small heifers is calving. She's giving the lads a lot of trouble. It's far too late for her to be calving anyway. She always lagged behind the rest. I told Turlough to sell her on. And now the calf is stuck and we're probably going to lose both of them. We'll be lucky to get twenty pounds from . . .'

There was a sudden yell. 'It's out, Hanna. A fine bull calf.' It was Turlough.

'Thanks be to God. How is the heifer faring?'

There was a low mumble of voices.

'It's Maddy,' I heard Mother saying. 'Wouldn't you know! Who else always manages to ring at the wrong time?'

Turlough came on the line, still panting a little from his exertions with the heifer.

'It hasn't been read yet,' I anticipated his question.

'Right so.' He hung up.

Carlos was back in LA on Friday and I was still no further advanced with my plans for the future.

Not that he noticed my distracted air. He was so blinded by his own good luck, so beside himself with delight, he wasn't aware of anything else.

The starring role in *Moonwalkers Two* was such a big a prize for an actor that I understood his preoccupation with it. His euphoria. All he wanted to do was talk about the role and wonder at his great good fortune in getting it.

'Even the publicity budget is huge. Humungous!' He practically danced with glee. 'One of the PR gurus was on my flight from New York. He says the advance publicity is gonna be bigger than anything we've ever seen before. Bigger than *Jurassic Park*! Bigger than

Titanic! He can't wait to get things rolling, plunge into the thick of it.' He laughed. 'You should have heard him, Maddy. Talking non-stop. The guy was practically orgasmic.'

'Get away.'

It was quite a while since I'd seen him look so excited. His skin was glowing, his brown eyes alight with happiness. 'I still can't believe I've got the lead. When I think of all those great actors I was up against. Wow!' He punched the air. 'The studio is throwing a publicity bash next weekend. They've invited the world and his wife.'

'Get away.'

'You too, Maddy. *I'm* inviting you.' He was like a big child.

He suddenly grabbed me and hugged me so tightly I could hardly breathe. I waited for him to let go.

He didn't. And what had started out as nothing more than a goodwill hug turned into something entirely different.

We were both on fire.

I forgot all about my concerns for my future, all about Lou Anne and the jungle, all about Bobby's thinly veiled warning. I forgot about everything except the sweet taste of his mouth, and the tantalising feel of his hard body against mine.

A bit like St Augustine, I *did* want to put temptation behind me. But not yet, Lord. Not yet.

Next morning, watching him dressing, I was still feeling the afterglow. No doubt about it, the man was the best. *The best.* He pulled a white T-shirt over his head, raising both arms at once, to reveal the little patches of inky black hair that clustered beneath them. He was the only man living who could turn such a small everyday gesture into a promise of carnal pleasure.

I must have sighed. Or let out a squeak or something.

He turned to me, smiling. 'Did I tell you that Lou Anne Bechal is playing the female lead?'

'You probably mentioned it.' I wimped out, reluctant to break the mood.

He didn't appear at all awkward, or uneasy, the way most men do when they have something to hide. There could be two possible explanations for this, I realized. Either he *had* nothing to hide, because he genuinely lived for the moment and thought I did too. Or he was a much better actor than Gloria had ever given him credit for.

In retrospect I would plump for the former.

'How long will the actual filming take?' I asked, watching him bend over to pull on his socks.

He stepped into his shoes. 'Oh man, I don't even wanna think about that.'

He was in front of the mirror now, checking his reflection, looking pleased with what he saw.

And who could blame him? Even in casual weekend clothes he was about as perfect a specimen of manhood as you are ever likely to encounter in this life.

Long after he had kissed me goodbye and left, I could still conjure up that perfect image, that incredibly toned body; that handsome face smiling at me from the mirror.

I lay back, thinking about it, cupping the bump lovingly in both hands.

'Pretty Daddy,' I whispered.

It kicked me viciously in the bowel. Some children are never grateful.

Movies, Is that All Anyone Ever Thinks About?

In the end there *was* no reading of Gloria's will. Not in public, anyway. Just as well, because if there had been there would most certainly have been a lot of long faces around the big mansion.

There was only one beneficiary. She left everything to Carlos. Everything she possessed. There wasn't a single mention of the loyal staff who had served her so faithfully down the years. Gloria sank even lower in my estimation. Then I learned that this will was nearly ten years old.

When she had signed it, Lilliput Productions had been in its infancy, which meant that she was worth very little.

When she died she was worth millions.

Bobby, who was, after all, her personal attorney and in a sense caretaker of all that she owned, surely should have arranged for her to have drawn up a more recent will. He squirmed uneasily when I said this, then got together with Carlos to work something out for the household staff.

Mrs Danvers appeared to have absolute faith in their judgement, as well she might because they *had* spent days trawling through Gloria's papers searching for a newer will, one that might possibly have been drawn up without Bobby's knowledge. One that would surely have been advantageous to her servants.

Gloria had always played her cards close to her chest. *And* thought nothing of playing one person against another. With her, anything was possible. Even a secret will.

There was none.

Carlos was back in New York when Bobby called us into the study, one by one. First Mrs Danvers, then Dong, then old Tomasino and finally me as if I were some kind of under-housemaid or something.

Whatever arrangements he and Carlos had decided on, the other three must have thought them satisfactory, because they all left the room looking pleased as punch.

Mrs Danvers was as close to smiling as anyone could reasonably expect. Dong practically sashayed his way along the big hallway and back into the kitchen. And Tomasino's wild head of white hair, that he had drenched with water in order to tame it for the big occasion, had dried out with excitement and was now standing up on his head again like tufts of fern grass.

There was an air of delight running through the whole mansion.

Then it was my turn to be called in.

Bobby stood behind Gloria's desk rubbing his hands together like a new curate about to count the Easter dues. 'I have to tell you, Maddy, that Carlos is very aware that if Gloria had made a later will she would obviously have made generous provision for you. So he's taken it on himself to do just that.'

Then he looked me straight in the eye and stabbed

me in the back. 'Carlos has arranged for the sum of one million dollars to be put into a bank account for you. In Ireland.'

I was the only one who left the study that morning with tears of disappointment running down her face.

'Maddy?' Bobby hammered on my door.

'Go away!'

'Why are you so upset? We thought you'd be pleased.'

'With a million dollars in an Irish account?'

'Isn't it enough?'

'Don't be stupid.'

'What is it, then? You said your family farm was badly in need of cash. They need to expand and your mother won't borrow. This way you can decide exactly how much to give them. Over whatever length of time you choose. It will be at your discretion, Maddy. It gives you complete control over their spending, even at this distance.'

I sat up. 'I thought it was your way of telling me to go home?'

'No! Carlos has also made provision for you here in LA. With no strings attached.'

I opened the door a crack to frown out at him. 'No strings attached for whom?'

'Maddy.' But he looked a bit shamefaced.

'How much money is he giving away?'

He grinned. 'A lot. But then he has a lot to give. I've been investing money for him and Gloria for years. He's not asking you to leave, Maddy.' He caught my hand through the narrow opening. 'And *I* don't want you to leave.' His blue eyes were warm.

I looked away. 'I haven't decided what I'm going to

do yet. I don't even know what I'd spend the money on. In LA, I mean.'

'You'll need it for the baby.'

I phoned Mother at seven o'clock at night. Of course that meant it was exactly three a.m. her time.

'How dare you ring me at three o'clock in the morning?'

'Oh dear, is it? I just wanted you to know, Gloria left me a million dollars.'

'A . . . A million dollars?'

'One million dollars, Mother. It's already on deposit in the Allied Irish Bank.'

'Jesus, Mary and Joseph!'

'Exactly. And Gloria earned every red cent of it. It's her money. But it's in my name. To spend any way I see fit.'

'In *your* name? What would you be doing with a million dollars?'

'Oh I'll think of something. I'll probably start with simple little pleasures, like sex, drugs and . . . Mother?'

There was a funny snorting sound. Then the line went dead.

I kept expecting Turlough to ring back. He didn't. And I wouldn't please him by phoning again. Who did he think he was fooling, pretending that he had no interest in a million dollars? The man still had his First Communion money.

Then it was time to get ready for the studio party and I was too busy thinking about that to worry about Ballyshannon and what they were up to over there.

For the first time since coming to Hollywood I was

anxious to attend a party. Of course, it wasn't the party itself that interested me, it was something much more personal. I wanted to watch Lou Anne and Carlos together. See how they behaved around each other.

I didn't have to tell Mrs Danvers that I wanted to make a special effort with my appearance for the big bash. She knew. Becoming a woman of means overnight hadn't changed her. She had already arranged for a beautician *and* a stylist to come to the house and make me over.

I have to say they did it with a minimum of fuss. And as little physical pain as possible. For me at least. I can't speak for them. Yet the end results were pretty startling and most satisfying. It hardly looked like me at all.

They dressed me in an ice-blue empire-line creation that had the finest silver threads running through its low-cut bodice so that it caught the light whichever way I turned. What impressed *me* most was that I didn't look at all pregnant in it, which was still a major requirement, if I was to be seen in public. According to Herman.

I might have appeared overly busty, flashing a little too much cleavage, but this was Hollywood, not Ballyshannon. Nobody would be calling the modesty police here. Besides, Carlos was hardly averse to a bit of heaving bosom.

The stylist began to fasten a wide pearl choker round my neck.

'But I never wear jewellery,' I protested as the egg-sized clasp snapped closed.

'You do now,' she said. 'It's a good trick. It draws the eye.'

'Where?' I asked dumbly.

'Away from the growing midriff.'

When I stood back to view myself in the floor-length mirror I saw what she meant. In this outfit, you'd have to become pretty intimate with me before you'd know I was pregnant. I stared long and hard at the slender, elegant woman in the mirror. Wait till Carlos saw this glamorous creature!

When the stylist had first arrived she had pointed to my middle and said, 'I know exactly what you need.'

'I'm not wearing a corset for anyone,' I snapped.

Seeing the result of her hard work, I was ashamed of this earlier outburst. 'I'm really sorry about my attitude,' I apologized. 'I'm just a bit nervous.'

'No need to be. You'll knock 'em dead.' She smiled.

'Go for it honey.' The beautician threw down her tail comb and raised a clenched fist in a supportive salute.

Mrs Danvers led me out to the waiting limo like a conquering queen.

She stood on the high steps to wave me off. The stylist and the beautician joined her, taking up position on either side of her to form an eye-catching little trio of feminine support.

'Go get 'em, honey!' the women's voices rang out encouragingly.

It would have made for such a dramatic departure if I hadn't spoiled it by having to climb out of the car and run back into the house to use the toilet.

If You're Not in the Business, You Don't Exist

The party was like I'd always imagined the Carnival in Rio might be, with thousands of paper streamers falling like coloured rain on to the heads of hundreds of happy carnival goers. Only this wasn't a carnival. This was a publicity bash, to announce the names of the cast members of *Moonwalkers Two*. Except that everyone already knew who they were. But then who was I to question the ways of Hollywood?

I was here to watch Carlos. And Lou Anne.

I hadn't seen him since early morning because he had gone directly from the studio to the party. With Lou Anne. And of course the producers and the director and the rest of the cast. Not forgetting Dieter the slimy cinematographer, the man I would hate to the end of my days.

They were clustered together in the centre of the big room, like Custer's last stand.

Only instead of being surrounded by whooping Indians, they were under siege by the world's press. TV crews and newsmen and print journalists of all denominations were firing questions at them. Shouting instructions as to which way they were to pose, and generally causing a lot of noise and disturbance.

But everybody seemed to be enjoying themselves, if the sounds of gaiety coming from that direction were anything to go by. There were loud peals of laughter and witty comments, and champagne corks popping in all directions.

And so much beauty.

Even with the big Super Trooper lights beaming down on them, none of the cast even perspired.

The heat in the rest of the big room made me feel faint several times.

Carlos and Lou Anne smiled untiringly at each other, obeying every call to 'Look this way, Lou Anne! That's it! Lean into him, honey! Hold her a little closer, Carlos.'

The great mock carnival continued to whirl around them in a dizzying kaleidoscope of colour, as dancers and wandering musicians, and girls dressed in fake leopard-skin bikinis thronged past.

Carlos was wearing a pale Armani suit. I recognized it. It was the one he'd worn the night Gloria died. It had certainly dry-cleaned well, but I suppose you get what you pay for, even in Hollywood.

Lou Anne was *almost* wearing a little slip of a black dress and I have to admit she looked stunning. Practically pornographic, but stunning.

'Maddy! I've been searching everywhere for you.' Bobby was beside me, a brimming glass in his hand, although I would have guessed that the last thing he needed was another drink. 'What a party. They've really pulled out all the stops on this one. The whole world is here tonight.'

'Except Gloria,' I reminded him.

'Poor Gloria. God I miss her.' Were his eyes filling up?

That was all I needed tonight. A maudlin drunk crying on my shoulder, while Lou Anne mauled

Carlos under the hot lights.

'Carlos is sure having a good time.' I couldn't tell if Bobby was being malicious or just dumb.

'He's under orders from the publicity department,' I snapped.

'Sure.' His grin was definitely malicious.

'The studio insisted that they arrive together.'

'Pimps!'

'What?'

'The publicity department. Pimps. Every one of them.'

'Well they have to garner publicity.' I couldn't believe I was defending them.

'They want a big romance, I hear.'

'Who does?'

'The publicity department. It's good box-office. Never fails.' He staggered slightly.

Lou Anne was licking Carlos's ear.

'Practically in their contract,' Bobby slurred.

I could see how much of a strain this make-believe romance was for Lou Anne. Having to keep nibbling at Carlos's ear for the news cameras must have been such a chore. And how wearing, having to keep kissing him full on the lips all those times for the clamouring photographers. And her nipples must have been worn flat from all that excruciating rubbing against his suit all evening.

Poor Lou Anne, she had my sympathy. My fists were aching to show her just how much.

Trying to get within speaking distance of the cast was a bit like attempting to line-dance at an IFA Christmas dinner. Three steps forward and two steps back. Then you had to bite your lip to prevent yourself screaming, when your toes were mangled by some heavy-footed Neanderthal who was moving to a beat audible only to him. And rabid dogs.

I waved, trying to catch Carlos's eye. No chance.

I kept hoping that he would look in my direction, see me standing there in my fancy pearl choker *and go get 'em* dress, and rush to my side, his eyes brimming with love.

It didn't happen.

The only people who got within touching distance of him were easily identifiable press men, media heads, studio moguls and, of course, the ubiquitous Lou Anne. She was practically inside his suit now, making little mock bites at his neck. But I couldn't hold that against her. Hadn't that been one of my foremost ambitions since I had first seen him cross that hushed court room in *People in Jeopardy*?

Bobby was spilling drink on my new silver shoes. 'So beautiful!' He swayed towards me.

I could see Carlos smiling down into Lou Anne's perfect little face. Then he suddenly moved away from her. Had he seen me? Was he hurrying to greet me?

No. He was turning to kiss Barbara Farrington's ring.

Bobby's hand was sliding down my back. 'You're the most attractive woman in the whole room, Maddy.'

Barbara Farrington made it her business to come and speak to me. 'How are you doing, Madeline? Well, no need to ask. You look marvellous. Such a pretty dress. I am so glad you finally discarded that terrible black. Will you be staying much longer?'

'Oh yes, I'm staying to the end.'

'I didn't mean the party, honey, I meant in LA.'

'I . . . I'm not altogether sure.'

'Well, I assumed that with Carlos going on location for a full year he'd be anxious to rent out that big mausoleum of a house. That type of property is in huge demand for rental in Beverly Hills. I told him I might be interested. He said I should talk to Bobby Kennedy. My place in Bel-Air is becoming impossible since that young brat-pack actor bought the Nowlan estate that backs on to mine. He has five motor cycles. I mean, what can one say? Five motor cycles!'

I fanned myself with my bag. The heat was really getting to me.

She leaned closer. 'What *is* he going to do without Gloria? She sat up half the night on the last day of her life to see that he got this great movie role and he can't be bothered to make arrangements about the house yet? Men!' She shook her hair, which was teased into a great big black mountain on her head.

'*Gloria* got him the movie role?' I tried to keep my voice even.

'Didn't you know?' The alcohol on her breath was lethal. 'She rang me from the Blue Pacific that night. Said she would be willing to change the *Moonwalkers* ending, *if* we guaranteed Carlos the lead in the sequel. Well, she was costing us a lot of dollars with her stubborn attitude to the *Moonwalkers* ending, so naturally enough we were happy to agree. She insisted that the papers be signed that night. It was straightforward enough, so she and Nathan and Saul met in my office and signed them. I feel quite depressed when I think back to that meeting, because they left my office so pleased with themselves. Especially Gloria. She looked radiant. Happier than I'd seen her for a long time. But she wouldn't hear of anyone taking her home. Stubborn to the last. "I don't need an escort," she said.' Barbara sighed loudly. 'Stubborn to the last.'

I kissed her warmly. 'Thank you for telling me this, Barbara.'

'What?'

We hadn't sent her home alone! Gloria had refused an escort. We hadn't sent her to cross by the pool in those ridiculous heels.

'Such a waste of all that talent.' Barbara sighed again. 'But then she always said liquor would kill her in the end.' She dabbed at her eyes and sniffed. 'But who'd have thought it would be so soon?'

'Does Carlos know about the deal she made?'

'No. We kept it quiet. The continued speculation over who might get the lead role was good for business. It generated publicity.'

I looked over at Carlos who was still posing for the cameras. 'Did Gloria realize how long the filming would take? Did she know Carlos would be away for a whole year?'

She frowned. 'But she was going with him, my dear. It was *her* screenplay and she told me she needed a break from Hollywood anyway. You think she'd let that man out of her sight for a whole year?' She laughed. 'Not the Gloria I knew. She was far too smart for that. And far too much in love with him, although she'd rather be hog-tied than admit it. Even to him. Stubborn and smart as they come, that was Gloria. And proud.' There was genuine admiration in her voice.

She looked over to where Carlos was still smiling at Lou Anne. 'He's almost too handsome, isn't he?'

'Almost.'

'Still, I wouldn't say no.'

'Barbara!' I was shocked.

'Did you think I was past it?' She gave me a wicked smile. 'Not when they're that appetising. *And* they're under contract to my studio.' She laughed. 'Ah, young actors. They're sometimes more trouble than they're worth.'

Her entourage was growing impatient, trying to move her along.

'*Five* motor cycles, can you imagine?' With a flick of the wrist she was off, her acolytes trailing obediently behind.

I had an even clearer view of Carlos and Lou Anne now. I could see their every movement, each little scene they played out for the cameras.

There was still quite a crowd of photographers competing for the best shot.

'Smile, Carlos. That's it, Lou Anne. Hold on to his arm. Fantastic! That's it, a little closer. Good girl! Make as if you can't get enough of him. Ooh that's it. And again!'

'Look at that Carlos. He's so stoned.' Bobby was back from the men's room, appearing anything but refreshed. He threw an arm round my shoulders, more to support himself than out of affection for me, I suspected.

'He is not!'

'What?'

'Stoned.'

'Yes he is. *And* he's been drinking bourbon all

night. You know what that does to him. I met Philip outside. He said Carlos is out of his head. Phil never gets it wrong.'

'Is that why he's been married three times?'

'Ouch! You're developing a nasty tongue, Maddy. Must be something in the genes.' He began to laugh.

'Don't say that!'

'Don't you wanna be like Gloria? You are, you know. When I looked across at you earlier I thought it was Glo standing here keeping an eye on Carlos. Oh my God, look at that Lou Anne, what's she trying to do, devour him?'

I turned away.

'There's Philip. Hey, Philip, you come here and tell Maddy what you told me. Is Carlos stoned or is he stoned?'

I took a cab home. I doubt if anyone missed me. Bobby and Philip were having far too much of a good time, slagging off Carlos and Lou Anne. Nobody else even noticed me leaving except the hotel doorman, who touched his hat so respectfully he must have mistaken me for someone else.

I stood in the shower for twenty minutes, scrubbing away every last vestige of the make-up the beautician had taken so much trouble with. Then I used a ton of shampoo to free my hair from the remaining traces of mousse and hair spray.

I had just slipped into bed when the phone rang. I ignored it, letting it ring and ring.

There was nobody I wanted to talk to. Not right now anyway. It was still ringing when I fell asleep.

I was woken by the sound of car doors slamming. There were loud shouts and screams of laughter just below my window. The voices carried clearly on the night air calling out to each other, joking and flirting. Then there was some more door slamming, before things began to quieten down again.

It was hard to guess how many people might be downstairs. It sounded like dozens, all shouting at once.

I checked my bedside clock. It was four fifty a.m. Almost dawn.

The noise outside had stopped altogether now. I heard a woman's laugh. I got up to look out across the garden. There were two figures leaning against the white balustrade, although they might have been one, they were meshed so closely. They were kissing with great enthusiasm, I noticed. I was smiling to myself when I suddenly realized who they were.

Carlos and Lou Anne. And there wasn't a photographer in sight.

Who's a Pretty Boy Then? Not!

Watching Carlos and Bobby suffer the next morning gave me a warm glow of satisfaction. There was *some* justice then.

One wicked part of me wished I had the nerve to go and get the state-of-the-art video camera that was lying in Gloria's study. It would have been interesting to have a videotape of the famous Carlos Garcia lying face down on the bathroom tiles, a little trickle of snot escaping from his perfectly formed nostrils.

It certainly would have made a memorable little going-away present to give to the wide-eyed Lou Anne. Or maybe even to the fastidious Barbara Farrington, who clearly believed that Carlos never looked like anything other than the *alter ego* of the super-suave Rick Hein, with his dark, sexy eyes and skin that shone like burnished gold under the studio lights.

His face was the colour of fish paste. His eyes twin pools of bloodshot misery, as he attempted to vomit and groan at the same time.

I would love to say that it was my compassionate nature that prevented me from using the video camera, but it wasn't. It's just that I was, and remain, a techno illiterate.

'Very bad.' Dong nodded as he half dragged and

half carried Carlos back to his room.

Mrs Danvers and I exchanged smug, satisfied looks.

'Very bad,' Dong repeated, thinking we had misunderstood him.

'Oh I hope so, Dong,' I said.

'No! Very bad!' He was becoming totally frustrated with my attitude.

Carlos was indeed very bad. So much so that when the call came from Herman for him to get dressed and hurry across town to some TV station to be interviewed, he could barely lift his head from the pillow when I yelled in his ear that he had an important phone call.

'What?'

I slammed the receiver against his head.

'Yeah? Yeah? Oh Jesus!'

'Is it bad news?' I asked gently.

'Yeah, I'm gonna be sick.' And he was. This man who was the sophisticated court-room king, the idol of millions, the suave lover whose perfect timing made women world-wide swoon in adoration, threw up all over himself and the satin coverlet. And then, in one last wild explosion of vomit, across my borrowed silk dressing-gown.

Herman was still screaming down the line. 'Maddy, you tell him he's gotta get here. This has been arranged for weeks. This is the highest rated talk show in America and they're doing a special phone-in. He's gotta be here.'

'What's the topic?' I tried to sound professional.

'*He is! He's the fuckin' topic! If he doesn't get here within twenty minutes he's a fuckin' dead man*!'

'That's not as unlikely an eventuality as it sounds,

Herman.' I looked down at Carlos who was lying half in and half out of the bed.

'*Please Maddy. If you have any feelings at all for the guy, get him over here! He has to be here. The topic is viewers who are obsessed with Rick Hein*!'

'Well who isn't?' I said.

'*Maddy*!'

The problem was, you'd be hard put to find Rick Hein this morning. There *was* a hung-over slobbering man lying here all right. But he was no Rick Hein. This man had an ice-pack tied to his head, his sunken eyes were half closed, his unshaven face was blotchy with sick and his mouth hung loosely agape.

No. There was no Rick Hein here.

I hung up.

'Carlos?'

'Uh,' he grunted.

'Did you hear what Herman said?'

'Uh.'

'Do you want to go to the television studios? Herman says you should.'

I'm not absolutely sure if I heard his reply. Not correctly, that is. Because what he said Herman should do was a physical impossibility. Even I knew that.

I left him to his misery.

Some time later I caught Bobby tiptoeing to his car, as if the driveway was made of broken glass.

'Bobby?' I yelled as loudly as I could because I wanted to make sure he heard me. I'm not a malicious person by nature. Or vindictive. Usually.

His hands shook as he attempted to put the key in the ignition. It took him several attempts before he made it.

'Will you be all right to drive?' I bellowed helpfully in his ear.

He ran his tongue along dry, cracked lips. ''Bye, Mad,' he whispered.

He manoeuvred the powerful Mercedes down the driveway at a dizzying ten miles per hour. At least he wouldn't be arrested for speeding.

Carlos spent the rest of that weekend hiding out. He refused to answer the phones. Or let anybody else do so. He was behaving like a little boy who has wet his pants in public. Shamefaced, avoiding everyone. Including me.

He hid away in his upstairs study with *the* script. The phone rang non-stop, but as everyone was under orders not to answer it I didn't touch it. Or turn the machines on.

I did feel sorry for poor old Lou Anne. What if she was trying to get through to her new co-star to discuss their shared love scenes? Or anything else they might be planning on sharing. Or even already had.

I had already made my decision about my future when the telegram arrived on Monday morning: MOTHER HAD STROKE. COME HOME.

'Why didn't you ring me?'

'Calm down, Maddy,' Turlough said. 'It was in the middle of the night. By the time we got her to the hospital and they diagnosed the severe stroke it was Saturday. I tried ringing but the line was engaged. Same thing Sunday. Nobody answered. When the lines weren't tied up there was no answer. Why do you think I had to resort to sending an expensive telegram?'

'You could have sent one straight away. I would have covered the cost.'

'Well I didn't. And you may as well know now, she won't walk again.'

'Oh God!'

'Or speak. She'll need full-time care. Hospitalization for the rest of her days.'

'She hates hospitals. And doctors.'

'She won't have any say in the matter.'

'I'll be home as soon as I can.'

'No rush. She's not going anywhere.' There wasn't an ounce of pity in his voice.

'Just one more thing, Turlough.'

'Yes?'

'Fuck off!'

It was only after I'd hung up that I realized he had actually used my name. He had called me Maddy for the first time in years. And they say money can't buy love?

I booked my flight without a word to Carlos. I would have had to ring him in New York to tell him and I hated explaining things over the phone.

He had left for the airport only minutes before the telegram arrived.

'Should have stuck to cocaine.' He had smiled weakly when I asked how he was feeling this morning.

'Just kidding,' he said, when he saw my horrified reaction. Then he hurried away, the *Moonwalkers Two* script clutched beneath his arm, his dark glasses firmly in place. I hoped he wouldn't throw up on the first-class stewardess. That would do his reputation as a serious actor no good at all.

He still had quite a few outdoor scenes to complete for *People in Jeopardy*, before he would be free to start work on *Moonwalkers Two*.

He looked so awful as he was leaving that I wondered how they could possibly turn him into Rick Hein by midday. But then my sister Gloria had turned him into Rick with a stroke of her pen. And he would make a splendid-looking Dr Mezzin when the time came, I knew that. The whole country would flock to see him on the big screen. And Lou Anne would make him a fine love interest. I tried not to choke. On screen she was as beautiful as he was handsome. And when I wasn't hating and despising her I had to admit that as Hollywood starlets go she wasn't the worst. She had a generous nature and her teeth weren't capped as I had first thought, and her breasts were all her own. They actually jigged up and down when she walked, which was a rare phenomenon in Hollywood. And she was never bitchy. God, I despised her. Her generous nature was bound to afford Carlos everything he needed. She would willingly share all she had with him. Insist on it. But better generous-hearted Lou Anne than some mercenary old boiler who would pull him around like a stuffed dog on wheels.

Poor Carlos, his problem was he drew women like pigs to shit.

And he loved them so much. All of them.

I thought back to the morning Gloria, Carlos and I had called in to Dr Wright's surgery together. This was shortly after I had agreed to go along with her plan to have a child.

All that was required of me that morning was that

I have a simple blood test. But because of my genetic abhorrence for all things medical, I had a feeling that it would turn out to be anything but simple. I was right. But it wasn't my aversion to the needle that had turned it into such an unforgettable experience.

Gloria and Carlos were with me because we were going riding in the hills immediately afterwards, a little treat to take my mind off the trauma of having to visit a doctor.

We were all dressed for our big day outdoors. I was wearing borrowed jeans and my comfortable brogues. Gloria was clad in masterfully tailored beige jodhpurs that clung to her like a second skin and knee-high riding boots.

Carlos was in faded blue denims, which on anybody else would have looked like faded blue denims. On him they were occasions of sin. Invitations to lust. He was also wearing shiny cowboy boots. If he was under the illusion that this would help him fade into the rough terrain of our proposed horse-trekking route and prevent him being mobbed by lascivious women, the man's judgement was seriously flawed.

Either that, or he had forgotten to look in the mirror that morning, which was an unlikely scenario for an actor.

Rick Hein in a superbly fitted business suit was always bound to attract a crowd. Carlos Garcia in faded blue denim and shiny cowboy boots was potential riot material, even I knew that.

When we walked into Dr Wright's office, two patients swooned outright at the sight of him. Well, perhaps not swooned, exactly, but close enough. Their knees had certainly given way at the sight of

Carlos in his cowboy get-up.

The receptionist launched herself across the desk like a heat-seeking missile. And it's not as if she could have mistaken him for a patient in need of urgent medical attention, or anything, because Dr Wright was a famous Ob/Gyn man. And nobody on this planet could possibly mistake Carlos for anything but a male of the species, even if he hadn't been wearing the tightest jeans west of the Pecos.

'I . . . I . . . I . . .' said the receptionist, or something to that effect.

'We wanna see the doctor.' Carlos was holding on to my arm, because Gloria had warned him that I might bolt if he didn't.

There were eight or nine women in the plant-smothered reception area, at least two-thirds of them visibly pregnant. Two of these appeared to be terrifyingly close to delivery. But without exception every one of them went slack-jawed at the sight of Carlos, even the two who should have known better. An almost reverential hush spread around the area as they watched him trying to peel the receptionist off his arm.

A pretty girl, dressed in Bermuda shorts and a low-cut halter top, *her* stomach uniquely flat, finally broke the silence. 'Could you . . . would you sign an autograph for me? Please?' Her voice was timid, almost childish, as she approached him, her eyes glued to his face.

And Carlos's eyes were sparkling.

'Where would you like him to sign it?' Gloria slammed in the door, having finally found a parking space for the big Cherokee jeep. 'On your tits?' she snarled.

The girl shrunk back, her face flaming.

'My God, have you looked at this lot, Maddy? I hope it won't put you off.' Gloria tittered cruelly at the line of hugely pregnant women. 'Well, at least it proves one thing. Their men can get it up. Eh, Garcia?' She elbowed Carlos in the ribs.

The women were all horrified. They suddenly discovered magazines, and notebooks, and bags that needed attending to. Anything but look at Carlos.

He walked out.

'Just kidding, ladies,' Gloria bellowed. 'No harm in keeping them on their toes. Huh?'

Even the cheeky receptionist turned away.

Gloria opened the door to the doctor's private room without knocking. 'You said eight thirty.' She looked at her watch. 'It's now eight forty-two and twenty seconds.'

When we rejoined Carlos in the jeep Gloria was in top form. The blood test had been pretty painless and I hadn't complained.

'Sorry for keeping you waiting, honeybun,' she said to him. 'No. Don't bother thanking me for getting you out of that situation.' She laughed. 'Just remember all those other times I've saved your ass. Okay?'

And Carlos actually smiled at her, before straightening his dark glasses and turning on the ignition.

'See what I have to put up with, Maddy? He can't go for a pee without putting himself in danger from marauding women. If he signed one autograph we wouldn't have got out of there before noon. Right, Garcia?'

Carlos grinned happily.

'Course you had to wear those damn tight denims, didn't you?' she said in a sly aside.

I slunk down low in the back seat, waiting for a row to break out between them. It didn't. Carlos just laughed and drove on.

I rang Ballyshannon.

Mary Kilmartin's relentlessly cheerful voice came on the line. 'You're not to worry, Maddy. I'm holding the fort. And your mother is holding her own. The boys are grand, the weather is lovely and you're not to feel guilty. It wasn't your fault.'

'What do you mean?'

'Well how were you to know that she'd have a stroke. When you told her about the money,' she added.

'That's what . . .'

'Oh yes. She barely got the words out to Turlough when she went all funny. Never spoke another word. Never will, according to the doctors. But the hospital has a lovely geriatric unit, it's the envy of the country. How are you, Maddy?'

'Oh I'm fine.'

'I can't wait to see you. I met Father Brennan at the hospital. He said you were blooming. He's a gas man. You won't know the twins, they're like two proper young men now.'

'How are they, Mary?'

'I told you they're great. Growing into fine, handsome chaps. Both of them picked for the county hurling team. Under eighteens. It's a great honour. They gave up that terrible kick-boxing. Grew out of it, I suppose.'

'Tell them I can't wait to see them.'

'I'll do that. And don't be worrying about all that money, Maddy. Don't let it be a burden. It will soon be used up anyway, what with your mother's hospital bills and those robbers in the nursing home. And the price of beef on the hoof is gone so bad that you won't be making a living from the farm, and you have the two boys to educate. You'll be as poor as the rest of us in no time.'

'Thank you, Mary. That's cheered me up no end.'

'Ah, you're a gas woman, Maddy. You hurry on home now and don't you be worrying. These things always work out for the best.'

Home Is Where the Heart Is

Mrs Danvers was helping me to pack when my bedroom phone shrilled. My heart gave a little flutter. Force of habit, I suppose, because I didn't really want to hear from Carlos. What would I say to him?

'Maddy?' It was Dr Wright, ringing to say that my medical charts were on the way and to wish me *bon voyage*.

'Before you go, Maddy, aren't you at all curious about the sex of the baby?'

I had almost forgotten that he knew. I had refused to look at the screen while they scanned me, still believing it to be unlucky.

'Tell me quickly, before I change my mind.'

'You're having a girl, Maddy. A perfect little girl!'

A girl!

I had to break off the conversation and search for a hanky. I had always wanted a girl. All the time I had been carrying the twins I had prayed and prayed that I would have a girl.

'It's a boy!' The senior midwife at Saint Columcilles had dashed my hopes. But all was not lost, I kept thinking, as I pushed and pushed. There was still another twin to come. I could still be lucky. I pushed again.

'Another boy!' The masked midwife compounded my misery.

I cried non-stop through every one of my eight stitches, internal *and* external, before plunging into the blackest depression imaginable.

And Turlough O'Toole, who knew all there was to know about the birthing process – of cows, skulked outside in the corridor, waiting for it to be all over.

When they wheeled me out of the delivery room I was still crying.

Turlough looked at me as if I was soft in the head. 'Stop that crying, you're making a show of yourself,' he muttered, passing me a big, grimy hankie.

And as if this wasn't enough, he then, in an act of unbelievable ineptitude that I would recall for the rest of my life, handed me the *Irish Independent*. The farming section.

Blue Tuesday!

But this time I was having a *girl*.

I was so elated I almost picked up the phone to ring Carlos.

Mrs Danvers read my mind. She reached for the phone and dialled the number for me. 'A call for you,' she said crisply into the receiver, then handed it over.

I put it to my ear. 'Maddy?' Mary Kilmartin's jolly voice said.

Mrs Danvers held my gaze steadily.

'Mary, my flight gets in on Saturday morning. But it will be at an unearthly hour. Would you pick me up? It will be around six a.m. I might even need to stay with you for a couple of days. Till I get something sorted.'

'Maddy! You'll be the talk of Ballyshannon.' She chortled.

'You don't know the half of it.' I giggled.

'Oh Maddy, I can't wait to see you. We'll have a right good laugh together.'

'That's a promise. Would you bring the twins?'

'Course I will, they keep asking when you're coming back.'

'Is that true?' I asked.

But Mary was too busy chatting again. 'You'll probably take our breath away with the glamour of you. Turlough won't know if he's on his head or his heels.'

'I can guarantee that,' I said.

I had already made my plans. For everyone. Turlough for a start. Hawthorn Farm was my family home. Not his. He could run the farm for as long as he wished. For a fair rate of pay. But he wasn't going to live there. Not even when I had the house completely refurbished.

Divorced women don't cohabit with their ex-husbands.

There were plenty of nice cottages to rent in Ballyshannon. He would be spoiled for choice. He could even have fat Marion to live with him if he wanted. Ten fat Marions, for all I cared. But she would never work on Hawthorn Farm again. And if Turlough had a problem with that, well, farm managers were two a penny in Ireland. Most of them with agricultural degrees and full knowledge of all the intricacies of EC farming policies. And they weren't all ugly either.

And I wouldn't neglect Mother. On the contrary, I would visit her with remarkable regularity. I would have to if I were to fill her in on all my adventures in

Hollywood. Her hearing was sharp as ever, they said. It was just that she couldn't speak or move.

She would be the ideal person to confide all my secrets in. I'd be able to tell her all about Gloria. And all the things we did. And all about Carlos. And all the things *we* did.

I won't keep anything back.

The twins and I will visit her every Sunday without fail. Bringing bunches of flowers like any devoted family should.

And when the time comes I'll bring the new baby to visit her. Baby Gloria.

I'll hold her on my knee for Mother to admire. I'll remind Mother of just how successful her namesake was. How people were already mentioning her in connection with an Oscar.

And we'll sit there, Baby Gloria and Mother and I, and we'll probably muse over the way things have a funny habit of working themselves out.

What goes around comes around, Father used to say.

Strange, that. It was Gloria's money that put Mother in the hospital. And her money that will pay for her upkeep in the nursing home. And make it possible for me to divorce Turlough. In fact, it was Gloria who made everything possible. Even for me to have Baby Gloria, when I think of it.

I hope wherever she is she's happy. Maybe even laughing, like Father Brennan said.

I certainly am.

Epilogue

I rewind the tape and give it to Mrs Danvers. She'll be the one handing it over to Carlos on Friday night. She knows what to say. She always does.

'Time to get dressed, Madam. You don't want to miss your flight.'

I throw my arms around her and give her the biggest hug imaginable.

'Incorrigible!' Her sudden smile startles me.

I puzzle over this as I rush upstairs. Incorrigible? Me?

I slip into my pale linen trouser suit and glance in the full-length mirror. The tall, tanned woman staring back at me doesn't look remotely like the Maddy who left Ballyshannon less than a year ago. This person looks so self-assured I hardly recognize her. I turn sideways and stick out my stomach proudly. The baby gives me a grateful thump. And I laugh out loud with the sheer joy of it.

'Your car is here, Madam,' Mrs Danvers calls from the hallway below.

I take one last look around, then hurry downstairs, anxious to be on my way, satisfied that I'm leaving nothing more than a waft of expensive scent behind me.

MADDY GOES TO HOLLYWOOD

ENTER THIS COMPETITION TODAY AND YOU COULD BE THE LUCKY WINNER OF TWO RETURN FLIGHTS TO HOLLYWOOD!

All you have to do is write and tell us in 20 words or less how a trip to Hollywood would change your life.

Send your entry, together with your name, address and daytime telephone number and enclosing either the voucher found on this page or your till receipt to either address below:

Hollywood Competition,
Arrow Marketing Department,
Random House, 20 Vauxhall Bridge Rd,
London SW1V 2SA
(if you are resident in the UK)

Hollywood Competition
P.O. Box 5769
Dublin 1
(if you are resident in the Republic of Ireland)

CLOSING DATE FOR ENTRIES IS 31st JULY 1999

RULES

1. Competition open only to residents of UK and Republic of Ireland aged 18 or over on 1st July 1999 (excludes employees of Random House UK Ltd, their families and agents).
2. The prize will be awarded to the entrant who, in the opinion of the judges, has submitted the most apt and original answer. The judges' decision is final and no correspondence will be entered into.
3. There is one prize of 2 return economy flights to Los Angeles from either London or Dublin to be taken before 31st March 2000. Flights are subject to availability and exclude all bank holidays. Airport tax, insurance, transfers and accommodation are not included.
4. The winner will be informed by telephone or mail by 31st August 1999. There is no cash alternative.
5. All entries should be on a plain piece of paper and must be accompanied by either the till receipt for the book or the voucher below. Photocopies or faxes are not acceptable. No responsibility will be taken for entries lost or damaged in the post.
6. For a list of judges, winners and results, please send a SAE to the competition address by 1st September 1999.
7. Closing date for entries is 31st July 1999.

ISP - Institute of Sales Promotion registration no 705.
Prize draw rules conform to the Institute of Sales Promotion recommended practice.

PROMOTER: RANDOM HOUSE UK LTD, 20 VAUXHALL BRIDGE ROAD, LONDON SW1V 2SA